I0838708

Division One:
The Bounty Game

by Stephanie Osborn &
A.G. Thompson

and

Complications:
A Short Story

by Stephanie Osborn

Chromosphere Press

Huntsville, AL

Chromosphere Press
P.O. Box 252
56 Hughes Road
Madison, AL 35758
www.chromospherepress.com

Table of Contents

Complications — A Prologue of Sorts

Arg-Dango Blehkar of the Lambda Andromedan Majestic Guard approached the Alpha One partnership as they passed through the floor securely reserved for the alien contingent on their patrol of the hotel. New York City had plenty of nice hotels, many of which were, in fact, equipped to handle their offworld visitors. A few were even run by offworlders. Most didn't try to cater to science fiction conventions like YuleCon, though, let alone a science fiction convention in conjunction with a major interplanetary trade negotiation. PLUS Christmas visitors to the Big Apple. The Pan-Galactic Law Enforcement and Immigration Administration, Division One — or just 'the Agency,' as most of the agents themselves called it — considered it ambitious, but appreciated the effort, nonetheless.

"Agent Echo? A moment, if you please?" Blehkar addressed the handsome human male with the dark eyes and broad cheekbones, and he glanced at his junior partner, a statuesque platinum blonde; both Agents paused.

"Yes, Blehkar?" Echo queried. "Is everything all right?"

"No, it is not, and I am very concerned," the muscular, chartreuse alien said, raising several tentacles as all three eyebrows tried to meet in a worried scowl.

The two Agents glanced at each other.

"Maybe we should find a less open place for the discussion," Omega, Echo's attractive white-blonde partner, murmured. "I mean, this is supposed to be a restricted floor, but there's still hotel maids and lost con attendees an' junk."

"Good idea," Echo agreed. "Blehkar, could we duck inside the guard quarters to discuss this?"

"I think that an excellent plan," Blehkar averred, turning and leading the way.

* * *

In Blehkar's own bedroom, he turned to the Alpha One

team.

"I am having problems with one of my guards, and I do not know what to make of it," he noted. "I thought perhaps you could suggest what might be causing such aberrant behavior on your world."

"What's happened?" Echo asked.

"Boogop was missing last night when he should have been on duty, guarding the Prime Minister as he slept. It left the Minister vulnerable, with one-third less protection than he should have had."

"Rationale for security structure?" Echo almost barked. Blehkar shrugged with all three shoulders.

"Multiple redundancy," the alien replied. "One to escort the Prime Minister to safety, while the other two lay down cover fire. Alternatively, if the Minister has been injured or become ill, two to carry him and one as rearguard. Optimally, the guard contingent would be four or better to provide for both point and flank, but with your people patrolling the area, I felt we could reduce the contingent."

Echo nodded. "That makes sense," he concluded. "So without the third guard, if the Prime Minister were injured, you either forego getting him someplace safer, or you forego the rearguard. Either one is potentially fatal for the Prime Minister."

"Exactly. As you now know, our physiological structure does not render us especially lightweight, even to our own kind."

"I noticed," Echo said, his tone dry as dust.

"What's your guard's excuse?" Omega asked.

"He does not have one. He swears he was on duty, by everything holy to our people."

"How do you know, then?" Echo queried.

"Because the other two guards — Dehman was one, Agent Echo, the one you helped out of her difficulties; Tortok the other — saw no sign of him, and they should have been together."

"Maybe he's just a bad egg," Omega suggested.

"Um…'bad egg'?"

"Oh, uh, we eat the eggs of nonsentient avians called chickens," Omega hastened to explain. "Occasionally one spoils, and it smells REALLY bad."

"Ah, I see. No," Blehkar demurred. "We brought no incompetents or idlers on this mission. Nor does such a one reach the levels of the Majestic Guard, for our qualifications are stringent. This is as out of character for Boogop as it was for Dehman going missing."

"And we know she got into something that left her… incapacitated," Echo noted, thoughtful, as Omega gave him a startled glance. "All right. Do you know he didn't have something similar happen?"

"I am fairly certain," Blehkar said, nodding…at least, as nearly as Lambda Andromedans could manage, given their very different physiques. "Another guard, Guglim, was off-duty and headed for the…filking, I think it is called? At any rate, Guglim saw Boogop walking through the hotel lobby, headed for the front doors, about…0100 local? Plus or minus," the captain of the guard added.

"What did Guglim make of it?" Omega queried.

"He thought perhaps Boogop was headed on an errand, for a special snack or the like, for the Prime Minister. He did think it odd that none of you were with Boogop, however. But he thought he might simply have missed seeing you in the crowds. After all, there ARE all those…'movie' people, dressed like you, attending YuleCon."

"Okay," Echo decided with a shrug. "Boogop's lying. Somebody bribed him."

"I have interrogated him," Blehkar protested. "With every means at my disposal, including electronic truth indicator equipment. He firmly believes he was on duty last night, guarding the Prime Minister. So I have confined him to quarters until this is resolved. He is…upset."

Echo raked a hand through his dark hair, standing it on end, and he and Omega stared at each other, puzzled.

* * *

A quick text message notified Fox of the situation, and Alpha One headed for hotel security. Their *carte noirs* morphed, displaying FBI identification, and they were immediately ushered in to see the security chief.

"…And we're concerned one of the movie people may be a plant to scope out security before the Russian Ambassador comes next month," Omega finished their cover story.

"And if he succeeds, it could be bad," Echo added. "Like, dead ambassador bad, with all that entails."

"Wow. Yeah, it sure would," Chief Jameson agreed. "So… what? You wanna look at the video from last night, see if he really did sneak out to meet somebody?"

"Exactly. It should be around one a.m."

"Okay. Hang on a sec." Jameson turned and fished the top CD off a stack, then popped it into a video player on his desk. Several live monitors on the desk depicted various angles through the hotel, but the player monitor was dark; it flickered to life as he hit a few buttons. "Okay, here's the lobby camera video from last night." He picked up a remote and hit <fast forward>. The player sped through the recording, showing everything onscreen at several times normal speed, but it was all discernible.

"There!" Omega said, jabbing a finger at the screen, and Jameson hit <pause>, then resumed at normal speed.

Sure enough, the imagery depicted Boogop headed out of the hotel through the front door. He didn't deviate, speed up or slow down, or make any attempt to be inconspicuous. He simply headed straight for the big front door, pushing it open and disappearing into the darkness outside.

"Well, that's that," Echo noted. "Mr. Jameson, would you burn us a copy of that video segment?"

"Sure," Jameson agreed immediately, sticking a blank disk into the other drive, and initiating the recording. "Strange. You'd think he'd have sense enough to take off the costume, so's he'd be less conspicuous."

"Maybe he figured he'd be less conspicuous WITH it," Omega suggested, trying not to bite her lip. "Science fiction convention and all."

"Well, that's true," Jameson said, as he extracted the fresh recording and slipped it into a paper sleeve. "Weird lot, that bunch. Here ya go. Yell if I can help. I sure don't want nothin' bad happening to the ambassador next month. Not on my watch."

"Thank you, Mr. Jameson," Echo said, accepting the disk and tucking it into one of his innumerable warp pockets. "You've been a huge help, and we'll certainly come to you if we need anything else."

* * *

"...And you've verified that?" Director Fox wondered. "It really was the guard supposed to be on duty last night?"

"Yeah, Fox, we did, and it was," Echo said, as Omega nodded. "Yet Blehkar's own lie detector equipment says Boogop believes he's telling the truth. And Blehkar swears up and down he's run diagnostics twelve ways from Sunday."

"And Lambda Andromedan lie detectors are damn near foolproof, anyway," Fox murmured, considering.

"Yup," Echo agreed. "What do you make of it, Fox? Some sort of dissociative fugue or something? Maybe a telepath?"

"Have there been any signs of a telepath?" Fox asked, sharp, and he and Echo both turned to Omega, who blinked, perturbed.

"Wha?" she asked.

"Well, baby, if anybody's capable of recognizing one, it'd be you," Echo pointed out. "You've got the experience, after Slug's attack this past summer."

"Um, okay, er, lemme think. No, I haven't noticed anything to make me think a telepath was about and probing, let alone attacking," Omega decided. "But unless I was one of the people being probed, I dunno if I'd know about it."

"Point taken," Echo sighed. "Fox?"

"Let me consider it a moment, Echo," Fox replied, putting

one hand to his chin in contemplation.

Omega and Echo remained quiet while Fox pondered.

"All right," Fox decided at last. "Here's what I want you to do. Check the convention membership for a pale man with dark hair and eyes, wearing sunglasses despite being indoors, and going by the name Jim, accompanied by a younger, somewhat scruffy guy named Sean. Jim's last name…well, it changes. Sean's name is…O'Donnell, if memory serves. If they're here, find them and get their help. Oh, and feel free to tell them what's going on."

"You mean this?!" Echo exclaimed, astonished.

"Like, the Prime Minister, trade negotiations, everything?" Omega added, as shocked as her partner.

"Yes, this. All of this. Everything," Fox said, emphatic. "They're authorized for full disclosure. Top level. And so are you."

"So they're agents from another Office?" Omega wondered.

"No, not at all. They've never been Division One agents, either of them."

"What planet are they from, then?" Echo asked.

"Earth."

"But…"

"Not everything falls under our jurisdiction, zun," Fox noted. "You know that. If it isn't alien, it's somebody else's problem. And in this case, if it's what I suspect, Jim just might consider it his problem, at least in part." He paused to consider. "Oh, just so he knows you're coming from me, with my authority, tell him I said, 'Die gedanken sind frei.'"

"What? 'Thoughts are free'?"

"Exactly, alter khaver. It comes from my days in the concentration camp; it's the name of a very old song. Certain Nazi resistance movements used it, and some Nazi concentration camps bastardized it. He should remember; it was our password."

"Wait," Omega exclaimed. "This guy knew you in the

concentration camps?"

"He did." Fox was calm.

"But I thought ECHO was your oldest human friend still alive?!"

"He is," Fox noted.

"So you're saying…" Echo began, as the light began to dawn.

"That's right, zun. Jim isn't human."

"Oookay…" Omega murmured, as Fox turned and headed back toward the negotiations.

* * *

It took some doing, and a couple of judicious brain bleachings, but soon enough, Echo and Omega had verified that Jim Hickey and Sean O'Donnell were indeed attending the convention and splitting a hotel room, the hotel being uncommonly full due to the convention — and a certain trade negotiation — occurring concurrently. A fen query had one of them pointing across the lobby to a very ordinary-looking man of average height and paler-than-usual skin. He was alone at that moment, studying the convention's pocket program. Echo thanked the fan.

"C'mon, baby," he told Omega, and they strode across the lobby.

* * *

Echo waited until he got close to the other man before speaking, unsure how he'd react.

"James Hickey?" he said, and Alpha One was surprised when the man didn't react to his name. It didn't take their coded communication to share the message, *That must not be his real name. Is he undercover…?* Echo tried again. "Jim Hickey? Sir?"

The man started and looked at them, a wary expression in his eyes. Echo held out his hands in a subtle, placating gesture.

"Sir, I have a message for you from an old friend. You would have known him as Franz Levy, but we call him Fox. He says, 'Die gedanken sind frei.'"

The man relaxed instantly. He eyed them up and down, a slight smile on his face; he seemed friendly enough.

"You work for Fox, eh?" Hickey said after a few moments. "Part of Galactic Division One's Agency?"

"We do, and we are," Echo averred. "I'm Echo, and this is my partner, Omega. We're part of Alpha Line, the new special forces department. We're Alpha One. Alpha Two is also at the convention, but…occupied at the moment. And there are others in the department, of course. Not many yet, but it's growing." Echo glanced around at the crowds milling through the lobby. "Um, should we go someplace more private to discuss this?"

"Not necessary." Hickey waved a dismissive hand. "I faded us as soon as I saw you."

"Faded?" Omega wondered.

"No one is paying us any attention now. I'll explain later. So how's Fox these days?" the other man wondered.

"Pretty well, if heading the Division counts," Echo said. "And doing as well personally, I suppose."

"Yes, I heard some time back he'd become director. And had a lady. Is he here?"

"Yes, but elsewhere in the hotel."

"Good. I'll have to find him and say hi."

"I suspect he'd like that, knowing him. But he seemed to think you might have a line on a developing situation."

Hickey's eyes narrowed. "Tell me."

* * *

"…All right, that's our side of things," Echo wound up the tale. "Now it's your turn, Mr. Hickey."

"I prefer 'Jim,'" the other male said. "What do you mean, 'my turn'?"

"Just what he said," Omega replied, not quite cold. "Who, and what, are you? You sure don't look old enough to have known him in Nazi Germany, but he said you were from Earth."

"Remember, Fox said WE were authorized for full disclosure as well," Echo reminded him. Jim sucked in a deep breath, then let it out in a sigh.

"You're not gonna like it," he told them.

"Try us."

"I'm a vampire."

"A WHAT?!" Omega exclaimed, in patent disbelief.

Jim rolled his eyes.

"Good thing I had us faded," he remarked, wry.

* * *

"All right, I see," Jim murmured, thoughtful, when both sides had finished explanations. "I was aware of some activity, but I hadn't realized there was an alien presence. At least, outside the usual."

"Quite a bit," Echo replied. "We're using the convention as cover for trade negotiations with the Lambda Andromedan system. Their Prime Minister is here, with his entire entourage."

"The chartreuse guys with three eyes and tentacles?" Jim asked.

"That's them," Omega confirmed, apparently having relaxed after the vampire explained his personal moral code — he only fed off those who were themselves heartless predators, often in an otherwise-untouchable position. "The ones everybody thinks are the aliens from the *Black Suits* movie that's being made."

"Which is a problem for us in its own right," Echo added. "But we're working on that. No need to concern yourself."

"I can see why. Okay. I knew they weren't humans in costume," Jim noted. "They didn't smell right."

"Smell?" Omega queried, lifting a silver-blonde brow.

Jim decided she was a curious little bugger, but seemed nice enough, though probably every bit as formidable as her partner, if she chose to be. She hadn't flinched upon discovering he really was a vampire, though her hand had floated near one of her concealed holsters initially. *Ready to 'smite' if need be, I suppose,* he decided with a rueful mental chuckle. *But then there's the... 'extra.' What the hell does it mean? And whose side is it?* He sobered instantly.

"It's...hard to explain," Jim sighed. "Especially to

someone who has never experienced it. Suffice it to say that my senses are…quite acute, in many respects. May I ask you a question, Omega?"

"I guess so." She shrugged.

"What are YOU? And what were you before you joined the Agency?"

"Um, what do you mean?" she hedged.

"You know exactly what I mean," Jim noted, folding his arms and raising a skeptical eyebrow. "Echo's scent — human, male, strong, intelligent. Just as it should be. Yours should be human, female, smart, strong…but it isn't. Quite. Oh, it's female, smart, and strong…but there's something there besides human. What are you? And does Echo know you aren't what you appear to be? Does Fox? Are you the original Omega, or a 'replacement'?"

The vampire watched, keeping his face impassive as Omega blanched, and she and Echo exchanged glances.

"Not again," she murmured. "This convention is just…"

"Yeah, I know, baby," Echo said, keeping his voice quiet. He took a subtle step closer to his partner. "But if he can tell, it's a reasonable inquiry. Besides, Fox vouched for him. And gave us orders, basically, to fill him in on whatever he needs to know…though this is your private matter, so…what do you want to do?"

They're in love, Jim realized abruptly, sensing the subtle thoughts and feelings that radiated from the pair, as well as the slight shifts in chemistry due to pheromones. *Except he hasn't really realized it yet, and she's afraid as hell to admit it. But he's protective of her, a lot. And whatever she is, he knows, in spades…and doesn't care. What the hell is going on here?*

A quick, brief — but gentle and specific — probe of Echo's mind confirmed the matter to his satisfaction, though Omega, to his surprise, was locked down almost as tightly as an elder vampire. *I could get in there,* he considered, testing carefully. *But she'll know if I do. Best I keep my distance and watch. I don't want to piss off two Division One agents, especially not from this new Alpha Line department. If they decided I fell under their jurisdiction, I'd be in trouble. And it's none of my business, provided it isn't HER doing some of this shit.*

"I guess he needs to know, just so he knows I'm not part of…whatever," she said; he wondered if she HAD caught his probe and understood why he'd done it. "Like some other folks apparently think. You tell him, though," Omega sighed to her companion, seeming tired. "I've had more'n enough talking about it already."

"Okay," Echo agreed. "I'll keep it simple and quick, I swear. It's like this, Jim — Omega was a scientist-astronaut before she came into the Agency. I was chasing a perp one night in rural Texas, and we literally ran across her with her telescope, doing some observing. Did hell to her equipment. But when nobody could find a brain bleacher setting that worked on her, we had to…draft her, sorta," the male Agent explained. "Only it turned out the reason we couldn't brain-bleach her was because…" He broke off and sighed, and Jim watched, sensing pain in both Agents. "Early on in my Agent career — I wasn't much more than of-age, if that — I made a deadly enemy. I captured a Snail assassin after killing its symbiote Shell, and the neural feedback fried some brain cells, turning Slug into a…full-blown psychopathic killer, fixated on revenge."

"Against Echo, specifically," Omega added, voice low.

"So…he kidnapped Meg as a kid — she's a few years younger than me; not much, just enough to make the difference — and, and genetically modified her. Pretty extensively in some respects, I've gathered…"

Omega nodded but said nothing.

"…And then telepathically programmed her to…to…"

"To kill Echo," Omega blurted, voice cracking. "That was the whole point of being unable to brain-bleach. So they'd have to bring me into the Agency, and I could get close enough to Echo to…to kill him. When the trigger initiated." She paused, then added, "I swear, I didn't know. Slug made me forget everything…until the programming launched."

"I gather, since you're both still alive, you found a way around that particular plan," Jim said, voice dry as the Sahara.

"Yeah, but it was a near thing, a couple times over," Echo noted. "Nearly killed her, nearly killed me…"

"What's keeping her from doing it now?"

"We had an Arcturan Deltiri deprogram her, once we figured it all out. They're telepaths, and Zz'r'p is a counselor." Echo's jaw firmed. "She's got control back. I know she'd never turn on me."

Jim took that in, then nodded understanding.

"She's got your six?"

"In spades."

"That's always good to have."

"Yeah."

"I guess, if you can smell the difference between humans and aliens, you could smell I was someplace in between?" Omega asked.

"Something like," Jim agreed. "Mostly human, but…with a twist. Like…the difference between regular black tea, and… masala chai, or something. It's still tea, but with a spicy kick."

"That's one way to put it," Omega said, wry. "Helluva kick."

"What can you tell us about our vampire perp?" Echo wondered. "I assume it IS a vampire."

"Probably, by the sound. And not…much, yet."

"Why not?" Omega asked.

"Simple — I didn't know there was another one here, until you told me as much. Experienced vampires can shield ourselves from others — sort of like that fading I mentioned earlier. Even others of our kind. Only an older, MORE experienced vampire can penetrate it…but we have to be looking, and I wasn't." He sighed. "I guess after the last couple of cons, I really need to get into the habit of looking first."

"There've been other incidents?"

"A few," Jim said, wry. "Only the last couple cons,

though. Couple vampires, a few demons, several deranged humans. I've been giving some serious consideration to not attending for a while, I just...haven't, yet. I enjoy 'em. But back to your situation. So we can erect shields of various sorts, mostly mental, but elders can see through 'em if we try. Oh, and magic users — which we are NOT — can raise a block that NOBODY can see through." He chuckled, rueful. "If we blunder into it, we kind of...'short it out,' is maybe a good way to put it. We can do that to any magic spell. But it feels a lot LIKE shorting it out, and if the spell is strong enough, it's like being electrocuted. Not fun."

"And you know this how?" Omega asked...

...Just as Echo began, "It sounds like you know first-hand."

Jim let out a lone bark of laughter. It did not contain humor.

"Let's say that, if a demon lord is helping with the spell, it can be plenty strong, even for an elder, and leave it."

"Elder? How old ARE you?" Omega wondered, astonished. Jim gave her a twisted grin.

"Um, millennia? I'd have to sit down and figure it up. And even then I might not get it right. When you're as old as I am, time tends to mush together."

"How many ancient civilizations can you remember?" a curious Echo asked.

"...Most of 'em."

"Can you help us?" Omega asked then.

"Well, to a point," Jim confessed. "I definitely don't want the bastard to keep doing this shit, but...well. I'm more a protector of humans than any kind of aliens. And while I'm glad to help, my lack of experience with said aliens might mean I'd actually make things worse."

"But Fox sent us to you," Echo protested. "You HAVE to be able to do SOMEthing. WE can handle the aliens, but Meg and I aren't exactly experienced with, uh, supernatural beings and shit."

"I can 'do' several things," Jim said, voice sharp. "I can

keep an eye out and notify you if I find out anything. I can kill the bastard. I can tell YOU how to kill the bastard. And I can put my…I suppose you can call them, my 'adopted family' on alert — the ones that are here, anyway — to keep watch. And any and all of us can show up if you find him or need backup. I can even send my best friend along with you, if you think you'll need him."

"Who's he? Or maybe that's 'what.'" Echo raked a hand through his hair, standing it on end.

"A werewolf. They have noses even better than mine, though they can't smell through the shields either. Nobody can, really. And since we have a blood bond…" he laughed, rueful, "blood brothers I suppose, he can notify me instantly if anything goes to hell, and I can be there within seconds."

Brown eyebrows and blonde rose precipitately.

"Seconds," Echo reiterated, tone skeptical.

"Seconds," Jim confirmed. "Those obstacle courses you agents test and train in? I can be in, through and out before anything has a chance to trigger, and you won't even see me do it. Yes, I talked to Fox, oh…ten years ago or so. Trust me. If there's any way to get there, I can be there."

"Shit," Echo muttered.

"And we kill a vampire how, exactly?" Omega wondered, dubious. "Just in case there's no way for you to get there."

"You lot still use proto-cyclotron blasters, right?"

"Uh, yeah," Echo answered, seeming a little put off by the vampire's knowledge of their systems and equipment.

"Perfect. One of you cinch the beam down as tight as it'll go, and slice off the head. The other one, open the beam as wide as you can, and fry his body as soon as the head's off. Continuous fire, as long as it takes. Barring that, if you can destroy the heart and the brain, it ought to do it. But decapitation and burning is the traditional method."

"What about wooden stakes? Garlic? Holy water? Crosses? Sunlight?" Omega wondered.

"A wooden stake is a distraction at best," Jim noted, ticking off fingers. "It does smart, though. Holy water'll definitely hurt, but if he has a demon companion helping, aim the holy water at the demon to melt it. Garlic, we're definitely allergic to, and smear enough of it on us, it'll work; but it works too slowly for your purposes. Holy symbols don't work, because being turned doesn't actually change our belief systems. Sunlight only works on the newbies, or an elder who's badly weakened for some other reason."

"Right," Echo decided. "Remove the head and fry the son of a bitch."

"Exactly."

"You're not afraid we'll use it on you?" Omega asked, eyebrow raised.

"If you do, you'll piss off your boss royally. Fox and I go back," Jim said with a reminiscent half-smile. "Like, World War II back. I was with the Allied forces in a couple different locations — I used it as an opportunity to kill off one identity and start another — and as the war neared an end in Europe, the Allies prepared to bring the soldiers in Europe to the Pacific, for a Japanese invasion. My C.O. sent me with a classified communiqué to a battalion commander in Europe. I was embedded with that battalion while I waited for a reply and, being what I am, as 'my' unit got close to the camp Franz was in, I did a quick reconnoiter — the C.O. thought I was a spy; he hadn't a clue about my real nature. When I saw what condition the prisoners were in, well…I was NOT a happy camper. Bad pun intended. More like appalled." He broke off and ran a hand through his hair, not unlike a certain werewolf of his close acquaintance. "Fox was the only kid still alive in his…cell block, for want of a better term. He was barely in his teens, nothing but skin and bones, and the bones almost poking through. His face was little more than a shock of dark hair and those hazel eyes, way the hell too big in a skinny face. He was slowly starving to death, just like all the others. But I could see the intelligence in those eyes, and I knew I had to keep him — and as many of the others as I could — alive until the battalion could get there and free them. So I snuck in and out as I found opportunity, taking out the nice well-fed guards for my dinner, bringing bags of chocolate bars, C-rations, whatever I could get my hands on, or the C.O. could find, to keep the prisoners going until the main force could get there and liberate the camp. Fox figured out what I was, and that I was there to help not hurt, so we devised a little routine to get me in and out. I kept an eye on him in Europe afterward, provided some assistance to get him across to Israel, stuff like that."

"So he owes you," Echo said flatly.

"Nah. He got me out of a couple scrapes involving pitchforks and torches in Europe, and did even better by me a few years later, as a Mossad agent. We're even. We're just old, trusted friends. And I don't have that many of those, so I try to do the best I can for 'em. It was good to see him again, after he came back from his galactic travels, back when you Originals started the Agency proper." Jim looked Echo up and down. "I heard you're his designated successor?"

"That's him," Omega said, grinning. The vampire didn't miss the proud light in her sapphire eyes, or the sheepish but pleased expression in Echo's chocolate gaze as he glanced at her.

"Good. Once he goes back to work with Entiyti, well… he'll tell you how to contact me if you need me, before he leaves. Hang on."

* * *

Alpha One watched as the vampire's gaze defocused for a few moments, then his attention returned to them.

"Yeah, there's a void, all right, but it's moving. I'll need to get someplace quiet where I can concentrate, and then I can probably get more information. I told everyone something was up, but I dunno if they'll come now or not. Sean's on the way; I'll introduce you to him, then we can spread out and look for the bastard."

"Who-all is 'we'?" Omega wondered.

"At this con, only a couple more," Jim said, "but those

16

couple more are…significant. My friend Raph — he's an angel, the real deal, and yeah, probably THAT Raph, though I never asked — and his lady friend Lil, who's a succubus he's trying to reform. Yes, it IS possible, because most of the rest of my 'family' consists of a reformed succubus, her husband, and their two sons…but it's complicated, so let's not go there and say we did, okay?"

"Uh…yeah," Omega said, blushing bright red, even as Echo's face turned dusky. "Not goin' there. Right."

"What she said," Echo agreed. "Are we gonna meet them, too? This Raph and Lil?"

"Eventually," Jim told Alpha One. "Maybe give me a chance to brief him first. He sometimes has a tendency to smite first and ask questions later."

Omega's mouth formed an O, but nothing came out.

* * *

A young man with sandy blond hair came striding up just then.

"Hey, Hickey," he greeted the vampire with a grin that, Alpha One realized, had far too many very sharp teeth. "These your new pals?"

"Yeah, fur-head, they are," Jim murmured. "Agent Echo and Agent Omega. I…knew their boss, way back when. Echo, Omega, this is Sean O'Donnell, the, uh, friend I was telling you about."

"Good peeps?" Sean asked.

"Good peeps." Jim nodded as Sean held out a hand, and the Alpha Line Agents shook it in turn. "We have a situation."

"Yeah, I gathered from the download. Another bloodsucker?"

"Looks like it, yeah. And active."

"But…I haven't smelled any blood," Sean protested.

"It won't smell like you're used to," Echo noted. "It's… a…a…"

Echo's voice tapered off as he stared at a couple drawing near.

* * *

The approaching male was moderately tall, well-built, and handsome, with dark hair and pale skin. The woman on his arm was a beautiful redhead, with distinct and well-rounded upper and lower 'assets.' More, the sense of straight-out, sheer, raw SEX that projected from her was nigh unto overwhelming. Even the vampire felt it, though it didn't particularly affect him. His companions were another matter, however.

"Uh, um, uhn," Echo stuttered, his heavy-lidded and unexpectedly sensuous gaze locked on the succubus. His pupils dilated, nostrils flared, and he impulsively stepped forward, then caught himself and took two stumbling steps backward. He looked around the lobby with a slightly wild expression, arms floating out from his sides, apparently seeking something. His stance suggested a fight-or-flight response — his legs were splayed, knees slightly bent, hands grasping for something that wasn't there. Then he abruptly sidled behind his partner, face reddening impressively, given his slightly darker half-Apache coloring.

What in...? Fox's second just...RETREATED?! Shocked, Jim's attention shifted to the other Agent.

Omega was in only slightly better shape; her pale eyebrows shot upward, but her eyes were also wide, the pupils dilated, and she instinctively sniffed the air. Jim realized the 'enhancements' had evidently heightened her senses relative to a 'standard' human, and she apparently detected the pheromonal components of the succubus' glamour. It still didn't stop a decidedly sultry expression entering the sapphire gaze.

"What the blazes...?" Omega murmured, leaning toward Echo with arched back until her shoulder blades brushed Echo's chest. His response was to grab her shoulders, push her away, and hold her still, positioned directly in front of himself, fully a foot from his own torso. "Ace, c'mere, you. Get out from behind me."

"No way in hell," Echo muttered. "Not until...whatever kinda shit just happened, stops happening." He glanced down the length of his body. "Uhm. Which doesn't look like happening, any time soon."

"But why…?"

"Because there's not a big enough potted plant nearby, that's why."

"I…don't get…waitaminit," Omega broke off. "Is…what's happening to you…the same as…what's happening to me…?"

"If by that, you mean I'm gonna haveta go find a room innaminit, probably."

Just then, Sean let out a soft whine, and Jim realized the werewolf was on the verge of shifting, himself. *Well, shit,* he thought, raking a hand down his face.

"Dammit, Lil," Jim grumbled aloud, "tone it down. You know how that affects Sean! Besides, these are MORTALS."

"Oh," Lil said, blushing. The glamour ratcheted down several orders of magnitude. "I'm sorry. I assumed you wanted to introduce us to some more immortals."

"That makes it better?" Jim fumed. "If you think you can't affect immortals, look at Raph."

"Sorry, sorry. I honestly didn't think anybody would notice."

"They NOTICE."

"Oof," Omega grumbled, as the glamour effect retreated. "That's better. You can come out now, Ace."

"Not yet, I can't," her partner griped. "That's gonna take a couple minutes. Damn. I thought I was gonna split a seam for a second, there."

Omega's mouth made an "Ooo" shape, and she blushed, but no sound came out. *Yeah, no, it's gonna take a few minutes for both of 'em, dammit,* Jim thought, irked. *Things almost got interesting in the not-good way. Those two are NOT ready for THAT.*

"In case you haven't guessed," Jim remarked, unable to keep the dry irony from his voice, "meet Raph and Lil."

"Lil is the…?" Echo confirmed, glancing at the vampire.

"The same. The glamour is pretty much on all the time,

but she can sorta control the volume. She wasn't thinking."

"Sorry about that," Lil tried again. The Alpha One team gave her somewhat stilted nods.

"So what's going on?" Raph wondered. "Is this the situation you were telling us about? And what do they know about it?" He waved a hand at the Agents.

"Lots," Jim said. "Let me explain the whole thing…"

* * *

"And you're sure she's not part of it?" a suspicious Raph said, eyeing Omega. Omega just winced.

"Positive," Jim and Echo said simultaneously.

"All right," Sean decided. "So we need to find this other bloodsucker and take care of 'im."

"Right," Jim agreed.

"Split up and start looking?" Sean wondered.

"I guess," Jim agreed, annoyed. "I'd really like just ONE convention where I didn't have to chase some idiot down to prevent an impending apocalypse."

"I don't think you've figured out the situation, then," Raph noted with the faint hint of a smirk on his face.

"I'm not sure Meg and I can be much help with that," Echo observed, "and I've got another angle we can pursue. How can we reach you if we come up with something?"

"Here's my cell phone number," Raph said, handing Echo a scrap of paper. Echo read it, then handed it back with a nod. "Text me if you need us. I can contact the others."

"Okay, that'll work. C'mon, Meg," Echo said, turning; apparently matters farther south had diminished enough that the male Agent no longer needed cover.

"I'll, um, I'll catch up with you in a sec, Ace," Omega said, glancing at him. "I'd like to, um, ask Raph something."

"Okay. I'll be at the Majestic Guard's quarters."

"Got it."

* * *

Jim and Sean headed out, grasping that the female Agent wanted to ask the angel something private; Jim fully suspected

20

what but he wasn't going to spill the beans other than a mental note sent to the wolf and the succubus of, *They need to talk.* Lil and Sean nodded at the mental communication, and turned.

"I'll see you later, hon," Lil murmured, stretching up to plant a kiss on Raph's cheek, and he nodded.

Then the others were gone and Omega faced the angel alone.

* * *

"I gather…you, uh, know what happened to me," Omega tried.

"More or less, to an extent," Raph confirmed. "And yes, I now know that you're innocent in all this."

"Good. So…you, um, know me?" she asked, seeming hopeful. "I mean…you know."

"Yes, I understand what you mean. But…no, I'm afraid I don't know you," the angel said, honest.

Omega's face fell, then crumpled, and the celestial being realized she was struggling not to cry. And he suddenly understood why.

"Well," she whispered, "I guess that answers THAT question."

"Wait," Raph said, grabbing her shoulder in a gentle but unbreakable grip as she started to turn away. "What question?"

"I just wondered…after everything that's happened to me…if it…changed things," Omega murmured. "Like THAT, I mean."

"You are a Follower?"

Omega nodded, then shrugged. "Believed. Always tried to follow, anyway." She sighed, a sound that seemed to come from the depths of her being…and in that moment, Raph knew that it did. "I guess that's all moot now, though."

Raph squeezed her shoulder.

"I'm not Himself Upstairs," he noted. "I'm not all-knowing. Just because *I* don't know you doesn't mean He doesn't. And…" Raph paused, getting the confirmation he needed before adding, "…He doesn't forget." He squeezed her shoulder again, then smiled.

"Oh," Omega said, then brightening, "Oh! You mean…?"

"Yeah." Raph's smile got wider. "Just…trust and keep walking."

Omega nodded her thanks, offered the angel a much happier smile, and she was gone, headed after her partner.

Cheered, Raph turned and started feeling out the hotel for a heretofore-unrecognized vampire.

* * *

It turned out Echo hadn't gone very far after all; he was, in fact, still in the lobby, screened by one of those large potted shrubs that hadn't been close enough earlier. As Omega passed it, he dropped in beside her. They headed past the Christmas tree, en route to the elevators.

"Oh!" she exclaimed, mildly startled. "I thought you were going back upstairs."

"I was," Echo said, "but then it hit me what you might want to talk to an archangel about in private. Not that you've ever mentioned it to me, but I get how you think. So I thought maybe I oughta stay around in case you…were upset." He scanned her up and down. "You don't look upset."

"I'm not," she told him with a slight smile. "I got the answer I was hoping for."

"So…nothing was affected by what Slug did…THAT way?"

"According to Raph, the Big Guy Upstairs has as good a memory as His reputation."

"Good. Kinda figured. I guess you're glad," Echo noted, putting a companionable arm around her shoulders as they headed for an elevator. "I know I would be, if the places were swapped."

"Oh yeah." Omega drew in a deep breath then let it out slowly. "Now I can quit worrying about THAT, at least. So Ace, what's your plan?"

"Okay. I figured, given how well you executed the plan against a certain assassin in Antarctica, it's your job to decapitate."

"All right. So I choke down my principal blaster beam as tight as it'll go."

"Right. And I'll widen mine and burn the thing to the ground. BUT."

"But?"

"I want us each to back up the other one. So take your OTHER blaster and open up the beam all the way and I'll take MY other blaster and choke it down."

"Oh, I get it," Omega said, as they got in the elevator. Two fen started to join them, but the Agents glared at them, and they backed off. The elevator door closed, leaving only Alpha One inside. "And if it came to that, just one of us could do it all."

"Right. No matter what happens. Now let's get to it."

After checking for security cameras and deactivating them, they got out their blasters and adjusted them per Echo's plan.

"Okay, that's done," Omega noted, as they re-holstered their weapons. "Now what? Shouldn't we be doing something to make sure the bad guy can't…like…mind-control us?"

"Well, me anyway," Echo pointed out, rueful. "I mean, when Lil showed…damn. Hot knife and butter."

"Nah, not quite, Ace. She had way more stuff going on than just a mental projection. There was…" Omega broke off, thinking. "There were…scents…in the air around her. Pheromones, I guess. I doubt I could pick up on 'em normally but she was just pumping 'em out in mass quantity, you know?"

"Oh. Well, that makes a certain sense. Embarrassing as hell, but…"

"Yeah."

"Uh, sorry about it, too."

"Don't worry about it. Once I understood what…happened, it was okay."

"By the way, baby, Jim said you were locked down. I mean, I guess an elder vampire could eventually manage to pry you open, but evidently after Slug, you've got a pretty hard telepathic block going, there."

"Still not good enough," Omega noted, stubborn. "I didn't let on but I could still 'hear' him."

"It's good to know, though, that a telepathic block screens you from vampires. And I got some ideas about that too. The first thing we'll do is swing by and talk to Fox for a few minutes."

"Okay. What else?"

"Well, it all depends on whether or not we can get a volunteer…"

* * *

"Ooo," Dehman said, uncertain, as guard captain Blehkar stood beside her. "It sounds…quite dangerous…in a way I am unused to."

"Indeed," Blehkar agreed. "Are you certain she will be safe?"

"Nothing is a hundred percent, of course," Omega said. "But we have…appropriate assistance, and knowledge of how to take down the perp."

"And assurance that, even if she's bitten, the creature's death undoes any ties the bite might create," Echo added.

"So you wish me to act as…bait?' Dehman verified.

"Only if you're willing," Echo said. "We'd be with you and you'd be bugged so we could listen, watch, and track you."

"You and Alpha Two?" Blehkar queried.

"Alpha Two will guard the rest of you, including Boogop," Omega said. "It would be typical vampire to gather a 'herd' of Lambda Andromedans to control. It's how they use wolves, werewolves, and bats, among others."

"Unfortunately, the bad ones think of us as cattle," Echo added. "Blehkar, you're welcome to come along. I understand how it feels as chief, to keep your people safe."

Blehkar drew the alien equivalent of a deep breath, letting it out in a sigh.

"You will have help?"

"Yes," Echo averred. "As soon as we decide to do this,

IF we do — either you or Dehman can veto it — I'll text my contact and let them know where to be, and when."

"I still do not understand why this…creature…is doing this," Blehkar protested.

"Near as we can figure, the vampire discovered y'all by accident," Omega explained. "And this sitch gives it a chance — by forcing Boogop to help — to stow away on your ship and go off-world when y'all finish negotiations and leave. And that puts it on a world where y'all don't know about vampires and have no defense against them."

"And chances are, it's decided alien blood makes an interesting addition to its powers, some kinda way," Echo added.

"How?" Dehman wondered.

"Who knows?" Echo shrugged. "Maybe it gives 'em visibility at additional wavelengths. Maybe it makes 'em stronger, or faster, or something. I dunno. I just know, according to what I was told by, uh, an expert on the subject, the blood transfers certain properties sometimes."

"But the end result is that your entire planet could wind up victim to a really hard-to-stop creature," Omega pointed out. "And I'd bet y'all wouldn't make it back home without either being bitten or outright turned. Assuming, I guess, that Lambda Andromedans can become vampires."

"So we need to stop this before it goes any farther," Echo concluded.

Blehkar turned to his subordinate.

"Dehman, agogla bop-doh? Adada pooh ding," he told her. Dehman pondered for a moment.

"Bop-doo, Blehkar," she answered. "Ding alin gda."

"You'll do it, then?" Echo confirmed, shooting a glance at Omega; his partner didn't understand the language, but Echo was trained in linguistics.

"Yes, Agent Echo," Dehman said. "Blehkar approves your plan, and I am willing to try. Only," she added with that odd Andromedan grin, "do try to keep me from becoming dinner?"

"You got it," Omega agreed, with a grin of her own, and Echo joined her.

* * *

Soon Dehman was outfitted with a personal sensor suite Fox ordered from Headquarters for the purpose. Alpha One tied it into a special app on their cell phones, then tested it.

"That works," Omega decided. "Echo, have you come up with a good location to plant our bait?"

"Not yet," he replied. "I'd been hoping that our, ah, allies would find something. Maybe even find the damned thing and take it out before we'd have to do anything else. No such luck, evidently." Just then, his cell dinged with an incoming-message notification. He extracted it and read the message. It was from Raph.

Agent Echo, Jim says he hasnt found the other vamp.
Its probably an elder, though not as much as him,
and its not staying in one place long enough to locate.

Echo studied the message, letting Omega read over his shoulder, then replied.

Any good ideas for placement of a sacrificial lamb?

There was a pause, then the response came.

Probably the lobby near the elevators.
Maybe btwn them and the dealers room.
Are you ready?

Yeah, as soon as we get her down there.

I will notify the others.

"Okay, now I know where to put Dehman," Echo said, looking up.

"That group of seats by the fountain?" Omega wondered.

"Exactly, baby. It should have a nice flow of people so our vampire will see Dehman, yet it's a little isolated with all those potted plants and shit."

* * *

Five minutes later, Dehman was sitting alone on one of the sofas, reading from the library on her personal tablet. Nearby but out of sight were two Division One Agents, a vampire, a werewolf, a succubus, and an angel.

"In fact," Omega breathed to her partner, "I kinda suspect the others are screening themselves and us too."

"I wouldn't bet against you, baby," Echo murmured, never taking his eyes off the ebb and flow through the lobby.

Why do you call her baby? suddenly floated through their minds…in Jim's voice.

"Did you hear that?" Omega wondered, shaken. She glanced around but saw nothing.

"Um, yeah," Echo said, also perturbed. "But I don't see him. Do you?"

"No…"

Sorry, came the answer. *I was just keeping everyone in touch. I'm faded. So you CAN hear me, Omega?*

"Yeah," Omega sighed. "I can."

For what it's worth, I can't really hear you, not mentally, anyway — your telepathic block is pretty damn effective. I've never encountered a human who can do that, at least not to this degree. But I'm near enough to actually hear you physically, and I wondered.

"Okay. That makes me feel a little better, I guess. As for the 'baby' thing, it's a nickname from my rookie days," Omega said sotto voce. "A reference to 'baby agent.' Same way I call him 'Ace' because of his awesome flying skills." Echo flushed.

Aha. That makes sense. Both members of Alpha One picked up on the grin in Jim's 'voice,' and knew it was because of Echo's embarrassment. Omega grinned at her partner, who rolled his eyes before getting serious.

"Do we need to cut the chatter?" Echo whispered.

No one else should notice. Between the three of us — me, Raph, and Lil — the six of us should be effectively undetectable even to our quarry.

"Good," Omega breathed.

They waited.

Nothing happened.

* * *

Until Echo's cell phone dinged softly. He pulled it and glanced at the message.

"Shit," he cursed. "Our perp didn't take the bait. That was Romeo—"

Of Alpha Two? Jim asked.

"Exactly," Echo verified. "Boogop's on the move. He was on duty and walked away from his post."

"There he goes." Omega pointed as the elevator disgorged Boogop. "He looks…"

"Like he's sleepwalking," Echo finished.

More or less, yes he is, Jim confirmed. *If we follow him, he might just lead us to our quarry.*

"Or he might be a diversion to get to Dehman," Echo observed.

Shit.

"Ace? You're the boss. What do you wanna do?" Omega wondered.

"Jim? Can you and your friends escort Dehman back to her quarters?" Echo asked.

We can, but hadn't you rather…?

"I'd rather she's safe," Echo pointed out, tapping out a quick message on his own phone, "and if she's with you four, she will be. We'll go after Boogop. As soon as you deliver her to Alpha Two, come find us, because we'll probably need help."

All right. You know we'll have to make them forget the… 'details'?

"Yeah," Echo sighed, "kinda figured."

Okay. Hurry; Boogop is almost out the door. And the sun set two hours ago.

Alpha One left their hiding place and headed for the door.

* * *

As unnoticed as any ninja, Alpha One trailed Boogop through the darkness outside the hotel. As soon as he exited, Boogop turned hard right, headed down the side of the building toward the street. But before he got there, he ducked right again, into the parking garage entrance. This was not much more brightly-lit than the hotel exterior, at least in the pathway to which Boogop kept.

Alpha One followed him up several levels to a skybridge, then across it and back into the hotel, staying far enough away that Boogop would remain unaware of them…thus, so would the vampire controlling him.

Boogop entered the hotel corridor then progressed to its end, where it teed into another; he turned left, then doglegged right. Alpha One trailed him while staying out of sight.

But when they peered around the dogleg, they were just in time to see him enter a door halfway down that corridor. Omega emitted a low hiss and Echo nodded.

They hurried down the hallway, looking for any sign of additional persons, but saw no one. They moved to the door, checking the notation on it; it was a spare laundry room and judging by the lack of traffic, not currently in use.

Echo glanced at Omega and raised an eyebrow; Omega nodded. The pair drew their primary blasters then stepped back. Echo delivered a powerful kick to the door; it flew open and Omega rushed inside, moving to the left, followed by Echo on the right.

The room was indeed an unused laundry room, empty of all save the equipment to handle copious quantities of bed and bath linens…and two figures.

Boogop lay quiescent on the floor, as a black-cloaked figure knelt over him. At the clatter of the Agents' entrance the figure looked up, allowing Alpha One to see a pale blonde woman with vivid amber eyes. As she raised her head, lime-green Andromedan blood flowed over her chin and dripped from her prominent fangs. Omega and Echo drew down on her.

The vampire growled, rising to her feet in a maneuver that was as inhuman as it was weightless. A flick of her wrist saw Boogop on his feet, advancing on the Agents with a snarl and all three eyebrow-equivalents drawn together in a scowl.

"Well, shit," Echo grumbled, holstering his weapon. "Didn't think about that."

"Nope," Omega noted, following suit. "We can't hurt him…"

But Boogop, under the influence of the strange vampire, had no such compunctions…AND he had three manual and three podal tentacles. Within moments both Agents found themselves grappling with one entranced Majestic Guard who had more tentacles than they had total hands…and a body which contained few major bones upon which to apply leverage.

"Dammit," Echo exclaimed as he pulled a tightening tentacle from his throat, "she's getting away!"

Omega's feet were off the ground as Boogop used two tentacles to lift her bodily but she twisted to see the vampire making for the rear exit into the adjacent corridor.

"NO!" she cried. "Zz'r'p! Somebody! HELP! Send help!"

* * *

Just then, Raph appeared in the doorway to the main corridor, crossbow in hand, bolt in place.

"DOWN!" he shouted.

With an effort, Echo lunged forward, carrying Boogop — with Omega in his tentacles — to the floor. Raph aimed and fired. A meaty *THUNK!* sounded as the smell of garlic wafted through the room…

…And Raph was gone.

The vampire let out a screech of pain; her body was transfixed to the wall of the far corridor, a crushed holly wreath between her body and the wall. She squirmed and clawed at the fletching, screaming, as the effects of the garlic — with which

Raph had thoroughly besmeared the bolt — and the holly made themselves known on her system. But the bolt had buried itself deeply enough that she could not get hold of it to pull it out.

Her distraction, however, meant Boogop was no longer under firm control so Alpha One quickly pinned him to the floor. Echo, having greater mass, sprawled across him while Omega pulled special force cuffs and restrained the Andromedan.

"Now for the main event," Echo grumbled as he and Omega strode to the far door of the laundry room. They peered into the corridor, looking both ways to ensure it was empty, before drawing their blasters once again. "Meg, be my guest."

"NO!" the vampire exclaimed, extending a pleading hand. She sniffed the air, then leered at Omega; Alpha One realized she'd recognized Omega's composite nature. "You, woman! Please! Free me; let me go with him and I'll trouble you no more! I can make you immortal! I'll show you how to control anyone!" Omega put a hand to her forehead as she felt pressure from without; the vampire was trying to control HER.

"Not interested," a scowling Omega muttered and opened fire, swinging her weapon in a short arc. The vampire's severed head fell to the carpeted floor, bumping and rolling several feet away, as Echo opened up with his own blaster to burn away the body.

"We're here," Jim said from somewhere behind them and Omega turned; Echo continued disposing of the body. Sean, Raph, and Lil flanked Jim as they meandered across the laundry room. "Huh. A bit late, I see. Good work."

"Thanks," Omega said, "but Raph pinning her to the wall is the only reason she didn't get away."

"She? Who is it?" Jim wondered, walking over and picking up the head. "Oh, damn. It's Irina Dalca. I was afraid she'd gone off the last time I saw her, and that was…what? Fifty years ago? Seventy-five?" He shook his head. "I'm sorry, honey," he told the decapitated head, "but it had to be done. We couldn't let you do this." He sat the head on the corner of a nearby sideboard that was bedecked with evergreen garland

and a big bowl of gilded fruit before turning to Echo. "Sir, if you please."

Echo turned his blaster on the severed head and moments later, there was nothing left to show Irina had existed except a crushed holly wreath, scorched paint, and the charred stump of a crossbow bolt, stuck in the wall. Jim sighed but said nothing.

"We'll take care of this mess and get Boogop back to his people, none the worse for wear," Raph noted, waving Lil forward. She raised her hands and began work eliminating the residual evidence and cleaning away all signs of their presence. "Jim, you and Sean escort our human allies back to the meeting point." He emphasized the word 'human,' and smiled at Omega as he did. She gave him a slight smile, then tucked her head, pleased.

"All over it," Sean said with a grin. "See, Hickey, that wasn't so bad. You didn't even have to do any of the fighting this time."

"True," Jim said, as the four headed down the hallway. "That I could get used to."

* * *

"What took y'all so long?" Omega demanded then. "Echo and I didn't expect her to use Boogop to keep us busy while she got away."

"Oh, there was a little matter of getting your 'bait' back to her quarters and then working out with Fox the best way to… ensure the Lambda Andromedan system remained free of… vampire lore," Jim explained, shooting a sidelong glance at Sean, who remained unusually impassive.

"Oh, did Fox brain-bleach 'em?" Omega wondered.

"Something like, yeah," Sean agreed. "Over here, Hickey. Lil said they'd meet us near the hucksters' room."

"Right," Jim said, veering left, toward the big room with the vendors. "Wasn't paying attention."

"So now what?" Echo queried. "This is gonna be one helluva shift report to write up."

"What do you mean, Ace? It's been a quiet shift," Omega

32

said then.

Echo stared at his partner as if she'd grown an extra eye, and it was on a stalk.

"C'mon, baby, quit joking," he told her.

"Who's joking?" she asked, confused.

"Agent Omega? Can I ask you some questions about the moon?" Sean wondered, drawing her to one side, just as Raph walked up with one arm around Lil.

"Sure," Omega agreed, cheerful. "I'm an astronomer; even if I don't know the answer, I can find out."

The two moved to one side, and Echo stared at the other three.

"What the hell just happened?" he pressed. "My partner just did something I've NEVER seen her do, in all the time I've known her. Not even with a brain bleacher on every setting we could come up with."

Jim sighed, turning to Raph. The angel held up a hand and stepped back.

"Thanks, pal," Jim grumbled. "You did part of it."

"You know why."

"Yeah, yeah. Look, Echo, the reason we were late was because security on the whole thing got...convoluted, as Fox might say. As he DID say. We three," he indicated himself, Lil, and Raph, "have some ability to control memory, and it works differently from any of your tech. Some of it doesn't even operate on the same plane of existence. So just because your tech doesn't work on your partner doesn't mean WE can't make her forget. Just like we did for Alpha Two and for all of the Majestic Guard."

"But not Fox."

"No. Not Fox. He's the Director of Division One. He has a need to know."

"And not me."

"That was one of the things we conclaved about," Jim admitted. "Fox decided it was time to read you in on our existence. You're his successor. You've got to know sooner or later. And if anything ever happened to him, you might need the information right away, not however long it took me to hear about it and come looking for you."

"Okay, I get that. But Meg?"

"She's not in the line of succession, Echo," Jim explained, earnest. "At least not yet. Truth to tell, Fox wanted her read in, too. But the rest of us felt it wasn't time."

"But she…she learned some personal stuff from Raph," Echo protested. "Will she at least remember that?"

"She won't remember anything about me except that I was an interesting friend of Jim's, I'm afraid," Raph said, voice very quiet. "I'm sorry, Echo. It wasn't my call. But YOU remember. Take care of her and help her walk the walk, okay?"

"Yeah," a glum Echo said. "That was NOT the way I expected this to end. You're asking me to keep a secret from my partner — my best friend. The person I haven't lied to, haven't really kept anything from, from the day I realized she'd have my back to her dying day."

"I'm sorry," Jim said with a sigh. "That's…the way it's gotta be, at least for now. Things may change in future; probably will. But for now, it is what it is."

"Hush," Lil murmured. "Here they come."

* * *

"Well, time to get on with things," Jim said, clapping Sean on the back. "You get your questions answered, wolf?"

"Yep," Sean said with that toothy grin. "Omega's a smart lady."

"I expect so. Echo, Fox knows how to get in touch."

"Right," Echo said, trying to hide his morose mood from his partner.

"Hey Ace, you okay?" Omega wondered.

"Yeah Meg, I'm fine. I'm…a little tired," Echo made excuse.

"Well, we need to go," Lil said, putting on a cheerful smile. "There's a panel coming up we wanna see. Good to meet you."

"Likewise," Omega said. "C'mon, Ace, we got work to

do."

"Right behind you, baby," he said.

And amid a chorus of "See you around!" the one-time team broke up, with Alpha One heading for the elevators and the immortals aiming for the panel rooms.

* * *

As the group split up to go their separate ways, a gray striped tabby peeped out of a dark alcove, watching as Alpha One, Jim, Sean, Lil, and Raph departed. It sniffed the air, curious.

Abruptly it shifted to a full-sized Bastian of the 6 Lyncis system, bipedal and nearly six feet tall...but there was something wrong: the eyes began to glow red and the already-long fangs elongated still further.

"Blood," it snarled very softly, then pulled back, vanishing in the shadows.

Moments later, the same little gray tabby trotted out of the alcove...

...Headed to the dealer's room.

Author Note:
The following story contains depictions of supernatural forces
and graphic combat scenes.
Recommended for mature audiences only.

The Bounty Game

by
Stephanie Osborn
& A.G. Thompson

Chapter One — Arrivals

Agent Pistol of Division One of the Pan-Galactic Law Enforcement and Immigration Administration leaned back the seat in his team's small SUV. With the top off, he was able to relax and keep an eye out for the incoming transport to the Division's Area 51 landing facility. He knew that the 'other' Area 51, on the eastern side of Papoose Mountain, operated by the U.S. Air Force, was currently on a maintenance stand-down and the inbound saucer would be clear into the Agency's own Area 51 spaceport. Said spaceport was on the western side of Papoose Mountain from the USAF base, with landing access along the eastern side of the Papoose Lake dry lakebed.

All the UFO nuts and ancient alien theorists and such had their attention firmly locked on what the Air Force was doing. In turn, the Air Force spent a great deal of time, money, and effort to keep said individuals' over-inquisitive noses out of U.S. military secrets. Neither group ever noticed the comings and goings of the heavily stealthed and cloaked saucers on the other side of the mountain. And that made life for Agent Pistol and his partner, Agent Mule, fairly simple and relatively comfortable.

"Hey, Mule, you ever think about applying for Alpha Line?" Pistol stretched and fished a can of soda out of the cooler mounted on the SUV's center console. "You want one?"

"Nah, I haven't finished the one I opened for lunch yet." Mule waved a half-empty can in the air. "And Alpha Line? I dunno, amigo. Too much of what they deal with leaves you stuck in some God-awful place like New York or Philadelphia. You know how crazy Headquarters, up in New York City, can get. Yuck. No thank you."

"How come? Afraid you wouldn't make the cut?"

"Callate, pendejo." Mule's grin in his dark face belied the

insult. "No, I like it here. I was born in the mountains and that's where I wanna stay. Besides, you can't hunt bighorn sheep on your day off when you're in New York. Well, not without having to get up early and travel a ways, anyhow. We have plenty to do here without sticking our necks out on a chopping block. Hell, you've read the reports about some of the crap Agent Echo and Agent Omega have been through." He paused long enough to take a deep swallow from his soda can. "I mean, hey, I admire the hell outta both of 'em, but there's a limit, ya know? You push the limit and eventually you wind up on the upper, right-hand corner of the envelope. You know, where your postage gets cancelled. I know my limits. Think I'll pass."

"So stomping through the mountains in Colorado or Utah, looking for some damn mountain goat, is better than being on the cutting edge up at HQ? Wuss."

"Cabrón, why don't you go apply, then? At least it'd get you outta my hair until some big bad turns you into roadkill."

Pistol chuckled at that. He had been partners with Mule for the better part of five years now, and despite constantly ragging on each other, they got along very well together — they were the best of friends, and usually hung out together, even in their off hours, as most partnerships tended to do — and as their records showed, they were excellent Field agents with a long list of accomplishments and commendations in their respective records.

But despite their experience and capabilities, neither of them had the least inkling of what was coming.

* * *

The local small animals were the first to notice. Squirrels, rabbits and such, sensed something was somehow wrong and quickly found other regions of the Gunnison National Forest to inhabit. The birds went next; even some large raptors took wing. Coyotes and cougars wasted little time making themselves just as scarce. In less than six hours of the first inklings that something very strange was coming, only a few elk, a wolf pack, and a grizzly sow with her three yearling cubs were still in the heavily forested hills twenty some-odd miles west of Colorado's Anthracite Range mountains. And even they appeared to be leaving the area; they were just taking their time about it.

Early that evening, as the saucer Agents Pistol and Mule were waiting for flashed meteorically through the upper atmosphere, reality — as embodied in the physical universe — was shredded and torn. The unreality of another, wildly differing universe pulsed and bulged into the mundane darkness, indefinable colors lashing out in arcs that left soil and grass and water twisted and warped. Those changes were incompatible with the existing world, but also irreconcilable with the energies that created them, energies from another cosmos. Everything transformed writhed and thrashed, rejecting that other reality before dying.

As the effect of the tear in reality spread, something oozed through that tear, forcing it into a portal as a multicolored, glutinous mass forced its way through the flaw in existence. It fell from ten meters in the air, the center of the rip in space-time, landing with a wet, sickening splatter, pieces of it flung away only to begin slowly creeping back to the larger mass. With the Entity through the portal, it closed with a thunderclap heard for miles through the mountains.

The Entity struggled with the new, bizarre environment to which it had escaped, fleeing an implacable hunter. The stress and energy required to break the boundaries between universes nearly killed it and left it in a stupefied state, barely aware of itself, much less its new environment. Slowly, it changed and adapted, struggling to breathe the alien atmosphere, absorbing what little life there was around it — only bacteria and a scant few insects.

A vulture, soaring on thermals, detected the scent of rot and corruption and slipped down the wind to investigate a possible meal. The bird flew within yards of the Entity before it realized that this was no meal but a...wrongness... that besmirched everything around it. That realization was too late as a pseudopod lashed out and yanked the bird out of the sky, engulfing it in its body. Death was slow and agonizing as the vulture was dissolved physically while the Entity slowly tore away the rudimentary mind and spirit of it, absorbing everything the bird was and had ever been.

This pattern continued, the Entity coalescing, becoming less of a shapeless, gelatinous mass. It grew optical sensors, olfactory cavities, and a sensitivity to audible waves in the air, abilities it absorbed from the luckless vulture and a very few other flying creatures it had attracted and snared. Intellect began to manifest in the Entity, and slowly it began to search for other lives to absorb and comprehend. It had no true self-awareness, at least not yet, only a vague sense that it was not safe and that it must feed, absorb life and spirit to become what it once had been.

As it slowly moved through the woods, it was attracted to powerful audible waves and strong vibrations through the soil across which it oozed. In a place without the numerous large, vertical immobile and inanimate lifeforms, it detected three large, mobile, animate life forms. Two of these crashed together again and again. A third, nearly identical life form stood on the far side of the clearing. At first the Entity lurked under the shade of the trees. It did not like the bright, concentrated, visible wavelengths of the great sky light.

It observed the life forms until the darkness began to fall. Their movements were less energetic and neither of the two larger ones attempted to flee as the Entity's pseudopods lashed out and buried long sharp beaks and claws, copied from the vulture, into their bodies. The third one bolted away, avoiding the grasping tentacle-like lashes by the slenderest of margins. Struggling and bugling, the two elk bulls were dragged into the Entity's body and absorbed. For the next hour, bulges and lumps reflected the elks' futile attempts to escape their fate.

The Entity's intellect grew as the minds and spirits of the elks were absorbed. Now it knew what hunters were and that they must be avoided. It now knew what, exactly, the elk feared.

Now, it knew what it needed to hunt for its own requirements.

* * *

Fred Rodriquez loved the mountains and the deep woods. The soaring evergreens and the deep green scent of pine filled his senses. A bit of a loner by nature, he was happier the deeper into the forest he traveled. He brought only what he absolutely needed with him and left little trace of his presence on the land through which he hiked. As much as he could, he lived off the land, emulating his distant Shoshone ancestors.

Fred saved his vacation time from the beginning of the year, using it to spend five or six weeks hiking the mountain woods before the start of the school year at the state university, where he worked as a certified Campus Police Officer. He had served in the Air Force Security Police many years ago. He knew he wasn't as young as he had been then, but he stayed in good shape and practiced regularly with his 1911 10mm pistol and his old 1895M lever gun in .45-70 Government. With those weapons, there was very little on two or four feet that he feared.

Fred's current camp site was a hundred meters or so uphill from one of the many little creeks in the local area. A half-mile further down, into the valley, was a good-sized clearing. He had heard elk bulls bugling earlier in the day and the rattle of antlers told him they were close, mostly likely down in that clearing, trying to attract females.

"Boys, yore sure lucky it's late August! A few more weeks and making that much of a ruckus will land ya in some hunter's freezer," he chuckled to himself. "Give it a rest, will ya? Be dark soon and the racket yer making will keep me from my beauty sleep. Lord knows, that's something I need."

Almost on cue the bugling abruptly cut off. He hadn't heard a gunshot, or he would have thought poachers had shot them. A dead silence fell over the woods, and Fred felt the hair on the back of his neck rise. He heard something bound through the brush along the creek and instants later, four-hundred-odd pounds of panicked elk cow crashed through his campsite, scattering his small campfire and knocking over him, his coffee pot and his tent as the terrified animal, the whites of its eyes signaling its desperation, thundered away up the hillside.

Fred stared after the cow from where he had fallen, stunned and confused. Elk normally gave humans a wide berth, so by any measure, this was damn strange behavior in the cow.

"What the hell?" Fred picked himself up and dusted off. "Something scared the pure hell outta that critter." Looking around as twilight began to fade to full dark, he recognized that an utter and unnatural silence had fallen, the receding sounds of the elk cow only emphasizing the quiet.

"This can't be good. What spooked her, a bear or cougar? Wolves? What happened to the bulls?" Unnerved, Fred picked up his belt with his pistol still holstered on it and fastened it securely before grabbing up his rifle and levering a round into the chamber. His hot handloads pushing a 430-grain hard cast bullet would drop anything that walked in North America. "What the hell is out there?"

He heard the sound first, grass and debris on the forest floor crackling as something slowly slid over it. Then he realized there was a vague black mass flowing toward him, flowing UPHILL. He could see the faintest reflections of starlight and the embers of his scattered campfire in the bizarre black mound. He reached over and flicked on the camp lantern hanging from a branch to get a good look at it.

For the smallest fraction of a second, he froze, his mind rejecting the reality of the thing in front of him. Then muscle memory kicked in, the rifle coming to his shoulder, and six rounds of heavy .45-70 slugs blasted into the thing, as fast as he could run the lever rifle. Dropping the empty rifle, his pistol flashed from the holster. He got off eight of the fourteen rounds in the magazine before the clawed tentacles grabbed him and jerked him screaming into the body of the creature. He joined the elk bulls in temporarily struggling to get free, before the thing suffocated him.

It stayed in that spot for several days, as it slowly and

completely absorbed everything that had ever been Fred Rodriquez.

* * *

The veils of the multiverse punished her during translation, leaving her sick and disoriented. The air ripped and tore at her lungs. Even in this supposedly remote area, she could nearly taste the acrid fumes of internal combustion engines. Her joints ached, and every old wound burned as if freshly inflicted. She coughed and spit, before retching and vomiting up the gel-like stuff that had been in lungs and stomach, bracing her internal organs against the pressure of translating from one universe to another. She dragged a hand across her face, clearing away the revolting stuff. Wearily sitting up, she raked her hands through long, bright auburn hair, stripping the protoplasmic goo out of it. More goo covered her naked body. Her skin twitched and shivered, trying to slide away from the rapidly decaying glop.

Well, Myclestra, you wanted to be alone. Now, you're alone. There's no one around. Not for two thousand ur-lans at least. Well, nothing but forest animals and plants. At least that damn druid and his unicorn partner, the ones responsible for getting me here, were right about nothing sapient nearby. By Alontora, how did I go from being a Shaeldrithan Slaver's Fetch, to fighting off Imperial Pyanjars, to being chased through some damn hot-rads ruins by cannibal mutants? From a battle-slave to a bounty hunter, and one that my old Masters want for a rug. Just because the Star-Drake ensouled in that Sword wanted out of their service and control! Surlianth just had to pick ME to become its next wielder.

She rolled to her knees and pulled the bio-pod containing everything she owned next to her. The bio-pod was, in a sense, alive, but it died as she drove her thumb into its release ganglia. The only way non-organic matter could be transmitted between universes was to be enclosed in a pseudo-living organism like the bio-pod. The thing flopped open and immediately began to decay. Within the hour, there would be nothing left of it.

Inside the pod were four cases, containing her scant

47

clothing, a few small valuables consisting of a dozen small gems and a single, pure gold nugget the size of her thumb, and her armor and weapons. She rolled on a synth-skin. The nearly transparent film melded tightly to her skin, allowing her direct neural access and control of her armor and any sophisticated weapons. The synth-skin regularly fooled human-norms and such into thinking that the Shaeldrithan Slavers' Fetches were nude or nearly so in battle. Despite appearing filmy and delicate, the stuff was tough enough to stop low-powered projectile weapons, as well as edged or pointed weapons, from penetrating, unless the weapon was magic, VERY high tech or swung by an inhumanly powerful arm. It might bruise, but it would not kill.

The armor harness, thin glittering straps and collar, slid on next, the field generators and energy packs no thicker than the tip of her little finger. Integrated with the synth-skin, it generated a powerful inertia-damping field, absorbing impact energy into recharging the packs and shedding forces that could knock her a thousand ur-lans across a battlefield. It would stop anything short of a Republic Battlesuit's railgun. The armor might stop a railgun round...once. The tech-wizards made many such items for the Shaeldrithan Masters, who then issued it to such of their Warrior Castes, Battle-Slaves and Fetches as they believed could be trusted with such powerful tech armor. A bad choice for them in her case.

The tech-wizards also made the plasma pistol she pulled out of the pod next. Maintenance was critical on plasma weapons as they tended to explode in the user's hand when tolerances got too loose. The underslung power pack gave her ten shots and she had a second pack on a carrier on her belt. Once she used both packs, she'd probably have to dump the weapon if she couldn't replace the barrel with its molecule-thick lining of collapsed neutronium. Not to mention lacking a way to recharge the packs themselves. There weren't any handy wizards here, she thought.

And then there was the Sword. A bit over an ur-lan and

a half long, the mono-molecular-edged blade could slice diamond with little effort. It was ornate, polished and inlaid with gems and metals completely unfamiliar to her. In her hands, it balanced perfectly. With it, she could take down one of the Free Republic's heavily armored, powered Battlesuits in a single swing. Assuming she survived the suit's deadly accurate long-range railgun fire.

She pulled on the short, snug tunic and skin-tight leggings before slipping on her tall pathfinder boots. Her belt locked around her slender waist. Pouches held the talismans for the few spells she knew, fire starters, and weather-wraps. Trail rations, a compact shelter, and what little spare clothing she had, it all went into a small pack she slung on her back. The plas-pistol locked into its holster, sealed there unless released by her unique handprint. The sword in its sheath slung next to the pack, its ornate hilt jutting up over her right shoulder. It would accept no hand but her own. And finally, to cover her blind, white eyes, eyes lacking pupil or iris, she slipped on her eye-shields.

The Shaeldrith had spent millennia tinkering with her people's genome. A distant ancestor born on the long-lost planet of Alontora would scarcely recognize her as a descendant. Her own line had initially been designed as pleasure slaves, and the lush contours of her body still reflected that purpose. But when her line had been repurposed as Fetches a millennium ago, massive changes were coded into her DNA.

Her senses were enhanced, but the cost had been the loss of actual sight in the visual spectrum. She perceived the world mostly through senses based on sound and pressure. Those senses were as good as sight, nearly. She did not perceive color, nor could she see through a window. Its greatest limitation was how far she could 'see,' barely two thousand ur-lans, an ur-lan being roughly the length of her arm, shoulder to fingertip. Beyond that distance, she depended on sound and scent. Her hearing was immeasurably keener than even the best electronic systems; she could sort a thousand human-norms by their scent alone, and her tactile abilities allowed her to differentiate between the thicknesses of human hair.

Her skeleton and musculature were also reinforced and enhanced, giving her strength and endurance almost even with the latest versions of Republic Battlesuits. A bio-optically enhanced neural system gave her unbelievably fast physical reactions. She could catch a butterfly out of the air between wingbeats and release it without disturbing the pollen on its wings. Despite looking human enough to pass among the norms with little notice, she was literally inhuman in her abilities and capabilities.

But here and now, she was the only one of her kind in this entire universe. If she couldn't hunt down and kill her target, capture its stolen life-energy, she would likely be stuck here for the rest of her life. The Warpwraith should provide the energy she needed to return. If she could not return, that would mean the loss of a very large payday, but perhaps the locals in this universe would pay very well to keep something like a Warpwraith from spreading and multiplying, infesting as many of their worlds as it could reach. If the thing found a power source to feed on, well, that would make it a challenge even for her.

And if she did wind up stuck here, then she would remain the only Alontoran to ever stand under the warm light of Terra's Sol. And she supposed that might be reward enough for her.

Who knows? At least the humans of this world shouldn't fear me on sight. Mothers' Blessings, what more could I want? She extended her senses to their limit. There was no sign of the Warpwraith. She had no idea how far away she was, but she had followed the Warpwraith through the tear in reality it forced when fleeing. Maybe not the smartest thing she'd ever done, but here, at least, she doubted the Masters could get their tentacles on her. She shouldn't be too far away from wherever the thing had fled between realities. She knew it was here, in this dimension, on this planet and within a reasonable distance from where she had arrived. She turned to face southeast.

Seems like civilization is that way. Time to start hiking. The Sword should recover soon. I hope. The bond is still there. In the meanwhile, maybe I can enjoy a little peace and quiet. She settled her gear and stepped out, following the hill contours, avoiding both the ridgelines and the valleys. She wondered what this world would be like, and if she might be accepted, hunter or hunted.

* * *

Kim Hallowell stretched luxuriously on the comfortable pad of sleeping bags, blankets and the light jackets that formed the floor of the tent. Her boyfriend, Ian Jose Soto, propped his head on his hand and enjoyed the view, all the more so since Kim didn't have a stitch of clothing on her athletic young body. She finished her stretch and smiled at Ian.

"Enjoying the view?" she asked.

"Oh, hell yeah. As Dad would say, muy bonita chica." He reached out and ran a gentle hand up her smooth flank. "You know both my Mom and Dad really, really like you. Mom says you're good for me, in lots of ways."

"Yeah, I know."

"I think they're expecting me to pop the question on you before the end of the year." He lay on his back as she rolled over and leaned on his chest, looking into his green eyes. "I mean, hey, you know I love you, but are we really ready for that?"

"I love you, too." A long finger tapped the end of his nose. "My parents don't, but they're stupid old stick-in-the-mud Boston Brahmins. They threw a fit when I accepted the cheerleader scholarship to Colorado. 'How dare I? Hallowell girls are NOT cheerleaders! They go to Harvard or perhaps Brown as a second choice, but never such a vulgar place as Boulder, Colorado!' I thought Father was going to have a stroke and Mother had to calm him down." Her fingers walked down his face to his chest.

"And then me, right?"

"Yes," she smiled and kissed his nose, "an Irish-Mexican

51

guy studying mechanical engineering, of all things. Not even a doctor-to-be, or preferably, a lawyer."

"Hey, Dad OWNS his own drilling company. We've got fifteen rigs working everywhere from Texas to Saudi Arabia and two offshore rigs in the Gulf of Mexico. He ain't Bill Gates but we're a hell of a lot more than COMFORTABLE. Guess oil money is too dirty for them, huh?"

"Yeah," she sighed, "Father will probably disown me. That is, if Mother lets him. She won't like it, your Dad being a naturalized American citizen who started off as a Mexican roughneck working on oil rigs. But one look at his company's stock portfolio and she'll yank a knot outta Father. She knows where the bread is buttered."

"Oh." He shivered as her fingers walked lower on his chest, tracing his ribs. "Quit that."

"What? Ticklish?"

"You know I am and you're not. Not fair at all, you cheater."

"'If ya ain't cheating, ya ain't trying.' Father's older brother, Uncle Connor, told me that one when I was in high school. Ha. Talk about black sheep! He went and joined the Marines. Now he's a Master Gunnery Sergeant. Father will just barely tolerate him, but Mother likes him, so he's still welcome." The fingers wandered lower. "Now, about a certain question, hmm?"

"You know, laying here stark naked and all sweaty from, hmm, certain highly *aerobic* activities, in a tent in the middle of a forest in the Rocky Mountains, well, I don't think this is a really great spot for, well, ah, hmm, certain, ah, proposals to be put forth. If your parents found out, I think they'd both have aneurysms. I wouldn't want that on my conscience."

"We don't have to tell them. Well?"

"You're being awful pushy, you know?"

"Us Boston types are like that."

"Fine. Will you marr—? Yurk!"

"Yes, I will," she rushed the answer as she lunged to

kiss him extremely thoroughly. Things proceeded quite satisfactorily from there.

* * *

The wolves wanted no part of Mama Grizzly when her sensitive nose led her to the spot of their recent kill. Half a dozen wolves were no match for the bear and her three yearling cubs, and they promptly made themselves scarce. There were other deer in the woods.

Winter was coming and the big female grizzly instinctively knew she needed all the protein and fat she could get before going into hibernation. Her cubs, as yet, weren't quite as food obsessed as their mother was, and after bolting down some of the deer, they wandered downhill toward the sound of a creek.

The young male preferred fish to deer and his two female siblings generally followed his lead. Unfortunately for the young bear, this small creek wasn't big enough to have anything in it but a handful of frogs. He caught one by surprise and stuffed it in his mouth before bawling and spitting it out when it urinated in his mouth. While the cub rubbed his face and mouth in the creek, the frog vanished into the water.

He looked up just in time to see something lurch out of the tree line on the other side of the creek. It was big and squishy and its surface bubbled and heaved. It was a bit bigger than the cubs' mother, but it was unnatural, a shape and scent that the cubs automatically realized was a hideous blot on the grass of the clearing. The male and one of the female cubs immediately turned and bolted away uphill, bawling in terror as they fled to the safety of their mother.

The other female cub turned to run an instant too late and a pseudopod lashed across the creek and wrapped around her hind legs. The thing shuffled across the creek, the water it passed through running darkly downstream as the frogs in the water twitched in agony before floating belly-up in the blackened sludge the creek water was quickly becoming. Screaming and clawing at the turf, the cub was dragged into the body of the thing.

53

The mother grizzly heard the cries of her cubs and recognized their terror. She dashed down the hill, meeting the two fleeing cubs just inside the forest. She slid to a stop, snuffling the pair briefly, before resuming her charge down to the creek to rescue her third cub. She reached the stream bed just in time to see her cub sucked squealing into the tar-like mass. With a roar that shook the trees, she crashed into the thing that had her cub, massive paws smashing aside flailing pseudopods and sending gouts of the foul black ichor of the thing flying.

But this was one time that a mother's rage and a grizzly bear's strength and power were insufficient to her need to save her cub. The bits and blobs torn from the thing stole back to the body of the monster as the rest of it reared up, above the eight-foot-tall bear, and fell on her like an avalanche. The thing lost whatever rudimentary form it had possessed as the bear ripped and tore at it, desperately attempting to get loose from the suffocating mass. But, like Fred Rodriquez and the elk bulls before him, there was no escape. The remainder of the day and through the night, bulges and swellings reflected the bear's weakening attempts to claw loose. At dawn, when the two surviving cubs came to the edge of the trees to seek their invincible mother, the thing lashed out and absorbed them into its bulk almost as an afterthought.

It lay there throughout the day, absorbing energy and mass. The potential life energy of the three young cubs was especially sweet, as was the strength of their mother, the powerful urges of the elk and, perhaps most importantly, the knowledge of Fred Rodriquez. Night fell and the thick, gluey mound of the thing thickened and hardened, becoming an irregularly shaped shell. With the dawn, that shell crumbled away into dust, absorbed by what now stood there. It stretched out human arms and flexed hands and fingers.

Finally, I am remade, forged anew from souls and spirits. It raised its face to absorb the energy of the morning light. *Not a source I can make much use of, but these beings that populate this world! The power and energy and intellect of their spirits! If the memories of this Fred Rodriquez are correct, the use of... what would they call it? Hechicería, sorcery or magic in the languages he spoke, it is unknown and unused here. Interesting. There should be deep wells of power to draw on here, at least in some places.*

And there are other energies here I may be able to use, this electricity, he called it. But these humans, they are warlike and possess powerful weapons. If his memories are correct. And the other things in his memories, what are called fantasy and horror stories. Those I might be able to make real, and the fear and terror and anguish they cause will also feed my power.

Still, I must move slowly and subtly here. I must ensure that there are none here who might challenge my power, or worse, seek to hunt me, as that damnable bounty hunter did. But I do not believe there is any means that she could have used to pass through the veil between universes. Not without help. So at least now I should be free of that bitch's pursuit. And who will dare attempt to claim a bounty on me when I rule this world and can spread throughout this universe? I do believe I shall enjoy it here. I shall need a name. That human's name will not do, for he will be known and eventually missed. His is not a place I would take. I shall have to ponder this. Names are powerful and I must choose appropriately. I can almost remember my old name, but not quite.

* * *

The sudden mountain thunderstorm caught her unprepared and in the open. The lightning was of no concern unless it actually hit her, and even that she might survive. But the crashing thunder and the pouring rain, a true Rocky Mountain deluge, drove her as close to unreasoning terror as she had ever been. Stumbling blindly along, she had reached a tree trunk and held on for dear life. The rain and thunder blotted out her senses, washing scent away, dulling sound and disrupting her ability to 'see' anything beyond arm's reach.

Myclestra feared few things, but being effectively blinded

by storms, snow, rain and thunder, those were some of the few things that left her feeling very helpless, blind and vulnerable. She couldn't sense anything at all beyond the shelter of the tree under which she huddled.

I truly hope this is a rare occurrence on this world. That damned Warpwraith won't care. It just grows eyes and ears as it needs them, until it takes a convenient shape. One that can see and hear. She shivered as a spectacular clap of thunder shot pain through her head. *Mothers! I can't sense anything beyond an ur-lan in this. Please, Alontora, home of my ancestors, end this soon.*

<Child, you know this will pass. The Warpwraith would not pick a world where the very environment might threaten it. You know this.> Surlianth's mental voice startled her a bit.

"What happened to you? I was beginning to think you'd somehow been hurt by the passage." Despite her snappy response, hearing the drake's voice in her mind was a great relief.

<No, child, not hurt, as you might say, but greatly discomfited. This world is…different, remarkably so. There is magic here, but deep and difficult to reach. Powerful magic but never accessed in any form that I can sense.> She felt the Drake's shrug in her mind. <That will matter more to the Warpwraith than to you.>

"Will my talismans still work? I mean, they're not exactly the spells of an archmagus or a ley-line walker, but they have their uses."

<Yes, your cantrips and hexes will still function. If by no other means than me lending them the power to allow them to function. They are minor enchantments, but you have always excelled at getting the most out of the least likely things, whether physical or magical.>

"Usually it's do that or die. What about Wruthas, the Warpwraith, will it still be able to pull power out of this world?"

<Perhaps. It was a powerful mage and sorcerer, made even more powerful by its very nature. I believe, however, that the

passage between universes will have been much harder on it than on you. Assuming it survived, which I do so assume, it will need time to recover itself. Time and energy. And it will only get that energy by stealing it from other living things, animate ones preferably but possibly even from the plants here, such as this tree that has sheltered you.>

"Ugh. I pity anything that crosses its path. If I could find it now, while it is weak, while the veil between universes is still weaker, I could slay it and return with enough to prove its death. Not to mention using its power to open the way. That would pay me enough to pass far beyond my old Masters' reach."

<Perhaps, child. And perhaps not. Only the greatest good fortune might lead you across its path while it recovers.> The drake turned its attention away from her. <The storm is passing. Come, let us go. The creature will seek out life, intelligent life, and then seek to hide, to blend into this world and plan to rot it from within. Something we must strive to prevent.>

"Or die trying?" She stood up and shook water off her weather-wrap. "Dead bounty hunters do not get paid. Keep that in mind."

<I shall.>

* * *

The wolf pack never really had a chance.

As scarce as prey had been lately, sighting the lone human trudging along the trail was good fortune. The man was following another creek a valley over from where the grizzly had driven them away from the deer carcass. Normally they would have never considered attacking a human, but hunger was stronger than fear now. The entire pack had come together, a dozen strong. The year had been hard and none of the pups under a year old had survived.

They stalked him carefully. Had they been human, they would have recognized his short black hair flecked with gray, black mustache with hints of silver, and dark brown eyes with reddish-tan skin as representing either Hispanic or Native

American heritage, if not both. He was somewhat shorter than average — several inches below six feet, perhaps only five-foot-seven or eight — and muscular for his build, though middle-age spread was beginning to catch up with him. He had a casual, easy stride that covered ground readily and swiftly, not unlike a member of one of the Indian tribes of the region. He carried nothing that was obvious, not even a backpack, and he seemed intent on something ahead of him, rather than his surroundings.

The wolves knew what guns were, but they neither saw a gun nor scented the smell of gunpowder and steel. They slunk ahead of the oblivious man and rushed him from less than ten yards. It should have worked; humans were so clueless, they couldn't smell anything this side of a skunk, and this man was just ambling along, paying no attention to his surroundings. Or so they thought.

As the wolves broke cover, lunging for the man, he flung up an arm and clenched his fist. All of the wolves were stopped stone still, whether on the turf or in midair. The man looked at them, smiled, and shook his head. He gestured with his other hand and the three yearling wolves floated through the air to his body and were absorbed into it, as if a stone were pushed into thick mud. He stared at the remaining wolves for a moment. Then he gestured again and all nine of them floated to within a few feet of him. His smile was as predatory as any wolf's had ever been.

"You lot will do for now. Let me see what can be done with you. Hmm." He delved into Fred Rodriquez's memories and thought about what he found there for long moments. "Yes, that will do. I think I can sense some more humans not impossibly far away. Perhaps I should see just how effective I can use the legends and stories of this world to produce fear and terror. And you, my loyal beasts, shall be the first of my… hmm, my experiments."

His eyes burned with an unholy black light as he forced the wolves' bodies together, creating six creatures where there had been nine. Then, with casual waves of one hand, he twisted and warped the resulting things, bending spines, stretching long-fanged jaws and growing claws much longer than the grizzly bear's claws. Burning red eyes met his, and he smiled.

"Yes, what was it he would have called you, ah, yes, el hombre-lobo, the werewolf. So, let me see how good a hunter you lot are. Go! Find the humans! Kill any males but bring me the females, alive, if you can! Enjoy the hunt, extend it as best you can." Howls tore the air as the reduced and twisted pack turned and ran through the woods. "Good. That is the direction I thought I felt more humans. They are at least on the correct track. If they are killed or die of exhaustion, then the spell of transformation will bring their energy back to me. The same spell will also bring me the life energy of anything they kill. I think I am only beginning to realize how rich with life and souls this world is. How delicious."

* * *

Kim hung her soaked clothes on the rope strung between two trees. Ian had already hung his up and gone down to the creek about forty yards away to wash up. The storm had caught them by surprise and soaked them both to the skin. And their backpacks had proven to be less waterproof than advertised. Their food, in its waterproof bag, was fine, but all their extra clothes were hanging on the line and they were both wearing just their skin. They put up their tent, the sleeping bags still dry on the inside and with nothing better to do with the time, cuddled together, and one thing led to another.

Later, Kim smiled and stretched next to Ian, wonderfully happy and content with the entire world at the moment. Her guy had proposed to her; oh, they'd do it again, properly for her Mother and Father, who could either deal with it or go hang. And their lovemaking was fantastic as always. She didn't know how she could be any happier right now. Then Ian sat up suddenly, startling Kim.

"What's wrong, honey?" she asked, raising up on an elbow.

"I heard something. Something wrong."

59

"What are you talking about? I don't hear anythi—?" She stopped mid-word as the faintest hint of a howl came to her. "What was that?"

"Don't know, but there's another one, and I think they're getting closer. Wolves, maybe. Sure ain't no coyote. Did a pack get on a scent? Lord knows, this area has been awful scarce with game…or any animals, for that matter. There it is again and yeah, I think there's another one, maybe three or more." Ian rolled over, pulling on his hiking shorts and grabbing the pistol he carried in the woods, an old cowboy gun in .45 LC, taking a second to check the loads in the old single-action revolver. "Stay here a second, babe. Wolves never want any part of humans. And I don't think wolves would be coming this way in midafternoon. If they're running a deer, the deer would head deeper into the woods, not down into the open ground near the creek. Something ain't right. Maybe get dressed?"

Ian stepped out of the tent, stuffing the pistol into the belt of his shorts. He shaded his eyes against the bright afternoon sun that followed the storm's clearing away. He could see a good way up the ridgeline. He froze as something ran over the ridge, followed by five others just like it, if not as big.

"Madre de Dios, that can NOT be possible." The remark was little more than a whisper to himself, then he got another look at the lead creature. "KIM! Get out here! Now!" he yelled.

"What's wrong?" came from inside the tent.

"GET OUT HERE NOW, DAMMIT!" When she poked her head out of the tent, he reached out and grabbed her by the shoulder, jerking her painfully out of the tent and to her bare feet. "Look there! You see those things?"

"What in the world are those thin—?" She stared in disbelief.

"I don't know, but they scare the shit outta me. RUN! NOW!" He pushed her toward the creek. "Just go, as fast as you can! There's an old fire tower on the other side of the valley across the ridge. You can climb up there and drop the ladder. GO, dammit!"

"What about you?" She stumbled and nearly fell from his shove.

"I've got the gun! I'll be okay, but just in case, will you please just go?! NOW!" He roared the last at her and Kim turned and bolted toward the creek.

As she crossed the creek and labored up the hillside to the opposite ridgeline, she heard the howls and snarls intensify. She stopped at the top of the ridge and looked back. Ian brought the old revolver up in a two-handed grip and the big .45 roared. She saw one of the…things…stumble, go down and then stagger quickly back to its feet. The pistol roared as fast as Ian could fan the hammer and each shot hit one of the creatures, blasting away fur and blood. But it didn't stop them; hell, it barely slowed them down. Then they buried him in an avalanche of fur, fangs, and claws. Blood spurted into the air and Ian's last anguished sound was a scream of "RUN!" He screamed again, a wordless shriek of agony as they tore him apart.

Stunned and mute with horror, terror, and grief, she turned and bolted down the hill, toward the old fire tower she could see now, all the way across the valley on the opposite hilltop. She stumbled and fell more than once, bruising and cutting herself. She ran her feet into bloody shreds as she leapt across the tiny rill-stream at the bottom of this valley. She looked back and saw the things stop and watch her from the top of the ridge between the two valleys. Then they howled as one and started down after her, the biggest one in the lead by yards. She didn't waste breath screaming, but put her head down and ran with everything she had, ran for dear life. Ran until she reached the edge of the trees and slammed directly into something, someone she never saw.

She hit that person, a woman from the substantial breasts she'd hit face first, hard enough to knock them both flat. But the stranger simply caught her and stopped her cold. She looked up into an odd set of mirrored sunglasses.

"We've got to run!" she gasped, "The monsters, the things

are coming, run away!"

"Karta pole midagi. Olete ohutu." The tall woman gently pushed her down, before laying something on her forehead. "Jääma." Kim tried to move, to get away, and found she could not move a muscle. Not even to scream.

* * *

The local sun was warm and bright. Myclestra thought it felt like the latter part of summer, assuming this world was even slightly similar to the one she had left. The gravity might be a bit lighter and she thought the air was richer, invigorating and pleasant as she strode along. The sun had traveled a bit more than a handspan when she heard it.

A long, quavering howl echoed through the forest then, quickly followed by another. Then another. She cocked her head, listening carefully. The howls were beyond the reach of all her senses save her hearing. And these howls did not sound in the least like a normal wolf. Not even a giant dire wolf.

I hope that isn't what it sounds like. But I'm afraid it is. I didn't think this reality extended to include preternaturals! And that certainly sounds like a kariskirlar *pack in full cry. And headed this way at a moderate speed. I wonder what or who they're coursing after. And if they scent me, probably they'll hunt me as well. Wonderful. I haven't been here a fortnight yet. Perdition, I haven't been here a day yet!*

<And what exactly did you expect, Child? We know the Warpwraith came here. And it would waste no time creating terror and horror. It feeds on such. Perhaps haste would be in order?>

"Just what I need, a magic sword with the soul of a snarky star-dragon housed in it."

<What? Doesn't everyone want such a boon companion, such a wise and powerful advisor?>

"Not once they realize that you never shut up."

<Please! Am I not a font of wisdom and advice for you? Not to mention the invincible blade my soul inhabits? Able to cut through nearly anything short of collapsium-enhanced

62

power armor? And the many other Gifts I grant you?>

"Let me think about it." She shouldered the light pack and headed off toward the howls at a dead run.

* * *

Wruthas, my name was Wruthas. Ah, there is so MUCH power here. And none who know how to wield it. It stood there and exulted as the life of the young human his creatures had killed flowed into him. Energy that filled it and brought power and memories with it. *They know to bring the female to me, alive, despite the distance. What did Fred Rodriquez call them? Ah, yes, miles. Several miles. I shall move toward them to secure my prize.*

The creature strode off, into the woods, following the distant howls of the monsters it had created. Ah, the power that a young female would give him, as he drained her and broke her soul, before consuming her to grant it even more power! It nearly salivated at the thought.

* * *

Myclestra reached the edge of the woods just in time to 'see' a naked, young, apparently human female run down the valley side, tumbling heels over head more than once. She detected the creatures as they stopped on the ridgeline and watched the human girl's futile flight.

Saa-haa, it has grown powerful already, if it can create a kariskirlar *pack so soon. Perhaps it arrived here well before I did. After all, dimensional portals don't have to connect identical timestreams.*

<So, what are you going to do about it? There are enough of those creatures to concern you, but only slightly. But while you deal with some, the others may slay that human. And I believe anything slain by the pack will feed the Warpwraith. There is a compulsion on the beasts to bring their prey, or the spirits thereof, to it.>

So, old snake, are you up to dealing with the rest if I slay the leader? I'd rather not use my plas-pistol if there is any other choice. I have too little in the way of supplies for it to last long if I use it frequently.

<I believe I could do so, but you will owe me more ornamentation if I do so.>

Oh, you...fine, I'm sure this world has gold and gems enough to satisfy even a greedy drake.

<Then yes, let us render succor to this poor child. I am ready.>

Myclestra sprinted silently to the edge of the woods, reaching a forest giant just as the girl ran into the wood's edge. She stepped out into the girl's path and caught her as she plowed into Myclestra at full speed. Gasping for breath, the nude girl spoke in unknowable gibberish, struggling to continue fleeing the pack.

"There is nothing to fear. You are safe." She knew the human wouldn't understand her, but hopefully she would at least understand the calm tone. And to ensure she didn't run off into the woods, she pushed the stunned girl to the forest floor before pulling a talisman from her belt and laying it on her forehead. "Stay." She activated the spell to keep the girl in place and walked out into the sunshine to confront the *kariskirlar* pack, drawing the Sword as she advanced.

The leader was well out in front of the rest of the pack. It howled, redoubling its speed as it leapt at her. A hand like a steel clamp shot out and grabbed the mutated wolf by the throat. It clawed and snapped at her, her armor flashing into visibility as the field protected her. The Sword flashed thrice as she sliced the monster into quarters and beheaded it. She spun the blade in a humming blur, to cleanse it of the polluted blood. The Sword swept out and pointed at the other monsters as they scrabbled to a confused halt.

"Tuld võtma!" she intoned. The point of the Sword unleashed a dreadful blast of elemental fire that flashed across the creek, instantly converting the water there into pure steam, and then up the side of the valley to the ridgeline. It reduced the monsters and everything else on the valley's side to either vaporized ash, or bubbling glass.

* * *

"Did you see that, Ace?" The tall, gorgeous, platinum blonde Agent in the pilot's seat of the saucer D1 *Calypso* suddenly focused out the saucer's window. She glanced over her shoulder at her partner and husband, sitting in the navigator's position to her left, pointing her thumb out the main window of the saucer, and off to one side. The Agent seated behind her there was a good bit taller than she was, broad-shouldered and masculinely attractive. His tanned features reflected his Native American ancestry. He raised an eyebrow.

"See what, baby? Agent Chi, did you see anything?" Agent Echo, Chief of Alpha Line and senior partner of the Alpha One team glanced at the brown-haired Agent in the co-pilot's seat.

"Negative, Agent Echo. I'm making sure we stay in the proper re-entry corridor. This IS my final check-out flight for my deep space pilot's certification, remember? If I wanna make the Alpha Line cut, it'll be a bonus in my favor if I'm already a certified pilot. And I'm lucky enough to have Alpha One giving me my check-out ride!"

"Okay, fair 'nuff. Omega, what did you see?"

"One hell of a thermal flash, big, bright and, I'd say, hot as heck. And well west, maybe southwest, of Denver, but in the mountains, I'd say way back in the back country. Maybe in one of the National Forests in southwest Colorado. And big enough to be seen from our two hundred thousand plus feet of altitude."

"Copy that. You see anything else, maybe a forest fire or something?" Echo leaned over to peer out the window. "Anything there now?"

"Nothing visible, no smoke or fire. But I've got a sensor on it now. Gimme a sec." Omega focused on her instrumentation, compensating for the effect of the thickening atmosphere. "Dear God," she whispered, "that can't be right."

"What can't be right, baby?" Echo sat back in his seat as Omega focused the sensors.

"If, and it's a huge IF, I'm getting accurate readings,

whatever that was, it was nearly as hot as the Little Boy bomb used on Hiroshima. There's no fireball or anything, but damn, I'm reading a residual heat over two thousand degrees Celsius. Why isn't the whole damn forest on fire there? This is freakishly weird."

"How so, Meg?" Echo asked.

"It's like an incredibly intense and hot, thousands of degrees hot, thermal pulse somehow lashed out and then instantly dissipated, leaving only radiant heat from the burned area." She sat back in her seat. "And there is nothing there, no structures, no vehicles — there aren't even any aircraft within a hundred miles. Nothing. This is beyond bizarre." She pulled her French braid around and briefly twirled the end between her fingers.

"Okay, Meg, what's going on in that head of yours?" Echo reached out and tapped her on the shoulder. "Is this something you've got one of your…FEELINGS about? Talk to me, baby."

"I…I don't know, Ace. I think, hmm, I think maybe." She twirled the hair for a few more moments while she considered. "Yeah, don't ask me why or how or what, but I think my brain is trying to tell me this is important."

"Gotcha." Echo turned to Chi. "Are we in too deep to divert to the Area 51 spaceport, Chi?"

"We'll have to abort the approach to Chicago and orbit at least once more. Depends on how visible you wanna be, I guess. I think I could manage it now, but we'd be a high energy object that'd be damn hard to cloak. I dunno, I'm still not one hundred percent on exactly what the cloaks and scramblers can and can't do. Depends on how important Omega thinks this is, I suppose."

"Baby, what's your thought? Either we divert to Area 51 or we contact them and have a field team sent out to evaluate the spot. You have any insights or flashes of pre-cog on this?"

"I…I'm not sure, Ace. This feels really strange, like things are somehow all jumbled up in time and space. It's giving me the beginnings of a nasty headache."

"Copy. It's your call."

"Contact Area 51 Ground Control and have them get someone out there ASAP. Soon as we're on the ground, you can finish Chi's paperwork while I get the 'Vette and check our gear, then grab anything else we think we might need. Then we'll get our own butts out there as quick as we can and let me eyeball it, whatever it is."

"Sounds like a plan. I'll contact Area 51 now."

"Fine," Omega sighed, a pensive look in her sapphire blue eyes. "I just hope that's the right call."

"Me too, baby. Me too."

* * *

Wruthas had felt his creations die, but no more than that. He saw the flare of light and heat that flashed up into the air above the ridgelines. He wasn't exactly sure what could have caused such a thing, but he was certain it had not been the human female the creatures had been pursuing. Something about it teased his memory, just out of his reach. But he knew for certain that he wanted no part of whatever was the source of that deadly burst of heat and light. Whatever it was, it was not something he was ready to challenge. Not yet.

He turned and headed directly away from the flare, *west*, Fred Rodriquez's memories whispered to him. *West* was rugged and mountainous, either only lightly inhabited or completely uninhabited by humans. He could stretch his senses, feel out the ley-lines this world must have and use them to travel much faster than his feet might carry him. In the meantime, he could delve further into Fred Rodriquez's memories and knowledge. He had already learned that he was in a kingdom or nation called the United States, perhaps the most powerful nation on this world.

Good, good. Where else might I suborn the rulers of one country and use them to bring the world entire to heel? He split his attentions, instinctively seeking out the ley-lines of telluric current amounting to magical power even as he considered everything Fred Rodriquez had ever known.

* * *

"You're going to be okay, honey." The gentle voice summoned her back to awareness. "Can you tell me your name?"

"Uh, Kim, Kim Hollowell." The world was a watery blur. She could barely make out the person leaning over her in a dark green uniform. "Where's Ian? What happened to those THINGS, those monsters?" She struggled and tried to sit up before hands pushed her back down. "Let me UP, dammit!"

"Okay, Kim, I'm going to let you sit up if you promise to take it easy. You're safe, there's no monsters or things here. But you were alone, we don't know what happened to…Ian, you said? Is he your brother or boyfriend?" The hands helped her to sit up, keeping a blanket wrapped around her. Her vision cleared and she realized the gentle voice was a woman in a US Park Ranger's uniform.

She was sitting on a stretcher at the base of an old fire watchtower. The valley spread out in front of her. She saw several trucks and SUVs, all painted in Ranger green. Other rangers were walking around the edge of the tree line with cameras. There was something covered under a large gray tarp just a few yards away from a large pine tree. Beyond that, no more than two long strides farther away, a scorched, black scar went down to the creek, then several hundred feet up the opposite side of the valley. It was no more than four or five feet wide where it began, and it stretched into a wedge shape as it extended up the valley's side, ending nearly seventy yards wide at the top of the ridgeline.

"Wha…what happened?" Kim realized she was nude under the blanket. "Where are my clothes?"

"Well, you were hiking up here, with someone else, right?" The Ranger knelt next to her, her name tag reading Ramos. "Where was your camp? Can you tell me?"

"Uh, yeah, it's in the next valley over." Memory spilled over her like a torrent. "Ian was there, we got caught in the rainstorm and all our clothes got wet. We were resting, well, he'd just proposed to me earlier, and then he heard something, and he got out of the tent with his gun and there were these things coming down the valley, howling like wolves. He told me to run, to go to the fire tower. He shot at them and then I heard him scream, oh my God, they, they, they killed him! Oh my God, and I ran, and I fell and tumbled. My feet were bloody and I cut my back and shoulder. I got up and ran again. Those, those things, they were just standing on the ridge, watching me, then the biggest one started chasing me and then the others followed. I was running for the tower and I knew they were gonna catch me and then I ran right into someone, a woman, I think. She grabbed me and pushed me down. She did something and I couldn't move and then there was this huge roar, like nothing I'd ever heard. Then there was fire and flames and heat everywhere."

"Ok, ok, slow down. Then what?" The ranger unobtrusively held a cell phone where it could record what Kim was saying, as she babbled in a near panic. "You're safe. Then what happened? How'd you get up into the tower? Would you recognize this woman if you saw her again?"

"Huh?" Kim stared at the ranger. "Ma'am, next thing I knew, you were asking me what my name was. The only things I remember about the woman…uh, I think she was really tall, and she had to be strong, 'cause I hit her at a dead run and just stopped cold. And she had on, like, mirrored sunglasses. Oh, and red hair. I saw that when she pushed me down. Then there was the roar and then I came to, here."

"Ok, Kim, now, just relax and lay back. There's a helicopter coming to evac you out of these woods. Someone will find your camp and get your stuff to you. We just need to finish our investigation first, all right? Just relax, you'll be okay."

* * *

Ranger Rosanne Ramos watched the medevac chopper clear the trees as it headed due south for the Gunnison Hospital in Gunnison, Colorado. She waited until the chopper was a dot in the distance before turning to the plainclothes Special Agent

69

standing next to her. Special Agent Jonathon Holland was retired Army and only a few years short of retiring from the Rangers and double-dipping his Federal retirement payments. He had been standing behind Kim Hollowell's stretcher, out of her view but within hearing range. Sneaky, but rumor had it he'd been a sneaky SOB when he'd led his scout platoon into the smoke and chaos of the First Gulf War.

"Well, sir?" she asked. "What do you think?"

"Of what, Rosanne?" Holland still wore his hair close-cropped, the blond shading more and more these days into white. He didn't care about the color, as long as the hair stayed put. "Miss Hollowell? Or this Charlie-Foxtrot in general? Or whatever it was that melted the top foot of soil into glass?" His green eyes crinkled as he grinned at her. "I have to kinda doubt her story about running until her feet were bloody and falling and cutting herself. Since she didn't have a mark on her anywhere. Not a bruise or a blemish. Not a single scratch anywhere."

"There is a good bit of blood by that big pine, where the ground is scuffled up a lot." Ramos shrugged. "I can't say how, but I bet it matches hers. Sir."

"Rosanne, how often do I have to tell you that you don't have to 'Sir' me, unless we're in court or such?" Holland rubbed his forehead. "It's Jon out here, dagnabbit!"

"Well, Jon, here comes your partner." She pointed at the heavyset woman headed downhill from the ridge line between the two small valleys.

Special Agent Caroline McPherson, known to her friends and coworkers as Spike, was about as big a contrast to Ranger Ramos as humanly possible. Where Rosanne Ramos was gorgeous with a café-au-lait complexion on her delicate, fine-featured oval face, straight, glossy waist-length black hair — when it wasn't in its work-time bun at the back of her neck — and a tall, slender, almost petite frame, Caroline McPherson was built like a tank. Short, bleached blonde hair bristled above a face that only a mother could love.

'Spike' McPherson was maybe five foot six, in work boots, compared to her partner's lanky six-foot frame. She was anything but petite, at two hundred and ten pounds of pretty solid muscle. One wag had described her as a 'refrigerator with a head.' His friends thought it was funny, until Spike invited him into the sparring ring with her. He didn't quite lose any teeth, and she didn't quite break any of his bones, but she proved she had a mean streak as wide as she was. And that she definitely did NOT fight fair.

"Jon, Rosanne," Spike wasn't short of breath, but climbing hills was not on her list of favorite activities. "We found the camp, right where she said. Found what was left of her boyfriend, too. Wasn't much left, mostly big bones where whatever it was didn't take the time to crunch open. Ya ain't gonna like this — I sure as shit didn't — but the whatsit did take long enough to break open his skull and literally eat his brains out of it. Gonna be a closed coffin funeral. Jist as well his girlfriend didn't see 'im. Wouldn't wanna remember my worst enemy like that. Brrr."

The trio paused, silent, as Holland and Ramos realized that the scene had been enough to shake up McPherson, and McPherson shivered at the memory.

"Found his pistol," she added then. "Nice old single-action in .45 LC. Six shots fired." She handed an evidence bag containing the handgun to Holland. "Might wanna have Forensics look his remains over real close. Some odd-looking teeth snapped off in a couple of bones. Weird, but this whole damn thing has me wondering jist what in Hell was going on here. Don't make no damn sense at all. What in Hell could eat a man whole up that fast?"

"Not going to argue with you, Spike." Jon gave the pistol a long look, before handing it to Rosanne. "Please see that gets into Evidence's locker, Ms. Ramos. Spike, you want weird, come over here with me and take a gander at this." As Ramos headed for her big SUV to secure the gun, Holland led Spike to the thing covered by the tarpaulin. He reached down and lifted it away. Spike took a single step back and a deep breath, all at once.

"Dear sweet Lord Jesus! What in th' bloody damn hell is THAT?!" She took another deep breath. "Ain't never seen no wolf look like that."

"Me neither. Looks like a Hollyweird special effect werewolf or something. Except it's daytime, werewolves don't run around in the sun, and, oh, yeah, werewolves don't exist. Can't wait to see what DNA tells us this freaking thing actually is."

"Dammit, Jon," Spike swore as she wiped more sweat off her forehead, "this is starting to look like some kinda horror movie setup."

"Oh, we aren't done with weird yet, Spike. Look at the cuts, three of them, one to decapitate, then two more to quarter the body. Whatever made those cuts went through skin, muscle tissue, internal organs, bones, everything in one swing. Sharper than any surgeon's scalpel, too. Look at the bones and the muscle. Sheared clear through, no hint of any ragged cuts or breaks at all." He pointed at the wounds as he knelt next to the pieces. "No blood or fluid either, 'cause next on the weirdo hit list, everything was cauterized. The body fluids did eventually leak out, which gives us the puddles around and under the pieces. Otherwise, with a wound this massive, blood would be splattered up in the tree branches and on the trunk. Zip, none of that."

"Okay, Jon, this is really starting to sound like some damn weird shit. Is there a sasquatch involved somewhere? Little green men from Mars? A chupacabra?"

"Don't know. Maybe, but I doubt it. But I wasn't done; I still got one more thing to show you." He used a stick to turn the head over. "Something grabbed this by the throat and crushed it, windpipe, neck vertebrae, tissue, all of it crushed nearly into a pulp. That happened first, *then* it was decapitated. And there's a handprint. I doubt we'll be able to get fingerprints, but who knows? I'll have the lab do what they can."

"Yeah, go on."

"It was a hand that looks as human as yours or mine, Spike. But I have no idea who or what could grab this thing in midleap, crush its neck into goo, bloodlessly slice it into five parts and then MELT a damn hillside. How about you?"

"Okay, Jon, now yer making me nervous."

"Oh yeah, and whatever did this is still out there somewhere."

"Dammit, Jon, I did NOT need that."

"Yeah, me neither."

* * *

Agents Pistol and Mule were surprised when they realized they were not the first ones to reach the site of the flash Alpha One had reported from orbit. Somehow, most of the local Forest Rangers and a couple of their plainclothes Special Agents were already there. Granted, they'd had to come from the Groom Lake Station, aka Area 51 spaceport, but still. They had tracked what must have been a Medevac helicopter leaving the area but lost it due to range before they could determine where it was headed. Even morphed and cloaked, their SUV simply wasn't fast enough. It was designed for rugged mountains and harsh deserts, not speed.

"¡Mierda!" Agent Mule cursed as the site came into view. "Amigo, this is a mess."

"Yeah, but don't fly us into a damn mountain while you're looking at said mess." Agent Pistol was focused on his instruments in the passenger seat. "I lost the chopper, but it could be headed for Gunnison or Montrose or even Colorado Springs if it's got extra tanks. And I've spotted two Forest Service vehicles headed AWAY from the area."

"Crap. That's definitely no bueno." Mule was looking for a clearing to set down in, one at least a little way from the Rangers. "The only way I think the Rangers could have gotten here so damn fast is if someone called them as soon as it happened."

"How? We get a signal out here only because of the

satellites. There ain't even a cellular tower within fifty miles or so."

"Probably that old fire watchtower. They all have radios and some of them these days have sat-phones. Otherwise, why bother putting up the towers, eh?"

"Mule, how the hell are we gonna track down everyone that's been here and brain bleach them? Not to mention that burn scar. For all we know here, some official government satellite may have picked the flash up, maybe not even a U.S. satellite. Especially a spy sat. This is getting outta hand, quick."

"Yeah, you're right. Okay, Pistol, I'm gonna set us down in that spot over there. Get on the horn back to our Office and give 'em a heads up. Then we need to figure out how to handle this right now."

"This is gonna be a mess." Pistol powered up the comm gear as Mule set the SUV down.

"Ya think?"

"Yeah, whaddaya think for our *carte noir* setting? Department of the Interior Special Agents?"

"Good idea, Pistol. But let's make it Senior Investigation Special Agents. I'm pretty sure there's at least one Ranger Special Agent already here. Might make this tougher than normal."

"Hey, even if we can get 'em all together and can brain bleach everyone, there's still that burn scar on the hill. We don't have anything with us that can deal with it."

"We can get a team up here from our Office in about four hours or less. They'll take care of it. We've just gotta deal with these guys. Let's go."

* * *

"Ok, lemme get this straight, you two are Senior Investigation Agents with Interior?" Jon Holland scowled at Agent Mule's *carte noir*, configured into the badge and ID of a Department of the Interior's Investigator. "From WHICH office, again? Far as I know the closest Interior Office is in Alamogordo, New Mexico and THAT'S a Bureau of Land

Management office. The BLM doesn't have any Agents, much less Investigators."

"Just look at the badge, buddy. Just 'cause we staged through the BLM Office, don't mean our credentials are any less valid." Mule didn't quite come up to the taller Holland's shoulder, but the scowl on his own face was just as menacing.

"Look, that looks real enough, 'buddy,' but I've seen a metric crap-ton of fake badges and IDs of every type, some so good they were better than the real ones," McPherson growled as she stepped up into Mule's face. "And there ain't no one in either Interior or our own Department of Agriculture that goes in the field in a black suit. Washington, D.C., well, maybe, but sure as shit not in the middle of the Colorado Rockies. So who the hell are you two bozos and whaddaya think yer doing out here? Cause, sure as shit, I ain't buying the crap yer selling."

Ok, now what? Mule signaled to his partner as he took a step back from McPherson despite himself. *There's too many of them to use stunners and not everyone is in range anyways.*

Yeah, and that guy over there just stepped out of his SUV with a 12-gauge shotgun. I think we're in deep shit and sinking fast.

You think? We pull anything that looks like a weapon and we're liable to get well ventilated.

"IF everyone will calm down and give me your attention, please?" A deep voice from the gathering dusk startled everyone. A tall, broad-shouldered man in a spotless black Suit stepped neatly across the creek, not getting even a spot of water or mud on his polished black cowboy boots. There was a bit of a lopsided smile on his handsome face. "Please, everyone, just calm down and I can satisfactorily explain the confusion here. Just give your attention to the video on my cell phone here and you'll understand." He waved the largish cell phone above his coal-black hair in his left hand while he slipped a set of odd-looking wrap-around sunglasses over his eyes.

Mule and Pistol immediately recognized Agent Echo and frantically shoved their own goggle-glasses on, split seconds before a multicolored, strobing holographic flash lit up the dusk under the pines.

* * *

"Well, that worked out better than I expected." Echo calmly watched the last of the Ranger green trucks and SUVs pick their way down the trail they had made getting here in the first place. "So, Agents Mule and Pistol, right?"

"Yes, sir." Mule answered as Pistol nodded his head.

"I understand you two are Field agents from the Groom Lake Station? You were available and closest and got scrambled out here when our call came in from Chicago?" While Echo was getting briefed, Omega was carefully moving around the beginning of the burn scar, and the tarp-covered object the Rangers had…forgotten about…as they left.

"Yes, sir." Pistol answered this time. "Most of our tasking is monitoring incoming arrivals after that one saucer crashed a couple of years ago. That and we handle issues with new arrivals and maintain local area security, mostly brain-bleaching the occasional UFO nut that's on the wrong side of the mountain from the Air Force's Area 51."

"Take it you boys don't get way out in the field like this very much anymore?"

"No, sir," they chorused.

"Okay, that's understandable, but you both need to be ready to handle things like this. It wasn't the worst approach I've ever seen, but it was far from being the best, either." Echo sighed. "Okay, make sure you both put in more time training, individually and as a team. I understand you're not Alpha Line, but regular Field agents gotta be on the ball, too. Are your training facilities up to Agency standards?"

"Yes, sir, they just were upgraded, but, yes, sir, I guess we've been slacking off a bit lately." Mule's shrug was an elegant understatement of embarrassment.

"Well, get back up to meeting your standard and maybe a bit more. It'll make getting out of a mess like this a lot easier next time. If you want, I'll have my partner Omega — she's head of training for Alpha Line — pop you some suggestions."

"Yes, sir," they chorused again. "That'd be great, sir," Pistol added. "It's hard to know how to train for stuff like this, when you don't know you're gonna GET stuff like this."

"Okay, we've got this now." Echo grinned at them. "You are relieved and can return to your regular duty station. I'll want to see a report on everything that happened here on my email in the morning."

"Thank you, sir." The pair of them vanished like smoke.

* * *

Echo sighed, then turned as his partner and wife walked up.

"Hey, Meg, whatcha got? Anything?" he wondered.

"Other than a gaping jaw, not yet, Ace," Omega replied, studying the readouts on her cell phone app. "We have obsidian up there. As in, the rock and dirt melted and re-solidified. Offhand, the only thing I can think of that might do that is a serious directed energy weapon of some sort. Not even our blasters would do whatever this thing did."

"What about a tachyon-splitter rifle?"

"Maybe. But the power output is bigger than a rifle. Maybe a cannon."

"Tachyon-splitter cannon? But there's no sign of one of those being trucked in here," Echo said, looking around, "and I'm not sure the terrain would cooperate with that, anyway. Flown in, maybe…"

"Yeah, except for the trees."

"Mm. Good point." He paused. "Have you been over to the campsite yet?"

"Not yet, no. I thought…eh." Omega shrugged. "It sounded pretty bad, from what I was hearing. I thought maybe it'd be good if we went together."

"Right. Let's go look at the dead beastie, then."

They walked over to the body under the tarp.

Echo watched as Omega pulled the tarp away from the butchered creature. He frowned at what he saw there.

"Well, what the hell is this, Ace?" Omega had slipped on latex examination gloves, but she still used a broken stick to manipulate the pieces of the carcass. "Doesn't look anything at all like a Tekulan, which is what I thought it was, based on what I heard from the rangers."

"No, it doesn't." He knelt down next to Omega and used a penlight to examine the head. "Looks like a giant monster wolf from some fantasy-horror movie."

"Yeah, actually if it wasn't for the fact that I know there's no such thing, I'd say it was a werewolf. But the legends all say that werewolves turn back into humans when they're killed, anyhow."

"Yeah, I guess." Echo frowned, remembering a certain Christmas-time science fiction convention a while back. And to what, or rather *who,* Fox had introduced him during that mission. "This is just…wrong." He stood and walked around the tree, shining the penlight on the ground. "There's blood all over the place here. Get a sample, would you, Meg?"

"Ok, Ace. I take it you noticed the nature of the cuts on the whatsit there?"

"Yeah, razor sharp and hard enough to slice through everything, and hot enough to cauterize the cut as it was cutting. That's a neat trick." He frowned and looked up at the fire tower. "I'll be right back, I wanna check the tower."

"You do know that when you split up in a horror movie, that's when the critter kills someone, usually the half-naked female who screams her head off."

"Well, then, keep your clothes on, silly." He grinned, then shook his head. "Give it a rest, will ya, baby? I know the scene is creepy as all hell, but we've got a lot to do here before the mop-up crew arrives. We still need to track down whoever it was on that Medevac chopper." He carefully examined the drops and smears of blood leading up the tower's steps. "This one is gonna be a real pain in the ass. I can feel it."

"Thought I was the one that had the premonitions, Ace."

"Yeah, me too. That's what's bothering me."

* * *

The convoy of Ranger vehicles was well down the mountain before Rosanne Ramos sat up in her Explorer to do more than just peek between the top of the dash and the steering wheel. She had been in the back seat, securing samples of the creature, the burn scar and the Ruger pistol when the men in the black Suits had walked out of the gathering dusk. She'd taken one glance out the window as they argued with Agents Holland and McPherson, then she'd ducked down, out of sight. She wasn't sure why she'd done that, but the third man in the identical black Suit confirmed her caution.

She didn't know what was going on here, but supposedly her great-grandmama had been a bruja, a witch, old family stories said. Maybe she had been, maybe she hadn't, but Rosanne had a long track record of getting 'bad feelings' about things. Some of the Rangers joked that they had their very own bruja, but only in a good-natured fashion. There were fewer jokes when she proved to be one of the very best at finding lost hikers and catching poachers and illegal miners red-handed time after time. And she was very glad she'd hid, and the black Suits hadn't noticed that no one had gotten in her vehicle once they were done flashing those bright, multicolored lights around, and everyone packed up quickly and headed back down the valley.

She'd been out of sight and the windows on her truck were darkly tinted. Maybe that was why she remembered things VERY differently from what the others were saying on the radios now. And she thought that, for now, she'd just keep her mouth shut and her head down until she had a better idea of what to do about the entire mess.

* * *

This is about the most pristine nature I've ever been near, much less having the pleasure of trudging through it. The only hint of civilization I can find is the very slight tang of internal combustion motors drifting in the atmosphere. I doubt any human could detect it. Huh, I doubt the local wildlife can smell it. Myclestra strode along through the wilderness, heading somewhat south of due west, at least according to the Drake whispering in the back of her mind.

"So, Old Snake, why do you think my quarry will head this way?"

<There is power this way, Child.> Surlianth's voice was calm as always in her mind. <This world has both mundane and magical power in abundance. Some of the greatest concentrations of mundane power are south and west of here. And some of that is power that can be easily twisted into corrosive use by something as corrupt and evil as the Warpwraith. But I do not believe the creature knows of the location of such sources of power. Not yet. And we should be there first, awaiting our prey.>

"Understood. And these humans, what of them?"

<They know little or nothing of arcane power, I believe. And therefore, they are vulnerable to the machinations of those with power. It was well done, to protect that human girl and to use their own devices to summon aid for her.>

"I had little choice," she sighed as she strode rapidly across a meadow. "I could not await whatever means the humans would utilize to provide succor to one assailed in the wilderness. And the girl was safe enough in that odd tower."

<Perhaps — no, I agree, she was quite safe.> The cold voice in her mind paused. <But there are other things here, signs of odd and powerful beings. I think, not all here is as it seems.>

"When is it ever?" Myclestra sighed as her stride settled into a long-legged lope she could maintain for hours. "And I think we have less need of speech and more of speed." For her, the fall of night meant nothing. Her senses made no difference between night or day. Only when she felt the Sun's heat on her body or face was she aware of daylight versus darkness. Her esoteric sense of the world she moved through was as detailed in many ways as any sighted being, even if that sense was limited in range. Colors were something she could not comprehend. It had been millennia since any of her race had been capable of perceiving something known as color. She was not aware of her loss in the least.

* * *

As Wruthas moved through the mountains, traveling along a weak ley-line, something new drew his attention. At first it was only the least of hints, the very slightest, subtlest scent of power, invigorating and intoxicating. He stopped and turned to face south, orienting to face that aroma of power. It was not a taste of magical power, but a purified, almost elemental power. It was different from anything he could ever remember detecting. Intrigued, he turned south, leaving the weak ley-line and extending his senses, seeking one leading toward this strange power he found so tantalizing. Leaving the ley-line slowed his progress, but seeing as he was in no particular hurry, he saw no concern in the length of the journey. And the strengthening allure of this new form of potential power quickened his steps as he trekked along the mountain valleys and ridgelines.

Chapter Two — Encounters & Complexities

Danny Hawkins was glad to get out of the car and stretch his legs. His big German luxury sedan was a great road car, massaging seats and everything, but even in its comfortable cabin, there was a limit. And driving through Colorado mountain roads was fun but tended to suck the large twenty-gallon gas tank dry in a hurry. He'd get better mileage if he could just keep his foot out of the throttle. But hustling the roomy Beemer down a curvy mountain road was so much FUN! He stretched both arms and his back and took a deep breath of the crisp Colorado air as he looked around.

The dilapidated sign read Hiway 50 Fuel Stop. There were a couple of the ubiquitous four-wheel drive pickup trucks parked at the store front, an older Japanese sedan, a grimy gray 4x4 station wagon and an old yellow dirt bike. His Beemer was undeniably out of place here on the west side of town, but the sign advertised 91 octane premium gas and the prices were twenty-five cents cheaper than the bigger, fancier stations back in Gunnison proper off State Highway 50. He figured it was worth it, as long as the bathrooms weren't too revolting.

But the store itself was clean on the outside, new signs advertising this week's special on hot dogs, beer and beef jerky. The owner of the dirt bike exited the building, helmet in hand, and the door didn't grind or rattle, only a bell above it jingling. He fed the pump his credit card and started refueling his car. He'd hit the bathroom and get a snack and some coffee or a soda after he fueled up. The biker headed north out of the parking lot, checking traffic before he crossed the highway, vanishing down a dirt road and behind a copse of pines. Danny noticed someone walking out of another tree-lined dirt driveway just east of the road the rider had taken.

The first thing he heard was the thumping of the bass, a

minute or two before a beat-up old Caddy El Dorado convertible pulled into the station, top down, blasting some God-awful rap song that Danny was embarrassed to even hear. He'd have fired any of his employees at Hawkins Financial Consultants in an instant for listening to such trash, at least in the office. A half dozen young men and one young woman were stuffed into the big Caddy, all wearing red and black checkered neck scarfs or head 'rags.' Black t-shirts, liberally adorned with vulgar slogans, were another uniform feature for the rough-looking males. The woman was just barely wearing enough clothing to be decent and looked just as feral as the rest of them.

The car knocked and rattled as the engine was shut off and its occupants scrambled over the sides, ignoring the doors. The driver started refueling the faded blue and gray monstrosity as the female and two males trotted off to the store. The remaining three males stared at his 750 and started circling it, prompting him to imagine sharks circling a wounded seal. The so-called music continued to assault everyone's hearing and sensibilities. He shook his head as he finished fueling his car and took the receipt from the pump.

"Oye, eso es un paseo agradable que usted tiene allí." The youngest and biggest of the three stepped between him and the front of the car, blocking his way.

"Uh, excuse me, uh, yo no hablo espanol, I think?" The short phrase was about all the Spanish he knew.

"Is okay, hombre. Ricardo don't speak much English," The other two blocked the rear of the car. The speaker had enough gold chains around his neck to start a jewelry store. "He said you gots a nice car, hey."

"Uh, yeah, thanks, uh, gracias, I guess."

"Si, bueno," Ricardo smiled at him, not a pleasant sight, not at all. "Me das un paseo."

"What'd he say?" Danny glanced back over his shoulder at the English-speaking leader.

"He wants you to give him a ride." The grin revealed stained brown teeth, a definite lack of oral hygiene, and cold, gray eyes.

"I'm sorry, I really don't have the time to give any ri…"

"Whasamatta, gringo?" The grin shifted into an uglier smile. "You 'fraid Ricardo'll fart on you fancy seats? Leave a nasty, Mexican smell in you shiny toy?"

"No! Not at all! I just don't have time to—" he stopped suddenly, startled by the black muzzle of the revolver the brown-toothed leader produced from his pocket. "Ah, let's not get hasty, now." Danny's attention was riveted on the handgun as he turned to face the leader.

"Tell you what, gringo, let's trade, hey? You fancy Beemer for Tio Enrique's old Caddy, fair enough?" The pistol, as well as the entire situation, was hidden from anyone in the store by the gas pumps. The bell over the door jingled as the female and her two companions exited the store, one of the males carrying two cases of beer. The girl, maybe in her late teens — it was hard to tell with all the makeup — sashayed up to the pumps and raised an eyebrow.

"Hey, Esteban, wha'da hell you think you doing?" Her kinky black hair and darker skin suggested African American somewhere in her ancestry; she could have been beautiful if her face wasn't spackled. "You crazy as shit, tryin' to take this guy's nice car."

The light-skinned, redheaded guy dropped the beer in the back seat of the Caddy and then came over to watch the fun from over the roof of Danny's car. His grin was just as cold as the others.

"Cállate, puta," Esteban, the apparent leader with the gun, snapped at the girl. "We ain't takin' this cabrón's car. We's trading it, you Tio Enrique's old piece a shit Caddy for this nicer car."

"Call me a bitch and tell me to shut up? You gonna be old and gray, pendejo, 'fore you get another piece of this!" The girl rubbed her crotch for emphasis. "'Sides, mi Tio will have your cojones, you give away his damn Caddy."

"You got a smart mouth, chocho! You uncle can have his

ugly ass Caddy back then and we'll just take this nice, new Beemer. 'Sides, you fat ass won't fit in the back seat no how. Puta!" Esteban snarled at her as the other gang members laughed at him. Danny stepped away from Esteban, backing right against Ricardo trying to get out of line with the gun's muzzle.

* * *

Over all this, the speakers in the Caddy had continued to thump out a nasty gangsta rap, not quite as loud as it had been, but loud enough. And none of them were paying any attention to anything but the confrontation.

"Palun lülitage müra välja." A hand like a steel clamp came down on Ricardo's shoulder and jerked him backwards. The owner of that hand, a very tall, redheaded woman, then stepped gently in front of Danny Hawkins. "Lülita see välja nüüd. Või muidu lülitan selle välja."

Everyone gaped at her as she shoved Ricardo away. He stumbled fifteen feet or so and fell flat on his butt. Ricardo had been the biggest member of the gang, but this woman towered over him and from the skin-tight tunic and leggings outfit she wore, they could see she was cut like a fitness model. A very odd pistol was holstered on her left hip and a huge, gold-and-gem-encrusted sword hilt jutted up over her right shoulder. Odd-looking mirrored, blade-style sunglasses covered her eyes.

* * *

Whatever that noise was, it was loud enough to definitely annoy and almost hurt her sensitive hearing. The noise was coming from a kind of canopy ahead, one with what appeared to be wheeled vehicles under it. One group, dressed in similar styles, had a surrounded a single human male next to the enclosed-type vehicle. The open vehicle was the source of the ghastly noise.

She was no stranger to gangs and their methods, and that was exactly what this appeared to be. She'd never liked gangs, since there was rarely a bounty on gangers worth the time it

85

took to apprehend them. Having the lone human male that was their target owing her a favor might be worthwhile. There was much about this new world, this new universe that she needed to learn. Quickly. Perhaps this was an opening to do exactly that.

She set her shoulders and headed to the incipient confrontation, gritting her teeth at that awful racket.

None of them were paying any attention to their surroundings, which was truly pathetic situational awareness, even for humans. She stepped up behind the larger male blocking the obvious victim's exit. She would give them a chance and ask them nicely to turn off the noise before she pounded some slight sense of civility into the gangers. Of course, she didn't want to be…too nice.

"Please turn off the noise." She felt the shoulder of the youngish ganger tense in surprise as she grabbed his shoulder. He started to turn toward her, and she simply tossed him behind her as she stepped in front of the older human male the gang was obviously threatening. She knew they didn't understand her, but she hoped her tone of voice might get it across — that, and the finger she waggled at the open-topped vehicle. "Turn it off now. Or else I will turn it off." She gave the one she thought was the leader a toothy grin that would not have been out of place on some fanged sea-beast.

He goggled at her in stunned immobility as she put her body between him and the older human. She saw the small-bore weapon in his hand, some type of slug thrower, probably chemically powered. She visualized the symbol that activated her tech-wizard armor. She doubted something like that would do much more than sting — she'd noticed her body tissues seemed to be stronger, more resilient, than the few humans she'd encountered — but no use taking needless risks. On second thought, her hand dipped into a belt pouch, coming out with the talisman for her strength-enhancing cantrip. A quick tap onto her forehead activated it. She stood there, in the frozen tableau, waiting to see what he would do. Taking in the gang, she realized they were young humans and most likely, on the stupid side. No surprise there. Most gangers weren't that bright, regardless of species.

"Last chance, child." Her smile was cold and menacing. "Put down the weapon, turn off the noise and leave. With all your limbs intact."

* * *

"Viimane võimalus, laps," her tone was cool, almost threatening, but the language was no more understandable to them than it had been when she first walked up. "Pange relv maha, lülitage müra välja ja lahkuge. Kõigi jäsemete puutumata."

Esteban stared at this giantess that seemed to have appeared by magic. He couldn't see her eyes, but her posture and tone of voice and the sneering grin got some of her meaning across. Yeah, she was tall as hell, but he had never backed down from a fight, especially not one with some dumb bitch.

"You asking for trouble, estupida puta! Get the hell outta my way 'fore I shoot the shit outta you! Like right now!" He thrust the old .38 revolver toward her.

"Unh-unh-uh." Myclestra smiled, shook her head and slowly raised one hand to wave an index finger in his face. "Akhandë, laps." (*Behave, child.*)

"Me cago en tu puta madre!" Rage flooded through Esteban. No one disrespected him like that! NO ONE! "You can die, gringo bitch!" He jerked the trigger on the revolver.

* * *

The .38 Special revolver was nearly eighty years old, a bit rusty and grungy these days, but it worked just as intended. The .38 Special 158-grain full metal jacketed bullet left the muzzle at just under a thousand feet per second. It stuck Myclestra just under her sternum and the tech-wizard armor vaporized the slug, converting impact energy into power that charged the armor's power packs. She never even felt it.

Before Esteban could pull the heavy, double-action trigger again, Myclestra grabbed his hand and crushed both pistol and hand, bending both the grip frame and trigger guard into his hand and fingers, forming a single compressed mass of torn skin, broken bone, twisted metal and gushing blood. His eyes rolled up into his head as he collapsed on the pavement, unconscious from the incredible pain. The rest of the gang stared in stunned astonishment.

Well, might as well see to the lot of them. She shook her head as all of them, including the older male, simply stood there, gawking at the gang leader and the bloody mess that had been his hand. *Great Alontora, do any of them have any sense of combat at all? They just stand there, like sathern waiting to be slaughtered!* She blurred into action, fists and feet liberally scattering moaning and unconscious bodies about the area. The female had been the most aggressive one, shrieking and leaping to shred Myclestra's face with long fingernails clawing futilely at the tall Alontoran. She was relatively gentle with that one. She only broke both wrists before knocking her senseless.

I think that takes care of them, so now for this horrendous racket! The Sword came off her back as she stalked toward the blue-grey convertible. A single swing of what, on Earth, would be considered a huge, two-handed sword cut the old Caddy in half, just behind the front seats. Annoyed, irritated and in a little pain from the auditory assault, she kicked the back half of the car twenty feet across the parking lot and into the compressed air hoses. The front half, she grabbed and dragged to the other edge of the lot before flipping it over into the drainage ditch there. She turned and started back to where the older male stood in disconcerted stasis, staring at her in what appeared to her to be a combination of mild apprehension, astonishment, and lust, as she approached him.

* * *

Oh. My. God. Danny Hawkins knew his mouth was hanging open like some clueless fan-boy meeting his favorite movie star. He wasn't the only one; he was vaguely aware of the customers and staff of the store that were standing on the sidewalk, goggling at the calamity the fuel islands had become.

88

The woman walking; no, prowling; no, strutting toward him was the most amazing woman he'd ever seen.

She's a taller, sexier, redheaded Julie Strain! She laid those punks out like something from a Chuck Norris movie! Oh, dear Lord. Where the hell is she from? People, even here in backwoods Colorado, just don't walk around with a huge sword hanging on their back, beat up a bunch of wannabe gangbangers without breaking a sweat, cut a car in half and kick the pieces away before strutting toward me like the latest, hottest Hollywood sex goddess! And she didn't even lose her sunglasses!

She walked up to Danny and stopped. He was six foot two, but he still had to look up at her a little bit. He figured she was six foot five, maybe six-six, and built like the proverbial bag full of bobcats. She had a very nice smile, he realized as she tilted her head a bit. She pointed at his car, which, miraculously, had survived without a single scratch, then at him, then at herself. She made a throwing motion with her hand and pointed at the road south.

"You want, er, need a ride?" he asked, puzzling out her sign language. He knew she could talk, but he doubted she spoke English. She gently put both hands on his shoulders, and then, just as gently, kissed him rather thoroughly. She smiled and pointed at the car and then at Highway 50, going south. Danny shook his head. *What the hell? WOW!*

She pointed again, and he nodded, then rubbed his hand with his face and shook his head.

"We need to wait for the police," he managed to get out. He was still off-balance and more than a little off-kilter from what had just happened. That kind of sudden, brutal violence was something completely unknown to him. He shook his head again. She frowned and then sighed, reaching into one of several small pouches on her belt. She raised something that looked like some kind of foil, then barely touched it to her tongue before quickly sticking it to his forehead, muttering something under her breath in what sounded like a different language. An electrical shock ran from where the thing touched his forehead around his skull and down his spine. She nodded as he shook his head to clear it.

"The cantrip won't last long, Man." She tilted her head as he jumped, realizing he understood her, despite the fact that she was not speaking English. "But I need you to take me south, quickly. There is a threat to your entire world, and I must stop it."

"We have to wait for the police, Miss."

"My name is Myclestra. Yours is?"

"Danny, Danny Hawkins."

"We do not have time to wait for any police, whatever they are, Danny Hawkins. I must hunt this thing down. The bounty on it will save my life and destroying it will save your world. We MUST go, now! Please. I wish no further conflict with any save my quarry, but I MUST catch it." Her hand came up slowly and caressed his cheek. "Please, Danny Hawkins. Lives depend on this. You must take me south, now. This instant."

"Ah, yeah, ok, get in, I guess." In the back of his mind a little voice was screaming, *What are you DOING?* at him, but her touch and the warmth of her voice promised that he would never regret doing this. She carefully placed the big, ornate sword in the back seat and settled in the passenger seat. He settled into the driver's seat, showed the seat belt to her and hit the 'Start Engine' button that woke the big, twin-turbocharged V-8 to life. He palmed it into gear and headed for the road... just as someone from the crowd in front of the store waved and yelled after him. But it was too late — the 750's broad tires scattered gravel as it rocketed onto the road.

* * *

Alpha One had only been airborne for forty-five minutes or so when Omega's phone rang.

"Omega," she answered. "Yeah, we turned the site over to a clean-up crew. What's up, Fox? Oh, yeah, I'll put you on speaker. There."

"Echo, Omega, I just heard from our contact in the Colorado

90

State Police. Have either of you ever heard of Gunnison, Colorado?" The speaker made Division One Director Fox's voice sound slightly hollow. The two Agents glanced at each other, Omega raising an eyebrow at Echo, who shook his head.

"No, Fox, neither of us? Why?"

"Well, it's about fifteen air miles from your most recent, ah, scene. Closest town of any size at all, really."

"And?" Echo's question hung in the air.

"As I said, I just heard from our informant at CSP. Another…weird event in Gunnison. Seems a gang started harassing some guy in a 'newish, fancy black sedan,' I'd guess something German."

"How's that affect us, Fox?" Omega looked out the window of the 'Vette at the passing mountains.

"Well, it seems a very tall woman walked into the middle of this confrontation, laid out all seven members of the gang in nothing flat, then took a damn big sword and cut the gang's car — an old Caddy El Dorado convertible — in half, with one swing, witnesses say, before kicking the back half across the driveway and throwing the front half into a drainage ditch. Then, she somehow convinced the driver of the black sedan to give her a ride. The sedan in question was last seen going like a bat out of Gehinnom, due south on State Highway 50. And no, the CSP has no available units outside of Gunnison itself."

"Hmm, I see." Echo smiled at Omega as he banked the 'Vette into a turn, headed back due south of the place they had just left as Omega punched up the local satellite maps from the orbiting Division One GPS-equivalent satellite system.

"We're turning around, Fox. ETA will be about twenty-five minutes." Omega leaned back and stretched in her seat. "Anything else? Is there anyone read-in on us in the area?"

"No, tekhter, unfortunately not. There's the station over in Roswell, New Mexico — it's a small station, a little short on manpower at the best of times, and you've been there — but no one up in the mountains this time of year."

"Understood, Fox," Omega answered. "Alpha One out."

"Fox out."

After a couple of minutes going over what little data was available, Omega leaned back in her seat.

"Mysteriouser and mysteriouser, Ace."

"What'd ya find, baby?"

"The owner of the gas station slash convenience store, Hiway 50 Fuel Stop, one William John Harrison by name, is an on-the-ball kinda guy. Building is about sixty years old or so, but he's kept it up to date. New, computerized fuel pumps, computerized check outs and — ta-da — computerized, networked security video system, updating the recordings to the cloud every half hour. And I just hacked the latest update from his system."

"Okay, and?"

"Flip on the auto pilot for a couple and watch this."

"Sure." Echo watched the video on the 'Vette's central display. "Holy…I thought you were fast, but this is ridiculous. That's what, a mid-70s Caddy? Those things were built like tanks and about as heavy. She kicked the back half, what, fifteen, twenty feet? Dragged the heavier front — with the engine and the drive train — over and flipped it into the ditch?"

"That ain't all, Ace. I took the known size of those gas pumps and the car, a Beemer by the way, and extrapolated her height. She's taller than you — six foot six if she's an inch."

"Huh-uh. And built like every teenaged boy's proverbial wet dream. She kinda vaguely reminds me of someone, I think…nah, not important right now."

"And look here, Ace," Omega zoomed in on a still shot of the woman to get closer. "You ever see a handgun like that one? Not to mention the at least five-foot-long sword slung over her back — an' that's just the blade? There's enough gold and gems on that thing's hilt and scabbard to buy a battleship like the *Genesis*. And watch this, she takes the stack of gold chains on that thug's neck, SNIFFS THEM, and then drops them back on him like they're trash. Like they're not good enough for her."

"Okay, I see," Echo was silent for a few moments, considering. Finally he ventured, "Baby, I know this might be a tender subject, but if you really, truly went ALL-OUT, could you match what she did?"

"Hmmm," Omega was quiet long enough for Gunnison's outskirts to come into sight. "I dunno, Ace. Maybe. I'd say from the video that she's stronger, but I'm faster. But either one of us could have laid out those punks as fast as she did. It's the car that gets me; maybe she was furious for some reason? Adrenaline, I mean. You know what that can do to anyone's strength and speed. I just don't know."

"You think she's from, eh, 'around here'?"

"She looks human, but I doubt it. That gun looks very, very odd. I don't think anyone makes pistols like that. Now, Hollywood, maybe. And she still used that sword to cleanly cut that old car in half. One swing, like it's no big deal. Dinner says Fox has orders for us to apprehend her after he sees this."

"No bet, baby."

"Yeah, thought so. I wanna see what that sword did to that car, ASAP."

"On the ground in sixty seconds, on site two minutes after that."

"Yeah," Omega sighed. "Here we go again."

* * *

"What in tarnation is an FBI Special Agent doing here, that is what I wanna know?" Gunnison PD Patrol Sergeant James Towers glanced at Echo's *carte noir*, morphed into an FBI badge and credentials, before staring back at Echo. Omega was kneeling by the rear end of the Caddy examining the very clean cut.

"Sergeant Towers, I understand this is your jurisdiction and I'm not intending to step on any toes." Echo gave the officer a half-smile and a shrug. "But when my boss says hop, I jump. Keeps him mostly outta my hair. And I'm actually on vacation at the moment, which didn't stop him from yelling for me and my partner. I'm guessing someone higher up the chain twisted his toes about this. I don't know why or who. But I was told to come check this incident out and report back. I dunno, maybe terrorism is involved somewhere."

"Terrorism? In Gunnison, Colorado, population sixty-five hundred or so? Oh, please, pull the other one, it has bells on it." Towers muttered a curse under his breath. "But okay, yah, FBI. Whaddaya want?"

"Well, allow us to examine the scene?"

"No problem, long as you share anything special you spot."

"Sure," Echo agreed, the lie smooth and practiced; 'anything special' was apt to be in their ballpark, and therefore even if he shared it, the police sergeant was unlikely to remember it when they were done. "And interview the suspects?"

"I got no issue with that, long as I can have an officer present. And yeah, this bunch, Esteban Navarro's second rate, wannabe punks, might be too stupid to get a lawyer, but there's a big 'but' in the way." Towers took his ballcap off and rubbed sweat out of his thinning brown hair.

"Oh, how so?"

"They got the holy, howling hell beat outta them. Multiple concussions, broken bones, mostly arms and legs, dislocated shoulders, broke knees, broken jaws. Oh yeah, here, check this out." Towers led them over to his vehicle, a big white SUV with *Gunnison POLICE* emblazoned on the side. He opened the rear gate and fished out an evidence bag containing a bloody, misshapen revolver. "Old .38 Special revolver. It was crushed around Esteban Navarro's hand. One round fired, I think. Grip frame and trigger guard bent in, basically mangled his entire right hand. He's gonna lose some fingers, I think. Maybe the whole hand. Anyways, they're all over in the ER in Gunnison Valley Health Hospital. I doubt any of them will be able to talk for a week or so, three, four days at best. You gonna hang around that long?"

"Hmm, probably not, unless something real odd pops up." Echo rubbed his chin as he studied the scene. "Honestly,

Sergeant Towers, I think my boss is just wasting my time. I'll try not to waste yours. Mind if we just look around?"

"Nah, help yourself, 'preciate the thought 'bout time, you know how it is."

"Thanks. I'll at least drop you a text or message when we head out."

"Great." Just then the radio in Sergeant Towers' truck squawked into life. "Dammit. Now what? 'Cuse me."

Echo smiled and turned away, walking over to where Omega knelt by the rear part of the car. She looked up at him as he approached, pointing at the cut in the rear floor pan.

"Looks like it was cut with a laser, Ace. That or a VERY high speed plasma cutter. Everything, body panels, floor pan, exhaust system, hydraulic and fuel lines, wiring — swoop, sliced smooth, as mah Daddy woulda said, slicker than owl snot."

"Any signs of heat a laser or plasma would leave, baby?"

"Nope. Nothing like that. I'm starting to consider there might be a true, monomolecular edge on that damn sword. Only signs of heat are from friction, and those are very minimal. You know of any tech out there that could actually put a monomolecular edge on a five-foot-long sword blade and keep that edge longer than the first cut?"

"No, baby, not off the top of my head. Edges that sharp, yeah, but mostly surgical stuff, scalpels and shit. Not on a weapon." He headed over to the other half of the Caddy, currently being dragged out of the ditch by a tow truck. Omega stood up and followed him. "Looks the same from here."

"So, Tall Lady," Omega spoke softly, almost to herself, "walks in like Chuck Norris, lays out the bad guys in nothing flat, sending them all to the hospital with serious but not life-threatening injuries, cuts a big car in half with a seemingly impossible sword, kicks and tosses both halves of the car away, respectively, then struts up..."

"Struts, baby?" Echo interrupted.

"Yeah, that's the only way I can describe the way she

walked up to Beemer man." Omega cocked her head at Echo. "Then she talks to him without any apparent understanding, then reverts to obvious sign language with him, kisses him thoroughly, puts *something* on his forehead, THEN apparently they suddenly understand each other. She carefully puts that giant sword in the back seat, gets in the passenger seat, and Beemer proceeds to haul ass down Highway 50, headed south. It blows through town and is gone. Did I miss anything?"

"Nope, pretty much sums it all up."

"Now, Ace, what does it all mean?" Omega brushed a loose strand of silver-blonde hair out of her face.

"I dunno, baby," Echo drew a deep breath and exhaled. "But I'm gonna bet it's gonna mean trouble of some kind for us."

"Nuh-uh. Not taking that bet. I'll keep my money. But I think we're done here. I suggest getting outta town and airborne and see if we can find that car. Any better ideas, Ace?"

"No, baby, not right now. I think you got a plan." They headed for the 'Vette, Echo waving at Sergeant Towers as he opened the passenger door for Omega.

"So, question for ya, Ace," she asked as the 'Vette pulled out onto Highway 50.

"Shoot."

"Ha, bang," she chuckled as he faked being shot with a smirk. "Seriously, have you ever heard of any race or tech that can do the kinda things we're seeing here? You've been around the galaxy more than I have…"

"No, baby, I can't, not off the top of my head. And I've been thinking, trust me on that. Maybe somewhere out in the galactic hinterlands, but no, this is new to me. Might as well be actual magic, somehow."

"Yeah, magic." She was quiet as they drove through the small town. "Magic. I can't come up with anything else, and that, Alex, my dear love, THAT…scares the hell outta me."

"Yeah. Me too."

* * *

Once they were out of town, she asked him to roll all the

96

windows down, and the mountain sage and fresh pine scent of the adjacent forest filled the cabin as the big Beemer hustled down the winding highway in the high desert. Danny Hawkins kept his eyes on the road, glancing over at his passenger from time to time. She kept saying to hurry, go faster, and he was pushing the 750 about as fast as he dared on the mountain road. It was hard to not stare at her. She was a walking wet dream, but if he didn't pay attention, slamming into a hundred-year-old tree, or worse, a rock cut, at eighty or ninety miles an hour would kill both of them right quick.

"So, Myclestra, right?" He looked over at her as the road straightened out down a valley. "So, where are you from? You a cop or peace officer or sheriff or what?"

"I am from another dimension of space-time, Danny Hawkins." She held one arm out into the airstream rushing past, using her hand like an airfoil, turning it to raise or lower her hand. A smile of pure delight turned her face — what he could see of it under the glasses — radiantly beautiful. "I am a bounty hunter. The creature I hunt is a malign being, feeding on pain, terror, and souls by its preference, although any energy source will do, at last resort. It is also from my universe, if you wish to think of it that way."

"Bounty hunter from another universe, right." Danny nodded to himself. *Maybe it was better when I didn't understand her? She must be looney-toons, and off her meds. What the hell have I gotten myself into this time?* Danny knew he was generally a sucker for little kids, puppies, kittens, and sob stories, but this was ridiculous. "So, you're after some kind of monster, eh? What's it look like?"

"It can look like any being it has absorbed. I think its 'natural form' is simply a black, colorless, gelatinous mass, but no one knows for certain."

"Ok, uh, wow, I guess." He was definitely bewildered now. "So, are you human, I mean a human being from Earth, like me?"

"No, not really. Many races in my universe look at least

somewhat…'human' I guess. Humanoid, I have heard it called. Some more than others. There are humans here on the planet you call Earth in the other dimension, but they are not truly the masters of the world, constantly fighting against others who would kill or enslave them."

"Ah," he said, as he risked a quick peek over at her. "And which side are you on?"

"Now, my own side. Before, I was a Slaver's Fetch, raiding to capture slaves, valuables and technology for the Masters. My people, the Alontorans, have been slaves to the Masters for millennia, changed by them to forms that suit their wants and desires better. We have been warriors, gladiators, slavers, pleasure mates," there was a long silence as she paused and bent her head, "food. Whatever the Masters wanted…or what their customers wanted."

"Food!" Danny was horrified. More, he was starting to believe; her story held together too well to be lunatic ramblings. "You mean they're cannibals."

"No, they do not eat their own. They only die if they are killed, being immortal otherwise. Compared to the differences between the Masters and you or me, Danny Hawkins, we are indistinguishable from each other and nothing at all like the Masters. To them, we of Alontora are naught more than playthings. Deadly playthings at times, because we remember what has been done to us. We have turned against them when and as we can. But they are the slavers of the universe, of my universe, with phenomenal powers and technology, and it is rare that any being escapes them as I have done."

Stunned, Danny drove on, a heavy silence in the car.

* * *

Several hours later, and well after dark had fallen, Danny pulled into the parking lot of The Abode in Santa Fe, shutting off the engine. Once they had come down out of the mountains, the roads had straightened out and they made good time. He stretched in the seat and several vertebrae in his back popped audibly. His stomach growled; her urgency had conveyed itself

98

to him, and they hadn't stopped for food.

She looked at him, a slim eyebrow rising above her glasses, which she still wore, despite it being nearly ten o'clock at night. The sun had set a couple of hours before. Danny also knew that whatever it was that had allowed them to understand each other had run out long ago. He patted her leg gently and made a 'stay here' motion with his hands. She nodded and leaned the seat back. He headed into the building to secure at least a room, if not a suite. He'd stayed here before and expected no issues at all. But it would be easier if Myclestra and her giant sword stayed out of sight.

* * *

"Well, Old Snake, now what?" Myclestra spoke to the empty car.

<He is a good man, but we should move on soon. We endanger him indirectly. And, perhaps, directly.>

"I will not countenance any harm to him." Her tone was short and sharp. "Yes, I agree, he is a good man. Could you gain his knowledge of the language here within a few hours of my close association with him?"

<Yes, the closer, the quicker and better.>

"You are saying I should engage him sexually."

<It would permit the greatest access and transference of his knowledge,> Surlianth's tone was sly. <And I have no doubt you would enjoy it. From the way he regards you, my guess is he would certainly not be opposed to the idea. Even if he does not truly know your reasons.>

"Enough, Surlianth. You are trying to embarrass me and that is wasted effort. He is pleasing to the senses, and well built, but there would be nothing other than temporary pleasure for each of us. Alontorans learned long, long ago that love and other such emotions too often lead to bitter betrayal and death. 'Tis simple pleasure and in this case the gaining of needful knowledge, naught more. And that is no different in this universe than in any other."

<Child, you close your eyes to possibilities, you realize

that, do you not?>

"Surlianth, stop. I know nothing will change for me. I am Alontoran. The softer emotions, love and friendship and such, those are not for my people, whether free or still enslaved. There is sisterhood between us and little else, save fury and hate for our enemies."

<Perhaps that is the reason the Masters eliminated the males of your kind long ago. Why all reproduction for your sisters is now controlled by the tech-wizards who are also enthralled to the Shaeldrithans.>

"Pah. Those creatures are given the power of their wildest dreams by the Masters. They would no more rebel against them than I can dance on the surface of a star." She heard the building's doors open and close and the scent of Danny Hawkins' approach filled her nostrils. "Enough, Old Snake. He returns. Be ready to transfer what knowledge of his world you can gain without harming him."

<I shall.>

She smiled at him as he reached the vehicle. He waved a square of something at her, smiling as he sat down in the driver's seat.

* * *

Myclestra had waved him to the shower first. He'd washed the road dirt off and shaved away his last two days of beard. Wearing his pajama bottoms and a fluffy robe the hotel provided, he bowed Myclestra into the bathroom. He'd stretched out on one of the two beds and turned on the TV. He listened to the water come on in the shower and tried to pay close attention to the TV. The image of Myclestra's magnificent body in the shower, long red hair cascading around her, kept intruding on the news.

Down, boy. Yeah, she is a walking wet dream, but damn, sit, stay. You ain't no hormone driven, sex-starved teenager anymore. I don't have any business making any assumptions about her. He looked over where that enormous gem-and-gold encrusted sword, with the sculpted dragon face on the hilt, rested in the middle of the other bed. He'd always had an interest in swords and medieval weapons as a bit of a hobby, but he'd never seen anything quite like that monster blade. After all, she'd cut that old Caddy clean in half with one swing. She could probably tie him in a square knot with one hand. Chastity might be a real good idea tonight. He could always take another cold shower.

He was waiting for the latest news on college football when he heard the water shut off. Despite himself, he perked up and kept an eye on the door. He'd turned off all the lights other than a bedside light and the TV itself. She'd had only the small, satchel-style pack with her, and he had no idea if she had sleepwear in there. So he'd do the right thing, and be the gentleman.

The bathroom door opened and Myclestra walked out, wearing nothing but her long, red hair, her glasses, and a few drops of water. She came straight to his bed, smiling at him. She motioned at the TV, putting a hand over her ear. He got the message and turned off the TV. She knelt on the bed, pulling loose the robe's belt and slipping it off his shoulders. She smiled again and her lips met his.

* * *

Myclestra closed the room's exterior door silently. She smiled to herself. Danny Hawkins was deep in an exhausted and satiated sleep. He was an attentive and thoughtful lover, as considerate of her pleasure as she was of his. She settled the Sword across her back and set off down the dark street, breaking into a long-legged lope as she left The Abode's parking lot.

<Well, you seem happy enough.> Surlianth's voice held a bit of mockery. And perhaps a hint of envy.

"Enough, Old Snake. Danny Hawkins is a talented and experienced lover. I truly expected no less."

<So you leave him asleep, and sneak out like a thief?>

"Surlianth, first, he has his own life, and second, I have a bounty to collect. And to do that, I have to hunt the Warpwraith down and kill it. I doubt Danny Hawkins would be pleased to be in the middle of battle when lightning bolts, fireballs and plasma blasts start flying. He would have nothing to add to such a fight and would be all too likely to get incinerated himself. Not exactly a fair return for his affections, now, don't you think?"

<Viewed in that light, I must concede the point to you.>

"And thanks to him, and you, Old Snake, I now know the language and much of his country, this United States." A passing vehicle's horn blared at her as she ran across a street. "And, if I understand him correctly, I need to find this place called Kirtland Air Force Base. Danny Hawkins believes there are atomic weapons there. Such weapons will have the power to draw the Warpwraith as sugar draws flies."

<Agreed. And how do we get to this place?>

"Danny Hawkins had a thought of a place called a 'truck stop' not too far from here. Heavy transport vehicles that travel on the roads called 'Interstates' should be a place where I can find someone traveling in the right direction."

<I see.> She raised an eyebrow at the Drake's tone. <And how will you convince one of these…'truck drivers' to give you transportation? Seduce one of them as well?>

"Morality? From you?" She grinned as she ran. "A creature of the deep dark between the stars would lecture me on morality?"

<Well…I've naught else to occupy my time at the moment.>

"Ha. Next you'll badger me on the evils of slavery."

<If there's nothing better to do, I guess?>

* * *

The brain bleacher's multicolored flash lit the room. Echo put it back in his pocket and slipped out of the hotel room, leaving Danny Hawkins to his comfortable bed and dreamless sleep. Omega leaned against the side of the 'Vette, an eyebrow arched as he walked up, shaking his head.

"Well?"

"More or less what you expected, baby. Yeah, he opened

up to my *carte noir* as an FBI badge and wasn't hesitant at all. This is getting weirder than snake mittens."

"So? Give, dang it!"

"Get in the car. I'll brief you while we go get something to eat. Any suggestions?"

"Yeah, a Burger Joint if one's reasonably close. Great burgers and their shakes are to die for. And I can get a chocolate malted."

"Good idea." Echo brought the 'Vette's engine to rumbling life. "I haven't had a good burger in quite a while."

"Meanwhile, what'd you learn?"

"Well, I have a name for our Tall Lady now. Myclestra is what she told him to call her. And here's the first head-smacker, she claims to be from another dimension or reality, take your pick."

"Ooookay. Now I know you're kidding! How could anything cross from one universe to another? That's just barely theory that there are other universes! Oh no, just no, no, not possible. She may not be, probably is not, from our galaxy, but she's GOTTA be from this universe, honey."

"Baby, I'm just telling you what she told this Danny Hawkins guy. This is what he supposedly knew."

"Well, she could tell him she's from Fairyland or something. She's pulling a fast one over on him. Or some such shit."

"That, I couldn't tell ya, baby. I'm pretty sure he didn't quite believe her, one way or the other."

"Good grief, extra-dimensional travel isn't even a theory, just speculation. Even if it WERE possible, and it just isn't, WHY is she even here?" Omega shook her head in frustration and denial.

"Yeah, well, as to that question of why. She's here because she's, of all things, a bounty hunter. And her target is worth enough to allow her to buy her own planet, or maybe even her own star system, or that's what she claims, anyway."

"Wow." Omega leaned back in the seat as Echo turned down a street where the orange-and-white peaked roof of a

Burger Joint restaurant gleamed in the very early morning dimness. "What else?"

"Well, when they got here, he cleaned up first, then she showered, came out of the bathroom and ravished him. Pretty sure he had absolutely no complaints. From what he said, I'd think that this Myclestra has fewer inhibitions than even 'dear old Ree-Ree.' She flat wore him out."

"Okay, wait, say what, Ace?"

"Hang on a sec." He pulled up to the drive-through and ordered enough for himself and for Omega's hyped-up metabolism. He paid and drove forward to the pickup window. When the food was delivered, he drove across the street into the parking lot of an auto parts business not yet open for the day. "Okay, to continue," he said around a mouthful of burger, "she's after a creature that feeds on energy. Any energy, but he said she told him it preferred life energy first and foremost, followed by concentrated sources, high radiation materials and shit. She told him it 'eats souls' and absorbs the memories and knowledge of anything it absorbed. And it's a shape-changer, too. It can take the form of anything or anyone it's absorbed."

"Great. That'll be a pain in the posterior to find. Anything about how to fight it?"

"Not really. According to what she told him, it doesn't like fire."

"But it's supposedly an energy eater? Why the heck would it be afraid of fire?"

"Beats me, baby. Maybe, to it, there's a difference between energy and fire or some shit like that? The oxidation effects? I dunno," Echo shrugged, "you're the one with the chemistry degree."

"What else?"

"Yeah, and this part is the scary bit, I think. It has the ability, or so he was told, to twist and warp other living beings. To 'forge such beings into weapons of fear and hatred.' I'll bet that's where that deformed 'werewolf' thing came from."

"Ace, do you realize how much this sounds like a steaming

pile of horse manure? Something right outta some really BAD eighties sword-and-sorcery B-movie."

"Yeah, but I liked some of those movies when I was younger."

"Why am I not surprised?" Omega finished her first double cheeseburger and took a long pull on her chocolate malted.

"Baby, there's still a big issue with this whole damn thing."

"What?"

"There's the 'werewolf' corpse. And the old Caddy cut cleanly in half. And no race I know of has tech like that. So maybe—"

"Oh hell no, Ace! Okay, so, there's new technology here we've never heard of. That doesn't mean either of these two — this 'extra-dimensional bounty hunter' or her target — had to come from another universe."

"Yeah, but baby, there's something else."

"What?" Omega dipped a couple of French fries into the little ketchup cup that came with the food.

"According to Mr. Hawkins, she was a slave to an extraterrestrial race she only called the 'Masters.' Those Masters' control was nearly absolute, literal power of life and death. Her entire race has been mutated and modified over thousands, maybe hundreds of thousands of years. Think about what Slug did to you…then do it to all of Earth. And KEEP doing it. Since, like, antiquity…"

"Oh, shit," Omega breathed, paling slightly, as she saw his point.

"So, in one sense," Echo continued, "she's a mutated, modified, escaped slave. In another sense, she's a powerful, dangerous fighter with little understanding of how our world works. And that all sounds like it holds, regardless of whether she's from our universe or not. How the hell do we apprehend someone like that?"

Omega stared at him in shock, her fries forgotten halfway to her mouth.

* * *

The air brakes on the massive semi hissed and the big diesel growled as it pulled back onto Interstate 40 East. Myclestra smiled briefly to herself for a moment. The woman driver had been willing to give her a ride closer to her destination, this 'Kirtland Air Force Base.' She'd also been quite willing to talk, and talk had led to the two of them using the sleeper on the big truck for a brief but intense lovemaking session. She had used that opportunity to learn more about this new world she now lived in, aided by Surlianth's ability to draw knowledge from unguarded minds. Myclestra knew that some societies found the very idea of same sex lovemaking to be horrible and revolting. Personally she didn't really care. If she was forced to choose, she probably would prefer another, compatible female. Women knew other women's bodies best. For her, there was little to choose from between Danny Hawkins and the driver, Selene Ochoa. Both of them had pleased her and in turn, she had pleased both of them. And her race only had but one gender, in any event.

This 'United States of America' sounded more and more interesting. It was, Selene Ochoa claimed, the most powerful nation on the planet, and the most tolerant. Myclestra was willing to believe the first claim, but the second one left her very skeptical. In her experience, powerful nations or empires or kingdoms, whatever they called themselves, those were anything but tolerant.

She was certain the Warpwraith would come here, drawn by the sharp scent of the atomics buried and guarded here. Surlianth declared the materials hidden underground here at the northeastern corner of the base were the 'ripest' and would draw the creature like iron to a lodestone. It was also closest to the edge of the base's perimeter and in some of the roughest terrain in the area. The area called Coyote Canyon was very lightly inhabited, with only a very few exclusive homes of the wealthy well off to the east of the base fence system, and the roughly defined Cibola National Forest was wrapped around the entire area.

She also knew the soldiers on the base would react to what

was going to happen. She hoped she could avoid causing any injuries or deaths in their ranks, but she knew the Warpwraith would have no such compunctions. If anything, it would cause as much murder and mayhem as possible, feeding off the chaos of wounds and slaughter.

The Warpwraith would never surrender, could never be captured alive. It could only be killed. She must be close enough to the thing to allow Surlianth to capture the raw energy the monster's death throes would release. Only then would she have even a slim chance of returning to her home universe.

If what Selene Ochoa said is true, well, being stuck here might not be the worst thing that could happen to me. I would have to find some way to blend into this society if I wanted to keep my freedom, or even my life.

<Remember that you are bound to me now, Little One, and I will allow no indignities or enslavements to MY bearer.>

"How would you prevent that, Old Snake?"

<Should they somehow slay you, I would be freed of this comfortable prison. I have grown to like my existence in this fashion. If I must be bound, then I find you a compatible and comfortable soul. But, IF you were slain unjustly, I would likely reject any other soul bond, break this adamantine shell, and burn this world to bare stone. I think it might make an acceptable grave marker. Do you agree?>

"Surlianth, do not even dream of doing such a thing, please! Punish my slayers, should you see fit, but only those responsible. As a world, as a race, this folk should not be destroyed as a species. You would only blacken your own soul!"

<We shall see, child, we shall see. I have existed for eons untold, and you know naught of any stains to my soul. Now, let us go and prepare for the Warpwraith to step into our web.>

* * *

The 'taste' of the power was nearly intoxicating as Wruthas neared it, using the ley-line to cross mountains in a single step. It was nearly teleportation, but he passed through all the

107

terrain, aware of its passing. Teleportation was simply 'here,' then 'there,' with nothing in between. It also drained immense amounts of power and left the user very vulnerable afterward. Teleporting wouldn't reduce him to imbecility again, but he would be defenseless, at least for a time. And why would he need to flee? These 'humans' were weak and powerless, lacking the slightest hint of any ability beyond the purely physical in any form. The power here would make him a god.

He reached the ley-line's closest approach to his goal. Perched on the highest mountain top where he must leave the ley-line's flow of energy to attain his goal, he looked down across the insect-like humans, swarming below him.

They are contemptible, huddling in their faceless hordes. Only the energy of their souls has any worth at all. I can feel this strange, purified power across this hive, calling to me, beckoning to me, promising me power undreamed of. I shall waste no time walking through their wretched hovels. My very first victim grants me the ability to avoid soiling my feet to achieve my desire. I come!

He called on his magic and abandoned the shell of Fred Rodriquez. Huge wings formed, fledged with black feathers, his neck lengthened, and eyesight and smell multiplied a hundred times. Toes became talons, and the monstrous vulture, over twelve meters from wingtip to wingtip, soared into the night sky.

* * *

"Okay, Ace, the general consensus we get from the truckers that THINK they saw her are that she got a ride on an owner-operator rig headed eastbound on I-40. No hard data; they might be willing to talk a little bit to an attractive female FBI Agent, but they're not fond of authority figures at best." Omega settled back into the passenger seat of the 'Vette as Echo pulled out of the truck stop parking lot and back onto the side roads nearby.

"No shit, baby." Echo had hit a brick wall, trying to talk to any of the current denizens of the truck stop. Omega had

had somewhat better luck. "So, east on 40, huh? What's out that way? Pull it up on the GPS system. Dammit, I'm missing something, just on the edge of my memory! What is it? There's something there that could be dangerous…"

"Oh, shit, Ace. You wouldn't be thinking of Kirtland Air Force Base, would you?"

"Yeah, that's it!" Echo snapped his fingers. "And, oh SHIT! Kirtland has one of the biggest Weapon Storage Areas in the US. I've got no idea how many nuclear weapons are stored there anymore, but I'm guessing it's still enough to blow up half the world!"

"Oh, yeah, not good, Ace." Omega paled at the thought of what stolen nukes could be used for. "And the eastern end of the WSA is reasonably close to I-40. What if she's after the weapons? Damn, get us morphed, cloaked and in the air. We can't be far behind her!" Dust and weeds swirled as the 'Vette leaped into the air. "Do we give the Kirtland Security Forces a 'heads-up' call?"

"No, Meg, let's see if we can keep this completely off their radar. Fewer explanations and brain bleachings needed afterward!" Echo turned the 'Vette southwest and floored it. It was about fifty air-miles to Kirtland and he was pushing the 'Vette for all it was worth. At full speed, Kirtland, just south and east of Albuquerque, was twelve minutes away from where they were in Santa Fe. The car's cabin was silent as the two highly trained and extremely competent Agents hoped they would be in time.

The lights of Albuquerque were filling the windshield when Omega suddenly sat bolt upright in her seat.

"What was that?"

"What was what, baby?"

"Something pretty damn big just occluded the lights, south and east of us. Big damn bird. Real big."

"You still see it? There's nothing on my sensors."

"No, I lost it, if I even saw it and it wasn't just anxiety. But Ace? Push it. Push it hard."

"Uh-oh, what's up?"

"You know that 'bad feeling' I had a while back?"

"Yeah?"

"It just got worse, lots worse."

* * *

"Whiskey Four, this is CSC. Status check. Over."

"CSC, this is Whiskey Four, we are secure and approaching Bunkers Four Niner, Five Zero and Five One. All clear and secure. Over and out." Staff Sergeant Bradley Norland hung the M1114's radio microphone back on its hook above the large center console. The radio continued to drone away as Master Sergeant Mike Conner in Central Security Control continued the hourly round of status checks with the remainder of the units that made up the midnight shift of the 377th Security Forces Squadron.

"Well, I guess we're good for another half hour." Senior Airman Wilson Bergenson shifted in the driver's seat, stretching enough to pop a vertebra in his back.

"Damn it, Bergenson. Don't do that. Making your bones pop like that is gross." Norland growled at his team member.

"Well, Staff Sergeant, if you hadn't had that little fender bender last week, you'd be driving, I'd be answering the radio and snoozing in between. Seriously, relax a little, catch a couple of Zs. We got four hours to relief and when we get back around to the Entry Control Point, I'm gonna stop long enough to go take a leak. Lieutenant Donley may be a prick, but tonight he's tied up with that wreck over by the Eubank Gate. I heard the LE net dispatcher say something about another drunk running into the ditch there."

"Yeah, and that's just the kind of shit some SMART bad guys might pull to get attention and responding units over to the other side of the damn base. There's a reason you ain't made Staff yet, and if you don't quit screwing around, you never will." Norland was a bit of an odd duck. He'd served a hitch in the Marines, of all things. He'd been deployed to the Sandbox twice and an insurgent IED left him with a small piece of shrapnel in his back that set off the metal detectors every time now. He'd seen the light and transferred from the Corps to the Air Force, leaving mech infantry for Security Force. The Air Force's 'Blue Beanies' were a sharp outfit in general, mean and nasty in a fight, but in garrison, stateside, they relaxed ever so slightly. Well, compared to the Corps, at least in Norland's experience.

"Aye-aye, Staff Sergeant." Bergenson grinned at his team leader.

"Why me, oh Lord? And to think I coulda just stayed with the Green Machine and wouldn't have had to put up with smartass E-4s." Norland sighed, shook his head and looked up at the M1114's roof.

"Nah, Staff Sergeant. Smartass E-4s are endemic. We're everywhere. Even in Uncle Sam's Misguided Children." The radio crackled before Norland could respond.

"Whisky Four, this is CSC. Be advised I'm showing an exterior perimeter sensor alarm just outside the fence near Bunker Five-One. Probably teenagers looking for a make-out spot again, or a big critter takin' a leak on the sensor, but I need you to expedite to that location and determine what's set off the alarm THIS time. Copy? Over."

"CSC, this is Whiskey Four. Copy exterior perimeter sensor alarm activation at Bunker Five-One. Expediting arrival. ETA, three mikes, Copy? Over."

"CSC copies Whiskey Four. Standing by. Over."

"Great," Bergenson grunted as he stepped on the gas, the big 6.5-liter diesel growling louder, "just what we need tonight, having to roust out a couple of horny teenagers too stupid to go find someplace else to screw around. That or somebody's damn dog, pissing on the sensor."

"Or no-shit bad guys thinking they can steal a nuke. Bad shit happens, Bergenson. You ain't been to someplace like the Sandbox. I have. Don't assume shit, troop. Assuming stuff can get you killed quick. So keep your head on a swivel, damn it." Norland reached around into the back seat and grabbed his

Advanced Ballistic Helmet and body armor, struggling into his gear as the M1114 accelerated up a hill, heading for the northeast corner of the WSA.

"Aye-aye, Staff Sergeant."

* * *

<It is near, Child. Prepare yourself. It will choose one of these three doors into the hill, desiring what is behind them. I think this one, closest to us, will be its first choice. The power is somehow 'purer' here. Much more of it, I think.>

"I will need to draw on your power this night, Old Snake. Will I have to barter for it this time?"

<No, Little One. The Warpwraith is an abomination, a stain on the fabric of the cosmos. I will not stint you in your need. This foulness must be eliminated from existence.>

"My thanks, Surlianth." A deep roar, engine noise, caught her attention first, then she sensed the moving air displaced by a large vehicle moving up the road inside the fence. The low hill blocked any direct view. "Oh, no, no, no. That must be some kind of guard machine. Why now?"

* * *

The M1114 slid to a halt with a screech of locked-up brakes. Norland unassed the vehicle, M4A1 carbine at high port, while Bergenson took enough time to grab his body armor and ABH out of the back seat and throw it on over his web gear. It took him a second longer to haul his M110A1 rifle out of its cradle.

Bergenson joined Norland where he crouched next to the HMMWV's front fender. Norland was staring into the night sky and Bergenson looked up to see what he saw. It took a second and then he saw something huge and black occlude the rising half-moon. Huge, black and moving fast, straight at them.

"That a friggin' condor? At night?" Bergenson brought up his rifle. The shape landed on the hill directly above the door of Bunker 51, shrinking and changing into a vaguely man-like shape. Huge eyes glinted in the dim light from dim streetlight on its pole next to the road. "What the hell is THAT?"

"Hell if I know," Norland muttered, flipping his M4A1's selector lever to full auto, "but it ain't good. No way, no how. Engage it, NOW!" He never got a shot off.

Bergenson got one round off from his suppressed M110A1. The 7.62mm NATO round passed harmlessly through the thing. It didn't even seem to notice the shot. A clawed hand flung toward them and clenched into a fist. The two Security Forces men were instantly crushed, the bodies forced together in a revolting splatter of flesh, bones and blood. Neither of them so much as screamed. When the warpwraith released them and turned away toward the bunker, the two were simply an indistinguishable mass of misshapen red pulp with bits and pieces of their uniforms, gear and weapons crushed into the grotesque remains.

* * *

<It comes. It is HERE!>

The Warpwraith coalesced out of the night, a foul, winged shadow that changed and shrank as it landed. Myclestra watched the creature turn to face what she realized was a manned vehicle with two occupants exiting it to confront the Warpwraith. Her jaw may have tightened ever so slightly as she heard the single, quiet shot from a projectile weapon, and then the sickening sound as the monster crushed those soldiers into a bloody paste. She activated the first cantrip she had placed on her brow, enhancing her speed and agility tenfold. It would last only a few moments at best. There were two other cantrips marked on her brow, all she could stand to use on herself at once. One of those quadrupled her strength, the other doubled her body's ability to absorb damage and continue to fight. None of them would last more than moments at best. If they did last too long, the stress the magic put on her body would burn her out and kill her within a handspan of minutes. They were powerful spells, but they came at a dreadful cost in the abuse of her body.

She came out of the concealing gulley in blurring speed, dirt and rocks rooster-tailing in the wake of her running footsteps. She reached the dirt road next to the first of the three fences and with a shout to activate the second cantrip on her brow into glowing life, she cleared the two-hundred-foot space enclosed by the triple fence system in a single bound. A second shout activated the third cantrip as she raced toward the nebulous black blot that was the creature, perched on the top of the concrete and steel entrance to the bunker below.

The plasma pistol flashed out of its holster, her esoteric senses putting it precisely on target. Her target was the black, vaguely man-shaped figure of the Warpwraith, and she pressed the trigger. Thunder and lightning split the night and everything within ten feet of a spot centered on the Warpwraith vanished in incandescent fury, the ground surface turned into bubbling glass.

But not the Warpwraith. The creature detected her the instant she moved from her concealment. It was surprised enough that she got off the shot before it moved, but it had its own defenses, and its own magic moved it fifty feet away, crossing the distance before Myclestra had actually pulled the trigger. This fight had just changed from a clean kill into a slugging match.

She turned hard across the rugged terrain, leaping across the paved road next to the bunker, charging the creature as the Sword swept out of its sheath. The blade glittered with its own power, brilliant arcs of cobalt and violet lightnings skittering along its edge.

"YOU!" the monster bellowed in surprise. "HOW ARE YOU HERE!?" A beam of intense, nearly poisonous green light flashed from Wruthas' hands, to be shattered and thrown aside by the Sword.

The plas-pistol fired again, creating another glassy crater as the Warpwraith dimension-stepped away once more. Undeterred, Myclestra altered course, sprinting to bring the monster within arm's reach. A wall of black flame raced toward her, burning from Wruthas' clawed hands. The Sword blocked some of the flames as the spell collapsed around her, but enough got through to smash against her armor. The tech-wizard-enhanced armor flared a bluish-silver as it absorbed the blast. There was still enough pure kinetic energy to knock her off her feet and ten yards through the scrub bushes that flared away in ash.

<Now, Child! He cannot cast the black-flame and still step away again.>

She brought the Sword up to target the monster, the power of a star gone nova lashing out. But before she could truly get the Sword's point on target, blinding light illuminated the entire hillside…not that she could see it. The voice that came with it was loud enough to partially disorient her.

"FREEZE! DROP YOUR WEAPONS! YOU ARE BOTH UNDER ARREST BY THE AUTHORITY OF THE PAN-GALACTIC LAW ENFORCEMENT AND IMMIGRATION AGENCY!"

The Sword's blast missed the Warpwraith. Terrified by the near-miss of so powerful a weapon, the creature instantly pulled enough magic from its reserves to do a true teleport, reappearing in a ley-line junction over sixty miles away. Instead, the blast melted everything in front of Myclestra, a narrow cone only centimeters wide where its apex touched the Sword, widening out to over thirty meters at the far end, half a kilometer away.

* * *

Echo landed the cloaked 'Vette in a dry wash covered by a stand of tall cottonwood trees. The couple grabbed gear out of the back of the 'Vette. Omega launched half a dozen cloaked drones that could provide real-time, over-the-hill images and act as high intensity flood lights and loudspeakers if needed. So far, the night was quiet, with only crickets and the drone of cicadas breaking the silence.

In addition to their dual proto-cyclotron blaster handguns in shoulder holsters and their Winchester & Tesla death-ray backups, Omega selected a Mark IV Tachyon Splitter rifle. Echo pulled out something that looked like a cross between a Deagle pistol and an old-school, cut-down laser rifle. They looked at each other with nearly identical rueful grins.

"Loaded for Arcturan were-bear, honey?" Echo checked the settings and safety on his weapon.

"Maybe," Omega answered, "and what's your excuse, Ace? And what the heck is that thing?"

"No one ever complained about having too much ammo or too much gun in a fire-fight, baby. And this is something I've been working on, off and on, for a few years now. A Colt-Westinghouse 2.5mm railgun pistol. We have them in the Armory at HQ, but this one's…special. I've been hot-rodding it, as you like to call it. They're no fun to take a hit from normally, but this one? This thing hits like an anti-tank cannon. Watch out, though; the recoil is a bitch. I've added compensation for a lot of it, but it still hammers back pretty damn good."

"Dear Lord, Echo! The Division One version of, 'Think you used enough dynamite there, Butch?' Yeah," she chuckled as she led the way out of the wash. "Time to get our game faces on, Ace."

"Right behind you, baby."

In less than ten minutes they reached the overwatch site they'd selected on the GPS map on approach. They had barely settled in when a sudden, incredibly fast movement grabbed their attention. They stared in shock as Myclestra cleared all three fences in a single bound. Instants later, lightning and thunder tore the silence of the calm night apart.

"OH, SHIT!" Echo started forward, running toward the fence. "Put the drones on her, Meg!"

Omega flipped a pair of switches on her remote, locking the drones on the sprinting woman. She followed as Echo was over the outer fence in two moves. His blaster pistol swept out and blew a three-meter gap in the middle, electrified fence. Omega was mere feet behind him as he reached the inner fence and her feet hit the ground on the other side before his did. Intense green light sprayed into the sky, a crackling, hissing noise coming from over the hill. Another blast of thunder and lightning shattered the night.

No doubt about it now, baby! That was a plasma weapon, and a powerful one. What the hell is going on here, and who's shooting at who? Thoughts flowed at near-instantaneous speed through their nd't'lq link as they raced up the slope to the top of the small hill. Omega was in the lead and came to a skidding halt, staring at the vague, humanoid black form.

WHAT the hell is that!? Ace, have you ever—?

No, baby, no idea!

A wall of black flame roared toward the strange woman. She used the huge sword to block some of the flames, bluish-violet energy crackling off the blade. Some of those flames got past the sword and hit her. A silver halo flared around her body as the fire exploded, hurling her ten meters through brush that flashed into ashes at her contact.

She landed on her feet and recovered, raising that ridiculously huge blade and pointing at an indistinct black figure further away on the hillside. Omega decided this had gone far enough.

"FREEZE! DROP YOUR WEAPONS! YOU ARE BOTH UNDER ARREST BY THE AUTHORITY OF THE PAN-GALACTIC LAW ENFORCEMENT AND IMMIGRATION AGENCY!"

As she watched, she realized her voice, amplified by the drones' speakers, was enough to make the woman flinch, the barest of twitches, but enough to keep the incredible blast of heat and light coming from the Sword from hitting the shadowy black figure. A figure that instantly vanished with a crack of displaced air. The woman vented a bloodcurdling scream of pure rage, spinning and charging Alpha One like a bullet train.

Omega was fast enough to hit her dead center with a shot from her Mark IV, but that silverish halo flared around her, and she didn't seem to notice. The deafening CRACK from Echo's pistol as the slug broke Mach seemed to stagger her more than the impact of the slug on the woman. Omega saw blood spatter as the silver halo flared brighter than ever. A second shot from

Omega's rifle had no apparent effect again, and Echo's second round was actually deflected by that ridiculous sword, but still, somehow, the shot hurt her. Then the banshee was on top of them in a flashing whirl of fists, boots and that sword.

Echo took a solid boot to his chest that catapulted him into the brush. The sword flashed by Omega's head and simply cut her Mark IV tachyon-splitter rifle in half. Omega blocked two punches, an elbow strike and a powerful spinning roundhouse kick. She was going all out, holding nothing back, faster than she had fought against Mark Wright, harder and stronger than the raid on Aggum's fortress on Kochav, pushing her enhanced body further and faster than she ever had before. And this woman, whatever she was, was actually FASTER and STRONGER. Omega got a punch, kick, roundhouse punch combination through the woman's guard, and it was like hitting battleship armor. There was that silver-blue flare around each strike and nothing, no effect at all.

Omega hadn't even been able to knock her odd mirror shades off. But she noticed there were three radiant symbols glowing on the other woman's forehead, almost pulsing like a heartbeat. The hand holding the sword hilt got through her block and smashed against her cheek, blood spraying from the cut the dragon-face on the hilt made. Omega staggered, stunned for an instant. *If that had been the blade, I'd be dead. She's not trying to kill me, but she could if she wanted to.*

Echo launched himself back into the fray, a perfect-form blindside block that knocked the woman off her feet and sent her rolling down the hill onto the paved road. She sprang to her feet and stared up at Alpha One. Echo picked up his railgun as Omega drew both her blasters. They stood motionless, waiting to see who would restart the fight. The woman screamed at them again, fury and frustration evident in every line of her body. Then she raised that sword and pure energy shot out the tip of the blade.

The blade burned a four-meter high, two-meter wide, fifteen-meter-long wall of pure, liquefied energy between them, a slice of a star come to ground. The radiant heat drove them stumbling backward as their specialized Suits heated toward their flashpoint. Omega felt her hair and eyebrows starting to crisp from the fierce heat.

"YOU IDIOTS!" The woman's deep voice roared from the other side of the molten barrier, "Take your AUTHORITY and be damned! It escaped, my bounty target escaped, and your world may die because of it. YOU MORONS! I should have killed you both! Stay out of my way, damn you!" Silence fell on the other side of the barrier and when it collapsed a minute later, the woman was gone.

"What the hell just happened?" a stunned Echo asked. "I feel like a gurfdin kicked me."

"Echo, she could have killed us both. She pushed me to and, I think, past my limits and she was STILL stronger and faster. Not to mention what she did with that damned sword. WHAT was that THING?" She turned and looked up the road. Sirens could be heard in the distance. And then she realized there was an Air Force Security Force M1114 sitting in the middle of the road, engine still running. "Uh-oh. There should be at least two troops in that thing. Where are they?"

* * *

Railgun still in hand and held ready, Echo snapped on a flashlight extracted from one of his many warp pockets and shone it down the road. Even so, he almost missed the rivulet of blood draining to the side of the road. But he realized what it was and followed it back to the source, something he regretted for quite some time afterward. And then Echo, that baddest of badass Division One Agents, the youngest of the Originals, the Head of Alpha Line, the Assistant Director of Division One, nearly lost everything in his stomach.

Echo had seen a lot of horrible ways to die, including his torture at the claws of the Cortians, and Omega's near death under the ion drive of their ship, but what he saw then was worse than either. The two airmen had simply been crushed into a ball of human clay. And he saw lights now, he was not just hearing the sirens.

"Oh shit," he stage-whispered. He ditched the flashlight in a pocket, pulled out his phone, and dialed Fox. "Hey, Fox, we got one hell of a sitch here. You updated on this possible illegal we've been following in Colorado and New Mexico?"

"Yes, what's up, zun?"

"How many Agents with brain bleachers can you get to Kirtland Air Force Base in Albuquerque? Inside the Weapon Storage Area?"

"How many do you need, zun?"

"All of them. Now. And maybe a certain special code sent to the Kirtland brass, as of five minutes ago. And keep listening; I think we're about to have fun with base security."

"Oy vey! All right, I'm on it."

Just then, he became aware of his partner and spouse coming up behind him, and he broke off the phone conversation to spin around and stop her.

"Don't look, baby." Echo turned to Omega, putting himself between her and the horror just off the road, half-hidden in the brush. He quickly shoved the rail gun into a standard jacket pocket, its butt hanging out over the top of the pocket.

"Too late," she gasped, turning away to vomit in a bush. "Much too late. Urgh!" She threw up, hard, and Echo was hard-pressed not to join her. When she finally got her stomach under control, she panted, then asked, "Dear sweet Lord God in Heaven. What in hell did that?"

Abruptly, from Echo's phone, they could hear Fox in the background.

"BOYS!" Fox roared. "I need two dozen Agents with fully charged brain bleachers on the way to Kirtland Air Force Base in New Mexico and as fast as you can. We need them there ten minutes ago! Oy, what a meshuginah shtik drek."

"He has no idea," Omega murmured at that.

"All over it, Boss-Daddy," Lima answered in the background. "What's the rush?"

"Anything bad enough to make Alpha One throw up is

something that gets top priority, zun."

"Oh shit! Gone!" a disturbed Lima responded.

"Then again, maybe he does," Omega added, rueful, just as her gut lurched again.

The phone clicked as Echo switched off incoming voice, but did not break the connection.

"What did that?" Echo asked, holding Omega's by-now very disheveled braid out of the way as she hurled again.

"I…don't think it was…HER," Omega braced her hands on her knees, "if it was her, then why didn't she…do THAT to us? I think it was the other one, the black shape that vanished. I'd say by teleportation, from the BANG of collapsing air. And SHE said that it was her target, her bounty target. And then SHE warns us…to stay…out of her way."

"Yeah, and where the hell did she go, baby?"

"Don't worry…'bout that, Ace. One of my drones…is still locked on her…ugh…ass, and will stay cloaked while it tracks her. We can catch up to her someplace where we don't have to worry about things like these guys." She pointed at a fire team of four Security Force troops slowly advancing on them, M4A1 carbines and an M249 SAW shouldered and aimed at Alpha One.

"Oh, shit."

Chapter Three — Pursuit

She had crawled into the low cave with the last of her energy, passing out until the midday heat roused her. Dragging herself out of the cave took all the strength she could muster. Something buzzed at her from under a bush, a snake coiled and ready to strike. As exhausted as she was, she was still quicker than some stupid snake, and she caught it in mid-strike. She twisted the head, with its venom glands and fangs, completely off, and ate the rest of it, whole and raw. There were some berry-looking things on the bush and she ate those next, followed by most of the green leaves on the bush. She considered the woody stems and smaller branches, but decided they would cost more energy to consume than she would gain.

She moved away from the cave and further into the sunlight. The warmth on her skin told her the local star was near its zenith. She went through the pouches on her belt again, but there were no remaining rations of any kind. She had her cantrips, but none of them did her any good now. Indeed, trying to use one in her drained state might actually kill her. The energy for wielding magic had to come from somewhere and in her case, being no wizard, the energy came from her body's own stores. Using magic could be addictive, and that addiction invariably killed the weak-willed.

She turned a few larger rocks over and ate the various things she found under them. Most were small, shorter than her thumb, and several fought back, gripping her fingers with clawed forelimbs as a tail-mounted sting struck repeatedly. The creatures' pathetic poisons had no effect on her. Slowly, she was recovering, but she needed a great deal more in the way of food and water. Desert crawlers and snakes were sustenance, but little more and not enough in any case. At least she no longer stumbled when she walked. There was other life in this mountainous desert, and she was patient. A couple of rocks, thrown hard and accurately, brought down a pair of small animals, long-eared and fast. Again, they were eaten raw and whole, leaving only entrails, fur and broken bones with the marrow sucked out. Feeling more like herself, she waited until the cooling air of night rose around her.

She climbed to the top on the highest hill there. To the south, six hundred odd ur-lans away, were the roads and some homes of the local humans. North, nearly a thousand ur-lans away, was a larger grouping of homes; at least she was pretty sure that was what purpose the buildings served. She had no doubt that she could get food and water at either place, but only at the cost of possibly revealing her whereabouts. One run-in with the 'Authority of the Pan-Galactic Law Enforcement and Immigration Agency' was enough, at least for the moment. She wondered if they would be willing to pay her the bounty for the Warpwraith when she caught and killed it.

"Well, Old Snake, now what? The creature has, at least for the moment, escaped me. And now there are these two from that awkwardly named 'Agency.' Sooner, rather than later, I will need more water than I can acquire by drinking the blood of the small creatures I kill."

<I know not, Little One. The timing of those 'authorities' was most unfortunate, confounding your attack and allowing the Warpwraith to flee through its magic.>

"And how shall I now find the trail? Waiting to pick up the thing's track after it strikes again, possibly at a place so far away I cannot reach it in time."

<I can at the least tell you which way it went when it teleported away. It can be no more than two days' hard travel by foot away from where we fought it. And I am certain that it went north by east, into a high mountain area, where the ley-lines will flow stronger.>

"Well, more than I knew a moment ago. Can you track it by magic, Old Snake?"

<Not with any great precision. I might, at best, get you within the range of your senses, two thousand ur-lans or so.>

"Well, that will have to be good enough. Now, darkness has fallen, as I no longer feel the Sun's heat on my skin. Can you give me a direction to begin hunting this beast again?"

<As I said, north by east, close upon the way we came here.>

"Retracing our steps," she sighed, "and I fear even my sturdy pathfinder boots shall be sorely worn before this race is run. North by east it is, then." Myclestra settled what little she had in her satchel, slung the Sword over her back and headed northeast.

Behind her and nearly a mile away, one of Omega's stealthed and cloaked drones whirred to life, lifting away from its observation spot and following her at a distance, uplinking its information through the Agency's satellite system to Omega's phone.

* * *

Wruthas smashed his way through another tree, pulling every least hint of life-energy out of it until the crumbled remains appeared as if they had decayed a hundred years ago. He had already engulfed all the animals his remaining power could draw to him. He wanted to obliterate the mountain side with lightning and fire in his rage. He could draw that energy from the junction of ley-lines here, but if he did so, he knew he would be waving a flag with *I am here* to that…that…that eternally and thrice damned bounty hunter!

How could that bitch have followed me here? She is no mage. She has barely enough ability to activate the paltry cantrips she possesses! How is she HERE?

His fury at least temporarily sated, he stood on the edge of a cliff, staring out over the valleys and lower ridges. *Wait, the last place she hounded me to, that ancient stone circle in that forest! Those woods were known to harbor an entire village of powerful druids. And where there are druids, there are likely a few unicorns. Those creatures are some of the most powerful sources of magical energy the universe has ever known. If one of those helped her — and they would, the interfering busybodies that they are — then that would explain how she had the power and the ability to pass through an opened portal and arrive close enough that she would be able to find me so easily. THAT is how she is here!*

Wruthas settled on the cliff top and meditated to recover some sense of calm. The bounty hunter was here and there were those others, the ones behind the thundering voice and brilliant lights, an 'authority' of some kind. He had only sensed humans there, one or two at most. He could have disposed of them as he had the first two who arrived in that machine. Only that gods-bedamned hunter had nearly incinerated him with that ensouled Sword. Individually, it was a rare human that could offer any threat to him. The threat from humans came in their numbers and their technological weapons. And they simply loved to use fire as a weapon. Fire was his one great weakness. He could wield magical fire, but he could not withstand it in any form, mundane or magical. And that gods-cursed bounty hunter knew it.

* * *

"FREEZE! DO NOT MOVE!" the leader of the team, who wore the stripes of a staff sergeant, ordered in what was just shy of a shout, then motioned with his rifle's muzzle at Echo. "YOU WITH THE WEAPON, SLOWLY PLACE IT ON THE GROUND."

"What?" Echo asked, confused. The sergeant pointed his weapon at Echo's side.

"THE WEAPON. PLACE IT. ON. THE. GROUND. NOW."

Echo glanced down at the butt of the rail gun, protruding out of his pocket; he had forgotten about it in his concern for Omega, who was still trying to retch.

Ohh, that ain't good, Ace, Omega thought to him.

I know. We can't let them get their hands on our weaponry. But there's already been too much bloodshed here. I hope Fox times this right, or we got a serious problem.

Ain't that the truth. And until I can stop throwing up, I'm not much help.

Unlax, baby. We got this, you and me. It's gonna be okay, one way or another.

Echo slowly pulled the rail gun from his pocket and placed it on the ground in front of him as instructed, making sure that the barrel was facing away from anyone…though mentally planning for sight lines, just in case.

"GOOD. NOW HANDS IN THE AIR ABOVE YOUR HEAD, BOTH OF YOU. TAKE TWO STEPS BACK AND TURN AWAY."

Echo raised his hands, and Omega started to do so, then heaved twice, spun to one side, and vomited again. The Security Force troops' weapons came up, aiming at her, but she threw out a hand in a *hold!* gesture, finished retching, then turned back to them.

"S-sorry," she panted. "I just…we just found what became of your colleagues, and…whatever did that, it was really gruesome."

"And I wasn't far behind her," Echo added the confession, cocking his wrist enough to point in the general direction of his stomach. "Only reason I didn't was because I was busy trying to take care of her; she's my best bud, and my partner. And we're not exactly inexperienced." Echo avoided adding that she was also his wife; that might have been taken amiss, in the circumstances.

The sergeant raised an eyebrow.

"You found Bergenson and Norland?" he wondered. "They didn't make it?"

Omega nodded, then pointed.

"Jackson, go take a look," the sergeant ordered, and the team's rifleman peeled off, the flashlight mounted on his M4 lighting his way, headed for the bush to which Omega had gestured.

"Um, you might not want to—" she began.

"Oh DAMN! Sergeant Mays!" Jackson cried, then spun to one side and began projectile vomiting. Judging by the quantity that came up, Alpha One decided this bunch had just had dinner, and it had been substantial.

"What the hell did you two do to them?" Mays snarled, shouldering his rifle again. Then he looked around the area, seeing several smoking craters and a five-hundred-meter burn scar carved across the nearby slope. "And what in hell happened here?"

"WE didn't do anything," Echo noted, even as Omega's face paled again, turning slightly green, as they listened to the airman barfing. An unfortunate breeze brought certain smells wafting past their noses, as well; she turned greener. "We had just arrived from Headquarters, trying to beat the alert and stop this from going down, but we were seconds too late."

"Headquarters? Stop it?" Mays queried, suspicious. "Where are you from? Who do you work for?"

"NSA," Echo offered. "We have…oh, shit."

"What?"

"Aw, I left my damn badge in my jacket pocket," Echo grumbled. "We stopped at a diner to grab a fast dinner a while back — hadn't had anything to eat all day — and tucked 'em in the chest pocket, and forgot to put 'em back on the lapel when we left."

"Heh," Mays chuckled grimly. "Ain't like I haven't heard THAT one before. Happens all the time. Okay. With your left hand, slowly reach into your pocket and extract your badge. Very slowly."

Echo reached into the breast pocket of his Suit jacket and produced his *carte noir*, which had already morphed into a perfect replica of an NSA badge, a Restricted Area access badge, AND a Common Access Card.

Huh, Omega thought at Echo. *First time I've ever seen those things split themselves.*

It only looks like it, Echo noted. *The clasp thing means it's all connected. These things are stupid-fanboi cool.*

"Hold it over your head," Mays ordered, and Echo obeyed. "Ma'am, where is your badge?"

"Sa—" Omega broke off as Jackson began another round of puking. "Um, can we get him out of the line of sight to the bodies, please? I already got a good look earlier, and every time he starts puking again, I wanna join him…" She choked back a gag, then added, "I could obey orders a lot better if I can stop heaving."

"Ah. Fair enough, ma'am. Hammond, run grab Jackson — don't look at whatever he's looking at; I don't want BOTH of you hurling — and pull him around to the other side of the . Stand by one, ma'am."

"Standing by, and thank you," Omega said gratefully, then began breathing deep, staring off into the darkness with a blank gaze, obviously trying to quell the nausea.

"I get it. To be honest, the sound and the smell aren't doin' any of us any favors," Mays admitted.

"Unfortunately, it isn't just his barf that smells," Echo observed. "Your deceased people are…pretty messed up."

"Oh."

By that time, Hammond had gotten Jackson out of sight of the bloody lump of oozing clay that had once been two men, and Jackson began to settle. Omega drew another deep breath and let it out slowly.

"Okay, Sergeant Mays, thank you," she said. "That's a bit better, I think. So, okay, my badge and access card are in my jacket's chest pocket, too."

"Left hand, bring it out slowly. Keep the right hand in the air, please."

"Um, could I use my right hand instead?"

"Why?"

Omega flushed slightly. "Curves. I can accommodate the, uh, slope a little better if I do a sorta cross-draw, as it were."

Several snorts came from the other members of Mays' team, and Omega grinned sheepishly.

"Hey, it is what it is," she pointed out.

"Troops, I don't want to end this massive Charlie-Foxtrot of a night by writing Letters of Counseling for my whole fire team. So zip it!" The staff sergeant glared over his shoulder at his men. "Yes, ma'am, go ahead and use your right hand, but very slowly," Mays allowed.

Keeping her left hand in the air, Omega produced her *carte noir* and held it over her head.

During this time, none of the airmen had come within some fifteen feet of their 'prisoners,' namely Alpha One. It was likely that the two Alpha Line Agents could take down all four members of the Air Force security team without any of the four knowing exactly what hit them, but there were more sirens en route, the lot needed brain-bleaching, the area needed to be secured, and the two Agents were united in not wanting to cause any more harm than their quarry had already caused in gruesomely killing the two dead airmen. So they cooperated, sure that Fox was listening in over Echo's still-open, quantum-ciphered phone comm, and expediting help. A quick flash, as of a shooting star, off to their northwest confirmed it to Omega.

Did you see that, Ace?

Yeah, baby. I'm betting the cavalry is about three minutes before arriving. We probably won't see 'em HERE for a bit, but base HQ probably will.

Which is good.

Which is damn good. 'Cause that particular shit will definitely flow downhill...to these guys.

"Airman Kanicky," Mays ordered his team's grenadier, "go check out their badges. We'll cover you." He gestured to himself and Hammond, who had left a slowly-recovering Jackson sitting on the ground, leaning against the HMMWV M1114.

Kanicky let his M4 with its underslung M320 grenade launcher hang from its sling as he moved over to Omega and carefully took her *carte noir* — which currently depicted an NSA badge with Omega's image and the name Margaret Tillman, along with an all-access Restricted Area badge and the CAC, a kind of universal key-card that government employees and contractors used at most US facilities. The wonder of the *carte noir* tech — it was Deltiri in design — enabled it not only to pick up on the needs of its agent, but access any needed information electronically via the specialized Agency comm sats. It normally relayed through the sophisticated Agency cell phones, but in a pinch could access direct. This meant that not only would the CAC function as a CAC, but the backflow of information also meant that if they checked out NSA agent Margaret Tillman, she would in fact be listed in NSA records.

"Oh damn, Sergeant," Kanicky exclaimed, having a look at the NSA badge. "It's a green badge!"

"Shit. Check his," Mays said, eyebrows going up.

Kanicky moved to Echo and took his *carte noir*, which likewise used an image of Echo in the 'NSA badge,' along with the name Alec Peterson.

"It's a green badge, too," Kanicky said. "These two are serious brass."

"Mmph. Lemme see," Mays demanded.

Kanicky carried both *carte noirs*, their temporarily-tripartite components held together by a clip lanyard, to his superior.

"Mm," Mays said, then produced a small scanner from his gear and ran each CAC through it. Fractions of a second later, it bleated and lit a green light. "Huh. This shows legit."

Much to Alpha One's relief, Mays waved for his men to lower their weapons — though they did not put them away. Likewise, Echo left the rail gun on the ground, though he casually stepped in front of it, obscuring it from view.

"So what are you two doing here?" Mays demanded, and they realized he was still suspicious. "And why didn't you come through the Entry Control Point and check in with Security?"

"There wasn't time," Echo noted. "We had a bunch of delays just in getting here — the ONLY reason we even stopped to eat is 'cause my partner, here, has blood sugar issues, and she was getting woozy — and by the time we arrived, the shit was already hitting the fan." He gestured to the still-smoking vegetation and the scars in the landscape. "We had just enough time to follow the terrorists through the hole they made in the fence and over here. Not in time to save your men, but we did scare off the terrorists."

"Who the hell were they, and how did they do…that…to Bergenson and Norland?" Jackson wondered in a weak voice.

Just then, another up-armored M1114 with an M240 MMG in a turret mount roared up in a cloud of dust. Five more men got out, armed and armored. A sixth stood behind the turret mount.

"STAFF SERGEANT!" the leader called. "Why don't you have these people in custody?!"

"They appear to be NSA green badges, Lieutenant Carsdale," Mays responded. "I'm still trying to sort it all out, but apparently they're responding to the same event we are… only none of us got here in time to save the Area Response Team."

"Don't look, sir," Jackson murmured, still pale and weak. "It's…bad."

Just then, two of the newcomers, who had spread out to form an area incident perimeter, began to retch in the brush on the far side of the paved base-perimeter road. Within seconds the sounds of nigh-projectile vomiting made itself known.

"Oh shit," a dismayed Carsdale said blankly. "You weren't joking. Those troops just got back from a tour in the Sandbox. IDEs make a mess of human bodies."

"Not like this, El-Tee," Jackson muttered from where he leaned against his team M1114. "Not like this."

"Jackson, here, was stationed at Kandahar AB, Sir. Mortar and rocket attacks were bad for a while," Mays noted, "and he did the same thing. And our female NSA agent over there was barfing when we got here, and her partner says he only managed to avoid it by dint of taking care of her."

"Whiskey Romeo Three, this is CSC. Do you copy?" suddenly blared from Mays' radio. He hit the mic button and responded.

"Whiskey Romeo Three here. Go, CSC."

"Do you have any persons in custody, Whiskey Romeo Three?"

"Yes and no, CSC. I have two persons detained, but they appear to be from the NSA with green badges — names are…" he consulted the *carte noirs*, "Alec Peterson and Margaret Tillman — and to have been attempting to ward off an attack. Which attack is evidently what the perimeter sensors picked up."

"Has Second Lieutenant Carsdale arrived?"

"On site now, CSC."

"Lieutenant Carsdale, can you hear me?"

"Roger that, CSC," Carsdale said.

"Good. This way you can all hear it at once. Stand by for orders from higher command. Go ahead, Sir," the CSC replied. Suddenly the voice changed.

"Thank you, Master Sergeant Conner. Whiskey Romeo Three, Whiskey Romeo Bravo Eight, do you copy?"

"Yes, sir," Mays and Carsdale answered simultaneously.

"This is Kirtland Base Commander Brigadier General Anders Miller speaking. This is an order: STAND DOWN."

"But Sir—" Carsdale began.

"That is an ORDER, Lieutenant. Code Delta One Alpha One Red One. Do you understand?"

"Um, with all due respect, sir, I've never heard that code before. Besides…spooks." Carsdale swallowed hard as he traded looks with Sergeant Mays. Mays pulled a plastic-coated card out of his pocket and handed it to Carsdale.

"Suggest authentication, El-Tee," he kept his voice just barely audible. Carsdale nodded.

"Sir, I request secure authentication at this time."

"Copy that, Whiskey Romeo Bravo Eight, stand by one," there was a sigh on the airwaves and a brief pause. "Ready for authentication."

"Sir, I read Mike, Tango, Zulu, Four, Seven, Niner."

"Copy that. I authenticate Hotel, Papa, Uniform, Five, Three, One. Confirm?"

"Good authentication, Sir. Whiskey Romeo Bravo Eight standing by for orders on that code."

"Good job, authenticating, Lieutenant. Smart. What I want out of my officers. Yes, that code would be above your grade, I suppose. All right, listen up, and listen close. These are essentially friends, they are here to help, and that is coming down all the way from the Global Strike Command MajCom. Code Delta One Alpha One Red One is one of the highest-level orders that can come down from MajCom. Whenever you hear that code, you stop what you are doing and offer aid to the ones issuing that code or for whom the code was issued, whether they're 'spooks' or not — and let me add, if they're using that code, they will ALWAYS be 'spooks.' Get over it. Do you copy?"

"Yes, sir."

"Um, General Miller, sir?" Mays asked, tentative.

"Go, Sergeant Mays."

"Could you please repeat that code again, sir, so we can ensure our teams remember it?"

"Of course. That makes good sense, Mays; good for you. Code Delta One Alpha One Red One: stand down and assist the NSA agents. Read back."

"Whiskey Romeo Three copies Code Delta One Alpha One Red One; standing down," Mays repeated.

"Whiskey Romeo Bravo Eight copies Code Delta One Alpha One Red One; standing down," Carsdale added. The rest of their teams nodded affirmation and lowered their weapons.

"Good," General Miller said. "I'll be sending you some more NSA personnel to back up the two you have there; evidently the two you have are the NSA's top response team, and it was hoped if they were sent ahead, they could get there in time, after the last-ditch intel heads-up that there was about to be a serious attempt to access and steal Special Weapons. Their backups are already en route to your location, after stopping by my office to ensure I had gotten the heads-up from their brass."

"Roger that, sir," Carsdale replied. "NSA backup en route.

Hopefully they can tell us what happened here; we have a mess."

"Most likely; can the two agents you have there enlighten us on anything?"

"Not much, sir," Echo said, enunciating and projecting so that Mays' mic could pick up his statement. "We got here in time to see at least one, possibly two, shadowy figures ignite some serious munitions, evidently in an effort to break into the top of one of the storage facilities. The signs of that effort are all over here, as well as the break in the live fencing where they entered. Unfortunately, the munitions temporarily blinded my partner and me, and our efforts to take them down missed. But we scared 'em off this attempt, and they escaped the way they came. Hopefully we can ensure there won't be a second attempt."

"Thank you. Agents Tillman and Peterson, you are free to continue your business," the general noted. "I hope, however, you'll work with us to ascertain what happened. Keep me in the loop. I understand there are two fatal casualties, two of my airmen dead? I want whoever did that, Agent Peterson. Preferably I want their hide nailed to a barn door, understand."

"We'll do our best," Echo agreed smoothly, bending and picking up the railgun before slipping it into a special holster he'd donned at the 'Vette. "We'll definitely be tracking them down from here."

* * *

By the time Echo and Omega could get themselves squared away, post the Security Forces teams to secure a maximum area perimeter, and start investigating the area of the altercation between Myclestra and the warpwraith, Alpha Two was on the scene, along with Firewall Teams Alpha Seven and Eight, Beta Fifty-Two, several other field teams that Alpha One didn't recognize, and a heavily-reinforced Event Control Team — the cleanup crews that the Agency used to remove, hide, or otherwise disguise evidence of alien presence, usually nicknamed the 'Et Cetera team' for the twisted acronym, ECT.

They were escorted by a platoon-strength flight of 377th Security Forces airmen and NCOs, relieving Carsdale's somewhat jittery troops, letting them hand over and take their upset comrades — Jackson and the others who had seen the bodies — back for medical assistance. The ECT team, however, had other ideas, rounding up the relieved teams and placing them inside the van 'for their safety,' while they ascertained if there had 'been a breach.' None of them had to ask what THAT meant, and they all agreed.

* * *

"Hey, guys," Romeo said as he and India walked up to Alpha One. "Y'all okay?"

"We are now," Echo said. "Thanks for the backup."

"Then why's Meg looking so pale and wobbly?" India wondered. "And where the hell did that nasty cut and bruise on her cheek come from, then?" India gently walked Omega over to Alpha Two's sedan, dug into the trunk for her medikit and swabbed some Rejuvic on the cut Myclestra's sword hilt had left on her cheek. "What happened, sis? You look really rattled; how come?"

"For the same reason several of the Air Force security teams are," Echo noted, as Omega sighed. "And I was almost right in there with 'em. The first people on the scene weren't Meg and me, but a couple of security guys on patrol."

"Uh-oh," Romeo murmured. "What happened?"

"There's a big ball of human protoplasm with embedded metal, cloth, and plastic over there, that used to be two men and their equipment," Omega pointed at the shrubbery on the far side of the military grouping, "so keep everybody away. Nobody's been able to stomach it long enough to set up crime scene tape, either."

"Oh damn," India said, concerned. "I better go see about that."

"No, India, trust me," Omega said. "I'm not sure HOW we're gonna get that taken care of. I hurled everything in my gut. So did nearly half a dozen of the airmen, including

Sandbox vets."

"Were the bodies mushed together?" India asked.

Both members of Alpha One blanched and swallowed hard before nodding wordlessly. Eyebrows flew up on all the gathered Agents at that; Alpha One had a reputation for toughness and resilience, and if it had upset them, the others knew it was Bad with a capital B.

"Then I'm probably the best person suited to handle it," India noted. "I've handled bodies brought into the ER from semi collisions, so I've seen it all."

"Not like this, you haven't, sis." Omega murmured. "Trust me on that, girlfriend."

"I'll be okay," India insisted.

"I hope you're right," Echo said, as India turned and headed in the direction Omega indicated. "No, Romeo, stay here this time," Echo added, grabbing the other man's arm as he turned to follow his mate and partner. "Trust us. That was… NOT good."

"But she gonna need help," Romeo protested.

"We got her back," one of the Et Cetera team interjected then. "We've dealt with similar gruesome scenes before. Sir, with your permission?" he addressed Echo.

"Go." Echo nodded.

Half of the ECT peeled off and followed India.

Moments later, India cried, "Oh, dear God!" and one of the ECT team retched loudly, but did not throw up.

"Told ya," Omega said in a low tone.

"Shit," Romeo expostulated.

"Something like," Echo agreed.

* * *

"Meanwhile, what do you want us to do, guys?" Monkey asked the heads of Alpha Line. "We need to develop a scenario, program it in, and do some, uh, forgetfulness training?"

"That sounds like a plan," Omega said, smiling at Alpha Seven and Eight; not so very long ago, they had thought she was a traitor to the organization and trying to turn Echo, but now were among the pair's most faithful backups. "Echo? You got any ideas for the scenario?"

"You're usually good with that, baby," Echo said with a shrug. "Go for it."

"Um, not right now, hon," Omega admitted, patting her belly. "After I emptied out my digestive tract the hard way, I'm kinda running on damn low blood sugar. I'm on my feet, but that won't be for long, unless I can get some food in me and manage to keep it down. Especially after that fight with the überfraulein, as Fox would say." She shook her head. "That alone took it outta me. Never mind all the throwing up after."

"Wait, what?" Tare said, as the new arrivals did double-takes. "'Überfraulein?' Took it out of you? You mean she BEAT you, Omega? YOU?"

"More or less, yeah," Omega admitted with a wry face. "She was damn strong and damn fast. If Echo hadn't got back on his feet and jumped back in after she knocked him flat, she might have taken me down. And with that monster sword, she could have killed us both, easy. She apparently just didn't want to."

"Shit," Yankee said blankly, and the others mirrored his facial expression. "This chick beat Alpha One. Together."

"HOW?" Chi wondered.

"She's enhanced, too, guys," Omega added, and the others gaped at her.

"Well, it's not just her that's enhanced," Echo elaborated. "Imagine if Meg and I were BOTH enhanced and then our kids, and THEIR kids…for literally hundreds, maybe thousands, of generations. That's what our perp is, according to our intel."

"Yeah, and I fought her as hard as I could, until I was close to fallin' down," Omega confessed, voice a little wobbly, "and then she got away, and I spotted the bodies and barfed everything I had left in me…"

* * *

"Oh damn," Echo, Romeo, Yankee, Tare, Monkey, Kako, Chi and Genova chorused. Echo grabbed Omega by the shoulder, and glanced around, looking for anything remotely resembling consumables on the M1114s. "Food, food, food," he mumbled. "Shit, it's all back in the 'Vette."

"I got it, bro," Romeo said, heading back to the car, parked interspersed with a couple of M1114s and a large 'souped-up' van that had brought the rest of the Division One agents to Kirtland. Moments later, while Echo got Omega seated on a large rock outcrop and the rest of the group quietly and surreptitiously discussed the best way to handle brain-bleaching the Air Force personnel, Romeo returned with a handful of Agency meal replacement bars and several half-liter bottles of water. "Here, sis," he said, putting the lot down on the rock beside her, then handing her a bar and a bottle. "India decided we needed t' be carryin' emergency food supplies around with us, on 'counta events on Kochav — 'specially when we're workin' with you. So now we got a special warp case in the trunk stocked with emergency rations. Knock this back, but take it easy. If you start to get sick, tell me an' I'll run grab India."

"Thanks, Romeo," Omega said, offering him a smile as she took the foodstuffs and opened them.

"Slow, baby," Echo warned. "Don't stuff your face." She nodded.

"So…what? It was a small group of terrorists after the nukes?" Yankee wondered. "That's our story?"

"What about the terrain?" Monkey asked. "It's a mess out here."

"Well, I already mentioned explosive munitions to 'em," Echo pointed out, as Omega ate the bar and sipped the water. "If some of that was, say, a specially-formulated thermite, it would explain the melted soil and rock, and the obsidian."

"True," Tare considered. "I know we discussed the whole superpowers thing, and comparing this to that film series, but I dunno if that would really work, with these hard-nosed military types."

"I'm thinking we could hit a happy medium," Omega suggested, around a mouthful of meal bar. It was already her second.

"Let's hear it, Meg," Echo ordered. She shrugged.

"Exo suits," she said. "Like that one movie character. Brilliant, no superpowers of his own, but damn, can he build a suit of armor."

Echo's eyebrows shot up.

"That…might just work," he admitted. "Because there ARE government agencies working on just that."

"I think we got it, then," Yankee averred. "You good to run with it, boss-couple?"

Echo and Omega exchanged glances, then both nodded.

"Let's go, guys," Tare said, and they all headed for the perimeter guard.

* * *

After the others left them, Echo sat down on the rock beside Omega, and she offered him a bite of her last meal bar — it was the fourth. He accepted, then took a sip from her water bottle.

"Take it," Omega said. "I got one more bottle over here. You didn't throw up, but a little cool water in your belly will probably make you feel better. I can feel through the nd't'lq that you're still kinda…perturbed."

"Point," Echo agreed, accepting the mostly-full bottle and drinking more. "Feeling some better?"

"Yeah. Not woozy and light-headed any more."

"Good," he pronounced. *So,* he thought at her as they shared the last of the meal bar, *I'm curious to know what you think happened here, based on what we saw. I have my own ideas, but I want to hear yours, unbiased by mine.*

I knew you were keeping up a light block, and wondered why, she told him as she opened the last bottle of water. *Okay, lemme think a sec.*

They were silent for a few moments, both surveying the scene before them with eagle eyes.

All right, Ace, Omega told him. *I think what we have is an interstellar — maybe intergalactic — criminal who fled into our jurisdiction, and the person sicced on him to bring him into custody. Maybe police, maybe a bounty hunter; I'm not sure yet, though I'm leaning toward the latter, based on some of the stuff she yelled at us when we screwed up her collar. She's been augmented like me, but I think there's something else going on there, too...she had, like, three lights glowing on her forehead. And none of the eyewitnesses have mentioned that, so it's like she triggered something that boosted her abilities temporarily.*

What about the...thing...she was chasing?

That, I dunno, Omega admitted. *But I suspect it's HER perp. I do know that it gave me the creeps, and that's hard to do. I did NOT get good vibes off the thing, and by vibes, I AM talking about my...special sense of things, like with the Cortians. And like we were talking about before base security showed on the scene, I think that thing is what killed the two patrol guys, not her. And think about the scene back in the forest, with the...werewolf-things.*

Yeah, I noticed that, too. Kind of a kluge of tissue. Only not fatal, like what happened to the patrol. Like...it was being used, rather than disposed-of.

Exactly.

So far, we're on the same page, Echo decided. *I'm just thinking this is a lot weirder than 'somebody from way the hell outta town.'*

Omega sighed.

I hate to say it, because that's someplace I haven't been trained to go, and I don't really wanna go there, she admitted, *but I'm starting to think you might be right, on several levels. What I saw...what that thing did, what this Myclestra did, too...well, I can explain away what she did a helluva lot easier than I can explain what the black thing did. And Ace?*

Yeah?

Their eyes met.

I'm not sure anything WE have can take that monster down.

Shit. You came to the same conclusion I did, baby.

Damn.

Yeah.

As one, they turned to gaze at the bizarre scene of battle, even as their colleagues worked to make it look less outré.

* * *

It took several hours to handle the scene to Echo's satisfaction. Once the ECT team informed him that Fox had released Alpha One and Alpha Two from the site, however, he gnawed his lower lip briefly.

"Everybody brain-bleached and reprogrammed with our cover scenario?" he asked.

"Yes, sir," Yankee avouched, walking up. "Including the ones in the van. Who India managed to get stopped barfing, into the bargain." He pointed, and Echo saw Staff Sergeant Mays and Second Lieutenant Carsdale shooing their teams into their own vehicles, heading back toward the main inhabited area of the base.

"What's the explanation for what happened to their two dead men?" he wondered.

"Real, or what they got programmed with?"

"Both."

"We don't have a real explanation yet," India said as she walked up. "I have the, uh, the joint remains in a body bag, which the Et Cetera team is gonna take back to Headquarters; hopefully Forensics can tell us a bit more. A quick discussion with Fox determined we're gonna cremate the remains, separate them in half, and return them to the base for disposition to their families." She shrugged. "First, we gotta pick out their equipment, though, or the cremation's gonna be tricky."

"Right," Echo said. "And the brain bleaching on that?"

"It was Chi's idea," Yankee said, grinning at the Field agent. "And it was brilliant."

"What?" Echo wondered.

"Hey, you said explosives, right?" Chi explained. "And we got all these boulders around here, and several of 'em tumbled down. Took a bit of work with the tractor beams on the car, and the ECT helped a LOT, but we moved a couple boulders to make it look like one of the explosions threw 'em up and squished the guys."

"Oh," Echo said in surprise. "Yeah, that works."

"So you run on and find the perps," Yankee told Alpha One. "Take Romeo and India with you, and the four of you should be able to handle 'most anything." He paused, then added, "Especially after that super chick that fought y'all to a standstill. Maybe four against one, and those four our top peeps, will turn the tide."

"Me an' India need t' go back t' the security building an' do a bit o' tidying first, I think," Romeo said. "Brain-bleach a couple folks an' whatnot. After that, we c'n head after y'all."

"That'll work," Echo decided. "Meg sicced her drones onto the female, and we'll track her that way." He paused, then added, "I dunno how to find the big black…thing."

"Me too neither, but I bet this Myclestra does. So if we can find her, we should be able to find the black creature. I can turn on the locator app on my phone," Omega offered, "and y'all can home in on us when you're able."

"That works," India agreed. "Where's the 'Vette?"

"Over the fence," Omega murmured, gesturing subtly at the large hole in the formerly-electrified fence, just in case any of the airmen guarding the perimeter happened to glance their way.

"Oh. Well, come on with us, and we'll go airborne over the fence, drop you off at the 'Vette, then head back to base security."

"And we'll make sure nobody remembers a flying car," the ECT chief said with a grin.

"Right," India chuckled. "Echo, Romeo, you two okay with it?"

"Soun's good," Romeo said.

"Yup," Echo confirmed, then turned to the rest of the PGLEIA operatives. "Okay, y'all, speak now, or forever hold your peace."

No one said anything.

"Okay, gone," Echo decreed, and he and Omega followed Romeo and India to their car.

* * *

"Well, Meg, we've finally gotten the Security Forces troops off our back." Echo led the way back to where the 'Vette was still parked, after Alpha Two dropped them off, just outside the clump of brush where they'd hidden it earlier. "Your drone still on our Tall Lady friend?"

"Yep," Omega strode along behind him as he broke a trail through the scrub brush, "and I was checking the video take while you dealt with the USAF officers. I'm still not sure I believe what she did. She ran nearly six kilometers like some kinda humanoid cheetah. Of course when she got there — wherever the hell 'there' is supposed to be — she pretty much collapsed and barely managed to crawl into a cave."

"Well, shit," Echo growled as they finally reached the hidden 'Vette, "so just when we're up to our eyeballs in scared-half-to-death Security Forces troops, trying not to get shot, we could've collected her with little effort?"

"Maybe," Omega settled into the passenger seat as Echo held the door open for her, "but she still has whatever the heck that sword is. That thing put out what I guess is some kind of nuclear plasma blast, but tightly directs and contains the heat that would otherwise turn everything within a thousand meters into glass slag. Instead, that attack she directed at the black figure was five hundred meters long and thirty-three meters wide. It was actually a cone, burnt down as far as it was wide. Then she used it to put a wall of...I dunno, plasma, between her and us before screaming at us to leave her alone."

"Well, yeah, and remember, she also said something about 'our world may die.' What the hell was that about?"

"Dunno, Ace. I'm trying to figure out just HOW a man-portable, directed-fusion bomb can be carried around in something that looks exactly like a sword from some heroic anime fantasy character."

"Yeah, baby, that thought's enough to scare me paler than the sheets. I hadn't thought about it in the immediate aftermath, being more concerned about making sure those Air Force guys didn't try to fill us full of lead." The 'Vette rumbled to life, morphed and cloaked as it lifted off. "So, now what?"

"Let's keep the drone on her and follow at a very safe distance, say fifteen, twenty kilometers. See what she does, which way she goes."

"Sounds good to me." He paused for a long moment. "Did you notice something else? In the fight, I mean?"

"You mean the fact that two shots from a tachyon splitter rifle hitting dead center had no effect, other than a silver-blue glow around her? Or that your railgun seemed to have little more effect than that? Or the fact that she managed to DEFLECT your second shot with that sword? Somehow I don't think that was just pure, dumb luck. Some kind of energy-field armor, maybe? I noticed a lot of things, and most of them did very nasty things to the way I learned that the rules of our physical universe are supposed to work. And that's giving me a furious headache while I try to think. But it's one of the reasons you're starting to sway me to this being more...bizarre...than normal." She pulled out a tablet computer and looked up the specs on the Colt-Westinghouse railgun. "Okay, tell me what you've done to that railgun of yours. I imagine I can improve it enough to make our 'friend' Myclestra sit up and take notice if you hit her with it again."

"Lord God, I hope so. So, you still think she's from our universe? After what we saw last night?"

"Yeah, I'm still using that as my basic hypothesis," she answered, somewhat absently as she paged through the railgun's spec sheet and manual on her tablet. "Maybe she's from so far away we can't even see the light of her galaxy without a hundred-meter telescope, but travel between different, maybe incompatible universes? No. She's just a good example of Clarke's Third Law: Any sufficiently advanced technology is indistinguishable from magic."

"Huh." The cabin of the 'Vette was silent for a while. "Then what about the corollary to that law: Magic is indistinguishable from sufficiently advanced technology."

"You're not helping."

* * *

She hit another animal with a rock, killing it. It was some kind of canid and it had clearly been stalking her. The rock crushed its skull, and she tore it open, pulled out its entrails, and then ate it raw. She didn't really like her food raw, and the thing was gamey and rank, but it was meat, meat was food, and food was energy. She couldn't afford to be picky.

She used its fur to wipe the blood off her face and picked up the pace a little, alternating a fast walk with an easy lope where it was clear enough to do so. She caught the scent of fresh, clean water and nearly drooled. She was within two or three hundred ur-lans of the human dwellings at the edge of the community. The scents were a curious mélange of humans, young and old, male and female, hot metal, fuel of different kinds, wood, trees, grass, flowers and shrubs, animals, mostly more canids, though different from the one she'd eaten, some felines and water. Lots of water.

"Oh, this is not wise, Old Snake, but I need actual water, not just blood. I'm not a *vampiir* as can survive on blood alone. I must risk it."

<Then be cautious and be quick.>

She slipped silently through the night, looking for the easiest spot to get water. In her pack, she had an expandable canteen that would hold enough water to last a week. She just needed time to fill it.

Some of the areas behind the humans' dwellings were open to the desert, but most had at least a rudimentary boundary wall, some only a handspan high. Others were quite tall, well above her ability to sense what was in the enclosure without jumping to get her senses above the wall. It was one of these that had the sound and scent of clean, running water and lots of it. She risked a quick hop. There were large ponds in the area, in what Danny Hawkins' knowledge told her were called 'yards.' Strange. A 'yard' was also one measurement of length, almost the same as an ur-lan. A quick two steps, a hand on the top of the wall, and she was over.

* * *

Christopher Tobias was enjoying a nice romantic movie with his wife, Marie, when the backyard motion detector alarm started beeping. He hadn't set it into 'night' mode yet, so the beep was just loud enough to get their attention. Chris was a business analyst for a big aircraft maker and looked it. He was about five foot seven or so, and a bit heavier than he had been many years ago as a nose tackle and center for his high school football team. He still wore his graying brown hair cut short and neat.

Marie was his antithesis, taller, willowy and a mass of long, tawny hair tumbling to her waist. They'd been married twenty-seven years and their last son had gone off to college now. Being home by themselves was still something of a new sensation for them.

"What the hell got in this time?" he grumbled as he got up from the sofa. Being able to sit on the sofa and neck like they had as teenagers was a pleasure they hadn't had in years, and he was annoyed at the interruption.

"Maybe the Allentons' dog jumped the front gate again. Trying to convince Shelia to have a 'good time' with him?" Shelia was their three-year-old Alaskan Malamute and their neighbors' Jack Russell terrier was infatuated with her. The reverse was not the case. Marie thought it was funny as hell, watching Shelia bat the much smaller dog heels over head when he annoyed her.

"No, it's not that damn dog," Chris had brought up the security camera feed on the alarm control panel and didn't quite believe what he saw. "Marie, come here and tell me I'm seeing this right."

"Oh, dear," Marie shook her head and leaned closer to the panel. "Who is that?"

There was a very tall woman in their back yard, kneeling next to the water garden, filling a canteen of some kind. She wore a tunic and leggings, tattered and burnt in spots. High boots came just above her knees. She had a belt with a holstered pistol of some kind and a simply enormous sword slung over her back. There was a large, dry bloodstain on the tunic, just below her ribcage.

"What should we do, Marie?"

"Christopher Tobias, what is wrong with you? The young woman is clearly injured and needs help. What kind of Friends should we be if we fail to at least offer her aid and assistance?"

"Marie, she is armed, looks somewhat desperate, and look at Shelia. She's crouched down in her doghouse, teeth bared at this woman."

"None of that matters, Christopher. She is clearly in need of aid and any person in need of aid should be helped as the Good Lord directs. Come with me, husband." Marie headed imperiously toward the sliding glass doors leading onto the patio by the pool and water garden. She stopped at the door a moment, watching the woman. "That's odd."

"What?"

"Christopher, the security lights all came on and I just turned on the flood lights, and she doesn't seem to notice. And she's wearing sunglasses after dark. I would imagine she must see us through the glass door, but she's shown no sign of doing so. How strange."

"Maybe the reflections are blinding her somewhat."

"Maybe?" Christopher put a hand on his wife's elbow. "Wait a moment. What's she doing now?" The woman released her hair from the top-knot in which it had been held and a curtain of red hair flowed around her. She shook her head once, reached up and gingerly removed her odd sunglasses and then immersed her head and shoulders in the water of the garden pool. She shook her head vigorously, scrubbing her face in the water with her hands. She raised up and flung her hair back in a spray of wet red locks. Pulling the water out of that hair with her hands, she glanced around the yard, looking straight at the glass doors.

"That's why she didn't notice the lights, Christopher," Marie stared at the pure white orbs of the woman's eyes. "She's blind."

* * *

The click of a lock was the first hint that she had a problem. What she thought was a wall panel was actually a sliding door. Now she sensed two humans at that door, one male, one female. There was no sign of any weapon, and the female was remarkably calm. Myclestra knew that they had seen her without her eyeshields, and they would probably be frightened, but to her surprise, there was no scent of fear at all from the female and very little from the male.

"Can we help you, Miss?" the woman asked.

"I needed water. Badly." She kept her own voice quiet. "I am afraid I scared your canine. Apologies."

"Did you drink the water in the pool? It's not really good for drinking; come inside and I'll get you some drinkable water."

"There is no need. This water is clear, there is no mud or filth in it."

"There is chlorine in it. Not really a chemical you want to be drinking. Please, we are Friends, let us help."

"How can you be my friends? I do not know you nor do you know me?"

"No, not personal friends, we are Friends to all. It's the faith or religion we follow. Some call us Quakers. We believe that once shown the light, all men are good inside. That is God's intent."

"Which god?" she cocked her head at the odd statement. "Not all gods, in my experience, are good. And there are beings in even this universe that are purely evil. There is no light that can be shown to those things."

"Miss, truly, there is only one God, the Lord God above all of us, Maker of all. Come inside, and I'll get you some clean drinking water and check the wound on your side. There is a lot of blood on your tunic. Please, by our Faith, we would help you as we would anyone injured on our doorstep."

"Ah, well, water would be good. Do you have any food? I can give you gold or a gem in payment. I am tired of having to eat things I catch raw." She ran her hand over the hole in her tunic. "Hmm. A powerful weapon to penetrate my armor. Very well, I shall at least get this clean drinking water you offer. Even the least morsel of food would be very welcome. But I must not tarry, lest my enemy elude my grasp." She followed the female into the house, the male shutting the door behind her.

"Careful. Let me guide you. I'd hate for you to stumble and fall." The female reached out to take Myclestra's hand.

"Why would you do that? I do not require guidance."

"But...but I saw your eyes. You're blind, aren't you, Miss?"

"Perhaps in one sense," Myclestra smiled at the female, "but only in that I do not 'see' light. For me the universe is sound and scent and pressure. Air currents. An esoteric sense some liken unto a bat, although I have no need to squeak as I move about." She suppressed a chuckle at the dumbfounded look on both of their faces. "Now, about food and water?"

"Ah, well, certainly, Christopher, get her a plate and warm up some of that roast left from dinner. I want to check her wound."

"No need, but I should get out a clean tunic. I only have two." Myclestra set the Sword down carefully, leaning it against a chair. "Do not, in any fashion, touch this." Then she set her pack down next to the blade and dug out her other tunic. It was wrinkled but clean. With a single motion she pulled the bloodstained tunic over her head, leaving her nude from the waist up. Both humans suddenly were speechless and staring. She scented sudden arousal in the male and even a sharp hint of it in the female. Then they both spun, putting their backs to her. "Do I give offense? Or perhaps you find me unsightly?"

With their backs to her, they did not see her wicked grin at their embarrassment.

"No, no, not, ah, at all, Miss—" The female stuttered slightly.

"My name is Myclestra. I remember now, many humans have a nudity taboo. Foolish. And so do you, then?"

"Well, ah, yes, I guess…ah, Christopher, hurry and get that roast." The female turned back to face her as the male left the room in haste. "Myclestra, my name is Marie, and my husband is Christopher. Please, sit down and let me see that wound. With that much blood…oh wait, there isn't a mark. How, wha—" She gaped at the smooth, unmarred flank under Myclestra's substantial breast. A breast which seemed to defy gravity. Her torso was superbly muscled, each group as sharply defined as an anatomy poster. Despite herself, Marie reached out and ran a hand up that smooth abdomen, pulling away from touching that perfect breast at the last instant.

"I do not have time for pleasure, sorry," She pulled her clean tunic down over her head, smiling at the flustered Marie. "Perhaps later, assuming I survive defeating my bounty target, an inhuman thing known as a Warpwraith. If I stay in this universe, that is." Marie simply gawked in disbelief. She was rescued by Christopher returning with a serving plate containing a large roast, utensils, and another plate. He'd peeked in first, to make sure this strange woman was no longer topless.

"Ah, Miss, uh, Myclestra, if you'll give me your canteen I'll empty it, rinse it out and refill it?" Wordlessly, Myclestra tossed him the water bag. He juggled it for a moment and disappeared into the kitchen again.

"This will not cause you a hardship, will it? Giving me this?" Myclestra didn't bother with the second plate when Marie shook her head. She pulled the serving plate over and simply attacked the roast. Between bites, she told Marie and Christopher, once he returned, her story, how she came to be here and what she was after.

"So, have you ever heard of the Pan-Galactic Law

Enforcement and Immigration Agency?" she asked casually while she mopped up the last of the roast's juices with a hunk of cheese and a slice of bread.

"The Pan-Galactic what?" Marie asked. "No, don't repeat it, I understood you. But no, not outside of some science fiction movie, maybe."

"Odd. I wonder." Myclestra shrugged. "Never mind. So your religious beliefs say you must help someone who needs it, correct?"

"That is the purpose of the Society of Friends, yes. It's been that way for over a hundred years." Maire smiled at Myclestra.

"Good. Prove it." Myclestra stood from the kitchen chair, shouldering her pack and picking up the Sword. "Help me. And in helping me, save your world and everyone on it. I need rapid transportation to the northeast. There's a truck stop near where I have to go. My quarry is up in the mountains near there. You can help me cut off nearly two days of going by foot. Allow me to catch it before it realizes I'm there. Catch it and kill it."

"Killing is wrong, Myclestra." Marie's voice was quiet but passionate. "There is good in everyone, if they are just shown the Light inside them."

"Marie, this thing, the Warpwraith, is not a person. It is a beast, an aberration, a horror that feeds on the souls of the living. It is evil incarnate, from my perception, and it would be from yours as well — what you might call..." she dredged the information she had obtained from those she had already encountered, and came up with, "a demon. Failing to help me could mean this monster escaping to wreak havoc on your world. Help me, please. I am only asking for transportation. I would never expect you to fight by my side. But please help. It is your world at risk."

"A demon?! Aha, I see. You're talking about the Petro truck stop on Santa Fe's southern edge, right? Just to there?" Marie's eyes flicked sideways to her husband.

"Yes, no farther. The creature will be up in the mountains, well away from any habitations."

"Let me get my keys." Marie stood up next to the much taller woman. "Yes, I'll help you. That's what Friends do."

* * *

Three hours later, Marie pulled her big SUV to a stop in the parking lot of La Cuenca de Santa Fe Spa & Ski Lodge. At three in the morning, the lodge was closed and the parking lot empty. Myclestra looked out the open window at the mountains.

"This is fine, Marie. I want you no closer. This beast likes to prey on friends and loved ones of those who oppose it."

"Did it do that to you? Hurt someone you cared about, that is?"

"No. No one loves an Alontoran. We are feared and hated, not loved," Myclestra sighed. "My sisters are slaves to monsters, creatures that treat all lesser races as slaves, playthings and worse. My line was modified, optimized for combat long ago. The humans of my universe called us Fetches, because that was what we did, we 'fetched' for the non-human Slavers that the Masters set over us. Obey, or perish. We obeyed…mostly. I am one of the very rare Alontorans who escaped the Masters."

"I see." It was quiet in the SUV for a very long moment. "Good luck, Myclestra. When this is over, visit us sometime, if you can. We…I would like to be your friend. You seem very brave to me, nearly heroic."

"Huh. That is something I've never been called. Heroic?" Myclestra turned all her attention on Marie, there in the truck. Suddenly she leaned over and kissed Marie on the mouth, tenderly at first, then passionately. Marie returned it just as passionately. The kiss held for what seemed to be an eternity, then Myclestra was moving, out the door, retrieving the Sword from the back seat and setting her hand on the open window of the front door. "Go home, Marie. Make love to your husband. Remember me. Perhaps, someday, if I survive this, I might visit you again. Until that day, cherish those you love. Farewell." And she was gone into the darkness, running like a deer into the forest.

"Farewell, Myclestra," Marie whispered to the night.

"Farewell and remember me, also." She rolled up the window and started back to her home.

Neither of them noticed the small, cloaked drone that lifted off the top of the SUV and carefully followed Myclestra into the woods.

* * *

"Okay, didn't see that coming," Omega muttered half to herself, as she studied the take from the drone. "Our tall friend is proving to be more and more complex the longer we follow her."

"Well, at least she isn't trying to do to us what we did to that rogue Glu'gu'ik, whatshername, Ke'ri Gla'd's." Echo chuckled from the 'Vette's driver seat. "Trying to lead us all over hell's half-acre on a wild goose chase. I hope."

"That's not what I meant, Echo and you know it," she grumped at him a bit. "In just a few hours, this Myclestra made enough of a connection with Marie Tobias that she left her with a very passionate kiss. We know a lot more about her now, from the drone eavesdropping on her at the Tobias' home, more than we got from Danny Hawkins. And she even keeps talking about coming from a different universe. And that's impossible."

"Well, then go tell her that, Meg." Echo held the morphed and cloaked 'Vette in a racetrack pattern, orbiting ten kilometers away from the drone following Myclestra. "I'm sure she'll agree that you're right and she's wrong."

"Oh, hush, Ace, and quit badgering me about that. Right now it's not important. What's important is, why is she heading into the Santa Fe National Forest in the middle of the night? Not quite at a dead run, but she's going somewhere in a hurry."

"What if it has something to do with the other party that was at the WSA? That vague, black, humanoid shape that possibly teleported away?"

"Probably a pretty good bet, Ace." Omega stared at her reflection in the 'Vette's passenger window for a moment. "Hmm, maybe you're right, honey. Maybe I should just go ask her about all this 'another universe' stuff?"

"Uhm, what?"

"Get some altitude and let's swing around and get in front of her. Set up and wait for her to come to us. See if she'll talk to us at all."

"Well, it can't hurt. I hope."

* * *

Myclestra loped steadily through the forest, following game trails in places and open meadows in others. The sooner she caught the Warpwraith, the sooner she could kill it. She knew she was taking a risk, trying to engage it again so soon. She dipped her fingers into the pouches containing her cantrips, examining them one by one as she ran.

<It is too soon, Little One. You could barely bear the cost of one. Two would kill you.>

"I've little choice, Old Snake. The Warpwraith will be weakened, too. A teleport spell is a tremendous cost to its strength as well."

<Perhaps, but here he will not need to use his own power. There are many ley-lines running through these mountains, and a node will be near the top of the one he fled to. He will have a vast amount of power outside himself to draw upon.>

"Can't be helped, Old Snake. The longer I give it, the more powerful it will be. I must depend on my combat skills and your abilities. I assume I shall not have to bargain with you?"

<Of course not. What I said earlier about this monster still applies. He must be destroyed.>

"Then we are agreed." She ran on, climbing steadily as the mountains rose before her. Surlianth was certain that the Warpwraith was lurking on the peak of the mountain just beyond the lower one Myclestra was traversing. She wanted to catch it just after sunrise, when it would be weakest and most vulnerable. She had time to spare, but not a lot. Time she realized she had just lost when she ran out of the woods into a large clearing. A clearing where a low-slung vehicle sat at the edge of the other side. And two humans, male and female, barred her path.

"Old Snake, this is a problem. It is those humans from that 'Authority.' And how did they get here in that vehicle?"

<A problem? Perhaps. Or possibly an opportunity.>

* * *

Omega watched Myclestra's progress up the mountain side on the monitor fed by the drone's take. The woman could really run. When she was within a hundred meters of the far edge of the clearing where Echo landed the 'Vette, she left the car and joined her husband standing next to the 'Vette.

"Well, here she comes."

"You sure about this, baby?"

"Not really, but I certainly don't think she's the problem. That thing, what did she call it, a warpwraith, I think it's the problem."

"Probably, but right this second, she," Echo pointed to Myclestra, who came to a sudden stop upon seeing them waiting for her, "is the problem."

"Your name is Myclestra, right?" Omega called out as she walked toward the very tall woman. "I am Agent Omega of the Pan-Galactic Law Enfor—"

"I do not care who you are," Myclestra's tone was hard and sharp as she interrupted. "And of your 'Agency' I only care if they will pay me the bounty I will be due for destroying the Warpwraith. Otherwise, as I warned you, stay out of my way." A silverish glow formed around her for a split-second before fading out of view. She strode directly toward Alpha One with a determined set to her shoulders.

Okay, baby, now what? Echo stepped slightly away from Omega, giving each of them room to fight if needed.

Well, shit. Stunners, Ace? Omega put action to thought as she drew her stunner an instant before Echo did. As both beams hit Myclestra, a silver-blue aura flared around her.

* * *

Stunners? They use stunners on me? Myclestra was surprised at Alpha One's choice of weapons. Her tech-wizard armor completely protected her from such things. She started to activate the cantrip for speed when Surlianth stopped her.

<No, Child, you must not use any cantrip. If you absolutely must assault these beings, do so without magic. The stress of such will surely kill you otherwise.>

Very well, Old Snake. And woe to them this time.

<It would really be better if—>

Myclestra burst into a dead-out sprint, straight at the pair of black Suited agents.

"OUT OF MY WAY!" She hit Omega at full speed, grabbing her to keep from being thrown. Many combat arts used an attacker's momentum against them, and she would not allow Silver Hair, here, to do that to her.

They went down in a pile of arms and legs, Omega trying to pin her and Myclestra trying to throw the Agent aside. They twisted around and bounced upright. She realized she was between the two Agents, and immediately attacked Echo while Omega was slightly off-balance.

<Child, they do not mean—>

I'm busy, Old Snake!

* * *

Myclestra's fighting style seemed to be based partly on spinning and circular moves, fist punch followed by elbow strike, followed by a kick or throw move. Echo blocked half a dozen strikes initially, but the next three got through his guard and sent him spinning into the open clearing, shaking his head from the last strike to his sternum.

The last move that put Echo at least temporarily out of the fight was the opening Omega needed. She bull-rushed Myclestra from her side, taking her down with a bruising tackle. The taller woman twisted like an eel, Omega lost her grip and suddenly flew into the trees. Myclestra popped to her feet, but not as quickly as before, head lowered and breathing hard. Echo hit her hard from behind and grunted as the silver-blue halo flashed around her.

Despite her armor, she went flying, launched hard enough

that she took down a smaller tree she hit full on. This time it took her a second to get to her feet. When she did, she found both the Agents standing side by side, between her and the forest.

"Why do you stop me from my goal? Do you fools think this is a game, the bounty going to the first to make the kill? Or do you want to watch your world be subsumed by this monster?" She spat on the grass. "If I wished, I would draw Surlianthet and you would both surely die. Let me pass!" As the two glanced at each other in consternation, she rushed them again, then leaped. Both of her feet hit Echo's chest solidly, blood spraying from his mouth as he flew backward into a tree.

"ECHO!" Omega screamed, rage and fear distorting her beautiful face. "What have you DONE?! YOU HURT ECHO! I'LL KILL YOU, YOU BITCH!"

Omega blasted into Myclestra with a blurring triphammer-like assault of punches and kicks, knocking her off-balance. She swarmed over the tall woman, realizing even in her fury that she couldn't get an effective hit through whatever that silver-blue halo was, but Myclestra had to be able to move her arms and legs. That was the weak point, and she attacked it. The pair went down in a tangle, and a sickening *CRUNCH* reverberated through the woods. There was another muffled *POP* and the two women staggered away from each other.

* * *

Omega's face was bloody and bruised, both eyes blackening and beginning to swell shut. Her Suit jacket was in shreds, and there were bloody abrasions all over her arms. Blood spatters covered parts of her white shirt. She wiped her mouth and spat out bloody phlegm.

There were no marks on Myclestra's face or torso. Omega had never penetrated her armor, but Omega had found its weak point, and her use of leverage had dislocated Myclestra's left shoulder joint and broken her left leg midway between knee and hip. Bone jutted from her torn legging and blood sheeted down her leg. She stood there, panting, using the sheathed

Sword to stay upright.

<NOW will you listen, Chi—>

I have matters under control, Old Snake.

<Oh, of course you do. At this rate, I will have to bring you back from the dead to finish your hunt.>

Shut UP, Old Snake! I have this!

<Very well. But you are going to regret it.>

* * *

"Has the Warpwraith perverted your mind, you fool?" Myclestra panted at Omega. "Do you serve it, now?" She was still lightning-quick as she drew her plas-pistol, faster than Omega could attack. "No, stand, or die. Your weapons cannot penetrate my armor, but you have no such protection. Enough. Get ou—"

The *CRACK* of Echo's Colt-Westinghouse railgun abruptly ended Myclestra's speech. This time, the two-point-five-millimeter penetrator managed to more than punch through her armor, penetrating into her body, breaking four lower ribs on her right side and three ribs on her left, where it exited her body in a huge bloody fountain. Passing from right to left, it hit both of her lungs, her liver, her spleen and a kidney. Somehow, it missed her spine and the great arteries and veins. She spun and fell, unconscious, a puppet with the strings cut, her eye-shields falling away from her face.

Omega stared in shock as Echo limped out of the forest, railgun in hand, a grim smile on his face. He looked up as he heard the faint whine of Alpha Two's car descending in VTOL mode to land in the meadow. He shook his head and sat down on a rock, leaning back against a tree.

"Ow."

"Ace, honey, are you okay?" Omega headed toward him.

"I think I'm in better shape than you are, baby," he said as he hefted the railgun. "Well, your mods worked. THAT got through whatever that armor of hers was."

"Yeah, but I think you killed her."

"Shit. I hope I didn't. I didn't want to kill her, but she had that…that…whatever that gun is, out and aimed at you. She had you dead to rights, baby." Omega settled gently into his arms and lost herself in his kiss.

* * *

<Younglings.> Had he lungs, the ancient drake would have sighed. <They never listen. Now I shall have to exert myself to keep my bond bearer alive. Or will I?> He carefully inserted himself into the minds of those beings that had defeated Myclestra. The large male had feared for his mate, the silver-haired female, who likewise had feared for him. The two that had just leapt out of their flying machine were compatriots and as close as family. The female was a healer and the other had been and was still an elite warrior.

<And this one, this Silver Hair, she is even more than merely human. She is a Splice, one made with great skill and cunning. And she forced my bond bearer to her limit, wounded her greatly, and with no option save lethality left…at least that the Child could see, in her fixated state. Let me see, what or how she was made and why?> His first attempt was unsuccessful; he had not expected Silver Hair, as he thought of her, to have such a powerful mind block.

As the kiss with her mate deepened, however, the telepathic block weakened enough for Surlianth to enter, gently but with purpose.

He moved silently, unnoticed through Omega's memories, seeing what Slug had done to her. <Huh. That one, this 'Slug' — it was insane, maddened beyond belief, but what it accomplished! A Splice that has survived for decades, mostly unknowing, with likely many decades left to her, if the danger of her occupation does not end her life for her. Not even I have heard of any Splice, much less one so complex, so many parts forced into such perfect alignment, living more than a few months, sometimes only weeks. It is a pity her maker is dead. I should have liked to talk with him, even as insane and evil as he was.> He felt Myclestra's life ebbing away through her horrendous wound. <Hmm, we cannot have that. I need

159

to give this young healer a slight assist, to keep her alive until they reach this HQ I see in their minds. I must learn more.> A sudden thought occurred to the Drake. <I wonder if this galaxy would make me a good hoard?>

* * *

"We're okay, India; go check Myclestra, see if she's still alive and if you can keep her that way until we can get her to Medical back at HQ," Omega said.

"You don't look okay," Romeo noted, even as India turned toward the downed female. "Meg got one big black eye f'r a face, an' Echo, man, you ain't breathin' great."

"Good Lord, there are pieces of her internal organs literally blown out of her body." India paled slightly. "What did you use on her?"

"Colt-Westinghouse railgun. Meg hot-rodded it for me. Nothing else could get through that armor field she had," Echo answered as Omega helped him clamber to his feet.

"Well, it got through," India growled. "You missed her spine, thank God, otherwise I think you'd've blown her in half."

"Is she still alive?" Omega followed Echo to their fallen opponent.

"Yeah, somehow, but don't ask me how." India dug into her medikit, packing the massive wound to stop the bleeding. "Maybe the slug partly cauterized the blood vessels. She shoulda died in minutes. They make 'em tough, wherever she's from. Here, take this. Weird looking handgun." She carefully handed it to Echo.

"Yeah, we think it's a plasma gun." He gingerly took the weapon.

"Plasma gun? That small? Is that even possible?"

<Silver Hair, only touch the Sword by the sheath. That is allowed. Keep it with her.>

"WHAT THE HELL?" Omega spun like a cat, both her blasters out. "Where'd THAT come from?"

"What's up, baby?" Echo had his blasters out a fraction of

160

a second later.

"Someone or something just whispered to me, telepathically, I think, something about the sword there."

"You kiddin', right, pretty lady? We're the only ones here. Well, the only ones not mostly dead, that is." Romeo had his blaster out as well, covering India as she worked on Myclestra.

"I don't know. I can't sense anything. But I know this much — that sword there, THAT is what is really dangerous." Omega dug around in a warp pocket and came out with a large silk handkerchief, bending down to wrap it around the sword's hilt and upper part of the sheath. "This is what burned that five-hundred-meter scar into the soil of the WSA."

"You foolin' me, right?" Romeo asked. "How the hell does a sword do that? Swords just cut things, right?"

"Not that one, Romeo," Echo said as he slowly lowered his weapons, grunting in pain at the movement. "That five-hundred-meter burn scar at Kirtland was done by her with that sword. She also used it to put a wall of…I dunno, plasma, hellfire, something between us and her to allow her to escape. Meg and I both saw it happen."

"Holy…well, shit," Romeo stared at the wrapped, sheathed blade in Omega's hand. "That thing did that!"

"I hate to be a buzzkill, but I've done all I can for this woman right now," India said and wiped a bloody hand over her brow. "I don't know how she's still alive, but she needs a fully staffed trauma ward five minutes ago. Echo, you and Omega look like you need some medical attention as well. Meg's beat to hell and back, and Echo, judging by the trickle of blood at your nose and the corner of your mouth, as well as your labored respiration, I'd say you have some busted ribs, maybe a punctured lung."

"I…don't think I'd argue the diagnosis," Echo admitted, panting slightly.

"Is either of you in good shape enough to drive?" India asked. "We don't have to go that far; there's a saucer hidden in the woods, just outside Kirtland. If we can get both vehicles back there, we can load 'em into the saucer, then take a suborbital hop back to Headquarters, and be there in minutes."

"You drive th' 600, hon," Romeo said. "I'll get th' 'Vette. Put the tall lady here," he gestured at Myclestra, "inna back seat. Meg, you ride with India, an' Echo, you hop inna passenger seat of th' 'Vette while I drive."

Omega and Echo exchanged a single glance, each feeling how much the other hurt through the nd't'lq.

"Done," they said simultaneously. "Let's get Myclestra loaded up," Omega said then. "No, Echo, sit tight. Not with those ribs."

* * *

The medium-sized saucer *D1 Marie Curie* passed low enough over the mountain top occupied by Wruthas the Warpwraith that the emanations from its drive system disturbed his meditations. He looked for the cause of the disturbance, but did not see the cloaked and heavily stealthed saucer in its climb to a sub-orbital hop to the Penn Station Spaceport.

What was that? he wondered. Seeing the beginnings of dawn in the east, he stood and considered his next move. *Returning to the place where the power is buried would not be wise. SHE knows I was there and knows how attractive to me that power will be. No, I shall not stick my head in yet another noose of HER devising! So much of this land is rugged, rocky and barren of life. While I meditated, I sensed that these humans spread much more thickly on the lands far to the east, lands richer with life and energy. They bury the burning lesser power of the sun here. Perhaps, where there are more of them, they will use more of that power in places easier to access. Places that hell-spawned, black-hearted BITCH can never reach in time to stop me. SHE must travel only by foot, or hope to hide aboard some crude vehicle or the other. And with no knowledge of where I have gone, SHE will never find me. Not until I am grown in power and control of this world and can find and crush HER like the annoying insect that SHE is. Crush HER and let HER know how foolish SHE was following me*

162

here and how utterly SHE has failed in HER hunt.

Wruthas sought out the strongest of the ley-lines at the mountain top node and bent it to his will, using its power to take hundred-league strides as he headed east.

Chapter Four — Trials and Tribulations

Once again, the world was only pain. Her guts burned, liquid fire surging through her stomach and lungs. Compared to this, passing between universes was a calm stroll in the park. Dying would hurt less. She was in a room somewhere, machines surrounding her, needles in her veins, skeletal metal armatures looming over her. Human norms, mostly males, but some females, did things to her. Others, strange scents and sounds, bizarre forms and shapes, stood and watched or aided the humans in the strange things being done to her. She heard them, them and the beeping, jangling machines and the constant passing to and fro outside the room's single door.

She was naked and strapped down on a padded table of some sort. She was weak and wounded, and Alontorans who could not keep up died. Often their compatriots killed them and destroyed the body, to avoid the dishonor of ending as nothing more than an appetizer for one of the Masters' tables. Where were her sisters? They would have ended her quickly and cleanly, not leaving her here to be tortured and mutilated before serving the Masters in one last humiliation.

Other than the humans, she most often sensed one she thought was an Elf, for he had the slender build and elongated skull, leaf-shaped ears and large eyes. What was an Elf doing here, in the Masters' experimentation rooms? Well, as anything other than an experiment himself.

<Child, Bond Bearer, you came near death. Release these foul memories. These folk are healers and medicine doctors. They work to salve your wounds, Child.>

Surlianth! Where are you? I cannot feel you near me. Are you lost again, fallen away and discarded? Help me, Surlianth! I am tortured and burning.

<Little One, you were badly injured battling the two

humans, the Agents of this Agency. You would not listen. And they came almost to slaying you in their own defense. Now they offer you aid and succor.>

"Surlianth! Surlianth! Where are you? I need you, Surlianth! You cannot be lost to me! Never in this life! Surlianth!" Her shout should have shaken the walls, but it was barely heard beyond those standing closest to the bed.

* * *

Deltiri Ambassador His Excellency Zz'r'p ob Tii'rkin was sitting at his desk, filling out certain forms on his computer, when he suddenly became aware of something nudging around the periphery of his mind. Deltiri were telepathic, fairly strongly so, and Zz'r'p stronger and more skilled than most; the ambassador held certifications as both a personal counselor and a PGLEIA interrogator.

So the notion of something trying to push past his personal telepathic block was not a pleasant one.

"Mmph," he grunted aloud — in both annoyance and effort — as he maximized his block, and the sense of something poking about ceased.

He sat there, unmoving, for long moments as he processed what had just happened.

Then he stood and headed out of his office, into the reception area of the Deltiri embassy in one of the upper floors of the Division One Headquarters building. He stopped dead in shock.

* * *

The room was filled with other Deltiri. Most were a paler shade of blue than normal, their fishlike faces depicting anxiety, and the room was an unusual hubbub of VERBAL commentary.

"…And suddenly there was this THING in my mind!"

"No, I was asleep. Whatever it was trying to talk to me woke me out of a sound sleep."

"Me, too! What in the name of the Maker IS it?"

"Is it still going on?"

165

"I think so, yes. I cannot quite force it out of my mind. NO, of course I do not like it!"

"Someone help me get it out of my head!"

A deeply perturbed Zz'r'p turned on his heel and headed back into his office before anyone could speak to him, closing the door behind him and returning to his seat at his desk.

What is happening here? he wondered.

Just then, he was contacted mentally…

…From his homeworld of Deltir.

* * *

Ambassador Zz'r'p? Zz'r'p ob Tii'rkin, can you hear me?

Prime Minister? Is this Rr't'n ob Kr't'k of Deltir?

There you are, Zz'r'p. Yes, it is Rr't'n. What in the name of the Maker is going on there?

Wait, what?

We have people at the highest levels of government, industry, education, and more, being mentally probed, Zz'r'p. We do not know what is happening, cannot identify the entity, and — and this is the most frightening — we CANNOT STOP IT. Whatever it is, it is cutting through our most powerful blocks as if they did not exist. My staff is being overwhelmed with calls for assistance and explanations.

Og'dm'n. Is anyone hurt? Is anyone dead? (damn, damnation)

No, that is the odd thing. No one is hurt. Upset, yes; confused, certainly. Harmed, no. But we do not know what information may have been taken in the course of…whatever this was.

Oh, my. Well, something similar seems to have happened to all my embassy staff and their families, Zz'r'p admitted. I have yet to determine what is going on.

Whatever it is, our specialists have ascertained it is coming from Earth, Zz'r'p. We cannot refine its location more closely than that, not at this distance and with no familiarity with that planet. You, however, are on location…

Aha. I see. Very well, milord Prime Minister. I will see

what can be determined, both myself, and with the aid of my staff.

Very good. Notify me when you can. Do what you can to stop it, if you can.

I shall.

And Zz'r'p rested his elbows on his desk, putting his head in his hands.

* * *

(Milord Premier,) the attendant murmured, dipping his carapace in front of the premier of the Persan Confederation in the Andromeda Galaxy, (the mistress of the harem requests an opportunity to speak to you as soon as may be.)

(Is there a problem with the harem?) Persan Premier Hsrs Syrsh wondered, in his concern bobbing up and down on the lower row of tentacles that served as his legs; his race, the Uzshei from the Andromeda Galaxy, resembled two-tiered octopuses. They were still on a diplomatic tour of the Milky Way Galaxy, aboard Hsrs' flagship, the *PCS Rtxrs*, having made first contact with the Pan-Galactic Coalition the previous annum.

(Not with the harem, milord,) the attendant responded, turning an odd yellow shade to denote his confusion. He did not closely resemble Hsrs, having a two-part shell about the majority of his body, with his face just above his tentacles; he was a Bofwai. It was still obvious, however, that he was a kind of cephalopodal creature, as was Hsrs. (She is alarmed, and I fear I have not been able to understand the source of the alarm.)

(Mm. Bring her at once,) Hsrs said. (That is not like Yeetoy, and I would hear what has frightened her so.)

(I will fetch her immediately, sire. She waits just outside your chambers.)

(Very good.)

* * *

(No, milord Hsrs,) Yeetoy, a member of the Pruug race, noted. (It was not a particularly detailed communication. Nor was it especially hostile, I suppose…)

(Did it speak to you?) Hsrs asked his oldest friend…whom he had given permission to return to their childhood habit of using his first name, after encountering Agent Omega the previous year. It had only deepened their relationship, and now Hsrs was starting to wonder if he had, at last, found his queen, and she had been right there all along.

(It did, Hsrs,) Yeetoy averred. (It said, 'Oh, hello. You are different, little one,' and I sensed it…explore me, for want of a better way to explain it.)

(Then what happened?)

(I sensed its focus move throughout the ship, rather as if it were curious. Each time it came upon a different species of our people, it spent especial time with that person before moving on.)

(As Agent Echo would say, 'Damnation,') Hsrs grumbled. (Was I one of those persons? Were any of my chief advisors?)

(Actually…no, Hsrs,) Yeetoy remarked. (I could tell, it knew who and what you were, but it did not spend any more focus on you than on anyone, and not as much as some, because by that time, it had already encountered another member of your species…)

(Mm. Interesting. That means it was less interested in the politics and secrets than in the types of beings here.)

(That was my impression, Hsrs.)

(All right, Yeetoy. I will see what I can find out about this. Meanwhile, are you available for dinner again tonight?)

(Do you want me to be?) she asked with a slight smile and a coy glance.

(Please.)

(Then yes. I will be there. And after?)

(Yes, please.)

(All right. I have missed you, Hsrs. So much.)

(And I had no idea how much I have missed you, Yeetoy. The perils of being too busy to sit down and ponder one's own situation, I suppose. I am glad I finally did…and I have the human PGLEIA agent to thank for that. Run on for now, though, so I can investigate this situation and see how far afield it goes, and I will see you at dinner. I will tell you how it goes, and what I have found out, then.)

(All right, Hsrs.)

They touched tentacles gently, and she was gone.

* * *

Bb'y'x, Jj'k'k, could you come to my office, as quickly as possible? Zz'r'p called mentally, after time to consider matters. *Come alone, please.*

Moments later, Bb'y'x ag Ogg'nii, a Deltiri inter-species telepathy expert, and Jj'k'k ob Dee'kyy, who was what Zz'r'p considered a 'power' telepath, entered his office, shutting the door behind themselves.

"Here we are, Zz'r'p," Jj'k'k, the big male Deltiri, said.

"Yes, what is going on?" Bb'y'x, a petite — for Deltiri — female asked. "Everyone has 'heard' something...or someone..."

"Yes, and it was not merely here," Zz'r'p said grimly. "I was just contacted by the Prime Minister on Deltir, and whatever it is has apparently gone through the hierarchy on our homeworld."

"Oh og'dm'n," Jj'k'k cursed. "That is...I have no words for how bad that is." (*damn, damnation*)

"Potentially, at least," Zz'r'p agreed. "The interesting thing is...no one was even hurt, let alone killed. Despite all telepathic blocks being overridden."

"So it was not an attack," Bb'y'x decided.

"I suppose it depends upon your definition of 'attack,'" Zz'r'p noted. "Certainly it appeared to be gathering information, but what information, and why? Is it preparing for something? What is it?"

"Why did the prime minister contact you?" Jj'k'k wondered.

"Because specialists on Deltir determined the source... was here on Earth."

"Ab, O'sh'n g'ar d'n," a fervent Bb'y'x prayed. (*Oh,*

Heaven help us)

"Could it have been Omega? Or someone attacking Omega?" Jj'k'k wondered. "Could everything she has been through have caused Omega to break through, and she is trying to find help to control it?"

"I do not think so," Zz'r'p said, after a moment to consider, and to mentally seek out his human protégé. "She tells me she is currently injured, in the medlab, awaiting being 'dunked,' as the physicians put it. She and Echo were rather badly injured in a recent mission, and Echo is already in the regeneration pod, as his condition was more serious…"

"But…then she is upset. Could it not be…"

"No, because she told me she feels it, too. It is not trying to force its way past her block, nor is it doing so with mine, but there is something moving out, through the galaxy, that telepaths are sensing. I need the two of you to help me locate it."

"You had but to ask, my friend," Bb'y'x declared.

Zz'r'p rose and moved to the conversation area in his office, gesturing the others to follow.

There, they sat down, joined hands, closed their eyes, and began to search.

* * *

In her hospital bed, Omega fumed and pondered, after Zz'r'p ended their brief mental conversation. *So I'm not the only one being bugged by whatever this is,* she thought. *And this is new, and I 'heard' that voice at the clearing…surely it isn't. It can't be.*

<Why not?> came the answer.

Aw damn, she thought. *Either I took a lot harder lick to the noggin than I thought, or…*

<No, your brain is not seriously injured, child, though you do have what the healers are terming a concussion. I need your help, and you need ours. Your very world — perhaps your whole galaxy — is threatened. You MUST help us!>

Shit. I know I'm gonna regret this, she decided. *What do you need...?*

<Let me show you...>

* * *

Zarnix frowned as the woman in the bed tried to shout for something, though she was so weak, she was barely audible. She constantly twisted and thrashed on the adjustable bed in the center of Trauma Room Three. She had proven strong enough, even as badly wounded as she was, to rip free of standard hospital restraints. So far the heavy-duty, thickly-padded ones were holding her. If she tore those loose, the next option was force cuffs.

"Something is greatly wrong here, Zebra. She was quiet and still for the entire flight here, short as it was, or so India reported." Zarnix Chifejuz sported a common Chesharilzi complexion of bright purple hair; large, currently-worried orange eyes; slightly pointed ears; and a blue tint to his skin. He was the chief of staff of Division One's Headquarters Medical Department. "And now she is damn near raving in delirium. I am not even sure how she is still alive. I am seeing some very, very slight tissue regeneration, enough to slow the massive bleed that should have killed her. And we are pouring blood plasma and cloned blood into her almost as fast as she leaks it out. Her organs are similar to human, yet very different in how they work. I think. I have not felt this much out of my depth since the first lunation of med school! As far as her physiology is concerned, I might as well be the village witch doctor, with a bone through my nose and a gourd rattle to shake."

"I feel you. What if she's calling for someone?" Zebra, the assistant chief of staff and Director Fox's wife, rubbed her chin as she watched Agency medtechs Yorker and Kaga struggle to hold her still enough to get another needle IV in her arm. They had tried the standard issue osmosive micropore hypodermic syringes and cannulas, but her skin rejected them time and again. Her delirium was not helping in the least.

"Not someone," a familiar voice spoke from the door, "I think rather, some THING." A weary Omega stood in the doorway, gingerly holding Myclestra's enormous, ornate sword in both hands. One whole side of her face was a massive bruise, and there was surgical tape supporting her lower jaw, which was badly swollen, further splitting open already-split lips.

"Omega! What are you doing out of bed? You shouldn't be walking, much less going down to Security to get that thing!" Zebra started to reach for the sword. "And how the hell are you talking with a broken jaw and cracked cheekbone?"

"No, don't touch it, Zebra," Omega exclaimed, jerking the sword out of the physician's reach. "I'm not sure what would happen, but I really don't wanna experiment right now. And we don't need one of our top physicians incapacitated." Omega gave her the best attempt she could make at a wry grin, given the damage to her face. "As to how I'm talking, let's just say, 'It's an effort,' and leave it at that." The others winced.

"Why have you done this, Omega?" Zarnix asked. "Zebra is right. You should be resting in bed. At least until we decant Echo from the regeneration pod later today. Then you would be next."

"She'd be in a regen pod right now, if we hadn't had that commercial transport saucer crash off the coast, coming in to Penn Station," Zebra grumbled. "We flat ran out of regen pods. Thank the good Lord all the passengers were Opdips, or we'd be in trouble."

"That's okay," Omega sighed. "Echo was worse off, what with the busted ribs and punctured lung."

"That is why we triaged you as we did," Zarnix acknowledged. "You have no potentially life-threatening injuries, and we can control your pain. He needed those ribs repositioned and the lung repaired quickly."

"What about her, though?" Omega gestured towards Myclestra, who had suddenly calmed. "She should be in a regen pod right now."

"I agree, Omega," Zarnix responded, "but as yet, we have no idea how to formulate the fluid for her rather unique body chemistry — I have worked on many of the peoples of the galaxy, but have never seen anyone like her, and frankly, we are at a loss. We must know how to formulate the fluid to work with her chemistry, or it does no good to place her in a pod. Now once again, why are YOU here, and what decided you to fetch that thing and bring it here?"

"The pressure on my mental block was what decided me," the tall blonde said as she rubbed her free hand through her hair, which was currently loose and spilling around her shoulders, instead of in its usual braid. The gesture spoke to the two physicians of her concussion, and its subsequent headache. "Whatever it was or is, maybe, it felt like a planet pressing down, demanding that I do…something. The problem was, I didn't really know WHAT. All I felt was a tremendous restlessness and the vaguest hints, images of Myclestra holding this sword. Yorker, Kaga, lemme try something. Step back a bit."

Omega stepped up to Myclestra's bedside and offered the sword, still in its sheath. The woman's right hand shot out, reaching for the sheathed sword, seemingly driven by instinct or perhaps her subconscious. The instant she touched the hilt, she calmed, becoming completely motionless, except for the rise and fall of her chest. All the monitoring instruments immediately showed an improvement in condition — heart rate, blood pressure, temperature, even the oxygenation of her blood — all of them settled down to something that looked like reasonable norms.

"Zarnix, look." Zebra pointed. The massive wound through their patient's lower chest had been a steady bleed, not quite faster than they could pour her own, cloned blood back into her, but close. Now, the bleeding slowed further, becoming a trickle and within a minute or so, stopping completely.

"What in the Maker's Name?" Zarnix was stunned.

* * *

"I am unsure that our Creator had aught to do with this woman or anything else about her." Zz'r'p, the tall, slender,

173

robed ambassador from Arcturus VII, known to his people as Deltir, suddenly announced from where he now stood in the doorway, his robes concealing his blue skin. "That said, SOMETHING has been prowling through minds here in Headquarters, something so powerful and stealthy that it has silently slithered through all but the most hard-held mental blocks. Most of the off-duty Deltiri are sitting outside my office, wakeful and disturbed, awaiting the conclusion of my visit here, hoping I return with answers. I myself, with one of the strongest telepathic blocks in the entire embassy, could feel it nudging about the periphery."

"Shit," Omega growled, "do we have another gastropoid in HQ? Some relative of Slug's, out for revenge…again!"

"No, child," Zz'r'p stepped over to Omega and laid a gentle hand on her shoulder. "Whatever this is, makes Slug — indeed, or any gastropoid — seem as telepathically weak as the average human. Weaker even, perhaps? For I was contacted by no less than the Prime Minister of Deltir, with news that it was happening there, too. Most notably to higher officials of government, commerce, education, and such. I have gotten further notifications from other worlds containing telepathic beings, as well. Someone is…exploring…our galaxy."

"Is it Myclestra, here?" Omega pointed at the now-comatose woman, lying quietly in the bed, her right hand locked around the hilt of the big sword. "We've seen no signs of telepathy or maybe quantum-foam manipulation, other than on the most basic levels."

"No, I do not think it is her," the powerful Deltiri telepath answered. He pointed at the sword. "I think it is…that."

"The sword?" Zarnix asked, eyebrows nearly reaching his hairline. "You are joking, right? It is only a sword, an inanimate chunk of metal."

"I don't know, Zarnix," Omega spoke up. "But once that thing was in her hand, that 'pressure' on my mental block went away. And I'm still a little — no, a lot — antsy about that thing. Y'all didn't see what she did with it. I did, and it scared me spitless."

<There is no need to fear.>

Everyone in the room startled in shock, staring at each other, even Yorker and Kaga.

"Huh, was I the only one that heard that?" Yorker stage-whispered. "Tell me I only thought I heard that."

"No, Agent Yorker, I think it safe to say we all heard the message. 'There is no need to fear.' Indeed," Zz'r'p glared at the gaudy sword, where Myclestra had unconsciously pulled it tight against her side. "Doctor Zebra, I believe that it is of the utmost importance that Director Fox be informed of this possible…development…at once."

"Understood, Your Excellency," Zebra acknowledged. "I'll take care of that just as soon as I get a certain beat-to-hell Alpha Line Agent back in her bed!"

"THAT, I understand, all too well," Zz'r'p replied, wry.

Omega flushed.

"All right, all right, I'm goin', already," she fussed, headed for the door.

* * *

A quick — by intergalactic standards — call back to the Andromedan capital planet revealed that a handful of empaths on the Milky Way side of that galaxy's periphery had picked up a few indications of contact with something or someone unknown, but it was extremely short-lived, and did not penetrate much past the outermost systems there.

Hsrs pondered for a bit, then requested a very specific communication be enacted, piped directly to his shipboard office, and carefully ciphered.

* * *

"You're kidding, bubeleh, right?" Director Fox leaned back in his chair, one eyebrow raised in surprise at the briefing his wife had just finished. "Zz'r'p said he thinks the SWORD is what has been driving those with even the slightest and most rudimentary hint of a psychic ability halfway insane? And then it SPOKE?! Oy vey."

"I know. And I know it sounds crazy." Zebra shrugged where she sat in a chair across from his desk. "But Omega gave me a quick briefing on what she, herself, has SEEN the thing do. At least in this Myclestra's hands. And she is rapidly improving since Omega brought the sword in to her. Really damn rapidly. You can almost see the tissue and organs healing. We're not even pumping any more of her cloned blood into her now. Two hours ago, we were pumping a liter an hour into her, and she was losing it almost as fast. It's bizarre, beyond bizarre, actually. It's like it's…it's…" Zebra glanced around the room blankly, searching for how to express it.

"I think magic is the word you're looking for, meyn gelibte." Fox leaned forward in his chair, resting his arms on the desktop. "I know, supposedly, real magic, like Merlin or a Romanian Scholomonar — some say even Hamelekh Schlomo, King Solomon, from whom the Romanian legends partially derive — that kind of magic doesn't truly exist, at least not in this reality. Oh, the Glu'gu'ik with their ability to manipulate quantum-foam might seem close, but still fits within what we know as science and the scientific method. And this doesn't, right?"

"No, it doesn't," she frowned, "but you weren't there when Zz'r'p walked in and pointed at that dratted sword. Like the thing is alive. And then the damn thing SPOKE. To ALL of us. Except it didn't."

"What do you mean, it didn't?"

"I mean, it was a telepathic voice."

"Mm. Sounds like I need to have a chat with Zz'r'p…and soon."

"I'd certainly suggest you do so, honey, emphasis on soon. Now, I need to get back to Medical. We're gonna decant Echo in a couple of hours and then it's Omega's turn." She paused. "You know, Fox, I would have said that no single individual could possibly stand up to both Echo and Omega in a knock-down, drag-out fight. But this woman, this Myclestra, whatever she is, rocked both of them back on their heels and then a day later, fought them nearly to a standstill. To the point where all three of 'em were about to take terminal measures, because they had no other choice. That worries me, Fox, a lot."

"Why, bubuleh?"

"If this woman is that strong, are there more like her and if so, where are they from? And what's her purpose in coming here?"

"Hmm, good question. A very good question, bubuleh. Hopefully, Zz'r'p can shed some light on that."

"Let me know what he says."

"I will."

"Well, gotta run, honey. Hopefully, I'll see you tonight." The door to the Director's office closed softly behind her.

"Hmmm." Fox leaned back in his chair again. "Magic. Oy vey. I think I need to make a couple of calls before I do anything else. Get an opinion of someone who's an expert on magic, before I take this forward to Pul. Hmm."

* * *

Pan-Galactic Coalition President Pulgey Entiyti was sitting in his office, doing some paperwork, when he suddenly became aware of a voice in his mind.

President Entiyti? Can you hear me?

"Hm?" he murmured absently, without looking up.

I know this is not an opportune time, and it is rather an awkward means of contacting you, but I have a bit of an emergency, and am already, and deliberately, violating our usual policy of non-interaction in order to gain information. And since normally Bozheen telepathy does not extend nearly so far, and we have neither biological speech nor visual centers, I have had to use technological means to boost my telepathy...the resulting headache is, I fear, most unpleasant, so if we could hurry, it would be appreciated.

"What?" Entiyti jerked upright, the word 'Bozheen' having gotten his attention. "You are the people from which the interstellar criminal, Slug, aka Azeln AbdohNeléKein, came?"

We are. And let me first apologize for that; we had no idea the nature of his contract until it was much too late to stop matters from unfolding as they did. And we as a people hold no ill will toward anyone in your polity for those events, and hope the feeling is mutual. Laws and regulations were changed here, in the aftermath, to try to ensure that such a situation never arises again, but I am certain the child he abducted and... modified...likely does not care. Entiyti heard what 'sounded' like a sigh. *But that is not why I contact you now, though later we should discuss it. We have had a very serious event here on Wontwuun...*

"Who are you?"

Ah! I am too worried to think straight! And this damn headache is NOT helping! Forgive me, Milord President; I am Ustrzir AbdohSarniKein, duly elected President of Wontwuun. We have just been contacted, more or less as a planet, by a strange entity...

* * *

Fox, who had previously opaqued his bay window for security, now placed an interstellar vid-call to a very secure and very little-known number. Abruptly a large white, reptilian face, possessed of black horns which were standing up in delight, appeared on one of the big wall monitors.

"Franz!" Pulgey Entiyti, the President of the Pan-Galactic Coalition and Chairbeing of the Ennead, the Coalition's version of the Security Council, exclaimed. "It has been too long, my old friend! I was just thinking about you! How is our 'family' doing? Is everything well?"

"Hey, Pul," Fox said, subdued. "The family is fine, though Echo and Omega have taken a few licks recently...but that's not unusual for them..."

"No, no, it is not," the big Draconan chortled. "They seem to get themselves into trouble on a regular basis, but they always manage to pull through. What of the others? And how are you and Zebra doing? Are you coming to work for me any time soon?"

"Um, Pul, this...this isn't a social call," Fox tried. "We

have a situation here, and even if it resolves well, we may only be exchanging one situation for another. I think there may be LESS of a situation if it resolves well, but you need to know what's going down here."

"Oh," Entiyti remarked, startled. "So tell me, my brother in all but blood."

"It's complicated, and it's going to sound damn near unbelievable, alter khaver. All I ask is that you don't call me crazy."

"You know I should not. Just tell me."

"Okay, you asked for it…"

* * *

Director Fox stood at the back of the hospital room as Zebra settled Echo, clad in a medical jumpsuit, into a bed in the room. Echo obviously wasn't happy about the fact that Medical still hadn't released him.

"I'm fine, Zebra, not even sore. There's no reason I can't put my Suit back on and get back on duty," he groused. "And Omega should have gone into the regen pod before me. She had a cracked cheekbone and a broken jaw."

"Echo, do you realize that, had this Myclestra hit you just a little bit harder or not quite so dead square center of your sternum, you'd be dead? Two of your ribs were driven through your right lung and within forty millimeters of your heart? Four centimeters farther — a little more than an inch and a half — and you'd have been dead when you hit the ground." Zebra crossed her arms and scowled at Echo. "You're lucky you're alive. Yes, Omega's injuries are serious, but yours were life-threatening. Therefore, you got dunked first. And I want to keep an eye on you for at least a couple of hours more before I release you to duty. And don't argue with me, and don't try to pull Alpha Line rank on me, OR bug Fox to override my better judgement. If you do, I swear I will keep you here OVERNIGHT. Am I understood?"

"Oh. Um. Yes, ma'am." A subdued Echo settled back on the bed. "I'll be good."

"See that you are. Now, Fox wants to discuss this whole messed-up sitch with you." She turned to leave.

"Zebra, one quick question." Echo pushed up farther in bed, then subsided as Zebra gave him the stink-eye.

"What?" she asked.

"How's Myclestra? Did she make it?"

"Hmm." Zebra paused a long moment, thinking, before looking back over her shoulder at Echo. "Yes, Echo, she did. But don't ask me how. She should have died within minutes of you shooting her with that God-awful railgun of yours. I honestly don't know why she didn't. And believe me, I've been racking my brains, and I'm not the only one."

"Huh. Why am I not that surprised? Thanks, Zee, thanks a lot. For everything."

"You're most welcome, Echo, hon." The door swung shut behind her.

"Concerned about an opponent, Echo?" Fox settled into the single visitor's recliner in the room. "That's not your usual modus operandi."

"Fox, I don't think this woman is a bad guy. And neither does Meg. I — we — think she's something like a bounty hunter. And she's either from another universe or from so far away we can't even see the light from her galaxy. Someplace where the physical rules are different."

"Well, I think that's very likely, zun." Fox steepled his hands under his chin. "And after I got the initial report from Omega and Alpha Two, and then the follow-up report from Zebra in Medical, well, I called a certain friend. One you met Christmas before last at the Con. Remember?"

"You mean you calle—"

"Let's not name names, not even here. Our mutual friend reminded me that in some circles, names have power."

"Any chance our friend might be interested enough to get involved?"

"No." Fox's answer was flat and harsh. "Not even in our dreams, he said. Same for any of his other…friends or family, he said. This is 'above our pay grade,' is how he phrased it to me. By all accounts that I can determine, this thing isn't much removed from the Judeo-Christian concept of a demon. In fact," Fox added, "I was so perturbed by the call with our mutual friend that I called the chapel and put all the chaplains on alert. Father Papa and Rabbi Yod have 'instituted the prayer chain,' according to Papa."

"Well, shit. That ain't good. Not in any kinda way. Did he say anything else? Our mutual friend, I mean."

"Oh, yes, I got an earful, and then some," Fox sighed and leaned back in the recliner. "He and 'others' have noticed a tremendous…metaphysical, for want of a better term, though multi-dimensional might be closer…upheaval in the mid-mountain American West. 'The fabric of the universe being torn asunder,' was how it was described to me. And it happened, not once, but twice."

"Mmph. I'd say that's pretty strong evidence for the 'alternate universe' theory. No matter how much it annoys Meg."

"Yes, zun, it is. I consider it confirmed at this point." Fox ran his hand through his hair in a rare nervous gesture. "And he warned me that TWO of the THREE entities that entered our universe were deadly dangerous."

"Oh. So the Sword really is an entity. Or else we missed somebody."

"Right. I've tentatively gone forward to Pulgey about it, just to make sure he's aware of the potential meshuginah balagan shaping up here. Please don't tell me that was all wet."

"I don't think so, no, and I think that was a smart move. And yeah, that all makes sense; Meg and I got the injuries to prove how dangerous Myclestra is. And we saw the black thing, not to mention what it can do, so there's number two. Dunno about three."

"Echo, this Myclestra is not one of those two dangerous entities. One is the thing she's chasing, this 'warpwraith.' The other one, I was told, was something completely different, something that might upset the entire fabric of galactic civilization. Upset it…or even destroy it."

"And that…must be the Sword."

"Exactly, zun."

Fox's voice was cold and flat. Echo shivered at the hard expression on his oldest friend's face.

* * *

"Gleetings, Roard Purgey," Premier Hsrs Syrsh said, once the secure vidcall connected. "How ale you doing? I heald about you' injuly in de tellolist attack awhile back, but we did not have a plopel chance to tark at de weddings on Ealth. But you seem to be doing werr."

"Ah, Oo Hsrs!" Entiyti exclaimed then, greeting the other leader in the Persan tongue. "Yes, yes, I am fine now. I had lost a wing, but a certain human female Agent we both know saw to its replacement!" He briefly flexed his wings to display the cybernetic wing. "To what do I owe the pleasure?"

"I am not sule preasule is de telm," a slightly hesitant Hsrs said then, in his oddly bubbling voice; his people had once been amphibian — not so very long ago, either — and that, combined with a dyslexic tendency in English, resulted in giving headaches — or desperately-stifled giggle-fits — to native English speakers. "No, dele is something velly long going on."

"Something is wrong? By all means, tell me, my friend! I will help as I can."

"Velly werr. I know dat youle peopurs have terepaths, an' you know dat my peopurs have empaths…"

"Yes. Go on."

"Have you heald anything flom de terepaths of a stlange, powelfur being in dis garaxy? One with terepathic powels?"

"Not yet, no, though I have received a peculiar report from a telepathic race not in our Coalition," Entiyti noted, then started in alarm. "Oh, but I have heard of some…incidents… in Division One, from Franz — from Director Fox. I wonder if they are related."

"Oh, learry? Was Arpha One invorved?"

"They were. I gather they have a…situation there, as Franz put it." Entiyti drew a deep breath, and his black horns crossed over his head in concern. "Do not tell me your people were contacted by one of those creatures."

"It appeals so," Hsrs noted. "The mistless of my halem, a good fliend since we wele chirdlen, is an empath of some skirr. She terrs me dat…an entity…exproled our spaceclaft about two houls ago, arong with arr of de minds on my ship."

"I cannot think that is good," Entiyti murmured.

"I aglee. I—" Hsrs began, when a sudden, loud, triple-bleat annunciated in Entiyti's office.

"Uh-oh," Entiyti said, jumping slightly in startlement. "Could you hold for a moment, Hsrs? That is an emergency call from one of my divisions."

"Standing by," Hsrs said immediately.

* * *

"Milord Entiyti," the blue, fish-like face pronounced immediately.

"Prime Minister Rr't'n," Entiyti said, recognizing the being onscreen. "Odd that you should contact me just now. Let me guess: a powerful entity has contacted your people telepathically, but is not itself on Deltir?"

"Wha- how did you know?"

"Because you are not the first to call me asking about the matter."

"Our people have managed to triangulate the source," Rr't'n noted.

"Earth?"

Rr't'n cocked his head in a kind of bemused amusement.

"Are you certain Draconans are not telepathic?" the Deltiri asked then.

"Very sure, my friend," Entiyti said with a rumbling chuckle. "I have been juggling several communications — from the Persan Premier, whose empaths reacted similarly; from the Bozheen on Wontwuun, if you can believe it — the gastropoids of Delta Scorpii are, after all, telepathic; from Director Fox on Earth…"

"The Bozheen?!"

"Indeed. I heard from them right after I ended the call with Director Fox, and as soon as I got off with their president, Premier Hsrs of the Persan Federation called. I was discussing the matter with him, when your high-priority call came in."

"I see. So they know, on Earth, of what is going on?"

"They are still working on determining precisely what is happening, but yes, they are aware that SOMEthing is happening. Does Ambassador Zz'r'p know?"

"Yes. The embassy there had much the same thing happen. I thought you should know, as well, but it seems I am late to the game."

"Not at all; I have several leaders currently on hold at this moment, so you are all jumping at once, as Lord Levy might say…or something like that."

"I see. Well, then if the Persan Premier is holding, I should let you go at once. We do not need an even bigger mire than we already have."

"I suspect, if this unknown entity is as powerful as all this — it seems he reached another galaxy mentally…"

"It depends upon how his telepathy works, milord Entiyti," Rr't'n explained. "If it is a 'transmission' type, then yes, you are correct. If, however, it is a kind of quantum effect, such as the Deltiri use, then distance is of little matter."

"I see. Which was it? Could you tell?"

"I think we are confident it was quantum in nature, though not quite like ours."

"Hm. All right. Well, that is something of a relief."

"Go, Lord Entiyti, before the Persan Premier becomes irritated."

"I think he is more apt to consider allying against any threat than becoming irritated at this point," Entiyti considered, "especially with all this going on."

"Point. Still…"

"Yes, I will keep you posted, Prime Minister Rr't'n."

"Thank you, Lord Entiyti."

* * *

"Hsrs?"

"I am stirr hele."

"Good. I apologize; the prime minister of the Coalition's principal telepathic race just called, to confirm that they, too, have had an incident similar to yours. And they have indeed traced it to Earth, to the situation of which Director Fox informed me earlier."

"Do you think thele is any dangel?"

"I am uncertain, as yet," Entiyti admitted. "So far, I am hearing a great deal of 'power' and not so much of malevolent intent. Given what I know, based on what Fox told me, we may simply have a curious being from another dimension, wanting to know more about us. Or we may have a truly frightening situation on our hands."

"I undelstand. But you do not yet know which?"

"No, not yet. Well, I do know there is one very malevolent and very powerful entity on Earth, but it does not seem to be the one making contact; there is another powerful entity there, except I do not know how malevolent it may be. I strongly suspect, based on what I have heard, that the POTENTIAL is there," Entiyti explained as best he could, "but the motivation may not be, for this one appears to be helping them against the other, the patently malevolent one…at least according to what has been reported to me at this point."

"I see," Hsrs murmured. "And so it may simpry be culious, o' it may be sealching fo' arries to assist…"

"Precisely. Or any of a hundred other possible motives."

The two galactic leaders gazed at each other.

"What do you think we shourd do?"

"I am uncertain there is anything TO do except wait to hear from Earth."

"I think pelhaps I wirr take de *Rtxrs* towald ou' home garaxy," Hsrs decided after long moments. "If nothing erse,

185

I can carr fo' leinfolcements…though it wirr take awhire fo' dem to allive."

"It may be better for you to leave our galaxy altogether, Hsrs," Entiyti suggested. "At least the distance will help protect your galaxy, if things in ours 'go south,' as Fox is wont to term it."

"You think it may? De entile garaxy?"

"If what Fox told me of the power of these beings is true, possibly. And if so, it could happen very quickly."

"You wourd not have ou' assistance?"

"I would, but you are friend as much as ally, and I wish to protect you, as well."

"Ah. Werr den, pelhaps I wirr take de *Rtxrs* back…to await de carr fo' leinfolcements, den come in folce."

"That…might be useful," Entiyti admitted. "As an ally, I can keep you apprised of matters as I know anything."

"Velly good, den. I wirr oldel a coulse change, and we wirr head fo' home."

"I hope to see you again soon, Hsrs."

"And I, my fliend, and I."

And he ended the call.

Pan-Galactic Coalition President Pulgey Entiyti sat at his desk, silent, wondering what would happen next.

* * *

With the pain finally receding, Myclestra managed, at last, to claw her way back to rational consciousness. She kept still, alert and aware, listening for the least sound and testing the cool air for the scent of anyone in her room. The Sword was at her side, clamped tightly against her torso by her arm, her hand now wrapped tightly around the sheath.

Surlianth? You are here, with me?

<Yes, Little One, and your injuries are mostly healed. Mostly.>

Why do you not heal me completely? These humans and whatever else lairs here, they have me at their mercy. Humans are not known for being anything but violently…short with

186

captured Fetches. I must escape, ere they slay me.

<Child, these are not the humans of your knowledge. I have been exploring while you have been unconscious and healing, and I can tell you this: No Fetch, nor Slaver, nor any other of the Masters' minions have ever breathed the air of this world, nor set foot on the soil of this Other Earth. They do not have any learned fear of you. Other, that is, than what you have already done to give them reason to exercise great caution in their dealings with you.>

They will hardly greet me with drink and feasting, now, will they? They confine me on this table, having removed all my possessions, ready like living meat to experiment upon.

<You are hardly being rational, Child. You are secured because you were fighting their efforts to heal you. If they wanted you dead, why, then, did they exert such effort into treating your wounds and rushing you to this place, a house of healing over two million ur-lans from where we were, and bending their every ability to ensuring your life and recovery?>

Are you saying these humans are then my bosom companions, that I should greet with a sturdy 'Hail, fellow, well met'? Please. I am no newling warrior fresh born from the tech-wizards' creches, knowing only the faint memories of our race's home, Mother Alontora and how to use a sword.

<Sssh-saaa, Little One, you can be so frustrating at times. No, they may not be 'bosom companions,' but then, what chance have you given them? Silver Hair was willing to talk, but no, you would NOT listen. Not to her and not to me. And, as a result, your chance to confront and destroy the Warpwraith, perhaps with their skilled and powerful aid, was lost to you. And you nearly died as a result.>

There was no time, Surlianth! You know that. Wruthas, that beast...I had to confront it as soon as possible, destroy it while it was still weak.

<Oh, weak, aye? Weak while it stood on top of the largest ley line node within thousands of ur-lans? It could have hardly been in a better place, for IT, to face your assault!>

You would have carried the day, Old Snake! You would have made the difference!

<Perhaps. And perhaps not. I am not all-powerful, Child, not in this form and not even when my soul was housed within its old body. Not even Star-Drakes…not even such as the few of us that ever existed, had the power of the Maker. Powerful enough to change the courses of stars and more, but not all-powerful. No Drake ever did aught save bow its crest before the Maker of All Things.>

Pah, the monster is hardly to be compared with the Maker you name. WE could have destroyed it! And then we could have returned home!

<And then what? Hoped that there was enough stolen power to recover from it to force a portal to return whence we came? To return to a world where you are feared and hated on sight? Where no hand is raised in friendship, only bare tolerance, if that? Where any stranger might kill you and face no censure? Where those who bent and twisted you into shadows of what your people once were, wait to hunt you down? That is the utopia, the Blissful Lands to which you wish to return? Have you considered the possibility that you might start afresh here, with no preconceived prejudice, and to that end, perhaps would do well to be more diplomatic?>

Myclestra was silent for a long time as she thought about her life on the Earth where she had drawn her first breath, sensed the lives of those like her, the memories of those uncountable generations that had come before her. What she had seen, what she had done. What had been done to her.

I have no eyes, no tears, Surlianth. I cannot weep. What else could I do? I am what the Masters have made me, and all my sisters of Alontora, to be.

<Child,> the Drake spoke softly in her mind, <Child, you are still so young, and yet so old. Your prowess in battle is as great or greater than any who have wielded me over the eons. Humans of only fifteen turns of the seasons are often considered to be as children, but at that age you are one of the

eldest of your race now living. The tech-wizards birth you and your sisters in their laboratories and creches. In six months you are fully adult, complete and ready for battle. And the Masters use you up with no more concern than a human has for the air he breathes. How many of you see even ten turns of seasons?>

Enough, Surlianth, enough. I will think on what you say, but I shall not meet the next being to enter this room strapped to a table like a sathern carcass about to be shoved into an oven for dinner! And I hear and scent one approaching who has come many times. Enough of this accursed table!

She focused herself and put all her strength onto the strap and cuff holding her left forearm securely against the rail on the side of the bed, and tore loose the metal tubing with which it was attached to the side of the bed. In an instant, regardless of the clatter of the broken rail, the straps on her other limbs were released. She dropped the broken rail with a clash of metal, leaping from the bed and drawing the Sword just as Zebra and Yorker slammed open the door, running in response to the racket of the bed being half-destroyed. They both skidded to a halt as Myclestra faced them, nude, with the Sword's long blade embedded a foot deep in the floor and her hands resting on the hilt in front of her. Blood stained the bandages on her sides and trickled down her arms, from where she had torn out the IV needles.

<Be amicable, Little One.>

Oh, very well. She smiled, her blind, white eyes seeming to meet the astonished stares of Zebra and Yorker.

"If you might be kind enough to offer a stranger mead and meat, it would be appreciated."

* * *

"There you are," a familiar, deep, beloved voice said, as Omega fought her way to consciousness. "Looking beautiful, as always, baby."

"Oh good," Omega sighed. "What with all the swelling, I wasn't sure how that cheekbone was gonna turn out, let alone the jaw."

189

"We know what we're doing, hon," Zebra's voice said then. "Zar and I, we've had plenty of experience putting you field agents back together after you've gone and played Humpty Dumpty. Never mind all Doron's training. And we're both trained in plastic and aesthetic surgery. It was just a matter of ensuring the bones were properly aligned, and the lacerations closed smoothly."

"Thanks," Echo told the physician, as Omega opened her eyes and pushed up in the bed. The covers abandoned her, slumping to her waist, revealing that she wasn't in a medical jumpsuit as yet. But only Echo and Zebra were in the room, so she didn't scramble to pull up the blankets.

"Yeah. From both of us," Omega agreed. "How's Myclestra?"

"She woke up shortly before you were scheduled to be decanted," Zebra noted. "She seems to be doing okay now. Why, I have no idea. We got her dressed, and she said she was really hungry. Her metabolic rates actually exceed yours, believe it or not — likely due to her larger stature — so we had to send out for a good bit of food from the deli. It's not back yet, but she's eagerly awaiting it in one of the medical conference rooms, with Fox and…well, it's the Praetorian Fox Team, but only a couple are in the room; the rest are standing guard outside the door, and around the medlab. Not that Myclestra knows that."

"She's indicated that she's open to discussion with us now," Echo told his partner and mate. "Though she requests we give her a chance to eat, first."

"Which will about give me time to check Meg's face and dentition, then get her into a Suit," Zebra affirmed. "Then you can both go talk to her."

"Let me slip in there first, and I think you should come along as well, Zebra," Echo wrinkled his brow in thought. "Or, well, when you're done with Meg. Then you follow a few minutes later, Meg, once you're dressed. Let's see if we can rattle her just a little bit, and get a better hold on what's going on with her."

"Don't rattle her too much, Ace," Omega put in. "She has a marked tendency to use violence first."

"Oh, I get that, baby," Echo agreed, "but we need to at least try to make her react to us a little. Seize the initiative, as it were. Think that'll work?"

"It's a plan," Omega agreed.

* * *

"That's her third, whole, roasted chicken, bones and all," Echo muttered under his breath to Fox, "and a gallon of beer, four extra-large baked potatoes and a half dozen large ears of corn. I thought Omega could put it away, but…"

"You do not have to mutter, Mr. Agent Echo," Myclestra spoke after devouring a chicken leg, bone and all, wiping the grease from her mouth with a napkin. She wore a pair of spandex workout shorts and a sports bra that was maybe a size too small…but had been the largest that the Wardrobe department had to hand. Her battered pathfinder boots were back on her feet, and the Sword in its sheath was slung over her back. Her auburn mane flowed loose, nearly reaching her waist. "I can hear you, no matter how quietly you are speaking. Fetches, such as myself, we were made to use everything and anything basically edible to feed our bodies. We leave little to nothing on the table. Unlike humans like you." She raised her face from her meal, her blind, white eyes seeming to focus on Echo, where he sat across the table from her next to Fox. Omega had not yet arrived; she was still getting dressed after Zebra's post-regen examination. Zebra herself had entered moments before, bearing that news.

"Agent Echo will do; there's no need for the Mister title. Agent is a title in itself. And no, we don't generally eat the bones and gristle. Some animals do, but not humans. We can't digest it properly; evidently you can."

"Yes; it provides us needed minerals. Ah, so it is only 'Agent Echo,' then?" Her eyebrows rose for a moment, then she returned her attention to her plate. "And who is Omega? The Splice with the silver hair?"

191

"That's AGENT Omega, thank you!" Echo's voice was a barely controlled snarl. "And what do you mean by calling her a 'Splice?'"

"Huh, you defend her?" Again the blind orbs appeared to meet Echo's glare. "Then you know she is a Splice. Interesting."

"Of course I defend her! She's my wife as well as my partner! And again, what do you mean by that, calling her a Splice?"

"Because she is one. The base is human, but there are… hmm, I do not know the word in your language, *geenid* in my tongue. The basic building blocks of life, they are."

"You mean genes, I think?" Zebra answered from the end of the table. "She's had other genes spliced in?"

"Yes, genes, exactly. She has been…extensively rebuilt, I am told, with the characteristics and abilities of many species forced into her."

"How the hell do you know this?" Echo's knuckles whitened as his grip nearly crushed the table edge.

"Partly because I can smell it. No human I have ever met has such a scent as hers. It is not an unpleasant scent; it is simply…different. I do not know the other races that are part of her, for I do not know this place, but she is not purely human. And partly, because I was told." She finished the last of the chicken, inhaled another potato in two bites, and leaned back in her chair. "In my universe, such as her are not unusual, albeit never as long-lived as she is. They are forced together, what you might term 'kluged,' built as combat fodder. If not killed in battle, it is a truly rare Splice that lives even two years. Some of the human nations attempt to duplicate what the Masters have done over the millennia to my sisters, the Alontorans. Lacking the Masters' immortality and patience, well, their results are inferior. And short-lived. She appears to be…very well-made."

"And who told you of her, then?" Zz'r'p asked from the other end of the table. Myclestra answered him only with a smile and a slow blink of the functional eyelids over the white orbs of apparently-useless tissue that should have been eyes.

Then she picked up her beer mug and drained it, setting it down with a thump.

"Myclestra, this is Ambassador Zz'r'p, a Deltiri from Arcturus VII, another stellar system in our galaxy." Fox spoke for the first time.

"Ah, the telepath," Myclestra answered with a nod. "I suggest to you, Zz'r'p, to stay out of my head."

"I do not attempt to reach into others' minds without permission unless it is a grave, even life-threatening emergency." The fish-like Deltiri's answer was formal, calm and cool.

"And when you tried to 'read' me when I was brought here, you hit a wall and bounced. Understood. I can see that being what you called a 'life-threatening emergency,' and I do thank you for your efforts to help heal me back to full life. But my warning remains." She turned her attention to Fox. "And now, is it Mr. Fox, or Agent Fox?"

"Director Fox is appropriate. I run the organization, at least in the Earth neighborhood."

"Ah, very well. Now, Director Fox, when will you return the rest of my possessions to me and allow me or perhaps aid me in tracking down and killing my quarry?"

"Excuse me? 'Killing' your quarry? No attempt to at least apprehend it?" Fox's answer was short and sharp, even as Omega, immaculate in her Suit, entered the conference room. "I think you might be jumping th—"

"No," Myclestra interrupted him, "you do not understand! There is no capturing a Warpwraith! You kill it, quickly and brutally. Offer no quarter. Given any chance at all, a Warpwraith will be in your mind, turning you literally inside out, faster than lightning striking. And this one, this beast, this monster, is worse than most. Not only does it have its own native abilities, it is a powerful wizard. Such knowledge will allow it to use this world's ley-lines and cover tens or hundreds of miles at a step. And it WILL seek a place of power, magical or mundane, to draw on that power and make itself nigh unstoppable. Of all creatures, Warpwraiths are most evil and cunning. It is well that they are so few and that they will always struggle against each other. This one will, at some point soon, calve another, a lesser copy of itself. But a copy that can become greater, and once the calving is over, the lesser one will flee and hide. Until it can return and strive against its creator for dominance and power. And when Warpwraiths war upon each other, they leave the lifeless, soulless, burned ashes of a dead world behind them. The ether of deep space, the void between stars, that is no impediment to a mature Warpwraith. I MUST find and destroy this thing quickly, before it either calves…or departs, after destroying your world. And if you are defenders of this world, this galaxy, you should at least not impede me, if you will not offer me aid. It IS your Earth, after all."

"Fox," Omega said then, "I have to say, I think she's right. Based on everything that Echo and I saw in trying to track her — and this…creature — down and figure out what's been happening, I think she's exactly right, and we won't have any choice but to kill it. And hesitating in doing so might just be the end of US."

"We might give it one chance to surrender," Echo suggested, "but it damn sure sounds like it isn't going to. I mean, I'm sure the guards at Kirtland demanded for it to surrender, and got mashed into one big lump of goo for their efforts." He and Omega both paled at the memory despite themselves.

"Easy, easy, there," Zebra murmured. "Why did you two just go white?"

"Because it was that gruesome," Omega noted. "I hurled my guts, and Echo came close."

"Alla that," Echo affirmed.

"And I heard the hurling," Fox confirmed.

"And that is typical," Myclestra agreed. "It will never surrender. It will fight to the death. If it spawns, your world is ash, and likely many like it."

"Farkakte, shit, verdammt, merde, glagaram, khro, abdab, gronk, and argdun!" Fox cursed fluidly, scowling, even as

Myclestra raised an intrigued eyebrow. "This is what I was afraid of, based on what little information I was able to dig out from some...allies."

The others stared at him, except for Myclestra, who resumed nibbling at what little was left of the food.

* * *

"So, you are paired together? Married, you call it?" Myclestra walked between Echo and Omega, following Romeo and India to the training room. "And you two as well?" She indicated the Alpha Two team.

"Yes. We are. Both Alpha One and Two consist of married partners," Omega answered. She glanced over her shoulder at the Alpha Seven and Eight teams following them.

"Huh, you still fear me, I see." Myclestra smiled. "Wise of you, but perhaps there is no need, now. You need me and what I bear to have any hope of dealing with the Warpwraith. Well, without destroying half of this country, this United States, at least. Your atomic weapons would kill it...eventually...but you would need multiple strikes."

"Myclestra, we don't fear yo—" Echo started to say.

"Oh, but you do. If you do not fear, then you are at least wary. All of you have elevated heart rates and are breathing faster. These two," Myclestra pointed at Alpha Two, "are very uncomfortable with me behind them. And these four following are sweating somewhat and keep checking that their weapons are loose in the holster. I am an Alontoran. Were matters different...well. I may be blind to visual light, but here in this hallway, within my reach...you should fear me." A tense silence settled around the group as Alpha Two stopped and spun to face Myclestra, bringing them all to a halt. "Hmm. Nervous, are you not? Well, in truth, there is now no real need to fear. In this, hunting down my quarry, we are allies, and no free Alontoran will ever break her word, once given. And I have given my word to Director Fox."

"That's good to know, then." Echo waved down the hallway. "Shall we proceed?"

"Certainly," Myclestra nodded at him. A moment later, she smiled to herself, waiting to see the response to her next question. "So, these other two Alpha Teams, Seven and Eight, are they mated pairs also? Married, as you say?"

It took longer than it should have to reach the training rooms, given the strident denials from Yankee and Tare of Alpha Seven, much less Monkey and Kako of Team Eight. Omega was silent the entire time, closely observing Myclestra. It was so very subtle, but she was certain there was a slightly smug smile on that beautiful face.

She's TRYING to throw us off, she thought. *Now, maybe that's just her sense of humor… 'cause let's face it, I'm about to die laughing at Tare and Yankee my own self, right now…but maybe it isn't.*

* * *

Omega watched every move Myclestra made once they reached the training rooms. Facilities personnel had brought a duffel bag containing Myclestra's gear. She picked it up, quickly checking the rest of her equipment for accidental damage, before walking into the combat simulation room. Then she moved slowly around the large, open space, examining everything in detail.

"Impressive. Very impressive." She tilted her head to pop the vertebrae in her neck. "But why the expensive machines? Live opponents are much more unpredictable."

"Um, Myclestra, if an Alpha Line Team, especially Alpha One or Two, goes full out against live opponents, well, people get hurt, bad." Omega answered her question, wondering just what kind of society had created Myclestra. "Maybe even killed."

"Based on my own experience with you, I can readily believe it. You are highly adaptable and intelligent."

"Right," Echo said. "Which is why we don't use live opponents."

"So? Surely, live opponents would be better training. And dying in training would weed out those unsuitable for the task."

196

All eight Agents were staring at her in various levels of shock and horror. "Hmm, not what you do, I 'see.' Then what do you do with those who cannot meet the requirements of your job?"

"We brain-bleach 'em and find a place for them back in regular society — the majority of this world doesn't know, isn't ready to know, that there's a galactic civilization, you see. Or they may not be up to Alpha Line standards or Field Agent requirements, but there are other needs in Division One," Omega answered her. "There may be other jobs they can fill. Diplomacy, Supplies, Wardrobe, Weapons Development, Facilities, Sciences…all these and more, are other departments we have, departments that don't require the need for prowess in battle."

"Yes," Echo confirmed. "Think of this organization… we're somewhere between a police organization and a military one, and there are logistics and such things that have to be handled. Just because you're not a soldier — or a beat co-uh, street officer — doesn't mean you don't help fight the war. Or help take down the criminals, as the case may be."

"Ah yes. I understand better now. Well, then, shall we see how you do against a prepared and fully empowered Alontoran Fetch? Allow me a moment to prepare." Myclestra leaned the sheathed Sword against the wall, then sat down on a bench and unlatched her boots before stripping off the restrictive sports bra and spandex workout shorts. All eight Agents gawked in shock at her unconcerned nudity. Myclestra's body was a vision of beauty, power and symmetry. She looked over her shoulder at them and sighed as one hand fished a shimmering, nearly invisible garment of some kind out of her equipment bag.

"Uh, Myclestra, we have dressing rooms to change in. Over this way." Omega was the first to recover her power of speech. The men were gob-smacked; even Echo and Romeo stared, despite themselves.

"Why?" Myclestra cocked her head at Omega. "We are warriors, are we not? What matter the flesh that all too soon will be ripped and torn in battle?" The red-haired alien shook her head. "Humans and your silly taboos about food and nudity and religions. If you wish to use a 'dressing room' then go do so. Otherwise, prepare yourselves for battle. Go, shoo." She waved a hand at them. The Agents quickly left the combat room to change. Omega delayed, watching Myclestra slide the nearly imperceptible synth-skin on over her smooth, tanned skin.

"What's that?" she asked.

"A synth-skin. It is a neural network system that connects me neurologically to any advanced weapons or powered armor in my personal armory. It also provides basic, light armor protection. It will stop pretty much any muscle-powered weapon. Of course, you figured out its weakness back in the forest. It is also why so many of our opponents and victims thought that Fetches went into battle nude or nearly so." A tangle of glittering straps was next. "This is my armor. It is a field generator of sorts, a molycirc powered generator that generates the armor 'field' that protects me. It must be connected to the synth-skin to function properly. As fragile as it appears, the power packs, here and here, generate a field that will stop pretty much anything up to a heavy railgun slug from one of the new Republican Battlesuits. Something else you figured out a way around." She smiled at Omega. "Very clever. And it hurt like hell. But I was too exhausted to use my cantrips. Today, you will see me at full strength. And this is what I was made for, the crush and brutality of close combat. Alontorans do not normally live long; we burn bright and fast. A few, a lucky few escape our bondage, but even then, we are feared and hated everywhere we go."

"You said you don't live long," Omega, almost against her will, took a step toward her. "How long is that? How old are you?"

"We are not like humans, for the tech-wizards 'birth' us physically mature. A few months of training, and a new Fetch is assigned to a Slaver. We die in combat, mostly. Few live past three or four years. I am an Elder. I survived nine years of combat as a Slaver's Fetch. Then I escaped and have eked out a bare existence as a bounty hunter. I think I would be about fifteen years now. I think. Much of my memories of the time after I escaped are…blurry. So I am not certain, but I am in that general range. But enough of me. Go prepare yourself… my friend."

Myclestra turned away from Omega, and the Agent stared at the hard-muscled woman in some surprise; aside from her shocking youth, she had called Omega friend, and it sounded as if she meant it, at least on some level. It seemed the red-haired alien woman was not finished with handing Alpha One surprises.

Dear Lord God help her, she's really only a teenager, as we would consider it. Fifteen years old and nothing but a life of brutal combat. Damn. Omega thought for a moment. *Well, maybe she really does need a friend. We'll see, I guess.*

* * *

The Alpha Line Agents came back into the combat training room as Myclestra was braiding up her hair into a compact top-knot. Over the synth-skin she wore the glittering armor harness, its energy packs fully charged. Over that, she wore a skimpy, thong-back, rubbery-looking black leotard. A sturdy belt held her plas-pistol and the pouches for her cantrips. The Sword, unsheathed, rested against one of the benches, its elaborate dragon hilt gleaming with the lavish inlay of strange gems and precious metals.

"That is the *coolest* sword I've ever seen, lady. I mean, whoo-hoo, shiny." Almost entranced, Romeo reached out to touch it.

<Silver Hair, I will not kill him, but he must learn respect.> Omega twitched as a mental voice she could only describe as primordial, slow and heavy with uncounted ages, insinuated itself through her mental block; it did not violate the block as such, but was rather as if she had been preoccupied and picked up on a comment spoken directly to her. It spoke a bare

fraction of a second before Romeo's hand touched the hilt of Myclestra's sword.

There was a flash of lightning, complete with deafening thunderclap, as Romeo was blasted, heels over head, across the room to slam into the far wall and slide down to lie in a pile. He shook his head very slowly as India rushed to his side. The other Agents spun in shock to watch.

"Romeo, talk to me, baby! Are you okay?" she half-shouted, partially stunned and half-deafened by the thunder, herself. "C'mon, baby, say something."

"Ow." Romeo raised his hand and looked at it, apparently wondering if it was still there. There wasn't a mark on it. The only bruise he had was going to be the one on his shoulder where he had hit the wall. "That kinda stung." He shook his head to clear it. "What the hell just happened?"

"You touched the Sword," Myclestra answered. Everyone 'heard' the capital letter implied in the comment. "Don't do that again. He may decide to kill you next time."

"You could have warned us not to touch that thing." Omega hadn't drawn a weapon, as Alpha Seven and Eight had done. "I mean, Romeo should have known not to touch someone else's weapon, but still — wait, HE? It's a sword, it's not alive. Is it?"

"Perhaps, Omega, it is. Alive, for some values of life. I am sure you have heard it by now; it seems to like you. I do not own the Sword, Omega. I am merely its chosen Bond Bearer in this cycle of life." Myclestra actually chuckled, "You might say it owns me. Now, let me show you a slight glimpse of what you may face when we find the Warpwraith."

"Okay, Myclestra, how are we going to do this?" Echo watched India help a mildly rattled Romeo to his feet, checking him over carefully with her medscanner, before giving the department chief a thumbs-up. "Any kind of scenario, or what?"

"Can you use the room to generate solid holograms? If so, create a thick forest, old growth, with tall, strong trees. At night. That is likely the sort of terrain where and when we will finally face the monster."

"Okay." Echo set the room's controls, and a dark forest filled the space. "How's that?"

"Excellent."

"Now what?"

"Prepare yourselves for a moment, then attack me. All of you. Full speed, holding nothing back. You may use any of your weapons, except the one you used, Echo, to nearly kill me. Now, silence…and wait."

* * *

Now, Old Snake, I will need to borrow of your power. They must learn what they will face. Show them what it will be like to have their very worldview distorted. Do not harm any you strike, only inflict the pain they would feel if the wound were real, or to stun them if it would be fatal. Lend me your strength that I might bear the burden of more cantrips. For I must pretend to be that which we face, or they will go into this at my side wholly unprepared. We cannot fully prepare them; I am not a Warpwraith. But we must try.

<How many more cantrips, Little One?> Surlianth's voice was dry in her mind.

A total of seven, I think: Strength, Speed, Toughness, Invulnerability, Accuracy, and Precognition. And a cantrip of attack magic, with the spells chosen and given to me through your own Power. And enough of your own magic to make this as real to them as we can. I want them to get a realistic feel of what we face. They must believe me, and they must be ready. Else they, and likely their world, are dead.

<Hmmpf. Would you also wish for the Bottle of the Four Winds as well? The Lance of Azrael the Deathless, perhaps? This WILL cost you. Child.>

I shall send them the bill.

<No doubt. Go; draw of my Power as you will.>

Magic flooded through Myclestra, bringing her to the absolute height of what she might be, if only for mere moments, at best. She laughed as she sensed the fear and trepidation of the humans facing her. Most of them. There were two that showed no fear, and two others powerfully controlling theirs.

"Woe unto you, puny Mortals!" she roared, an inhuman resonance to her voice. The room reverberated with the power of her shout. "Flee, Mortals, for your Doom is come!" And she attacked.

* * *

Later, Omega could barely string together a coherent account of what had happened. Myclestra had moved with impossible, blurring speed, even greater than that which Echo and she had seen at the Air Force base. She remembered one of those 'Pathfinder' boots blasting her across the room, an attack she barely saw coming, and somehow she blocked that dreadful, radiant Sword, losing a blaster in the process. She had another vague memory of Echo cartwheeling past her as Myclestra contemptuously tossed him aside.

The Sword loomed large in her memory, flickering, dancing, like heat lightning over hot summer nights, the lightning of distant storms.

She recalled Tare, Yankee, Monkey and Kako dropping bonelessly and bloodily to the forest floor as that terrible blade gutted them, clove them in half or lopped off a head…or at least, that was what Omega thought she saw.

India, blasted into a carbonized skeleton by a deadly blue ray that shot from Myclestra's open hand.

A grieving Romeo, screaming insanely as he charged, stopping with a horrible gurgling sound as Myclestra's fist punched through his chest, before ripping his heart out.

Then the most horrible of all…

The Sword pinned Echo to the floor like a bug in an insect collection, twisting as he shouted — more than half screamed — in pain and fury, his blasters pouring fire into Myclestra that her armor shrugged away. He paled, weakened, and finally lay still, those beautiful brown eyes that she loved glazing in death.

Then Myclestra was stalking her, the Sword spotless and

unbesmirched, Romeo's life blood dripping from her other hand, a cruel smile on that beautiful face.

"Now, little Silver Hair Splice, let us see what you are truly made of, if you are worthy of my blood and pain," Myclestra said as the Sword hissed back into its sheath and she set it down. "Against Surlianth you cannot stand; few can. But now, against me, the slayer of your belovéd, stand and deliver. Or die."

With a blood-curdling shriek of raw fury, Omega flung herself at Myclestra, fists and feet blurring as they hammered at the alien woman. She pushed herself to her absolute limits and beyond, but was unable to truly touch the alien.

In her turn, Myclestra landed blow after blow, powerful kicks driving the air out of Omega's lungs, leaving her bruised and bloody, yet not stopping her.

Omega tried again and again to gain the leverage she'd used in the forest, but this time Myclestra slipped away, an oiled eel in her futile grasp. With a last gasp, Omega landed a powerful kick straight into Myclestra's chest. This time, she heard ribs break, and blood spurted out of the tall alien's mouth. But Myclestra landed her own potent snap kick into Omega's face in the same attack, and the two women flew away from each other, crashing through solid holographic trees to finally stop when they slammed into opposite walls.

Omega coughed, spitting blood on the floor, before coming to her feet. In the dimness of the nighttime forest, she could see Myclestra lying motionless against a huge tree. Shaking her head, blood spraying from a broken nose and pulped lips, she headed for Myclestra, hatred burning in her heart. *She KILLED them! She killed Echo! It was all a ruse! Forget that 'my friend' shit! She's DEAD MEAT!*

The alien staggered to her feet, wiping blood from her face. Omega accelerated into a hard sprint, and was only an arm's length away, when Myclestra responded to her charge.

"Hold! Mortal, be thou Still, Held So by the Power of a Drake's Will." Something gleaming and sparkling shot out of her hand and stopped Omega cold, hanging in mid-air as if caught in a tractor beam. Myclestra gave her a crooked smile. "You believe I have betrayed you, slain those dearest to you, reaved away your own mate. Not so. Look around you, my friend, and watch Surlianth's Power make all right again, all as it should be."

* * *

The blood coating the combat room, the holographic trees, the forest floor and even the contorted bodies slowly faded to nothingness. The Agents groaned as they sat up from where they had fallen, each of them gingerly feeling the 'fatal' wound they had suffered at Myclestra's hands. Romeo felt his chest once, then scrambled across the floor to India, wrapping his arms tightly around her.

"You BITCH!" Romeo twisted around to snarl at Myclestra. "I oughta kill your ass dead for that!"

"For what? For showing all of you what you may face against the Warpwraith? I told you in advance, this was what I must do. I comprehend your feelings. But you cannot afford such sentiment, my allies, else he will surely make use of them, and in a far more real fashion." She walked carefully around Omega and picked up the Sword with a wince of pain. Then she slowly waved her hand, releasing the spell on Omega. Omega immediately spun and ran to Echo, helping him to his feet.

* * *

"You could have warned us, Myclestra." Omega controlled her voice, but the ache of watching Echo die was still there. "You could have explained what would happen."

"You would not have believed me, I think." Myclestra sighed. "But I am sorry for your distress."

"Yeah, damn you," Yankee growled from where he still sat on the floor, carefully feeling around his neck, where the Sword had 'beheaded' him. "NOW you regret it. After damn near giving alla us heart attacks."

"No, I do not regret it, Agent Yankee. I am sorry for your discomfort, but I have no regrets. Alontorans...do not feel

204

regret. We cannot. Something else the Masters did to us as they molded us to be the perfect slave warriors. I can, however, sympathize. And for the emotional anguish I inflicted, I am… sorry."

"Still, damn it. That was way the hell more than we ever expected." Omega wiped blood off her face. "And, damn you, the injuries you gave me are real enough! Shit! I just got outta the damn regen pod!"

Myclestra spat blood on the floor as she slowly approached Alpha One. Echo moved in front of Omega, shielding her with his body.

"Yes, those wounds are real, as are the ones you gave me. However, I can offer a curative for that. I can heal you of those wounds. Please, if you will." She watched Omega and Echo closely, until they both nodded at her. Slowly the Sword hissed from its sheath. She balanced it on her hands, the blade flat on her palms. "Reach forth, Omega and but ever so slightly touch the edge of the blade. It will draw blood, but only in the slightest amount." Hesitant, Omega touched the tip of her forefinger to the edge. There was a slight cut, leaving a trace of her blood on the Sword. A trace which disappeared within seconds. "Now, place your hands over mine, touching the flat of the blade. Then take a deep breath…and relax." Myclestra drew a simultaneous breath with Omega. "Surlianth, *Tervendama meid kui õdesid.*"

<Well, that is a strange request from you, Little One.> The same ancient, heavy voice slid into Omega's awareness. <And you, Silver Hair, please, release your mental block. It will interfere with my healing if you maintain it. You may trust me; by my word and my life, I will do you no harm.> There was laughter like continental shelves grinding together. <And in some ways, as my Bearer has requested, the pair of you are much like unto sisters. Or lovers. Now, each unto the other, be thou revealed.>

Omega wanted to scream, as she fell into a vast space. She felt a hand on hers. She looked over to see not Echo, but

Myclestra holding her hand as they fell. Echo was still there, oddly distant, but there through the nd't'lq. Then she became aware of the eyes, gigantic, glowing eyes, pure white with a reptile's vertical pupil. Eyes the size of the Moon. Eyes that held depths and knowledge beyond anything known in the entire Galaxy. But eyes that watched her with a distant, warm regard. *Almost as warm as Echo's gaze,* she thought vaguely. *And more so, in some ways. I...don't understand. What's happening?*

<Look, each of you, into the past of the other. Understand and learn to trust, to believe. In no other fashion shall you save this world, or perhaps even this Universe entire.>

Omega did scream then, as she experienced an unending cycle of war and battle and blood shed in rivers and lakes and fields. Incomprehensible alien minds, minds twisted and bloated with death and horror, Myclestra kneeling naked before them as the lives linked to her stretched away into darkness, each life one of terror and death. Agony twisting through life after life, as bodies and minds were perverted and warped into patterns that pleased other minds so bizarre and freakish, that merely glimpsing them in these memories threatened her sanity. A life only of cruelty and blood and death, with no real hope of any other ending.

Myclestra fell beside Omega, living and feeling the cruel, callous viciousness of Slug's unbenumbed vivisection of young Megan McAllister, forcing her into the shape he wanted, not a shape forged over generations, but within a single day. The pain of burning under the Cortians' ion drive, the crash on the proto-planet, the Deltiri telepath Tt'l'k mind-raping her, attempting to kill her and Echo. Mark Wright attempting to rape her physically, even as her own body betrayed her. Losing Echo while rescuing a crude spaceplane, retrieving Echo's mutilated body from the Cortian slave ship, her fear that she was nothing more than an animal, created to kill the man with whom she had finally found love. Pain and heartbreak and sorrow, but balanced by love and devotion and family.

They were no longer falling, but rising, floating on a cloud of peace and empathy. They each saw…a kind of resonance in the other. With a gasp for air, they opened their eyes, facing each other across the Sword.

Their eyes met, one pair bright blue and sighted, the other white and blind. But somehow, each aware of the other, for the first time.

"I understand," they said in unison…

…Even as Echo whispered the words himself.

* * *

"Omega, baby, what happened to you when she used that sword to heal your injuries?" Echo had just stepped out of the dressing room, neat and sharp after a hot shower, and clad in a fresh, clean Suit. "I felt some of it through the nd't'lq, but only distantly. Is that thing really alive, or haunted or what?"

Yankee and Tare were sitting on a bench just outside the dressing room door. India leaned against the wall, waiting on Romeo. They all perked up at Echo's question. Monkey and Kako had been the first ones out, and neither of them really wanted anything to do with Myclestra. They had quickly headed out the door to get coffee in the Alpha Line briefing room.

"Hmm?" Omega was watching Myclestra reorient her magical talismans in her belt pouches. She still wore only the synth-skin, her armor harness and the skimpy leotard. The outfit left little to the imagination. "Sorry, woolgathering there," she said and blushed as she turned to face Echo. "What did you say?"

"That sword, any idea what it is?"

"It is the domicile of an ancient being, Agent Echo." Both Agents startled a bit as Myclestra turned and spoke to them. "For now, let that be enough, please. Not all secrets need be revealed." She turned her attention to Omega, "You are well now, battle-sister?"

"Yeah, I'm fin—" Omega stopped mid-word. "What did you call me?"

"Battle-sister." Myclestra straightened and slung her equipment bag over her shoulder. The Sword was slung over her other shoulder, gems shining in the overhead lights. "A term of endearment among my people. Despite what the Masters have done to us, we are still individuals, like any thinking being. We feel antipathy to some of our sisters, warmth, friendship and, yes, even love to others. We must have care in that. The Masters tolerate only submission and obedience from their creations, and no affections at all between others. Great Alontora Herself help any who display the least sign of caring or concern for any other than those above your station. If discovered, you are lucky if you are only sentenced to die in the arena. The greatest offenders, those suffer a terrible fate, to be devoured alive by the Masters, slowly, aware of what is happening until the very end, when the flesh is consumed, and the trapped soul is slowly torn apart and absorbed. That is the true nectar of life for them, the very souls of beings deemed lesser by the High Lords of the Masters."

"Oh dear God! What a horrible, horrible world you come from," Omega blurted out, eyes wide in shock at the existence Myclestra's words revealed…and that she now knew to be true. Even Echo was a bit pale.

"It is simply what is, Omega, of no more matter than light or darkness to me. And not a fate which concerns me any longer. Surlianth is my Bonded and he protects my soul. The Warpwraith might kill me, but no more than that. And I have danced before Death's door many a day, and live yet. Much as the two of you do, risking life and love in your chosen tasks." She stopped, turning her attention from Omega to Echo and back.

"It's a lot to take in, all at once," Echo met her scrutiny with his own frank assessment. "YOU are a lot to take in, as well."

"Perhaps, Echo, perhaps." An odd sound, half laugh, half sob, slipped out of the tall alien woman. "And you are fortunate, very fortunate, in the affairs of the heart and of love."

She stopped, with a sad half-smile on her face. "And were you not so fortunate, ah, well, perhaps my new battle-sister would be more to me than sister." She walked toward Alpha One, stopping between them. She reached out and gently touched Echo's face, running her hand along his jaw before turning and bending down to quickly kiss Omega, who froze in surprise. She broke the kiss, leaving Omega staring at her in shock. "Perhaps, in another reality, Omega, perhaps." Then she was gone so quickly that neither of them made a sound before the training room door swung shut.

India, Tare and Yankee stared in befuddled astonishment at Alpha One. Echo gazed intently at a beet-red Omega. Her confusion was obvious.

"It would seem that she finds you attractive, baby." Echo reached out and put a gentle hand on her shoulder. "She certainly has great taste in beautiful women."

"Why does that never happen to me?" Yankee muttered, just loud enough for his partner to hear. Tare couldn't help himself — he burst out laughing as Yankee scowled at the still-swinging door.

"Okay, what'd I miss?" Romeo walked out of the dressing room, straightening his tie.

India slapped her hand to her forehead; Omega turned even redder.

The rest of the room broke up laughing.

Chapter Five — Analysis, Planning...and Waiting

"I dunno, Fox, you've seen the video." Echo leaned back in one of the chairs in the Director's office. "She went through us like shit through a goose. Ninety-nine seconds, start to finish. The last thirty-nine of those were spent fighting Meg hand-to-hand. Truthfully, she scares the holy howling hell outta me."

"Me, too," Omega added, "and honestly, if she'd used that God-awful Sword on me, I wouldn't have lasted any longer than anyone else did. That armor field generating rig just shrugs energy weapon fire off, like rain on a windshield. That's a huge advantage, and we don't have anything like it. Oh, we can generate shields, but they're big and bulky and relatively immoveable. Nothing like this thing she has. It looks more like a glittery negligée than anything else."

"Think we could come up with something like it, Omega?" Fox steepled his fingers together, leaning back in his chair.

"Maybe, but damn if I know how, off the top of my head. She called it molycirc, short for molecular circuitry, I guess. Not something available on Earth. What about elsewhere, Fox?"

"I'm not sure off the top of MY head." Fox made a note on his tablet." I'll have the Boys look into it, but I doubt it."

"I'm not sure it'll matter," Echo decided. "I think there's a combo of what we'd consider magic, along with the tech, in her universe. I think that's how she can outfight Meg. I think that's how she has offensive and defensive weapons like she has. And I don't know that we can make anything like 'em. At least not in a short time."

"Good points all, Echo," Fox said. "But I think we're all dancing around the real concern. Remember, I was told that TWO of the three entities that came through those...portals, I guess we'll have to call them, that two of them were deadly dangerous. On a planetary or even galactic level. For all her ability and ferocity, that isn't Myclestra. Only thing we'd need to do to deal with her is stay out of her reach."

"Oh, she's killable, all right," Omega stated. "It ain't easy but it's doable."

"Exactly," Fox answered, "therefore, she isn't the problem. No, from what you've told me, whatever it is that…resides in that damn Sword…is one, and this warpwraith thing is the other one. Myclestra admits that a nuclear weapon or weapons would destroy the warpwraith. What about the Sword?"

"I dunno, Fox." Omega exchanged looks with Echo, before shrugging. "I haven't the foggiest idea what it is. Or what it's really capable of doing. What I've seen it do so far, scares the ever-lovin' colly-wobbles outta me…though it did heal me after the fight in the training room, and I was in about the same shape I'd been when we came into the medlab after our FIRST fight with Myclestra. I don't think there's any real way we can deal with whatever it is. Not currently. Sorry."

<You have no need to fear me or 'deal' with me, Silver Hair.> The ancient voice smoothly insinuated itself into her mind. <Unless, that is, you harm my Bonded. Then…well, just do not. Much as you and your mate in your chosen profession, my Little One chooses to risk her life in what she does, and that is her choice. But IF she dies to such as the Warpwraith, I shall need a new Bonded.>

"OH SHIT!" Omega jerked bolt upright in her chair, sapphire eyes wide. She pointed to her head as Fox and Echo both snapped to attention. "Hmmm, uh, it would seem our conversation here is not entirely private, guys. Gimme a sec, here."

* * *

<Silver Hair, there is no one at all, including your fish-like blue friend, who can keep me out of their minds if I decide to enter. You are the most powerful human Esper I can find on your entire world, and your hardest-held barrier is a mere inconvenience at best. And I should think I have already proven

211

I bear you no ill will, have I not?>

Perhaps, but it's rude to pry into an individual's mind without permission.

<Not when one's life and the life of one dear to me might be endangered. Would you grant this 'privacy' to an enemy sworn to do you ill? Such as the Cortians, perhaps? Ha, I thought not. Nor have you, as your own memories of rescuing your belovéd betray your alliance with these Deltiri to do so. And your Agency's attitude toward me and my Bearer are… uncomfortable, at best. So far.>

Still, it's…rude. And if I may, who, or what, are you?

<I am Surlianth; at least, that is the use-name I give mortals such as you, Silver Hair, or my dear Little One. It is not my True Name. Names have power, although I doubt there is a sorcerer or wizard anywhere in this galaxy that is strong enough to bind me. I am the mind, soul and spirit of an ancient being, one who now resides within the star-forged blade borne by Myclestra. In the beginning, as the stars, galaxies and universes of the multiverse formed at the Will of the Maker, I and others like me, came into being, the splinter of a thought in the Maker's Mind. When thought and intelligence rose on the worlds of the galaxies we chose for homes, they called us Star-Drakes. Some worshipped us, others feared us.>

I…see. An image formed in her mind's eye, multiple universes springing into being at a command. In one of those universes, colossal leviathans came into existence, behemoths who briefly warred against each other, before parting, each massive titan claiming an entire galaxy as its home. Or its lair. Creatures so gigantic as to be nearly unimaginable to Omega, as an ant attempting to comprehend the fluke of a whale.

<I am OLD, Silver Hair, as old as your universe perhaps, certainly older than your entire star system. Eons ago, I tired of my lair, the galaxy that was my hoard. I allowed the powerful mortal wizards who thought to league against me to 'defeat' me and despoil me of what was mine. They could not kill me, as I did not allow it. Instead, I allowed them to place my mind,

soul and spirit into an unbreakable weapon, one forged by magicks incomprehensible to most, in the heart of a neutron star. I caused them to send the Sword forth, cast out of my own galaxy, my own universe. I wanted to travel the multiverse, experience the wonders of the Maker's brilliance, the glory of all Creation. And in this fashion, I could do so, as I could not in my original form. I saw such wonders then that even I cannot relate them to you. And to do so might damage your mind. Though,> and Omega heard the smile in the voice, <I have no doubt that you would love to hear it.>

I...see. Echo, are you getting all of this? Omega reached out and grabbed Echo's hand, nearly hard enough to hurt.

Yeah, I am. Dear God in Heaven! What...I mean how...? Holy shit! If you're so powerful, Surlianth, why don't you just destroy the warpwraith and be done with it?

<I could do so. But I am bound by my own choice into this form, this Sword. And there are limits I cannot break without destroying my vessel. And that, destroying my vessel, that would be...unfortunate.>

Why? The question came from both members of Alpha One simultaneously.

<I would then need a new vessel, a new body. Quickly, lest my being dissipate and come to an end. I could make a new body, using what materials are available, but if I did, well, this entire star system would no longer exist. After all, Star-Drakes are QUITE large.>

* * *

Both Omega and Echo paled in near-shock.

Fox was deeply concerned at that...but held his questions.

* * *

You mean— Omega quietly asked.

<Yes, child. Your star, the planets circling it, including your world and all on it, would be destroyed. I would regret that, but I WILL, I MUST preserve my own existence. It is as instinctive for me as your next breath is for you. And a drowning man, you know, fights for his next breath. I am, in some ways, an

integral part of the multiverse, and my destruction would be… unfortunate, in its own right. But being in a newly-made body would affect my outlook, my mental state, and…well, I am not sure but that I might not decide that THIS galaxy would make me a nice, new hoard. And I doubt that your Galactic Alliance would freely pay the homage I would demand as my right.>

Oh— Omega had never felt quite so small and insignificant before in her life as Surlianth showed her a vision of what might be, if the Sword was destroyed and he was reborn into a physical body.

<So, I think we should avoid that outcome, no? Besides, I quite like my Little One. I am very fond of her and would be most…unhappy…were anything to befall her resulting from any nefarious plots. And I am also fond of you and your mate, Omega. More you than him, for I believe I know you somewhat better, but if needful, either of you might make a MOST satisfactory Bearer of my Bond. I do you both great honor in that, for I do not, I will not, Bond with just anyone; I require someone of distinct courage, strength, intelligence, and moral aptitude. But I would prefer NOT to find that needful, as the end result for you could prove costly and unpleasant. And as I said, I have grown fond of you both already. So now, I leave you to your own devices. Remember, betrayal would have a cost nigh to being unbelievable. I do not intend that as a threat, simply as a statement of fact. I am what I am; it cannot be changed.>

Omega leaned back in her chair, almost limp, as she felt Surlianth's presence depart.

* * *

As the Director watched his premier team, he was worried. Whatever had just happened had affected Omega the most, likely due to her innate psi capabilities; her face was as white as a sheet. A pale Echo held onto her hand and rubbed his face with the other, and Fox realized he was deeply affected, too.

"You both look like you've seen a ghost," Fox spoke up then, seeing the change in their body language that denoted they were 'back' in his office. "I take it, that was whatever lives in that damn Sword? Are you two all right?"

"Yeah, Fox, okay but…badly rattled. There's a LOT more at stake here than we've realized until just now. Lemme give you a quick brief on the conversation we just had." Omega proceeded to inform Fox of everything she had been told by Surlianth.

"Farkakte, shit, verdammt, merde, glagaram, khro, abdab, gronk, and argdun!" Fox cursed fluently in…well, not EVERY language he knew, but quite a few of them. He was just as shaken as Alpha One. "I have GOT to get this information to Pulgey immediately, if not sooner!"

"Assuming Myclestra's 'friend' will let you do that." Omega spoke into a Director's Office that suddenly became very quiet.

* * *

Once Alpha One left his office, Fox, who had previously opaqued his bay window for security, now placed another interstellar vid-call to the same very secure and very little-known number he had called earlier.

"Franz," the white, scaly face said immediately. "Two calls in such a short time! I cannot think this bodes well."

"I don't think it does, Pul," Fox noted. "I have some more information."

"For that matter, I have news for you, as well, old friend."

"You go first, then. Maybe it'll bear on what I have to tell."

"Very well. But this may take a while…"

"Don't I know it."

* * *

"Bravo, Lima, where is Alpha One? And where is Myclestra?" Fox stepped into his assistants' office after that long call with Lord Pulgey. Pulgey was Fox's oldest friend, but this time the big Draconan had been skeptical, then incredulous, and finally very, very apprehensive.

"Echo is working on paperwork in the Alpha Line Room. Omega and Myclestra are down in the Weapons Development

215

Lab with Madrid. Omega and Madrid are going nuts, trying to figure out how someone squeezed a plasma rifle's firepower into a pistol smaller than a standard proto-cyclotron blaster." Bravo looked up from his computer to answer Fox. "Omega and Myclestra seem to be getting along like the proverbial 'house on fire,' Boss."

"I've noticed." Fox's eyes were hooded in thought. "I think I'll wander down there and see how they're coming along on that."

"Boss, quick question?"

"Go ahead, Lima."

"This woman, Myclestra, does she really use magic, you know, abracadabra stuff?"

"Yes, she does. Have you seen the video from the training room with her and four Alpha Line teams, including Alpha One and Two?"

"No, sir." Both assistants chorused the response.

"Watch it." Fox sighed. "Then ask yourself that again. I don't think you'll need my answer, zun." He turned and headed for the Weapons Lab.

* * *

"The chamber is the most critical part," Myclestra said as she shone a bright light down the barrel of her disassembled plas-pistol. "The chamber is integral with the barrel. The least amount of impurities in the barrel or chamber can make the charge flare when the lasers fuse it. If there is any weakness in the barrel, well, you are then holding an atomic grenade. IF you are lucky, only the charge in the chamber will detonate and IF you have decent armor, you shall only need a cyber-arm. IF you are not so lucky, the entire magazine will blow, leaving the user a smoking hole in the ground and killing anyone within, oh, say thirty or forty ur-lans or so. Anyone not protected by at least a full-up battlesuit further away might survive the explosion, only to die later of the elemental...poisons...released."

"Radiation," Omega supplied, as Fox walked up to the open doorway of the lab, then watched in silence, unwilling to interrupt their brainstorming.

Because I know, he thought, *sooner or later, my people are going to have to work with that strange woman to stop this warpwraith, this tayvl, this shlekht mazzik, this...evil demon. Because from all I've been told, what she wields may be the only thing short of HaShem that CAN.* So he waited and watched.

"Ah! Yes, that is the term," Myclestra averred.

"Dear God!" Madrid exclaimed. "How often are these weapons used?"

"They are issued if medium to heavy resistance is expected. I stole this one when I fled the Shaeldrithan Masters. Losses among shock troops and slaves are either acceptable, or of no concern."

"You said 'thirty or forty ur-lans,' Myclestra," Omega was paying very close attention to the field-stripped plas-pistol. "How far is an ur-lan?"

"The length of my arm, Omega, similar to your world's 'yards' or 'meters,' if I have understood correctly what I have learned since my arrival. Very little difference." The tall alien shrugged. "I know what it does and how to maintain it in the field. I know what happens when one fails, for I have known it happen; I was far enough away to survive, but I had a clear sense of it. Do not ask me the 'whys' or 'hows' because I fear I do not know. Alontorans are...discouraged from learning such things."

"I can imagine," Omega murmured at that.

"Yes, I expect you can, now," Myclestra responded with a smile. "And that...that, alone, is appreciated, my friend."

"Do they deliberately discourage you from learning?" Omega wondered then.

"Yes. No one wants highly educated slaves," Myclestra gave Omega a bitter smile. "It tends to result in rebellions and dead masters. That hurts sales."

"I say, then, Myclestra, have your people ever rebelled against the Masters that, well, that created you?" Madrid's face twisted in distress at her cold, flat tone.

"Not in thousands of years. Rebel against lesser beings the Masters sell us to, yes, that happens. Often. Against the Shaeldrith? No. They truly are inhuman, with powers and abilities you cannot imagine. It is well that they are actually so few. And are more interested in being merchants than conquerors. We do not rebel against them; we merely take the most desperate chances available to simply…escape their reach. Their powers are near to god-like. Were it not for Surlianth bending his every power to aid my own escape, I likely would still be there, screaming under their tortures. Or worse."

"How do you deal with that, Myclestra?" Omega asked as she watched the alien woman quickly and skillfully reassemble her pistol.

"One tries never to be taken alive. Or one never attempts to escape. Not all of my sisters are unhappy with their station in this life. Only between a third to a quarter of all Alontorans even wish, deep in their hearts, to be free. Few attempt escape from the Masters. Fewer succeed. Life for us is often brutal and short. And then the tech-wizards make more of us."

* * *

Fox still stood just outside the door, listening closely to the conversation going on around the workbench. *Damnation,* he thought in deep sympathy, remembering his own past. *Godlike Nazis. HaShem help them all.*

"Well, I think I understand the concepts, here," Madrid remarked then, interrupting Fox's brooding. "But I don't think this is a weapon we'd want to try to rush to completion, because as Myclestra here points out, it's a bloody damn big mess if you get it wrong."

"No, that is a wise statement," Myclestra agreed, as Fox slipped through the door into the weapons lab, continuing his efforts to be silent and avoid interrupting their work. "Still, if it gives you some ideas about what you CAN do, it will have been worth it."

"That, I think it does," Madrid said. "And you say this works on this creature?"

"The Warpwraith," Myclestra said with a nod. "He is susceptible to fire, and from what I have been told, fire is simply one form of plasma."

"It is," Omega confirmed. "So…yeah. I'm starting to get some ideas, too, Madrid. How far along did you ever get with miniaturizing the plasma rifle?"

"Pretty far, all things considered," Madrid averred, "though nothing like this pistol. Still, I think we're thinking in similar directions, Omega, old girl. I've got it down to standard rifle size, by using compressed helium nodules and a miniaturized semi-Medusan array, as well as factoring in an accelerator similar to what's in the proto-cyclotron blasters; that also increased the range, while we were about it. I'm thinking that Myclestra, here, may have just given us our breakthrough in further miniaturization, though. That will help considerably, at least in future."

"Good," Myclestra remarked. "I take it, you have something similar in a rifle, then?"

"Not far off," Madrid said. "It used to be just one step up from a flamethrower, using hydrogen for fuel instead of napalm, but Omega here had several ideas when she first came on board with us, and it jumpstarted our work on the thing. Now it's maybe about an order of magnitude less in power than your pistol, but that's only because we were working on the further miniaturization."

"That sounds great," Omega determined. "Should we demonstrate for Myclestra? She has the knowledge of what can harm the warpwraith, we don't. So if it's a weapon we can use against it, she'd know."

"I think that is a likely plan," Madrid agreed. "Especially if the creature can be harmed by fire and plasma."

"That is acceptable to me," Myclestra decided. "Director Fox, do you have any problem with that?"

"No, I don't," Fox said, stepping forward, as Madrid startled badly; Omega just grinned tightly. "I think that whatever we can do to hurt it, to slow it down or stop it, is going to be a good thing. I just don't know if we can do enough."

"It will be difficult," Myclestra agreed. "Have no doubt of that. But I think our chances have increased considerably by combining our capabilities."

"Myclestra…"

"Yes, Director Fox?"

"Is that which your Sword carries…will he, she, it…"

"He."

"Will he be involved in the fight?"

<Most certainly, Director Fox,> came the inaudible answer. Myclestra and Omega merely nodded; Madrid startled badly yet again. <This vile creature is an abomination, a stain upon all Creation, and I will not suffer it to live any longer than we can manage it. And you may call me Surlianth, as I have invited Silver Hair to do. My Little One, here, is very good, but she does not have the ability to defeat the monster alone. Nor do any of you, not quickly, at least. Destroy it you could, but it would lay waste to a goodly part of your world first, and reveal your organization to those who are not yet ready to know of it. Even I would have difficulty doing so alone, and would risk dissolution in the doing.> Surlianth paused. <I know you fear me, and I understand why. And as Myclestra has said, such fear is reasonable. Especially in light of what I have told the lovely and intelligent Silver Hair and her mate. Understand something important, however.>

"What?" Fox wondered aloud, aware by their reactions that the being had spoken to everyone in the room.

<What I told Silver Hair of myself was never intended as a threat, merely a sort of warning. I have been with Myclestra for many years now, and our bond is deep. I am extremely fond of her — the word 'love' might even apply, I suspect — and I want nothing to happen to her. Should something happen to her, my grief, after all these long millennia alone, would be deep, and my response strong and swift. And emotionally

driven. So there is that...>

"But there's more," Omega interjected. "All that other stuff you told me about re-manifesting a body."

<Yes, my little Silver Hair. And again, I did not tell you that as a threat, but as a warning. You see, I know myself all too well, and I know the...I believe you term it, a 'knee-jerk' response...which I should have, in the event of the Sword's dissolution. For almost all living creatures, survival is a basic instinct, and I am no different. But I know how much material would be required to remake my body, and I know the temptation that would come with once again inhabiting the body of a Star Drake. It would be catastrophic for your star system. And I do not actually want any of that to happen; I am growing fond of you and your mate, as well as my Little One, here. And certainly your...'family,' the people I see in your mind, the people you have gathered about you...which I also see includes Director Fox...should have my protection, in addition. I told you what I did...because I am trying to prevent it happening. Neither Myclestra nor myself wishes anything terrible to befall this world, let alone by my doing, or we should not be here; we had actually already discussed it, long before we met you. And so I tell you in order to prevent such a possibility. Do you understand? Especially you, Director Fox?>

"I...think I may be starting to," Fox murmured then, considering what Omega had told him earlier in the light of this new information. "You're trying to warn us off a path, a plan of action, that might lead that way. A way none of us want. Including you."

<Exactly. I do not wish your fear of me to become a kind of self-fulfilling prophecy. I do know you have called your friend, the being in charge of the galactic government, twice already, so as to give him the entire story...but I also know you tempered that story with how my Little One and I are attempting to defeat the Warpwraith, how we brought you warning of it.> There was a pause, then Surlianth added, <For

whatever it is worth, I wanted Myclestra to stop and discuss matters with Silver Hair and her Echo, after the first fight with the Wraith, for I sensed that was what they wished, as well.> Surlianth paused again, and Myclestra flushed slightly, tucking her chin. Then, humor in his mental voice, he continued. <But she is impulsive and sometimes too eager for battle. And so she nearly forced them to kill her, instead.>

"He speaks truth," Myclestra said quietly. "He did try to get me to stop and talk. But I could only think of getting to the monster and destroying it." She turned to Omega and knelt. "Can you and your mate forgive me, my battle-sister?"

"I think they already had, when they brought you to our medlab for healing," Fox noted, when a surprised Omega gaped at the kneeling woman, speechless.

"Um, yeah, pretty much," Omega admitted then, finding her speech center once more, as she put out a hand and raised Myclestra to her feet. "I mean, by that point, we'd kinda figured out that the wraith-thing killed those two men, not you, and…"

"Wait. What men? You mean the guards at the power depot?"

"Power depot?" Fox wondered. "Oh, oh, oh. Yes, the weapons storage unit. The warpwraith would have been trying to get inside, to an energy source?"

"Yes," Myclestra confirmed. "Yes, I had temporarily forgotten about them; forgive me. It was, indeed, a terrible death, and one that I was too late to prevent, though I would have, had it been in my power to do."

"Right," Omega said, nodding. "Echo an' I KNEW you hadn't done that. It just didn't feel right to assign it to you, but it DID feel…appropriate," she pulled a face, "to the big black creature, the wraith-creature. And the things you said, well, Ace an' I were pretty convinced by the time we tried to talk, that you were actually chasing it, that it was your perp." She shrugged. "We really did just wanna talk, and I was tryin' to introduce myself, though I guess, after what happened at the storage unit, it mighta sounded different…"

"Ah. And I misunderstood," Myclestra realized, "thinking that you were attempting to assert authority again…when likely, you were simply trying to break up the fight before, not knowing the danger of the Warpwraith…"

"Alla that," Omega averred.

<And so the battle-sisters finally come to an understanding,> Surlianth said with a deep chuckle. <It is high time.>

* * *

"Surlianth, since you're feeling talkative," Omega tried, "can I ask you some things? It sorta pertains to what we're trying to do here. And yes, Fox, I want you AND Madrid here to hear it, 'cause I got a wild-ass idea…if it would even work. But only Surlianth can tell me if it would. And then Madrid and I would have to figure out how to make it happen."

Fox shrugged. "You have excellent ideas, tekhter, so I suppose I'm game to hear it, if Master Surlianth is willing to discuss it with you."

<And I am,> came the response. <Go ahead, Silver Hair.>

"Well, we're looking at weapons that can affect the creature," Omega pointed out, "and we have ways we can probably beef those up, no problem. What I'm worried about is…wait. Lemme back up and punt, because I might be off in the weeds about something…"

"I have no idea what you just said," Myclestra murmured.

<Fear not, Little One; I do, for she shows me in her mind. To punt is to kick an oddly-shaped ball in a kind of war game; it gains the kicking team time to regroup. Off in the weeds is just what it sounds like, lost in the wilderness, at least mentally.>

"Oh. All right."

<Keep going, Silver Hair.>

"So, if I've understood Myc right, this wraith uses ley lines to travel…"

<It does not have to, but yes, it can do so. It can cover ground more rapidly, so.>

"Wait," Madrid said. "What the hell is a ley line?"

"It's a magical sort of term that turns out to have some

physical reality," Omega explained. "It's a telluric current, a flow of electricity that runs through the soil, down at least as far as the upper mantle, and runs through bodies of water, too, but the flow of water changes things…"

<Yes, and interferes with the Wraith's ability to use it,> Surlianth added.

"So it's a real thing?" Madrid wondered.

"Yeah, it's been measured, and even used to run stuff," Omega averred. "And it's stronger in some places than in others, and certain places just naturally generate these currents. Some human activity can generate them, but most of it is driven by the geomagnetic field, and that's also affected by solar activity, so it can vary…"

"All right, I see," Madrid said.

"You are very learnéd, battle-sister," Myclestra said, seeming almost in awe. "I have only ever heard the mages speak as you are, now."

<Yes, she is, and very intelligent, Little One. You chose your battle-sister well.>

Omega blushed almost scarlet, but managed to continue.

"So this warpwraith is using the electric currents to power it as it goes from place to place," Omega observed. "Right?"

"Correct," Myclestra confirmed. "The stronger the line… this 'current,' as you call it…the faster and farther he can go."

<True.>

"And is there anything that can prevent it from accessing the current?"

<Not readily, no,> Surlianth replied.

"Is there anything that can prevent it from using the current to move?"

<I suppose that depends upon your definition of 'prevent,'> Surlianth decided. < It can dimension-step and avoid projectiles, or beam weapons that are too narrow.>

"Huh. Sort of like a Glu'g'ik," Omega murmured, thinking swiftly.

<If it attacks, if it casts the black flame, it is tied to that

spot for a moment. The energy it uses to do so comes from itself, and it cannot manage enough energy to cast the flame AND dimension-step,> Surlianth explained. <But only for a moment. And it CAN teleport; however, it must draw its own energies to do so, and it will be weakened for a time after it arrives at its destination.>

"Which means it's likely to head for a power source, whether a ley line or something else," Omega reasoned.

"Yes," Myclestra confirmed. "Which is what it did when it left the…the weapons depot. Optimally for a Warpwraith, it will do these things while either at the height of its power, or while feeding on a power source. And what you may not have realized, battle-sister, is that this creature actually prefers this power source to be…living beings."

Omega, Fox, and Madrid gaped in horror. Echo, who was absently following the discussion via the nd't'lq, suddenly focused in on the conversation, and Omega could feel his horror as well.

"You mean," Omega began. "The two soldiers, the guards at the Air Force base who were killed…"

"No, probably not, actually," Myclestra said then. "Had the Warpwraith fed on them, there would have been nothing left to find. It even incorporates the bodies into itself…after it feeds on the souls."

"Shit," Fox cursed.

<No, there is no waste left to expel,> a bleakly-humorous Surlianth said at that. <A Warpwraith's 'digestion' is… extremely efficient.>

* * *

It took a few minutes for the now-pale Earth humans to assimilate that and deal with it intellectually and emotionally, and while they did, both Myclestra and Surlianth waited patiently, fully comprehending the horror they felt. Finally Omega continued her line of questioning.

"So…so we, we need to be able to hold it in place," she managed to get out.

<Yes,> Surlianth confirmed. <Your force fields are apt to hold it as is…provided he is not on a ley line or the like…but it will be difficult, and the power required is likely to draw him to you, rather than your controlling him.>

"That's good news and bad news," Omega decided.

<Yes, and I see the notion taking shape in your mind, Silver Hair, and yes, it will likely work…until such time as I must take control of my energies to eliminate the abomination from All Creation.>

"Yeah, and I get that," Omega said. "I was just hoping you'd be willing to work with us to figure out how to…" she shrugged, "pin him in place, long enough for you TO zap him."

<This, I believe we can do,> Surlianth agreed, <provided we can devise a way to store my power in your weapons for the few seconds it will require me to unlink from your equipment, join with my Bond mate in battle, and deliver the maximum force of which I am capable in this form.>

"Oh, well," Madrid piped up, "that's where I come in."

"First, weren't you going to give Myclestra and Surlianth a demonstration?" Fox wondered.

* * *

Madrid set up the weapons test room for the demonstration, which Omega would perform, while Fox ensured that Myclestra had the appropriate sensory input to perceive the demonstration. Surlianth explained that he would be able to perceive it through all the observers, including Myclestra and Omega herself. Then Fox settled back to watch, and was soon joined by Echo, who had wandered down from the Alpha Line Room to watch, having finished his paperwork.

Upon Omega's request, Madrid set up a 'sporting clays' scenario, much like the one upon which she had been tested when first introduced to the Agency. Unlike the plasma rifle she had wielded at that time, what she currently held was something roughly the same size as a proto-cyclotron blaster, but with a longer barrel-slash-nozzle and an extendable, adjustable-angle stock. This latter she quickly adapted to her own body while Madrid finished programming the clay pigeon scenario, then Echo cycled the blast doors on the test room and Omega entered.

"Don't forget your goggle-glasses, Meg," he told her as she walked past him. "Otherwise you'll be seeing spots for the next three hours."

"Oh, good point," Omega said, pausing to drop a kiss on his lips. "Thanks for reminding me."

Moments later, the blast door was locked, Omega donned the eyewear and hoisted the weapon, and the others watched.

"Ready, old girl?" Madrid asked through the microphone.

"Yup," Omega replied, hefting the plasma rifle to her shoulder, as she took a forward-and-back stance. "PULL!"

Madrid hit the initiate button.

Solid holographic clay pigeons began flying into the room from all angles.

Omega calmly brought the stock to her cheek, sighting along it, as she swung the weapon from point to point, pressing the trigger each time.

Jets of plasma, almost beam-straight, shot from the barrel, incinerating each clay in turn, as fast as the computer could fire them into the room.

"Pow…pow…pow…pow…" Omega could just be heard murmuring to herself over the whine and sizzle of the repeated discharges.

It went on for nearly five minutes, with nary a missed clay, before the simulation ended. Omega lowered and safed the rifle, and upon Madrid's nod, Echo moved to the blast door to cycle it open.

"I like this one," Omega said, patting the stock. "Can we add it to Alpha One's arsenal?"

"If you want to, of course, Omega, my dear," Madrid said with a smile. "I don't know that you can 'hot-rod' it much; it's already as hot as I've dared make it, at least until I add a few more bells and whistles. But yes, we do have a goodly number of them, so I can supply Echo with one as well, if he wants it. And yes, Fox, I can supply all of Alpha Line, and the rest of the Praetorians…and a significant number of the Field agents, as well, though not all of them, by any means. But I had a sneaking suspicion that this particular weapon would be of use at SOME point, so I had a good two or three dozen crates' worth manufactured. We have somewhere in the vicinity of two gross to work with; I'll double-check the inventory, because it might be closer to three gross. I don't think so, but I'll check."

"Four hundred and some? That would be nice," Omega murmured. "Still, almost two hundred an' ninety ain't shabby."

"Then I think we have part of the system," Fox decided. "We do need the boosted force field, as Omega says…and possibly a decoy, just in case."

<I like the way you think, Director Fox,> Surlianth declared.

Myclestra's eyebrows shot upward, and Fox grinned wickedly.

* * *

Hours and then Division days passed with no word on anything odd enough to be the Warpwraith. Fox began assembling the strike force he felt would be needed to stop, drive and eventually trap and destroy the monster, placing them under the joint leadership of Alpha One.

Facilities assigned Myclestra a small apartment just down the hall from Echo and Omega's quarters, and the tall blonde and taller redhead were often found together. Obviously Myclestra could neither read nor watch any type of television or video, but then Omega had the idea of introducing her to audiobooks. Myclestra was fascinated and spent an entire day listening to Tolkien's *The Lord of the Rings*.

When she wasn't listening to nearly hundred-year-old novels, she worked out with Omega, teaching her the various fighting styles the Alontoran Fetches used; she, in turn, taught what she could to Echo, and repaid the favor to Myclestra by teaching her martial arts moves.

Sparring together proved that Omega had been right, back

when she had watched the security video from the Colorado gas station. Myclestra was substantially stronger — partly because she was bigger — but not quite as fast as Omega was, although she always pushed Omega to her absolute limits. Echo remarked more than once that the pair of them were starting to look like a superhero movie's special effects. Omega noted that sometimes a light flared on Myclestra's brow, then faded, and wondered if there were some sort of temporary enhancements upon which the Alontoran could call.

As more and more of the strike team assembled at Headquarters in preparation for whatever was coming, Alpha One, Alpha Two and Myclestra began to hold briefings for teams and individuals about what they were going to be doing and what, exactly, would be their target. Often, these briefings were met with incredulity, disbelieving stares and outright scorn. These attitudes raised problems and issues at times. Many of those attitudes were realigned after watching the video from the Training Room of Myclestra flattening four of Division One's premier Alpha Line teams, including Alpha One and Two, in under two minutes. Of course, there were always a few who either didn't see the video, insisted it was faked somehow, or that the Alpha Line teams had laid down to make Myclestra appear more dangerous than she was. Usually a quiet chat with Echo or Omega sorted them out, but not always. There were always some people who had to learn the hard way.

* * *

"Yeah, I've seen that ridiculous video," Agent Rho scoffed to his partner, Agent Scout. That partnership was a bit of an odd couple from the get-go. Rho was one of the biggest human Agents in all of Division One, standing six foot, ten inches in his sock feet and weighing in at two-hundred-ninety-five pounds of solid muscle. A very black-skinned African-American, light gleamed off his bare scalp, dark brown eyes were friendly or cold as needed and his Suit did little to hide his massive build. His recruitment into the Agency pre-empted a promising career in pro football, but he never seemed to regret it.

Scout could not have been a bigger contrast to him physically. She was of Irish descent, a pale, freckled, red-haired, green-eyed beauty who put more than one person to thinking of the Tuatha de Danann of Irish legend. She was a slender five foot two, about a hundred-twenty or so soaking wet, and often referred to herself as "fun-sized."

"Rho, you really think Echo or Omega would falsify something like that? Or that Director Fox would let them do something like it, either?" Her voice was a light alto compared to the deep bass rumble of her partner. "And didn't you hear, this Myclestra has offered to spar with any who doubt her ability."

"Okay, yeah, I'll grant you she's probably way quicker than I am. Hell, half the Division is quicker than I am!" He added weights to the bench press bar, bringing the weight to an even five hundred pounds. He knew Scout could never spot for him, so he looked around to see who else was available in the weight room, just as Myclestra walked through the door, clad in her usual skimpy attire of skin-tight spandex shorts and her black leotard. Her hair was gathered in a top-knot tail and a pair of mirrored eye-shades covered her blind eyes. Rho smiled wickedly.

"Oh, shit." Scout muttered under her breath behind him. "Don't do it, Rho, just say no."

"Hey!" Rho called out, ignoring his partner. "Ain't you that Myclestra woman everyone's been talking about?" The alien woman cocked her head quizzically at him for a second before nodding.

"I am. Why?"

"If you're as strong as I've been told, you think you could spot for me?"

"Spot for you?"

"Yeah, come over here and watch while I'm lifting, 'case anything slips, ya know."

"Ah. And you are Agent Rho, from the Atlanta Office, and

she is your partner, Agent Scout. You wish me to 'spot' for you? Very well. I shall do so." She stalked over to the bench press, immediately riveting the attention of every humanoid male in the room and a couple of the females, including Scout, as well. Rho swallowed hard as she stopped at the head of the bench. "Now, are you ready? I wish to use this apparatus myself, if no one else is awaiting it."

"Uh, um, yeah." Rho slid under the bar and settled his hands on it before slowly lifting it from its rack on the bench. "Okay, this is five hunnert pounds. You sure you can handle it if need be?"

"Oh, me boyo, this canna end well," Scout murmured to herself. "Use some sense, mate."

"I can. Easily. You may begin."

Rho was every bit as strong as he thought he was, and he easily pumped out ten solid reps with the bar. After the tenth one, he stopped and held the bar up.

"Hey, can you rack this for me?"

"Certainly." Myclestra reached over with one hand, took the bar at the balance point in the middle and slowly lifted it out of Rho's grasp, raising it effortlessly to her shoulder level and holding it for a slow five count. Still holding it straight out, she looked down at Rho and gave him a cold smile. She gently racked the bar without making a sound. Of course, a pin dropping at that moment would have sounded like an avalanche as everyone stared. "Are you done now?"

"How the hell did you do that? There's no way someone built like a porn star can do that! No damn way!" Rho jumped to his feet, the dark skin of his face hiding some of his flush from exertion and embarrassment. "Where's the trick? Someone using a portable tractor beam or something?"

"I tolerate much, but you, Mortal, tread dangerously close to insulting me. I tell no lies and use no 'tricks.' I do what I do, no more, but also no less. Now, again, are you finished?" That flat, cold voice should have frozen the sweat beads on Rho's chest, but he wasn't listening.

"Lady, or whatever the hell you are, you ain't pulling your bullshit on me! You may have fooled Alpha One somehow, but you ain't fooli — urk!"

The video replay later showed a light flaring on Myclestra's brow. Impossibly fast, she reached back and grabbed a spare lifting bar and wrapped its seven-foot length tightly around Rho's chest, pinning his arms to his side. Unbalanced by the forty-five-pound bar trapping his arms at his side, he staggered and half-fell, half-sat onto the bench. Scout jumped and grabbed his shoulder, keeping him from falling over.

Myclestra reached over and grasped the bar around his chest and effortlessly tossed him ten feet in the air, catching him above her head and holding him there as he stared down in shock at her.

"I think you are done for the day. At least until you can find someone capable of freeing you from the slight impediment this bar represents. Now, go away. If you are still bound when I have finished my workout, I shall consider freeing you from your predicament. Assuming, that is, that you trouble me no further." She carefully lowered him to the floor, considerately sitting him on one of the extra chairs around the room. She stepped over to the racked weight plates and added an additional five hundred pounds to the bench press, settled under it, and began her workout.

Other than Rho — who was rather stuck there — and Scout, who stayed by her partner, the weight room emptied quickly.

* * *

"You look tired, Myclestra." Omega watched the alien woman closely as she shoveled food into her mouth at first lunch. Myclestra's appetite was enough to put even Omega to shame at the table. But Alpha One had invited her over for the meal, thereby ensuring she ate, and ate well; she had been a bit moody of late.

"Hmm?" she swallowed, then added, "No, not tired, exactly. I do not like being cooped up in this place. Your 'space-warps' disturb my senses somewhat. I know it is larger inside than outside, but at times, part of my mind says it is bigger than it should be. There is no sense of time. I may not see the Sun, but I feel the warmth of its passage, from light to dark to light. That is lost inside this warren of rooms and passages where none should be. It is…uncomfortable."

"And incidents like Rho and Scout don't help much either, do they?" Echo's warm voice broke the silence that filled the room then.

"No, they do not," Myclestra growled. "Were I allowed what is considered 'proper' training on my homeworld, there would be a few heads on the combat training room floor and this nonsense of doubting me would be ended. Abruptly, in some cases."

"Hey, battle-sister," Omega reached across the table and gently took Myclestra's hand, stopping her fork in mid-stab, "I know, trust me, I know. I've been there, too. You're not a machine, you know. You have feelings and emotions, not that different from me. If nothing else, I learned that from Surlianth when he healed us."

"Omega, Echo, if I release these frustrations, currently held with bitter control, people will die. Especially idiots like that Agent Rho. He fears me, justly so, but in that one, fear may turn to hate. I will not allow him behind me with any weapon."

"You did kinda humiliate him, you know." Echo was calm and relaxed as he brought the point up.

"So?" the alien woman snarled. "He doubted me, all but called me a liar to my face. Aloud, so that all in this… gymnasium…could hear! I wanted to pull his arms and legs off, slowly, for his insult!" The table bounced slightly as she slammed a fist down.

"Myclestra, dear sister, it sounds like you need a good cry or something." Omega held her other hand firmly.

"I am Alontoran, Omega, Echo. I have no eyes, not truly. I cannot weep, I have no tears to shed. I am as the Masters have made me and each one of my sisters. When a human like you — yes, I know you are a Splice, but you are as human as any — when your emotions overwhelm you, you can weep, cry, rage at the uncaring gods. My tears are made of blood; they run down my cheeks as the blood of mine enemies drips from my face."

"Dear God, Myclestra," Omega half whispered, "You're free now. You don't have to do that."

"You still do not realize what I am, battle-sister. When these 'Cortians' kidnapped him, had your Echo been a captive of my sister Fetches and our Slaver, you might have recovered him. Might. But had you not done so, a year later he would have still been screaming, as we would have been directed to destroy him slowly, not shedding the first drop of blood until a year passed. And, long before then, he would have told us all he knows, willingly, anything to stop the pain." A very uncomfortable silence descended on the table. "Then, he would have been given to those my Masters considered true artists in the art of inflicting pain, using his screams as you would use soothing music."

"Dear God." Echo's brown eyes reflected the horror of the brutality the Cortians had inflicted on him many months ago. "You mean it's worse than what I went through?"

"The Cortians are amateurs at best, my friend, fumble-fingered idiots in the art of inflicting pain," Myclestra spoke into that leaden silence. "Forgive me. I give offense to those who would befriend me. I shall return to my own quarters then, that you may console each the other."

"NO, Myclestra, wait!" Omega called after the tall alien as she nearly ran from their dining room and shot out the front door. "Dammit, she's just so freaking FAST!"

"Shit. Now what?" Echo leaned back in his chair. "Do I need to have Fox get Rho and Scout the hell outta here?"

"No, I don't think so. Myclestra meant it when she said she would do us no harm. Though I don't know that they're going to be much use in what's coming, if they can't believe it's real." Omega crossed her arms under her breasts and tapped her chin in thought. "Stress has been defined as the inability to choke the ever-loving shit outta somebody who desperately needs choking. And that's where Myclestra's stress is coming from. But I think I know what to do."

"And what's that, baby?" Echo asked...very cautiously.

"The same thing women have done over the centuries when someone angered them that much."

"Well? Spit it out."

"They go shopping, of course. And then they go out with their girlfriends, dressed to the nines to show all you poor males what you're missing." Omega smirked at her husband. "Imma gonna take her shopping, and then to a fancy dinner. Let her get out in the fresh air for a good long while."

"Oh, Lord help us," Echo said as he paled slightly. "Will New York still be standing when you two are finished?"

"Most likely."

* * *

"You want to what?" Myclestra's tone was flat and hard, as Omega stood there, smiling.

"I want us to have a girl's day out," Omega explained. "A bit of pampering. I think you might not have ever had that, by the sound, and I'd like you to know what it's like."

"I...am not sure what that involves, battle-sister." Myclestra's face was as blank as her tone.

"Do you trust me to lead you through it, to guide you?"

"Yes, but..."

"But what?"

"I would rather not embarrass you, and I might, from the sound, let alone what Surlianth is telling me you have in mind. And...he is laughing at me." Myclestra looked uncomfortable.

<Not AT you, Little One. Never AT you. At the reaction you are having now, yes, but not at YOU. You are uncertain, child, and that is so unlike you that I am unused to seeing it. It is amusing, after a fashion. But Silver Hair is right. I think this would be good for you. Very good.>

"I think, if you'll relax, and realize you're among friends

and people who WANT to pamper you, it'll be okay," Omega said, still smiling. "Have you ever had a massage?"

"From a…another battle-sister, when I was mildly injured, yes. We had gotten separated from our Slaver and the other Fetches, and we…" She paused. "You recall that I told you we, as Alontorans and Fetches, had no one, and why?"

"Yes."

"We were friends, well, more than friends, we had become lovers. We, Aerwanath and I, managed to keep it hidden… until we got back to the Slaver. He had used things like your drones, monstrous eyes floating in magical crystal spheres. They were…are efficient spies. And even for an Alontoran, they are almost impossible to spot. And we…both of us had become distracted, each by the other. We did not see them, but the Slaver saw what the Eyes saw. When we returned, the Slaver reported to the Overseers, and…before long, the Masters knew. She was taken to the Masters by other, more horrible servants, the Khainceans. Even the memory of them is dreadful; ask me no more of them. She was taken before the Masters and mind-raped, before being physically torn apart and her soul devoured. She did not live long. Fortunately."

"Damn. How did THAT turn out, and how did you manage not to wind up following behind her?"

"Ah. The Masters well understand the fear and terror that anticipation can bring. I knew they would have stripped every secret from her as they slowly flayed off her skin, and that I was, indeed, next," Myclestra admitted. "Knowing what had happened to her, I…" She broke off, head bowed and quiet for a long moment, then finally said, "That horrid expectation is what moved me to escape. Better to be killed attempting to flee than to suffer what they did to my poor Aerwanath. Or worse." She was silent for a long moment before Omega gently broke the silence.

"So what did you do then?"

"So that night I broke into the armory to steal weapons and equipment, and that is where I found Surlianthet. He told me he had been hanging on the wall for quite some time."

<Several of your centuries, children, I think. The time tended to get away from me, and I am uncertain exactly how long it was. I have a tendency to kill bearers I do not like, so the Masters grew tired of having their favorite minions incinerated. But when Myclestra entered, I knew we would be an excellent match for one another. More, I was bored to tears; that was not the exploration of the Maker's worlds I had wished, so I called to her. I still do not know if she understood what she heard. But she reached for me, and I finished the healing of her shoulder. And we departed together.>

"And he helped me evade those sent after me," Myclestra wound down the tale in succinct fashion. "Shortly thereafter, he helped me find work as a bounty hunter with a trustworthy client — meaning one who would not sell me back to the Masters — and here I am." She sighed, then added, "But…yes, my Aerwanath, oh, Omega, she was rather like you, pale and beautiful, at least to me. She worked my injured shoulder and was able to loosen it after I popped it back into place. Her own leg was injured, but both of us would heal if we could only get back to the Slaver's conveyance, his battle floater. So we worked together to do so. And to enable me to help her walk, my shoulder had to function. So she massaged it."

"How did it feel?"

"Once the initial soreness was worked through, it was… nice, I think."

"Okay. Now imagine having that done just when you needed to relax."

"Oh. That…yes, I think I like the sound of that." Myclestra paused and cocked her head. "Would you be the one giving me this…massage?"

"Oh, well, I'd thought we could go to a spa, and get facials and stuff, too," Omega said, startled. "But, um, well, I could. I'm a certified massage therapist. So is Echo," she added.

"I should prefer you to do it," Myclestra noted. "And then we could follow on to other matters, perhaps. More enjoyable matters?"

"You mean the shopping?"

"I was thinking more in terms of finding a bedroom and perhaps, lovemaking? The shopping could wait."

"Myclestra, you do need to understand, if you haven't picked up on it already," Omega murmured, keeping her voice gentle. "I'm very, very flattered, but…Echo is my one and only. He's the other part of me. It hasn't been that long since we had to deal with another woman going after HIM, and trying to interfere in our marriage…"

"He might join us, if he wishes. I can do that. The reason I have the form I do is that one of the first uses of the Alontorans was as sex slaves. It was not the worst usage of us. We were repurposed into battle slaves when war broke out between several of the Masters' client races, and the Masters found that we made better warriors than lovers…especially when the lovers are not allowed to love. I think we took out our hate on our enemies."

"That…makes sense," Omega murmured. "But no, honey. Never mind I don't go that way, Echo and I don't…don't share our bed with others. I don't want to hurt you, but…you're too late, Myc. My heart was given…a long time ago, I think. Even before I met him."

Myclestra's breath caught. Then she slowly nodded.

"Aha. And now I understand some of the memories that were shared with me," she replied, voice soft. "It was when this Slug brainwashed you, implanted the information about your target in you, was it not? That was when you fell in love with Echo. For he was your target."

"I think so, yes," Omega sighed. "Between that and his torture, I…well. Let's just say, there never really was anybody before him, for sure."

"And likely will not be, after, should you outlive him."

"Which I probably won't do, unless we get as far as retiring together," Omega noted, jaw firming temporarily.

"I…understand," Myclestra said, and laid a light hand

on Omega's shoulder. "Then battle-sisters we are, and shall remain, but we shall be no more than that." She rose. "Let us have this 'girl's day out,' then, my battle-sister. I will share this with you, at least. And you shall guide me through it. What should we do first?"

"I think the first thing is…we need to make you look like an Earthling."

"What? Oh, you mean my clothing? Or my eyes?"

"Yeah, your clothes. We need to get you into jeans and a t-shirt, so you'll pass on the street as an Earth woman. You're tall, but that happens sometimes, so I think we can make this work. Your shades will be fine for your eyes. And if anyone notices, well, we just tell them the truth, or rather, part of it. You ARE actually blind, after all."

"Lead on, then."

* * *

It took a while, but eventually Omega found jeans and a t-shirt that fit Myclestra's tall, curvaceous frame, and felt comfortable to her. It took more convincing to get her to leave Surlianth behind.

"Honey, do you have any idea how fast the police would be on top of us if you carried a big-ass sword through Manhattan?"

"I thought you were the police."

"We are, but we aren't the ONLY police," Omega explained. "And remember, most people on Earth don't know about us yet. So we have to blend in, not stand out."

<She is correct, Little One. I am not happy about it either, but I have no real way to disguise myself, and I am much too large to hide under your clothing. Which I note fits you quite well, if the view I see through Omega's eyes is anything to go by. It is most appealing, I think.>

Myclestra flushed slightly.

"Are you all right remaining here, Old Snake?"

<For the time, yes. You will return, and Silver Hair will help you get 'gussied up,' I believe she puts it, and then you and she and Agent Echo will go out to dinner. And then you

will be back. It is only temporary, a few hours, less than a day. I have, as I mentioned earlier, been alone for many hundreds of years; this is nothing. And you can tell me all about it when you return, and I shall live it through your mind.>

"All right," Myclestra sighed. "Am I ready to go, then, my battle-sister?"

"I think you look great," Omega said with a grin. "It's getting well into morning out there, so we have the whole day before us. Let's go."

They headed out in the 'Vette, with Echo's full knowledge and blessing.

Chapter Six — Girls' Day Out

They went shopping first.

Omega promptly headed for the island of Manhattan, and the couture design houses there, along Madison Avenue. Unbeknownst to most humans, a couple of those designers were 'not from around here,' as she and Echo were wont to put it, and there, she and Myclestra could get proper service without many questions being asked — at least, questions to which humans didn't need the answers. In addition, one of those designers, in particular, was used to handling some of the female Agents, notably Omega and India. More, it meant considerations of payment would be handled discreetly, enabling Omega to put the whole thing on her personal account at Headquarters.

But when the pair got out of the 'Vette after Omega parked it in an alley off East 78th between Madison and Fifth Avenues, they became the inadvertent focus of unwelcome attention.

"Whoa, baybee!" The catcall was followed by a chorus of wolf-whistles from a group of young men loitering on the street corner.

"Are you two ladies models?"

"Of course they are, Jimmy, look where they're headed!"

"Can I have your autograph?"

"Forget autographs! Can I have a date?!"

"What is a date?" Myclestra wondered, turning to the apparent leader of the group, who was grinning from ear to ear.

"Oh, honey," Jimmy said, growing seductive, "it's a lovely little time spent together in very…intimate…surroundings. I'm sure you have those in your country, whatever word you use for it. And trust me, I can make it worth your while."

"You do not know me. Why would you wish to become intimate?" Myclestra cocked her head at the youth, puzzlement obvious in her body language.

"All I gotta do is look at you, honey, and I'm all ready to be intimate with you."

"I'll bet." Omega rolled her eyes, then grabbed Myclestra's elbow. "C'mon, Myc," she murmured. "Just ignore the peanut gallery."

"The what?" Myclestra asked, perplexed.

"The onlookers. We have an appointment and we need to go, so we're not late."

"Awww," came the chorus from the 'peanut gallery.' "C'mon, ladies, ya don't wanna leave us hard up, do ya?"

"Of course, Sil-uhm, Meg," Myclestra replied, hastily changing her mode of address to the one Omega had instructed her to use for this outing. Omega tugged her arm, pulling her away.

"Hey!" Jimmy exclaimed. "I was talking to her!"

"Emphasis on 'was,'" Omega decreed, straightening her shoulders and glaring at the man as she extracted her goggle-glasses with the left hand — holding tight to Myclestra with the right — and donning them.

"You think you're goin' incognito that way?" Jimmy growled at them, brash.

"No, I think YOU need to go, before you get into something you have no idea about," Omega responded, cold.

"And I think you need to get your hand off my new girlfriend," he shot back, trying to knock Omega's hand off Myclestra's arm. Suddenly he found his wrist gripped tight, as his arm was bent back behind him. "What the hell?! OW! That hurts, dammit!" he exclaimed, as Omega spun him around, putting his hand into the small of his back. Myclestra stood behind Omega, grinning as she 'watched' the interaction with her esoteric 'sight .'

"All right," Omega hissed into the man's ear, "you're going to take your friends and get lost, understand?"

"Says who?"

"Me." Omega pulled Jimmy's arm a little farther out of position, and he squirmed, turning to try to face her. Instead, she followed him, staying behind him. "Keep this up, and I pull your arm out of socket at the shoulder."

"The hell you say!" one of his friends exclaimed, reaching for the Agent. Suddenly he fell over backward, landing ass-first on the sidewalk, rubbing the dirt-encrusted welt that was rising on his forehead. "OWWW! WHAT THE SHIT?!"

"You will not harm my sister," Myclestra declared, hefting another piece of gravel from the sidewalk. "I tire of this. Go. All of you. Before we become angry. You will not like us if we become…angry with you fools."

Omega released the man's arm, shoving him away, and the group hastened off at some speed.

"And that takes care of the peanut gallery," Omega decided. "Thanks for the assist."

"He was attempting to attack you from behind, while you were occupied with the first one," Myclestra noted. "I will not stand by and allow such a thing to happen to my battle-sister. It rapidly became obvious that they did not mean well, and you understand this environment much better than I do. So I thank you, in turn."

"Team, then?" Omega offered.

"Of course. Always, my friend."

"Good."

Omega guided the other woman down the street to the side entrance of the design house with no further incidents.

As they entered the building, soft sighs and groans of disappointment went up from down the street, as what little was left of the small crowd slowly dispersed. They had gathered to watch the confrontation between the two imposing women and the latest group of wanna-be tough guys attempting to claim territory here.

* * *

Inside, they were met by the receptionist — who was from Kref, and personally knew Travis Taylor.

"Ah, there you are," she said with a smile. "Pleased to see you again, Agent Omega."

"Likewise, Libala," Omega responded, returning the smile. "I hope we're not late; we had a little, um, delay on the street."

"Yes, I saw on the security monitors," Libala replied, frowning. "I am glad the two of you were able to handle them. Occasionally the gangs invade our area and things get… interesting."

"I'll pop Echo a note to see about that," Omega said. "I don't think that's what these guys were, but if there's problems, we need to check into it. Some of those gangs absorb some bad influences from the 'imports,' and get cocky."

"Yes, they do," Libala agreed in no uncertain terms. "Thank you. Is this the friend you said you would bring?"

"Yes, this is Myclestra," Omega said, introducing them. "She's not from Earth either. I met her recently, on a…case… we're both working. She was sent here to capture a perp, and Echo and I are helping. Myc, this is Libala Sudarlit. She's not—"

"Not from Earth," Myclestra finished for her. "I can tell by her scent."

"Excuse me?!" Libala responded, not sure whether to be offended or not.

"Oh, no, no," Omega soothed. "Myclestra, here, is visually blind, Libala. Her species is all blind; they use other senses to compensate. She can literally smell the difference between humans and Krefans."

"Ohhhh," Libala said in understanding. "Um, pleased to meet you, Myclestra." She offered a hand, then wavered, thinking better of it, but before she could pull back, Myclestra accepted it.

"I am pleased to meet you, as well, Libala Sudarlit," she replied. "Your voice is pleasant to the ear."

"Thank you," Libala said, offering a tentative smile, patently unsure what the tall woman could perceive. "Come now, let us get the two of you in with Kiaiala, or she will chew me out. She was looking forward to seeing you again, Omega.

The images of you in your wedding dress were lovely, and she was excited to see what you needed this time."

"I'm sorry neither of you were able to attend the wedding," Omega said sincerely. "But yeah, this should be fun."

* * *

"Oh my," Kiaiala Heltor, the head of the design house, an older, female Dabanoran, remarked, as she surveyed Myclestra. "She is lovely! So statuesque! And the hair so beautiful! What color are your eyes, child?" the elder remarked. "Pull off those sunglasses and let me see."

"Um, Kiaiala," Omega began, as Myclestra stiffened. "Myc's people…they don't have eyes, as such. I mean, they do, but they don't. It's just…white tissue. It's…a long story, and not really mine to tell, but…her race is blind. They use other senses…"

"Ahhh," Heltor murmured. "Then forgive my presumption, children. I only wanted to ensure that I chose the proper colors to set off Myclestra's beauty."

"Thank you, elder sister," Myclestra said softly. "I appreciate the consideration. I have never had such garments before, so my battle-sister Silv-uhm, Omega, is helping me learn."

"Myclestra's had a hard life," Omega told Heltor. "Most of her people are…slaves. She's one of the few who escaped."

"Where are you from, child?" Heltor wondered. "I thought most of the slave planets in the galaxy had been freed, long since…"

* * *

Myclestra shot a kind of 'glance' at Omega, uncertain how to answer, and the Agent responded with a sigh.

"Really long story, Kiaiala," she said. "The gist of it is that Myc, here, isn't even from our universe, let alone our galaxy."

"Oh my," Heltor gasped. "That is…unexpected."

"My people, the Alontorans, were once as the two of you," Myclestra said then, having determined by Omega's response that it was safe to explain. "But my world was taken over many thousands of years ago by the Masters; we were enslaved, and genetically manipulated as they saw fit. The result is what you see. I think we once had eyes and sight, though I am unsure; it has been millennia, our racial memories of them are faded, and there are no records. There are also no longer male Alontorans; we are cloned, not born. I managed to…escape…and became a bounty hunter. When my latest quarry jumped between the universes, I…followed."

* * *

"And that's kinda where Echo and I came in," Omega finished the abbreviated explanation. "And, based on what Myc, here, has told me, the Masters are just flat evil."

"I see," Heltor said, considering the Alontoran with sympathy…and a certain degree of creativity. "Then I will ensure you are beautifully dressed for this evening out, my dear girl. You have earned it, it sounds like."

"I think so, too," Omega agreed.

"And if you have befriended this one," Heltor patted Omega's shoulder, "then you are in good hands, and will enjoy this evening, I am certain."

"I think you are right," Myclestra agreed with a smile.

"I know it's a quick turn-around, Kiaiala," Omega said, "and Myc, here, is rather taller than most Earth women…"

"Quite all right, actually," Heltor answered. "I had occasion to knock out some costume concepts for a Broadway production recently — there were some characters in drag, and the costume designers were having difficulties making it work, so they asked for my assistance — and I think, with some fitting and tailoring for the more voluptuous body shape, there is one that would work for Myclestra, here, very nicely. And it is a lovely shade of green that should just set off her hair and skin." She smiled. "As for you, youngling, I already have a beautiful, soft blue dress waiting. You have not changed your measurements since last time, have you?"

"I don't think so," a smiling Omega said. "But we can check, just in case."

"That is wise. Come, let us see about taking measurements, and then we can fit you both and make any needed adjustments."

* * *

In short order, they found that the pale blue evening gown fit Omega perfectly, and the deep-green gown, while requiring considerable tailoring to fit Myclestra's decidedly curvaceous figure, did indeed bring out and enhance Myclestra's complexion. More, it was long enough for her height; apparently the actor for which it had been designed originally was quite tall…or had been, with high-heeled shoes.

"And it will show off her figure to perfection, when we are done," Heltor promised. "Now, since you told me you wanted a proper 'girl's day out' when you made the appointment, Omega, I have taken the liberty of calling some friends at my favorite shops, so that you may shop for accessories and makeup with no hindrance from humans not in the know — I will notify them of colors and styles, and they will have some excellent recommendations when you arrive, for shoes and handbags and makeup — and then I scheduled you for the afternoon at my favorite spa."

"Oh!" Omega exclaimed. "I was going to ask you for a recommendation…"

"Oh good; I feared you already had appointments made," Heltor said in relief. "But I do very much want to help. Especially now. Never mind the things you and Echo do for those of us who are 'imports'; it sounds as if Myclestra has been busy helping defend my new home, as well, and she deserves some good things in her life."

"I think so, too," Omega declared, staunch. Myclestra bowed her head. "Now, now, Myc. You okay?"

"I am…unused to such consideration," Myclestra said in a low voice.

"All the more reason, then," Heltor decreed. "Come back by here when the spa has finished with you both, and I will have the dresses — and perhaps a few dainty lacy bits for you both — ready for you to take back to Headquarters and don.

Echo will have to put his eyes back in his head when I am done with the two of you."

Omega grinned.

So did Myclestra.

"Libala?" Heltor called.

"Yes, madam?" The receptionist-slash-assistant popped into the doorway.

"Do you have the itinerary ready for Omega?"

"I sent it to her phone already, madam."

"Great!" Omega said, grin growing wider. "Send the bill to my personal account, Libala."

"The matter is already taken care of," Libala replied.

"Wait, what?" Omega wondered, surprised. "What do you mean, 'taken care of,'?" She glanced between Libala and Heltor. Heltor remained stubbornly silent. Libala bit her lip.

"She means that she comp'ed Myclestra's and your dress," Libala finally answered.

"No, I'm paying for it," Omega insisted.

"What is wrong, battle-sister?" Myclestra asked.

"She's trying to give us our dresses for free," Omega responded.

"No!" Myclestra exclaimed. "I will not take it for free! I will earn what I have!"

"It is quite all right," Heltor replied. "You have the stature and the figure to wear it. The theatre did not take it, and I have no other clients it would fit. You do me a favor."

* * *

"No. Damn. Way," a seething Jimmy decreed to his friends. "Nobody treats me like that! I WILL have that red-headed model, dammit, if I have to do it the hard way!"

"Dude, are you sure you wanna do that?" another asked. "That's a good way to get arrested."

"Not if we get rid of the blonde bitch," Jimmy snarled.

"That's even worse, Jimmy," someone else pointed out.

"I'm not talking murder, you idiots," Jimmy grumbled. "Get her out of the way, I can make time with the redhead.

She's not from the States, and I can talk her into it. Didn't you see how she was responding to my banter? I bet she's got some serious moves, too; those foreign chicks are always so hot! Not to mention the curves from here to there. It wouldn't even be forced then!"

"Hell, I thought the blonde was hot," the first friend replied. "If you don't want her, I'll take her off your hands and outta the damn way, no prob. Besides, they gotta have friends in the industry who are just as gorgeous."

"Done," Jimmy said. "Dan, you get Blondie, I get Redhead. Deal?

"Deal," Dan agreed.

"Do we get 'em when you're done?" a third asked.

"Maybe," Jimmy said. "Depends how it goes, Pete. I might just want her for a regular. But otherwise, sure, why not? Long as you don't mind sloppy seconds."

"So," Dan asked, "are the rest of you with us?"

A chorus of, "Yeah! Hell yeah!" went up.

* * *

It took a bit of diplomacy and negotiation, but in the end, Omega got the matter worked out to everyone's satisfaction: She would pay for the alterations to Myclestra's gown, as well as paying — though at a discount; Heltor insisted — for her own gown, and in exchange, Myclestra would take the dress off the design house's hands.

"Because otherwise, it is only sitting in the back, taking up space," Heltor pointed out.

This satisfied both Myclestra and Omega, and the pair headed out on foot, to the first shop on their itinerary, down the street.

* * *

Jimmy and his posse watched from a cul-de-sac until the blonde and the redhead emerged from the design house across the street and headed down the sidewalk toward another shop.

Then they slipped out of the cul-de-sac and quietly meandered down the street, some distance behind the two women, watching for a good opportunity to split up the pair.

* * *

Shortly thereafter, in the first boutique on Heltor's itinerary for them, Omega found herself the owner of a pair of lovely silver pumps with stiletto heels, and a tiny matching envelope clutch, just big enough for a lipstick and a cell phone — though a warp pocket would significantly increase that volume, if she decided it was warranted.

Myclestra, meanwhile, settled on a pair of soft brown, flat-heeled, gladiator-style sandals that laced up her calves.

"But I do not understand the purpose of this 'clutch,'" she noted, waving around several small hand-held purses. "It is not nearly big enough for a change of clothing, or even my plas-gun."

"It's kind of a decorative equivalent of a pocket," Omega explained. "It's not supposed to be a case or pack. It's just big enough to stick in a cell phone — um, a communications device, maybe a lipstick…"

"What in the name of Mother Alontora is a lipstick?" Myclestra demanded to know.

"It's makeup," Omega began…but got no farther.

"And what is MAKEUP?!" Myclestra exclaimed, frustrated. "Battle-sister, I am trying VERY hard, but I do NOT understand your world! Do you honestly paint your face with mud, as the clerk, there, said?"

"Allow me, madame," the shop clerk, who wasn't from Earth, suggested. Omega nodded, and the clerk tried, "Ms. Myclestra, on Earth, many women, and some men, choose to enhance their appearance through the use of something called makeup. And yes, some forms of makeup contain minerals — some taken from soil — to tint the skin, or to improve the skin's health. The spa that Ms. Heltor has scheduled for you will explain more, but there are various items of makeup which help even skin tone, sculpt the bone structure of the face, and bring out the color of the eyes and lips. I realize that, since you have never experienced sight, this may make little sense to you. But stop for a moment and think: what is the difference in your perception of a small woodland stream, flowing over the rounded stones in its bed, as compared to, say, a flash flood in a slot canyon?"

"Oh," Myclestra said, eyebrows ascending as understanding dawned. "Oh. Yes, the flash flood is rough, almost angry, churning, roaring, hurtful to my hearing, but not to my limited form of…well, of sight. A kind of sight, but nothing like humans and other sighteds perceive the world. Flash floods always come with storms, thunder and the deluge. I fear those, for such things make me, make any of my sisters, truly blind. Our senses are finely tuned by the Masters, but they are far from perfect. Rain — unless very, very light, snow, dust, strong winds that roil the air and carry leaves, dirt and such, those render us nearly helpless, unable to sense anything beyond arm's reach. But the little stream has a musical, rather happy sound. It is soothing to the ear. On the rare occasions when I can, I like to sit and listen to it."

"Exactly. The makeup will create, for sighted beings, something of that effect on the face, especially when combined with an appropriate hairstyle — not that either of you truly need the makeup; you are both lovely as you are. Still, it can be fun to play with it! Now, since lipstick, being applied to the lips, tends to be eaten off when one is at a meal, it is good to take it along so it can be reapplied after eating. You can also tuck a small cell phone into the clutch bag, as well as keys, payment cards, and similar small things, and it is easier to keep up with it, so."

"I do not see any reason for this…lipstick," Myclestra wondered, tapping her pursed lips with a forefinger. "But, if it is truly necessary, I could learn to apply it by feel, perhaps. Or, if you might be willing, my battle-sister? And I have no keys, or phone, or the like. Omega, do I really need one of these 'clutch bags'?"

"Hm," Omega grunted, pursing her lips and twisting them to one side, as she considered. "You know, Myc, you have a point…"

"She does," the clerk agreed, "and maybe, if the two of you will be together, any small objects Ms. Myclestra needs can go into Ms. Omega's clutch. Even if she does not use a lipstick, perhaps a lip balm, which as she says, can be applied by feel, and gives a hint of gloss…"

"That would work. Or she can use Echo's pockets," Omega averred. "I think that's a plan."

"Good," Myclestra declaimed in some relief.

The purchases were made and placed into dainty shopping bags, and the pair headed on to the jewelry store.

* * *

Jimmy, Dan, and their gang — for they were a gang, of sorts, if not the usual kind — trailed Omega and Myclestra from the leather goods shop and down the street once more.

"There's gotta be a good spot here someplace," Dan muttered. "This part o' the City is all elbow to elbow, dammit. Gotta hang in a doorway or something and watch; there's no alleys much around here, and what there are, are all gated up."

"Maybe we shoulda stayed back where they parked, and got 'em when they come back," Pete speculated.

"Hell, we can always follow 'em back," Jimmy noted, then called to a laggard. "Keep up, Bill. Stop window-shopping."

* * *

The jewelry store visit went quickly; Omega already owned some lovely jewelry, and didn't really need more. Some had been inherited from her parents, some had been acquired over the years as she saw this or that, and some had been gifted by Echo after their marriage. This visit was mostly to acquire some nice sparklies for Myclestra.

Myclestra did not have pierced ears, and did not take well to clip earrings, declaring they were uncomfortable in no uncertain terms, and Omega couldn't argue with her there.

A small pendant of pearl and emerald, with silver chain, however, set off the slightly pearly sheen of the Alontoran's tanned skin, as well as contrasting nicely with her red hair, and that, and the matching bracelet, was acquired — and Myclestra permitted it, as it was not especially expensive.

The purchases were made, and discreetly sent to Headquarters to await their return, by an employee who 'wasn't from around here' — thereby ensuring the two women did not wag around bags that might draw unwanted attention — and they made for the spa.

* * *

As they reached the block in which the spa lay, the two women passed a small alleyway between buildings.

"Mm," Myclestra hummed as they continued walking.

"Yeah, no shit," Omega muttered. "They're getting closer, finally, so I guess they're about ready. Which means we need to be ready, too."

Myclestra stopped dead.

Omega stopped beside her. Together, they spun on their heels.

Jimmy and his posse stood behind them, only about ten or fifteen feet away.

"I have had enough," Myclestra declared.

She stalked toward the group of young men, grabbed Jimmy by the back of the collar — she effectively grabbed the 'scruff of the neck' — and dragged him across the sidewalk and into the alley.

"Ooooo!" the young men said, grinning from ear to ear and elbowing each other. "Whoa, baybee! Go, JIMMY!"

"Hey, sweet thing, how 'bout you?" Dan wondered, still grinning, and indicating Omega.

Arms already folded, Omega held up her left hand and waggled her fingers; the hyperdiamond engagement ring sparkled in the sunshine, emphasizing the alien-alloy band next to it.

"Already spoken for," she noted, and Dan's face fell.

"So?" one of the others said, insolent. "What do we care?"

Omega scowled.

The others backed up a bit.

* * *

Inside the alley, Myclestra looked around, still grasping Jimmy by the collar.

"Over there looks like a nice corner," Jimmy said, pointing to a small alcove between the buildings. Then he reached for the fly of his jeans. "I'm always up for a quickie, sweetie."

Myclestra said nothing.

Instead, she pulled him close, until she was nose-to-nose with him, staring into his eyes — as he thought. At the mouth of the alley, his compatriots all began crowing and cat-calling. He smirked, letting his eyes flutter closed as he leaned toward her for a kiss.

She tossed him over her shoulder…

…And into the nearest dumpster.

With a clang, the lid fell down. She turned and latched it, then effortlessly bent the steel latch shut, trapping him in the mostly-full — and VERY 'aromatic' — dumpster.

Then she stalked out of the alley. Myclestra paused long enough to cast a baleful 'glance' toward Jimmy's posse.

They paled and backed up again.

"Come," she told Omega, and they turned, headed for the spa, as banging and muffled yells came from the alley.

"That worked," a grinning Omega decided. "And was funny, to boot. Taking out the trash."

"Thank you," Myclestra said with a smile. "And…yes."

They saw no more of Jimmy or his posse.

* * *

In short order, Omega and Myclestra were checked into the spa, stripped down, and lying face-down on adjacent tables, while massage therapists worked their strong, curvaceous forms.

"Mm," Omega sighed.

"Yes, this feels…good," Myclestra agreed.

"That's what I wanted to hear," Omega murmured. "Most people tend to drowse, or even fall asleep. You're safe here — this is where the local offworlders go to unwind, and it's got a highly-trained security guard team on it, nearly equivalent to the Galactic President's security team, to make sure nobody gets outed — so just relax and take a nap, if you can."

"I…think I can."

"Good. I'm probably gonna go out soon, too."

Moments later, both of the prone female bodies softened into a state of deep relaxation, as spliced human and Alontoran dozed, content in each other's company and friendship.

* * *

Then it was on to the facial. In a set of reclined chairs, their faces were gently cleansed and exfoliated, then a moisturizing mask applied, along with soft, cool compresses for the eyes… or, in Myclestra's case, what would have been eyes. Again, both women sighed in relaxed bliss.

"Battle-sister," Myclestra decided, "I must admit that this was an excellent idea you had. I cannot recall ever being so… at peace. And I have never been so pampered."

"Well, since we're in the process of gearing up and locating your perp, we might as well do what we need to do, to be rested when the time comes," Omega pointed out. "You and I are a lot alike; we both tend to stay wound up when we're waiting for the big fight to go down. For that matter, Echo does, too."

"I do hope he is not back at Headquarters, all wound up, as you say."

"No, he promised me that he'd go down to the gym, find one of the full-time massage therapists on staff, and get a nice long massage, too, while we were gone."

"Good. He could have come with us, I suppose."

"No, he couldn't, actually; most spas here won't work on a mixed group like that. I mean, if it was only him and me, they would, but with more than just a couple, it gets…complicated."

"Ah. I underst — no, I do not understand."

"Okay. There are some unscrupulous spas, not around here, but there are some in various parts of the city, that illegally hire prostitutes, not certified therapists," Omega noted. "So going to one of those with a group is tantamount to an orgy of sorts."

255

"Ohhhhh," Myclestra murmured. "And so the scrupulous ones do not wish to be mistaken for…"

"A brothel. Bingo," Omega confirmed. "So Echo couldn't come with us. It's against the rules."

"Well, at least he is getting a bit of pampering of his own," Myclestra decided.

"He is. I made him promise me."

"Good. And he will abide by his word. He is a good man."

"Yes, he is. And yes, he will."

"You love him deeply."

"I do."

"I am glad you are so happy with him."

"Thanks, Myc."

"You are welcome, Meg."

The pair smiled at each other as their aestheticians lifted away the compresses and began removing the masks.

* * *

In short order, the makeup artists were honing the sculpted features of both women, using a light hand; both Omega and Myclestra were beautiful women, and unless on stage, Omega used very little makeup — she simply didn't need it — and Myclestra had never known it existed. While that was in progress, stylists worked on their hair, putting both women's hair into simple yet sophisticated, elegant updos.

An hour later, both women walked onto the street looking utterly gorgeous, even in jeans and t-shirts.

And they were wonderfully relaxed, yet alert.

* * *

Half an hour later, they had verified that the new dresses fit beautifully, enhancing their figures divinely. The dresses were carefully placed inside garment bags, and those bags gently laid in the warp trunk of the 'Vette.

Then Omega and Myclestra were off, back to Headquarters.

* * *

Back at Headquarters, Omega went with Myclestra to the quarters assigned to her; Echo — aware through the nd't'lq that they had returned — waited for the pair outside the door of Myclestra's quarters, and took the garment bag Omega held.

"Gonna help Myc get dressed?" he asked, as Omega leaned up and kissed him.

"I thought I'd make sure she had help with zippers, if she needed it," Omega said. "Extra arms are sometimes useful on these evening gowns! Then I'll be back home to get dressed myself. I'm sure she and Surlianth can chat for a few minutes; I'm picking up that he's really curious about our day, but he gave us privacy for some girl time, so…"

"Right," Echo said, leaning down to kiss her again, while Myclestra waited amiably nearby. "You go help Myc, and I'll go get myself ready, then help you if you need zipper help, once you get home."

"It's a plan."

Oh, just so you know, Echo added mentally, as he turned. *You look even more dynamite than normal, baby. And tell Myc she looks great, too. I'm a lucky man tonight. More so than usual, I mean.*

Omega grinned.

* * *

It didn't take long to get Myclestra into her sandals and dress. It was a rich emerald-green satin, sleeveless, with a low-cut back, a plunging neckline, and a side slit to mid-thigh, and Myclestra looked stunning in it. Omega told her so.

Just then, Surlianth interjected his opinion.

<Oh my,> he said, both women able to hear. <I must agree, Silver-Hair. My Little One is strikingly lovely tonight.>

"How can you tell, Old Snake?" Myclestra wondered, blushing slightly; Omega was silent, watching the interaction.

<With her permission, I am using Omega's eyes,> he responded. <The dress sets off your figure and your hair quite beautifully. My Little One is an exquisitely lovely woman.>

"Can you show her, Surlianth?" Omega wondered, as Myclestra blushed deeper.

<Not really, child. Long, long ago, the part of the Alontoran

brain that, in you, would interpret sight, was repurposed for other matters. I could show her, but she would not understand what she was being shown, for her brain cannot interpret it.>

"It is what it is," Myclestra said then, bowing her head. "I am only glad you both like what you see."

"We do," Omega said with a smile. "Echo said you looked great, too, by the way."

<Run along now, Silver-Hair,> a tolerant, cheerful Surlianth said then. <I wish Myclestra to tell me about her day, and you need to get dressed, as well. Echo tells me you have reservations at a very elegant restaurant, and you must not be late.>

Without question or demur, Omega scurried out the door, headed for Alpha One's quarters.

* * *

Three-quarters of an hour later, everyone was ready, and the 'Vette was en route to Manhattan once more, with Alpha One, plus one.

"So we're going to that penthouse restaurant at Rockefeller Plaza?" Omega confirmed, as Echo started the engine.

"Yup, I thought that would be a damn nice place to squire two beautiful ladies out on the town, and it's somewhere we don't go often, you and me," Echo averred, heading out of the vehicle hangar toward the street. "I mean, I know Myc, here, can't really see the view from the restaurant windows, but the food will be good, and I'll ensure she gets plenty to eat…"

"This sounds very nice, and I can observe 'the view,' within certain limits, two thousand ur-lans, no more," Myclestra noted. "I assume it will be in a…what are they called here… skyscraper?"

"Yes, it's on the 65th floor," Echo told her. "We'll be up a good ways. That doesn't bother you, does it? And what's an 'ur-lan,' Myc?"

"I do not think so," Myclestra decided. "Should it? And why do you call me this odd sound, Mick or Myc, however you say it? That is not my name. And an ur-lan is the length of my arm, similar to a yard or meter of your world."

"Ah. Got it," Echo said with a nod.

"Some people on Earth are afraid of heights," Omega explained. "He was just making sure you weren't. As for calling you Myc, ah, hmm, well, it's a 'nickname.' Made by shortening your full name. A form of affectionate address. And it's a lot like one that already exists on Earth, so it blends in, sorta. Kind of how I told you to call me 'Meg' when we're out and about. Is it a problem?"

"Ah, now I understand. No, it is not a problem, but it is not something Alontorans normally do, so I have been mildly confused by it. I…appreciate the level of…trust implied by it; thank you. And as to heights, no, that is not a consideration," the Alontoran said. "I am looking forward to the outing."

"Let's go, then," Echo said. "We can discuss the menu while we're on the way."

* * *

After a detailed conversation in the 'Vette about how to make it look as if Myclestra was simply an unusually tall, blind woman to the other patrons of the restaurant, as well as those waiters who might be local, they arrived at Rockefeller Center. A quick trip up in the express elevator, and the maître d' led them to a window table in the corner. Omega was on Echo's left arm, and Myclestra was on his right.

"There we are, ladies and gentleman," the waiter said as he presented them with menus, then filled goblets with water.

"Um…" Myclestra said, waving the menu in some confusion.

"Is there a problem?" the waiter, whose name tag said 'Dave,' asked.

"Our friend Myc, here, is blind," Omega explained. "She can't read the menu."

"Oh, I'm sorry," Dave exclaimed. "And that's why she's wearing the sunglasses! But I didn't see a cane when she came in…"

"It, uh, got broken in her trip here," Echo lied smoothly,

"and we haven't received the replacement yet."

"Oh. Well, I'll see if we have a Braille menu."

"That won't be necessary," Echo said with a smile. "We discussed the menu with her on the way, and I can order for everyone."

"Ah, very good," Dave said, responding to the smile. "Please proceed, then, sir."

"We're going to start off with Caesar salads," Echo said. "Meg, do you want extra garlic?"

"Yes, please," Omega replied.

"Myc?"

"That sounds good, yes."

"Extra garlic, all around, then," Echo said with a grin, and the waiter smiled. "Then we'll have the mushroom bisque. For entrées, Ms. Myclestra will have the porterhouse, medium rare, with balsamic glazed asparagus, carrot cavatelli, and please give her an extra side of the grilled leeks. My wife will have the mushroom and pork risotto with steamed Brussels sprouts and the glazed asparagus, and I'll have the maple-glazed salmon with pommes frites and…you know what, I'm gonna have the glazed asparagus, too."

"Very good, sir. And to drink?"

"Let's have a bottle of your best cabernet."

"Excellent choice. Do you wish to order dessert now, or wait until you've finished your entrées?"

"Let's wait until after the entrées, and see if we have room," Omega suggested. "Myc, is that okay with you?"

"That sounds like a good idea, Meg," Myclestra responded. "I am looking forward to the meal!"

"Then let me go submit your order to the kitchen, and I'll be right back with your wine," Dave said, and hurried off.

* * *

In the end, all three ate until they were stuffed, and even Myclestra was impressed with the deliciousness of the food.

"I have never been given such wonderful food in my life," she murmured, keeping her voice low so that it did not carry to another table. "Thank you both, so much."

"From what I've been able to tell, it's high time, and past it," Echo noted. "And Fox agrees, and is personally helping foot the bill for our little outing tonight, on that account. You've fought, been betrayed, been tortured, escaped, took out perps, and even left your own universe to chase what sounds like one of the most dangerous perps you could chase…and he understands that, because in some measure, he's been there, too…"

"What Ace is trying to say is, we think you've earned this, and then some," Omega finished for her spouse. "Now, before we get maudlin, chocolate torte, limoncello cake, or pear tartlets? Myc?"

"I am uncertain what any of these 'desserts' are, but they all sound delicious," Myclestra responded.

"Then let's get one of each, and share, between us," Echo suggested. "That way, we all get a taste of each."

"Done!" Omega decreed, delighted.

* * *

The evening was a rousing success. Jokes, funny stories, and tales of derring-do were exchanged between the three, and laughter — genuine, unrestrained mirth — was shared. Given the fact that Myclestra also got to take out some of her ire on what she and Omega took to calling 'Jimmy's Posse' that afternoon — they filled in Echo over dinner, and he laughed his head off over the dumpster incident — had been pampered and massaged, complimented by no less than Surlianth on her beauty, and eaten the first gourmet meal of her life, she was exceedingly happy, and said so.

"And I have you both to thank for that," she told them, as Echo helped her into the warp seat in the rear. "As well as Director Fox. I will thank him for his financial assistance in the morning."

"And we have you to thank for notifying us of this deadly threat to our world," Echo pointed out.

"Even if we don't know where the damn thing has gotten,"

Omega grumbled, easing into the front passenger seat.

"Patience, battle-sister; a wise hunter does not rush after prey such as a Warpwraith when it has gone to ground, lest the roles of hunter and hunted be reversed," Myclestra said, somewhat uncharacteristically. "He will show himself soon, I am sure."

* * *

Once they dropped off Myclestra at her quarters and ensured that all was well with Surlianth, Alpha One headed for their own quarters.

"Ohhhh, there we go," Omega sighed as the door closed behind them, shutting out the rest of the world, at least for the time. She bent down and slipped off the stiletto-heeled shoes she'd worn all night, then wiggled her toes in the pile of the soft blue carpet.

"Tired, baby?" Echo wondered, unfastening his bow tie and cummerbund before removing his Suit jacket and tossing it all over his left forearm.

"Maybe a little," she decided. "It was a good day, and a great evening. My feet were ready to come out of those shoes, though. I am NOT used to wearing high heels these days."

"Why did you wear 'em in the first place, then?"

"Kiaiala picked 'em out for me. Said they'd help set off the dress."

"Which, let me say for the umpteenth time, looked damn great on you, sweetheart," Echo noted. "I had a hard time looking at anybody — or anything — else."

"I'm glad you liked it," she said with a grin.

"I liked what — or rather, who — was in it even better," he admitted, returning the grin. Then he sobered. "I, um…"

"'Um' what?"

"I'm sure you didn't mean for it to happen, but I…" Echo hesitated, then confessed, "I 'heard' Myclestra ask you to make love this morning…through the nd't'lq. I wasn't eavesdropping, I swear," he said quickly, "it just came through, and, and I sort of…stopped dead and…well, Romeo said my jaw dropped and

I turned pale…" Echo bit his lip.

"Aw." Omega took him by the arm, and they wandered deeper into their apartment, headed for the den. "Did you hear what I told her, then?" she asked.

"Yeah…but I still can't help but wonder…"

"Wonder what?"

"Who you really wore that dress for."

He said nothing more, but Omega could 'read' the thoughts behind it through their bond: Just because she had no intention of sleeping with Myclestra didn't mean she wasn't trying to impress her, wasn't herself attracted. They had, after all, noted others responding to the Alontoran in such fashion, during their initial surveillance. She remembered his previous experiences with his girlfriends, as well as how the breakups had been one-sided and had damaged his self-esteem, and she decided to act on those considerations.

Pausing behind the sofa, Omega silently placed her shoes on the floor.

Then she took Echo's discarded garb from his arm and laid it all carefully over the back of the couch, before slipping her arms around his neck and pulling him down into a tender, deep, passionate kiss. They both sighed then, and stayed like that for long moments. At last they broke the kiss, but she refused to let him raise his head, instead lacing her fingers into his hair and keeping his forehead pressed to hers.

"Who do you think?" she breathed then.

Echo swept her up in his arms and headed for the bedroom.

* * *

Several hours later, they lay in each other's arms, quiet. Echo had found the lacy lingerie that Kiaiala Heltor had placed in the garment bag alongside the evening gown for later use, laying it on the bed to await his wife, and it had received its due attention on Omega before being discarded in favor of bare skin. Now, even that passion had subsided, sated for the moment. The occasional stroke of fingers through hair or light kiss of lips was all that broke their stillness in those minutes.

263

"I love you," Omega murmured.

"I love you, too, baby," Echo replied, voice low.

"So…did that answer your question?"

"In spades, and then some."

"Good. For what it's worth, though, I also wore it for me. I like getting all dressed up now and then."

"I think that's a healthy attitude to take," Echo said, considering thoughtfully. "Maybe we should do it more often. We go out a fair amount, but not necessarily to such fancy digs."

"I wouldn't argue the idea. I don't wanna break the bank, but all it really means is a big night on the town more often than we currently do; I don't need to buy a new dress every time. I already have several really pretty evening gowns and cocktail dresses now. Plus the accessories for 'em."

"You do, at that, and I like seeing you in 'em," Echo told her. Then he grinned wickedly. *I also like seeing you OUT of 'em,* he told her mentally.

I'll just bet you do, she snickered. *What's under YOUR Suit fills it out very nicely, too, for that matter. Naked Cowboy an' all.*

Right. Time for the Naked Cowboy to make a reappearance?

Not tonight, I think. I'm too tired now to properly appreciate him. But he's welcome any time he wants to show up!

"Heh," Echo chuckled aloud. "Maybe tomorrow night?"

"Maybe. For now, let's cuddle up an' get some sleep. While it was a good day, today was an exercise in diplomacy from the start, and frankly, I'm slap worn out."

"C'mere, then."

Echo gathered his wife and partner close. Omega snuggled into his warm, strong body, and in moments the pair was asleep.

* * *

"Ah, there you are," Fox said from behind his desk as Myclestra stood at the open door. "Come in, come in and have a seat." He pointed to one of the various visitor chairs, rising and coming out from behind his desk as Myclestra sat in one of the larger, better-padded chairs.

"Omega said you wished to see me?" the alien woman remarked, as Fox closed his office door. "Is something wrong?"

"Yes, I wanted to see you, but no, nothing is wrong," Fox said with a smile. "I see you have your Sword with you. Surlianth?"

<I am here and aware, Fox, and I think you have an excellent idea. Little One, Director Fox has some personal things he wishes to discuss with you. I want you to listen carefully; you already know you have a battle-sister who understands much, let alone her mate, as well. You may have more friends here than you had thought to have.>

"I will listen this time, Old Snake, this I swear to you," Myclestra said with a smile. "Director Fox, what did you wish to discuss?"

"I wanted to tell you a little about myself, Myclestra, and about a place called Majdanek, a place I once knew all too well…"

* * *

"Oh, yes," Myclestra hissed, as Fox came to the end of his personal tale. "Such a tale is one I well understand. You have seen much, as well. Like Omega, like Echo…and like myself."

"I have," Fox confirmed. "And I know what it is like to be treated as…well, as slave labor, at best. For most of my adolescence."

"Adolescence is very brief for my people, but not for yours," Myclestra sighed. "Omega tells me, and Surlianth confirms it, that I would be an adolescent to your people."

"Yes, that's true, if we looked just on the basis of years lived, but you've seen and done much, and that matures one mentally and emotionally," Fox pointed out.

"Oh! That makes me think," Myclestra said, sitting up and smiling slightly. "I did many things yesterday that I had never done before, guided by Omega. I found out from Echo, and confirmed with one of your assistants earlier today, that you financially aided them out of your own monies in doing so much for me, and I wanted to thank you, sir. It was a wonderful day, like something from a dream, and I shall remember it dearly for whatever time is left to me." She grinned at him, "Of course, I still expect to be paid my just bounty. I am a bounty hunter, after all."

"You're very welcome, tekhter," Fox murmured, touched by her gratitude and the way her face lit up when talking about the 'girl's day out,' as Omega had expressed it to him. "I was happy to ensure it went smoothly, and made some new, and more pleasant, experiences for you. And yes, you will be paid for your efforts in saving our world."

"I appreciate that, Director Fox. But I have a question. 'Tekhter'? What does that mean? I have heard you call Omega that…"

"It's a word from one of the languages I speak, called Yiddish," Fox explained. "It is my native tongue. The word means 'daughter.' I use it with those younger females I'm becoming — or are already — fond of."

"Oh," Myclestra said with a smile, blushing lightly. "And this is why Omega calls you 'Abba Fox' sometimes?"

"It is. Yiddish is a mix of several languages, including one ancient language, Hebrew, which my people spoke millennia ago. 'Abba' means father in Hebrew. I'm the father figure of the little family-like group Omega put together, you see."

"Then…thank you, Abba Fox."

"You are most welcome, Tekhter Myclestra."

They both 'heard' a pleased rumble from the Sword.

Chapter Seven — Preparation

"Hey, Meg?"

"Yeah, Ace?"

"You at a stopping point over there?"

She looked up from her laptop, then glanced over her shoulder at where Echo sat at his desk in the Alpha Line Room.

"Pretty much, yeah. I just finished the shift report an' sent it to Fox, and I was gonna have a look-see at some of the requisitions, but that can wait a bit. Whatcha need?"

"I was just thinking…you recall your buddy out of the Chicago Office? The one who's into all kinds of weapons, and military history, and is a gunsmith, an' all that?"

"Who, you mean Agent Zulu?"

"That's him, yeah. I'm thinking…maybe we ought to call him in for this. I want him here with his whole arsenal of anything remotely apt to poke a hole in the warpwraith."

"I can do that."

"Good. Do it."

"Alpha Line Chief authority, or…?"

"Or."

"Aha. All over it, hon."

* * *

Agent Zulu was an odd character, even for Division One. Assigned to the Chicago Office, he was one of the rare Agents who maintained his permanent residence away from the Main Office. Under the auspices of a small shell corporation, he owned a medium-sized farm in rural Indiana. The actual farmland was rented to his closest neighbors, several miles down the road. He kept enough land for an elaborate shooting range.

Agent Zulu had been a naturalized American citizen when he was recruited into the Agency from the United States Army ten years ago. His Military Occupational Specialty,

267

or MOS, was a 91Foxtrot, repairing and maintaining Army weapons, everything from huge artillery cannons to standard issue handguns. His last posting had been as the small-arms master armorer in the 115th Brigade Support Battalion, part of the Army's First Cavalry Division. In his time as an armorer, he discovered a love for firearms, often the older the better. He carried an Agent's standard proto-cyclotron blaster when on duty, but the secure basement under his modest farmhouse held more firearms than the Chicago, Illinois National Guard Armory. In short, Agent Zulu was a dyed-in-the-wool gun nut. And proud of it.

Zulu wasn't an especially big man, being a solid, well-muscled five-foot-ten inches or so, somewhat under two hundred pounds. He kept his dark brown hair and mustache neatly trimmed. There was usually a lively sense of sardonic humor in his brown eyes, and he had a rare talent for pointing out things that some of his superiors would have rather ignored. More, he had a gift for telling stories that often illustrated those things others wanted ignored. He was sometimes ordered to keep his mouth shut…but he rarely did.

He had been more than a little shocked when he received a call at his desk from Agent Omega, the Alpha Line Assistant Chief herself. Zulu was a good Field agent, sharp and ready, keeping up to date with his training and proficiencies, but he honestly never even considered applying for Alpha Line. He liked being a Division One agent, partly because it paid well enough that he could freely indulge in his hobby of gun collecting and shooting. It also kept the ATF off his back. Mostly because they didn't know he was still alive.

His surprise deepened when Omega asked him directly if he owned any man-portable weapons, old or new, human or alien, that could effectively shoot any kind of fire or plasma. Of course, he answered in the affirmative, and was immediately ordered to pack anything whatsoever that met those requirements and report for duty to the Alpha Line Office no later than eight hours after the call.

And ninety minutes later, his secondary vehicle, an original, mil-surplus High Mobility Muultipurpose Wheeled Vehicle M1114, rose from the hidden 'basement' of the large and very secure barn behind his farmhouse, and rolled out, its tires crunching onto the gravel drive. He'd affectionately named the huge SUV 'The Beast.' He'd modified it to Agency standards, including the new sensor scrambler, cloaking and morphed flight capability, of course, but he had never expected to actually need to use the thing, let alone fly it anywhere. Or use any of the weapons he'd just cached in the warp-space chest in the back of the vehicle, for that matter. It was an almost ridiculous amount of hardware and ammo, but Omega had said, "Bring everything," and his only answer there had been, "Yes, ma'am."

He wondered why in the world Omega wanted his gear, and he kept puzzling about it as The Beast rumbled along at its best morphed cruising speed of two hundred and sixty miles per hour; Alpha One's 'Vette, by comparison, could top three hundred miles an hour, and as the pair kept tinkering with it, its top speed kept climbing. Speed was certainly not The Beast's forte — an M1114 wasn't designed for aerodynamics — but the brute mounted enough guns and blasters to make the USS *Iowa* blush in envy. It was armored heavily enough that Zulu thought he could take on anything short of an Abrams tank in a fair fight. Of course, fair fights were for suckers. Which, he considered, meant he could probably take out the Abrams, too.

While in flight, he went over every possible little tidbit of information, speculation and rumor available on the Agency's secure servers. There wasn't much there.

Finally, he checked out some of the regular Internet's online 'scream-sheets.' There were LOTS of kooks, nuts and crackpots out there, but sometimes, one or another of them actually had a clue what they were talking about. Maybe not much of a clue, seeing as too much of a clue would get said nut a visit from someone with a brain bleacher. But there was enough there to give Agent Zulu a whole new set of worries.

Especially about the southern Rocky Mountain region.

And when he reached HQ in New York City almost three hours after leaving Chicago and was briefed by Agent Romeo of Alpha Two, he learned that his worries did not even vaguely reach the reality of the threat.

* * *

"Okay, that's not possible, just flat out impossible," Agent Zulu muttered to himself as he watched the video of Myclestra destroying four Alpha Line teams in ninety seconds flat. "No way anyone humanoid can be that fast. And watch here, against Agent Yankee, she moved like she knew, in advance, what he was gonna do." He rewound the replay and slowly clicked through one section, frame by frame.

"I grow tired of being told what I do in combat is impossible," Myclestra growled from where she sat next to Omega's desk. "Believe it, Mortal, that film is nothing less than absolute truth. Or would you call me liar and I then be forced to prove to you otherwise?"

"Easy, Myclestra, let's cut Agent Zulu some slack." Omega reached over and gently rubbed the tall alien woman's shoulder. "He has NOT been in the loop on this at all. It's coming at him cold. And my reaction, when I saw video of you in action, was initially kinda the same, girl. You bring abilities to the party that we're not used to seeing in this world, because our universe doesn't normally allow for things like that to happen. Give him a little time to deal with it."

"Very well. For the moment, battle-sister."

"Agent Zulu, what you are seeing there is honest-to-Merlin-the-Wizard magic. Myclestra is not only alien, she's from another universe entirely," Echo explained. "One where the rules of physics are a bit different than ours, but not so different that they don't apply here. Trust me on that. And Director Fox has confirmed that. Don't ask me how; I don't have a need to know." Agent Echo DID know how Fox had confirmed that what Myclestra used was real, actual magic. But at least for now, that information was restricted to himself and Fox only, as Director and Assistant Director. "And, yes, she did, in fact, waffle-stomp eight Alpha Line Agents, myself included, in well under two minutes."

"I…see, Agent Echo." Zulu was hesitant answering as he watched the full video again. "My apologies, Agent Mycl—"

"I am no Agent of your Galactic Agency, Agent Zulu," Myclestra interrupted him. "I am a bounty hunter, and I DO expect to get paid. Handsomely."

"Ah, I, er, hmm, I see, Myclestra," Agent Zulu stumbled a bit at the interruption. "Ah, well, then, given what you can obviously do, what do you need me for?"

"Your flame weapons, Agent Zulu," Omega answered. "Your presence and skill. And maybe that rolling bunker you call a vehicle. The Agency is a little short on tanks and armored personnel carriers at the moment."

"You're kidding me, right?" Solemn stares from brown and sapphire eyes answered him. Myclestra snorted, her mirrored eye-shields reflecting Zulu's own image.

"I have better things to do with my time, battle-sister. I shall be either in my kitchen or the exercise room, should you need me. I have no need to hear the story again." Myclestra stood, and Agent Zulu finally realized just how tall she was as she stalked out of the Alpha Line Room. Her skin-tight leggings and gypsy-style midriff top left little to the imagination.

"Wow." Zulu strangled his wolf-whistle stillborn before it could get him in deep kimchee. "She's really something else, isn't she?"

"You have NO idea." Echo grinned at him. "Now, pay attention; here are the problems we think we're gonna have, and how we hope your equipment can help with it." Echo pulled up a briefing list on his computer screen and started going over the highlights.

* * *

The auditorium was packed. Fox had called in every one of the Agents and Teams from Alpha Line, Field, and Security departments, as well as Weapons Development, for a meeting to discuss organization and tactics. Agent Zulu had contributed four military grade flamethrowers, an American Army M9-7, a Vietnam-era weapon and three World War II era weapons, notably a pair of German Flammenwerfer 41 flamethrowers and a British 'Lifebuoy' flamethrower, named for the circular fuel tank on the pack frame. He also had two XM43 commercial flamers and three commercial modified butane torches. The butane torches and XM43s had provided examples for the Weapons Division to copy and produce enough of them to issue a butane torch to each individual Agent and provide at least one two-Agent flamethrower team to each ten-man squad.

He showed them the training room video with Myclestra, and the room began to murmur in displeasure and disbelief, the volume growing by the second.

"Stop right there," Fox ordered firmly, holding up a hand. "I can assure you right now that the video is the real deal. Myclestra does NOT come from this universe, and she, and the Sword, which houses a sentient entity, are therefore not required to follow our personal expectations in terms of abilities…so deal with it. By way of explanation: As you all know about Agent Omega's 'enhancements,' if not officially then through the Agency grapevine, imagine an entire race on which an advanced culture has been experimenting in similar fashion…for MILLENNIA. Now imagine the abilities of that race if each generation was tweaked a little more each time…and each generation gets shorter and shorter due to artificial gestation, until it takes mere months to create a new generation. That is Myclestra's species, most of whom, in her home universe, are enslaved to that advanced culture…or sold as literal cannon fodder to other species. She is here largely for the simple reason that the entity in her Sword helped her escape her slavery, and she became a bounty hunter, chasing what we would consider a demon through a rift between realities. I gather Agent Omega has been working on the physics of that rift, so if you have questions, go find her after the briefing."

The murmuring resumed, but this time was quieter, more

curious.

"The training session you just saw was intended to give our Alpha Line Agents a better feel for what a standard fight against this demon would be like. Obviously, it would be like nothing we've ever done before, and the video depicts as much. The demon-creature is called a warpwraith, and it does have the ability to turn your own thoughts and feelings against you. It can also teleport extremely fast, and use that ability to dodge your weapons fire. It is effectively impervious to any weapon that is not plasma-based in its attack. To that end, proto-cyclotron blasters, while normally our preferred weapon, are of somewhat limited use, as verified by Alpha One in their first, and so far only, encounter with the creature. Tachyon-splitter rifles are likely a bit better, and we will be using those and tachyon-splitter cannons, mounted on vehicles. We will also be issuing plasma rifles, newly released from the Weapons Development lab. Tactical nukes are also an option, if it comes to that. We hope it does not, for obvious reasons."

A hand went up.

"Go, Chi."

"Sir, why don't we give it an option to surrender? It sounds like we're going in armed for Aurigan were-bear."

"We are, and it's been given an option to stand down by Alpha One already," Fox noted. "Never mind by Ms. Myclestra, and at least two U.S. Air Force security guards. You don't want to know what became of the guards."

The room grew dead silent.

"Fox, I think maybe we do," Crutch said then.

"Are there photos?" someone asked.

"NO PHOTOS," Omega declared then, moving forward and holding up a staying hand, from where she and Echo backed up Fox, alongside Myclestra, on the stage of the auditorium. "Trust me on that."

"But why?" cane another query.

"Because they, along with their uniforms and all the equipment they carried, were crushed into one big...lump," a pale Echo said then. "Nothing was distinguishable from anything else, except for some protruding shards of bone and metal and plastic. Well, the blood and body fluids that were oozing out everywhere. Maybe a trailing piece of intestine or something."

Omega went white.

"Enough, Ace," she murmured.

"Oh shit. Sorry, baby," he replied, turning to her.

"The first ones to discover them were Alpha One," Fox continued, as Echo led Omega back to Myclestra's side and eased her into a sitting position on the floor; India slipped onto the platform to come to their aid, and Myclestra crouched beside them, concerned. "I listened as they tried to report in regarding what happened, and discovered the bodies. Can you imagine listening in your office, in utter helplessness and horror, while Alpha One — the toughest, most battle-hardened team I have — retched for five minutes straight? From what I understand, and by the sound, Omega basically purged her gut, and Echo avoided it only because he immediately started seeing to his partner and wife, which took his attention away from the horror of the remains. Even so, he had hard work to control his own nausea."

"No shit," Echo murmured, though the acoustic systems picked it up and transmitted it to the room as a whole.

"Given that Omega had already been operating at maximum in order to apprehend the warpwraith and its hunter," India added, as she dosed Omega with an antiemetic via osmosive micropore syringe in her neck, "the one-two combo very nearly resulted in a severe hypoglycemic episode."

"It didn't, quite, but she was awfully damn wobbly," Echo added.

"Damn," Crutch murmured.

"Alla that," Chi agreed. "Are you okay now, Meg?"

"The memory doesn't do either of us any favors," Echo admitted, seeing as Omega was still trying to get her belly settled. "But it does get worse."

"How can it get worse?" Nab wondered. "Crushed beyond recognition is about as bad as it gets."

"No, it isn't," Fox countered. "Because, never mind the power of its innate weaponry — and the beings of that universe do have access to what we would consider powerful magicks — the warpwraith's preferred energy source is living beings."

"So don't get eaten," Rho said with an indifferent shrug.

"It isn't quite that simple," Fox declared. "You see, not only is it lightning-fast, it's kind of like an amoeba — it reaches out and grabs people, and then it…absorbs them. From what I gather, the first thing it does is feed off your fear, as it gradually and painfully begins to dissolve your body…slowly, to heighten the fear and the pain. Then, for want of a better way to put it, as your body is finally dying, it consumes your very essence — your soul. I'm not sure how that appertains to those of us who believe in an afterlife, but I can't think it's a good thing, regardless."

"Nope. That's not good," Crutch opined.

"No, and that's why we're going to be making heavy use of force domes and force fields in general, because those apparently can stop this thing, or at least slow it, especially in lock-out mode," Fox pointed out. "And," he added, then broke off, dropping his gaze to the stage floor.

The room was silent for a long moment, waiting for their Director to finish his statement. Finally he drew a deep breath as if steeling himself, raised his head, and looked at them all.

"And that is why," he continued, "I am issuing the following order: If anyone is grabbed by the warpwraith, that person is to be targeted by nearby agents…and killed before he or she can be contained within the creature."

The room was dead silent for long minutes.

"Damn," a shocked Rho said then. "Shit just got real."

* * *

"The distribution of personnel will consist of three force teams and a command team, broken into four squads each, as well as a diversion team," Fox continued. "Apple Force will be staffed largely from Headquarters personnel, or from those I've called in to Headquarters; the Commanding Officer will be Agent Romeo of Alpha Two, and his XO is his partner, Agent India, who will also be our on-site medic. Baker Force will also be staffed out of Headquarters, and commanded by Alpha Seven. CO is Yankee, XO is Tare. Dolphin Force is the command team, in charge of C-cubed operations, and will be headed by Assistant Director Echo. The Diversion Force will be headed by Agent Omega, and will be placed at some distance from wherever the warpwraith next appears."

A hand rose.

"Go, Crutch." Fox waved a hand.

"You're missing a force, there, Fox," she pointed out.

"No, I just hadn't gotten to them yet. Charlie Force will come from the field agents of the closest Office to the warpwraith's location, once it surfaces again," Fox said. "To that end, it'll be more of a last-minute thing, and will be first on scene, tasked with setting and maintaining the perimeter. It will be up to Apple Force and Baker Force to go in and confront the wraith."

Silence descended over the big room. Fox broke it once more.

"If you are here in this room, you are capable of participating in the attack," he said. "Those who are on medical leave, or who have other duties, will remain here at Headquarters. Unfortunately, while Echo is going with you, that means I must remain here. It isn't according to my wont, but one of us has to stay out of harm's way, to run the Division. Echo, I expect you to stay in the rear, and I expect the others to ensure he stays safe."

"Yes, sir," Echo responded.

"Now, I do have some tentative assignments, but given that all of the force leads volunteered, I'd like to give you the opportunity to volunteer for which force team you'd like to be on," Fox continued. "So please pull your cell phones and text your first and second choices to Lima," he waved at the Boys, who were at a small console in the front stage-right corner, "and he and Bravo will coordinate the responses, put together the forces and squads, and send them to my tablet, and from there, back to you as assignments. Go."

Everyone pulled out their phones and began texting.

* * *

"All right," Fox said, about twenty minutes later. "That's that. You should all have your assignments now. Go to the armory and fetch your personal armor and equipment, and consider yourselves on call for BATTLE. This isn't just a mission, it's a small war, ladies and gentlemen. I want us ready at a moment's notice; it'll take us long enough to get where we need to go, without having to wait for readiness."

"Fox, how are we getting to wherever we end up going?" Nab wondered.

"Oh, a glaring omission on my part; thank you, Nab," Fox said, smacking his forehead with one palm. "We'll be taking four *Phoenix*-class saucers, with stowage and berths gutted or stowed. That way, if you all cram in tightly and stay friendly, we should be able to get roughly one force per ship, along with armor and equipment. In addition, you'll be using the ships' tractor beams to carry along several smaller craft, such as Agent Zulu's personal armored vehicle, which he calls The Beast, and which is itself a small tank, and some four to six airskimmers each for additional air support. All craft have had their offensive and defensive armament significantly boosted over the nominal specs, and will be suited to function as something between a destroyer and a corvette. They will also have tachyon-splitter cannons mounted as door guns, and each craft will have a pilot, co-pilot, and door gunner, in addition to the landing troops. Is this clear to everyone?"

Nods went around the room.

"Good. Go get ready. And may HaShem help us all."

* * *

In two hours, everyone was ready and on standby.

All that was left was for the warpwraith to show up.

Somewhere.

* * *

The next few days were quiet, save for the preparation for action that never seemed to arrive.

Each day saw a meeting of the various force teams, who kept themselves in shape and well fed and in a state of continuous readiness. And each day saw the leads, plus Myclestra and Surlianth, meeting up in Fox's office for the latest intel…which was always that there was no intel. No one knew where the warpwraith had gone, not even Surlianth.

"This had better go down soon," India grumbled one evening to Romeo, over dinner, "or I'm gonna break something."

"Careful what ya wish for, babe," he told her. "Been my experience, you'll get it in spades."

* * *

They were gathered in Fox's office for another intel meeting. He'd just told them that there was still no news, and they all sighed, then fell silent, pondering where the thing might have gone, and how they might scare it into showing itself again.

The chirping of Fox's phone broke the uncomfortable silence.

"Fox here; go," he answered it. "WHAT?! Where? Shit, merde, verdammt and farkakte! Oh, dammit all to hell and back. Okay, Lima, keep me updated."

"What's up, Fox?" Echo asked.

"Myclestra, I think we might have just found your monster," he said as he glanced at her. "The Browns Ferry Nuclear Power Plant in Alabama just went completely off-line. For no discernible reason. All of northern Alabama went dark as a result. There's no communication with plant personnel, and there are reports from a tug pushing barges on the Tennessee River of something 'huge and black, like a solid cloud' settling over the plant. Could that be this warpwraith?"

"Oh shit," a perturbed Omega whispered. "Oh shit. That's

it, Fox! That's this thing!"

"Most certainly. My battle-sister is correct." Myclestra was on her feet instantly. "Now, shall we go?"

"We shall," Echo said, as Fox nodded, deferring to him as the operation's commanding officer. "Fox, please issue a Level 2 Planetary Alert. Meg, send out the Alpha Line Alert. Operation Takedown is a go. Start loading up."

Chapter Eight — Power!

It had taken far too long to reach this source of power. The great river that nearly bisected this continent had broken the ley-line he had used to flee the ambush. Crossing it had greatly delayed him. While he feared fire, water was mostly an annoyance or inconvenience. Unless in truly massive quantities, such as this accursed Mississippi River, or so he had learned its name from the humans he had used to transport him across the flooded river. Humans he had used and then consumed, stealing their knowledge, lives and souls as well.

Now he spread himself wide and settled out of the sky over this place, this 'power plant,' and greedily absorbed the glowing energy of burning nuclear cores. Power so great, he found he could not simply take it all into himself at once. The three greatest supplies of energy were close together, easy to absorb. Once he dealt with the pestiferous humans infesting the place, he could siphon off the pure, raw energy. There were some few other concentrations of power, depleted and lesser. Perhaps the remnants of the fuel this place used. No matter, for those places offered him power he could easily and immediately devour, increasing his capabilities at least two-fold. He shuddered in pleasure at the potential the raw power of this place promised him, fueling his desire for power and dominance.

* * *

While there were about two hundred employees at work on the graveyard shift at the Browns Ferry Nuclear Power Plant, Joe Buckley was really only directly responsible for about thirty of them. He was the night shift Control Room Supervisor, with three other employees with him in the Control Room itself, monitoring the output of the three boiling water reactors and the generators they powered. The others were maintenance engineers and techs, a janitorial crew, and the roving fire watch and security officers, all positions inside the reactor buildings and the entry control point.

The remainder — those that weren't his people, and therefore external to the power-generating station proper — included the techs at the actual electrical distribution station, delivering the electrical power produced here through the Southeastern United States, as well as line workers, another janitorial crew for the office building, exterior security patrols and others.

When it happened, when whatever it was blanketed the plant, those exterior employees were the lucky ones. They escaped with their lives, and some even kept most of their sanity.

* * *

Lawrence 'Larry' Gamble was the head of security on the night shift, and rather than sit on his butt in the Security Office, staring at an endless bank of monitors, he preferred to be out and about. Walking the plant kept his people on their toes, because you never knew just when the boss would turn up. And putting in a couple miles walking the corridors kept him in better shape than planting his rear end in a chair and eating doughnuts and beef jerky all night.

He knew he had a couple of employees who liked to smoke, and sporadically he had to remind them not to spend too much time in the authorized smoke shacks sited the correct fifty feet away from any TVA buildings. It was part of the job, keeping his eye on his people. But tonight, his conscientious attention to his duty meant that he was among the first to die.

"Hey, boss." Miles Chaffington was one of the smokers and always called him, 'Boss.' Amanda Arlington, or AA to her friends, was the other smoker and she rarely spoke to anyone. But she was a regular and heavy smoker. And therefore, she spent as much time as she could get away with at the shack.

"Miles, AA, how's the shift going?" He nodded to them as he walked up. He smoked a butt or two on rare occasions, himself, and now bummed a light from Miles for his own

281

smoke.

"The usual, Boss, quiet, no drama. Haven't quite got used to this new schedule, starting third shift at twenty-thirty instead of twenty-three hundred."

"Yeah, I hear you on that. But some 'efficiency expert' did a report, blah, blah, blah and here we are at twenty-two-fifteen, nearly two hours into our shift. I can growl about it, but the head honchos don't listen to me." His cigarette glowed in the shadows of the shack cast by the building's bright yellow sodium exterior lights. "You know that. What about you, AA? Any moans, whines, bitches or complaints?" He noticed the middle-aged African-American woman was staring up into the night sky beyond the lights.

"Not really, Larry. But where did the stars go? Look up. It's like someone threw a wet, shiny black blanket over the sk—"

The wave of foul corruption that washed down out of the night strangled her scream before it had barely begun. Miles and Larry, at the back of the shack, had just enough time to draw their Glock 19 duty weapons, but neither of them got a shot off before they were engulfed and crushed, too.

* * *

"What the hell?" Arnold Carter suddenly sat bolt upright in his chair. Every warning light on his board for Reactor Number Three had flashed into yellow warning mode simultaneously. Yellow warning lights quickly began to change to red emergency lights. Buckley snapped upright in his desk chair.

"Arnie, SCRAM the reactor, NOW!" was his instant and instinctive order.

Carter's hand slammed down on the red SCRAM button, activating the hydraulic system that forced the control rods, made of high boron steel and boron carbide, into position to drop into the reactor vessel, bringing the fission reaction within the containment vessel to an abrupt stop.

Before Buckley could get another word out, the warning lights for Reactors One and Two flashed yellow, then red. Casey

Winston was Reactor One's operator and he hit the SCRAM button instantly. Irene Delgado was only fractions of a second behind him in SCRAMing Reactor Two.

"What the hell is going on here?" Joe Buckley stared at the constellation of red warning lights lending a garish scarlet hue to the entire Control Room. "All three reactors? At the same time? That's so far out on the edge of probability, I can't even imagine! Dammit! I mean, all three? At once?"

"Yeah, and Joe, look at the readings for decay heat." Irene was frantically paging through her post-SCRAM checklist. "It's dropping, dropping fast. Like it was freezing solid or something. That's not possible! Not improbable, it's IMPOSSIBLE. Like something is draining the radioactivity out of the reactor core. How in God's Nam—"

"Your pathetic god has nothing to do with it," a strange, warped voice whispered behind them. "I require the power you hold here. And that which Wruthas requires, is his at his will. And now, I require your souls."

The four of them spun to face that uncanny, impossible voice. A…black thing…stood there. It was basically humanoid but lacked anything other than rudimentary facial features. There were no legs, just a column of a shiny, gelatinous black sludge holding up a torso with the disturbing head and a pair of tentacular appendages where a human would have arms. Dozens, scores of black pseudopods stretched away from the base of the thing. They thinned into hair-like tentacles and seemed to fit under the cipher-locked door and into every crack and crevice between instrument panels. Thicker ones twisted into each air vent.

All four humans gaped at this bizarre apparition. But only for scant seconds. None of them had the chance to speak before Wruthas moved like a striking cobra, enveloping all of them in an instant. There wasn't even time to scream.

They kicked and twisted against the monster enveloping them, slowly suffocating as the Warpwraith eroded their souls and melted their bodies. When they tried to scream, the black corruption of the creature forced its way down their throats. It kept them alive when they should have died quickly, feasting on their terror and pain. If Wruthas had had a face, he would have smiled in pleasure at the hopeless struggles.

Buckley was the last to die.

* * *

The cloaked airskimmer's magnetic propulsion systems whined softly as it dropped out of the dark sky, hugging the ground as it ducked under the main power lines leading out of the Browns Ferry Nuclear Power Plant. It settled onto the asphalt at the intersection of Nuclear Plant Road and Hawkins Drive. The skimmer immediately put up a solid hologram of a TVA electrical maintenance truck before it dropped its cloak.

Agents dashed out of the side hatch and began setting up solid hologram roadblocks — not that there was a great deal of traffic in the pitch darkness. And none near the nuclear plant. What there WAS, was an odd feeling of…dread. Which probably explained the lack of traffic.

The last two agents off the skimmer pulled a fold-down table and awning from the side of the vehicle before turning high-powered night vision devices toward the distant, blacked-out looming hulk of the reactor plant buildings, which should have at least been silhouetted against the glow of Decatur, Alabama across the river…but even that was dark. A dozen other morphed and cloaked vehicles coalesced out of the night sky, adopting solid holograms of TVA pickup trucks and Limestone County Deputy Sheriff patrol cars as they landed.

"You see anything, Tau?"

"Not a damn thing in any spectrum. And, buddy, that's SO very not good. From here we should be able to see the damn plant lights, easy. And maybe the exterior personnel. But, yeah, it's quiet as the grave over there." Agent Tau, Alpha Forty-Two's senior team member, and the Charlie Force commander, answered his partner.

"Not a good simile, man, not with what we've been getting outta HQ. Not at all." Agent Upsilon was the taller of the Alpha

Line pair, just shy of a lean, solid six feet tall. His blond hair and blue-eyed good looks attracted more female attention than was good for his partner's ego. Agent Tau was short, blocky, dark haired and dark-skinned, rough-hewn and beetle-browed, only redeemed by an intense pair of brilliant green eyes. Still, Upsilon was a good partner, and so was Tau…so he played the hand he'd been dealt. It was what it was, and right now, there was a damn serious job to do.

"Probably not, buddy." Tau answered absent-mindedly, scanning the nuclear power plant. "Probably not." He lowered the image intensifiers and turned to where Charlie Force was slowly getting organized. "Ok, guys, we need to get busy clearing out the local subdivisions and getting the exterior perimeter established. You know the story — possible containment vessel failure, radiation leak. Get a move on, people. Alpha One is inbound, ETA in about an hour, so let's show some hustle, troops."

* * *

"We need to hurry up, Madrid," Omega murmured to her coworker as they worked frantically on a very special device in the weapons lab; it would, hopefully, enable them to capture and store the amazing energies produced by Surlianth via the Sword, then release them as needed to either boost their energy signal, or enhance certain other functions of the ship on which they were about to debark. "Echo and his task force left Penn Station ten minutes ago."

"I know, Omega, old girl, I know," Madrid muttered, as he concentrated on adding the last few parts to the device. "But I can't go any faster, or this thing won't work at all, and might blow up in our faces. Hand me the acoustic turnscrew."

Omega placed the tool in his hand, then held the part steady as he worked to fasten it in position.

"Okay, it's tight enough I can finish this," Madrid said. "Grab the next piece."

Omega reached for the next part.

* * *

Nearby, Myclestra, with Surlianthet sheathed on her back, observed the two agents working frantically.

<This is taking longer than I expected,> Surlianth told Myclestra in private.

It is, Old Snake, but they are working hard, and they are aware of the time, Myclestra responded to the telepathic remark.

<I know. Silver Hair is brilliant to have even devised a way to do this, and her friend there is as brilliant in his own right, to have figured out how to construct it.>

They are very good at what they do. I am amazed at Omega's learning and knowledge.

<I know. If we can all survive this little adventure, do away with the Wraith, and catch our breaths, I would like to encourage you to sit at her side and learn from her. I think there is much she can teach you, about many things. And it would only make you a better bounty hunter to understand those things.>

You make a good point, Old Snake. If she is willing, and we all survive, I will try. From what I have seen, she is an excellent teacher, and I understand that she does teach on the side, at this...Division One University.

<So I understand, as well. Still, if this device is not finished soon, it will all be moot, for we none of us will survive the destruction of their world.>

"DONE!" Omega cried just then.

"Good timing, Old Snake," Myclestra said aloud.

"Huh?" Omega wondered, glancing in confusion between Madrid and Myclestra; Madrid looked just as puzzled as Omega felt.

<My Little One and I were only discussing the fact that we should depart, and soon, if we are to make this work,> Surlianth replied 'aloud.' <Just as you finished the device.>

"Ah. One last test, then," Madrid said. "Myclestra, would you draw Surlianth and place him into the device?"

"You are sure it will not hurt him?" Myclestra wondered.

"No, it won't hurt him," Omega soothed. "The worst that would happen is just that it wouldn't work."

"Very well. Are you ready, Old Snake?"

<I am, Little One. Let us do this thing.>

Myclestra carefully drew the Sword from the scabbard on her back, then strode to the device, which looked rather like a high-tech mailbox, or perhaps a giant coin bank, about four feet high, two feet across, and shaped like a hexagonal pedestal…not that Myclestra knew what any of that was, but the two Earth humans did.

"The blade goes into the slot?" Myclestra asked, pointing.

"Exactly," Madrid confirmed. "Slow and easy."

She positioned Surlianthet over the slot, inserted the tip of the blade, then gently slid it home.

Immediately the status lights on the device lit up, indicating a good interface.

<Ooo,> Surlianth said then. Madrid and Omega both went on alert.

"Is everything okay, Surl?" Omega wondered, concerned.

<Yes, yes, everything is fine, Silver Hair,> the ancient star drake replied. <But I did not expect it to tickle!>

Myclestra and Omega snorted in unison, and Madrid turned away to hide his efforts to control mirth. Finally he turned back around.

"All right, Omega, girl, let's pack up and head south," he decreed.

"Not…quite," Omega determined, a bit hesitant. "I appreciate the intent, Madrid, but you're the top weapons designer on the planet. You can help me load this into the *Prydwen*, sure, but then you have to stay here, at Headquarters. Fox's orders."

"Aw," Madrid sighed, face falling. "I never get to see my devices in action."

"Wasn't my call, hon. I'd love to have you along," Omega admitted.

"Come along, then, and let's get you on your way, or this

whole thing will come apart at the seams," Madrid said. "I've an antigrav tow platform right over here…"

Fifteen minutes later, the "Surlianthet Capacitor," as Madrid had dubbed it — though the name was more joke than anything, and only conceptually bore a resemblance to an actual capacitor — was loaded, with Surlianth, into the D1 *Prydwen*, waiting for Omega at Pennsylvania Station.

The D1 *Prydwen* was one of the largest ships that could be berthed on-planet, but that meant several things: one, it could maneuver in-atmosphere readily. Two, it had a big power plant, with circuitry corresponding to big power. And three, while it normally had a crew complement of five, in an emergency, it could be handled by one person. And Omega knew how to handle it.

"Are you sure about this, Omega, old girl?" Madrid said, worried, as he and Myclestra parked the 'capacitor,' with Surlianth still in it, the lot still on the antigrav platform, in the rear of the flight deck, near the deck's main exit hatch. Having already been shown how, Myclestra bent and locked the platform in position. "You won't have anyone to help you…"

"No, this is as Omega and I have discussed," Myclestra said. "We do not wish to put anyone else in harm's way, and Omega is the person I trust to pilot this vessel, and to help me do what is needful. Never mind to initiate the force fields to trap the Warpwraith."

"And I'm good with that," Omega agreed. "I don't want to risk any more personnel than we already are, if something doesn't go right. I've got enhanced shit to help me handle things, and after everything I've been through, it's hard to really scare me, anyway. But if we have another pilot, and he or she sees this monster and panics, we'll have problems."

<Fear not,> Surlianth told Madrid privately. <By doing this, Omega may be able to escape, should matters go ill. Knowing her, I doubt she will, but she may be what we need to, as she says, 'pull our fat out of the fire,' if things DO go badly.>

"Oh," Madrid said then. "OH."

"You okay, buddy?"

"I'm fine, old girl. Listen…be careful, all right?"

"Always," Omega averred. "But we take this thing out, one way or another. So know that, hon. If we fail, Earth — and probably the whole damn galaxy, eventually — is doomed. As my old employers used to say, 'Failure is not an option.' Not at this point. I'll do what it takes to prevent mission failure. Understand?"

"Right." Madrid sighed. "All right, let me get out of here so you can go."

* * *

Three minutes later, the D1 *Prydwen* was exo and hauling ass, with full cloaking and sensor scrambler active, headed on a tight, swift, suborbital hop to a point along the line between northwest Alabama and south-central Tennessee that had been determined as the final showdown.

* * *

"ETA ten minutes. Strap down tight, boys and girls, it's gonna be rough and bouncy the rest of the way down." Agent Dog was at the controls of the *Phoenix*-class transport saucer *Eagle*, currently slicing down the re-entry corridor of a high-speed sub-orbital hop from HQ.

"How's the corridor look, Dog?" Echo was in the co-pilot's seat, displacing Agent Hypo, Dog's assigned co-pilot — Dog's Alpha Line partner, Quebec, had been on personal leave when it all went down — to the navigator's station, where he was maintaining a careful surveillance of the area around them. Below the flight deck, half of Apple Force was crammed into temporary aluminum seats that would have looked perfectly in place in a C-47 Skytrain flying over Normandy on D-day. Three airskimmers and Agent Zulu's modified M1114 were tucked in tight to the saucer's hull, locked in by tractor beams, in order to be covered by *Eagle's* cloak and scrambler system, let alone the force field protecting them from re-entry.

"We're in the pipe, five by five, Echo. But the skimmers and Zulu's monster truck are playing merry hob with the airflow, despite the force fields. The additional lumps in the field shape, pulling it in so tight, just create all kinds o' turbulence. Makes for a rough ride."

"How's the cloak holding?" Echo sat back in the seat, ready to grab the controls to help Dog if needed.

"Good so far," Dog growled under his breath, "but we ARE raising the Devil's own amount of turbulence, and the saucers coming in behind us are only going to make it worse. If there's any standard aircraft that comes through the airspace in our wake, they're gonna wonder what the hell is going on with the weather."

"They'll just have to wonder, Dog," Echo said with a shrug. "I hear you, but it shouldn't be bad enough to take an aircraft out, so they'll just have to wonder already. Besides, given it's dark as Hades down there — including Huntsville, where the international airport is — I sorta doubt any aircraft are up, at least in our target area; any incoming were probably diverted, and those on the ground are gonna stay there awhile. But I'll ping Fox to have something ready to insert into the aviation weather reports, just in case."

"Good plan. And you're prob'ly right. Which may be the only GOOD thing comin' out of it." Dog checked his instrumentation. "Where you wanna set down and establish a command center?"

"Well, we need to tag up with Charlie Force first off," Echo noted. "The Atlanta Office personnel were here in about half an hour after Fox issued the orders, and they should have the area secured from civilians, at least. I wanna find out what they've seen, and then adjust the plan from there if need be. Hopefully they haven't had to interact; their orders were to wait until the main force arrived, if at all possible. They won't have plasma rifles or flamethrowers, anyway."

"They'll have tachyon-splitter rifles."

"True, but I can speak from experience that blasters do nothing, and we don't know yet how well tachyon-splitters will work on this wraith-thing. At least, I hope we don't know yet. But that's another reason for checking in with them first."

"Aha. No battle plan ever survives first contact with the enemy?"

"Something like, yeah," Echo offered him a tight, mirthless grin. "But really more a case of on-site recon. I want the latest intel."

"Roger that. Gonna make that the main command post?"

"I'd thought about it, yeah. Prob'ly will, at that. As the commander of this whole operation, Alpha Line Chief AND the Assistant Director, well…" Echo sighed. "I had specific orders from Fox NOT to lead from the front this time, for several reasons, the most notable being what's in my brain doesn't need to get passed to the wraith if I'm et. And I'll get the sideways stink-eye from Meg if I disobey."

"Aha. It makes sense, pal. And your wife is your chief bodyguard, remember — she heads the Praetorians, after all. She loves you, AND she has a good strategic head on her shoulders. They're both right: You're the brains, here; we need you around to direct the units and respond to enemy action, and NOT wind up helping said enemy by getting noshed, and everything you know found out. Okay, I have Charlie Force command in view; it's at the intersection of Nuclear Plant Road and Hawkins Drive, which I'd say is a good location for an overall command post, just for the record…"

"Good, and I agree. Let's do it."

"Okay; I'll notify the other spacecraft. We'll offload the various craft, then put down the *Eagle* just outside the perimeter. If we need the spacecraft, they'll be in reach."

"Copy that; good plan."

* * *

By the time the main forces arrived, Charlie Force had evacuated the area from the Tennessee River north to some five miles out, setting up roadblocks and checkpoints along the way, as well as aerial patrols in airskimmers. This included the river; all of the nearby industrial facilities on the south side of the river had likewise been evacuated by a team from

Huntsville Station, coordinating closely with the Atlanta Office contingent, all under Alpha Forty-Two's command. Between them, they'd also cleared all the barges and river traffic, and established a cloaked aerial patrol over the river proper, as well. Another primary roadblock had been set up at the intersection of Shaw Road and Douglas Branch, and there were secondary roadblocks everywhere a main road tied into either Shaw or Nuclear Plant Road, just to make sure.

"But no, Echo," Tau noted, "we haven't seen a damn thing. No lights, no heat signatures, no rad signatures, no nothin'. And the northern third of the state is dead in the water."

"What do you mean?"

"This plant provides the electricity for the northern third of the state of Alabama," Upsilon interjected. "When it goes down, everybody sits in the dark."

"Has it happened before?" Echo wondered.

"Yeah, EF-5 twister came through here during the 2011 superoutbreak," Tau noted. "Just missed the plant, but took out all the lines coming out of it. Wadded up all those big high-voltage towers like tin foil."

"Shit."

"Yeah. Only place that had power was Decatur," Upsilon pointed, "across the river, 'cause the main cables for them run UNDER the river."

"But now they're dark, too," Echo observed, glancing south. "Because nothing is coming out of the plant. Not even radiation signatures from the reactors. It isn't a meltdown, like Fox was afraid might happen. The whole damn plant is stone-cold. Reactors and all."

"That's how we read it," Tau agreed. "But the scariest part is, there should be human infra-red signatures over there, a bunch. And there's none."

"Shit, hellfire, damnation," Echo cursed under his breath, then raised his voice. "All right. All hands meeting to coordinate this shit. Now. Tau, have your people stay on station, but tie in via comm."

"Roger that, sir."

* * *

"Apple Force," Echo called.

"Here!" Romeo responded, as the groups under his command went on alert, listening closely.

"You have your squad assignments?"

"We do, Echo," India averred. "And everyone knows where they're supposed to be, at least according to the plan when we left Headquarters."

"Good," Echo said, "and nothing's changed, but I'm gonna verify that as we go, just to make sure. Listen up."

"Yes, sir," came the chorused response.

"Apple Force, you have the river side," Echo noted, studying a map on his outboard brain tablet. "Apple Force Squad One: Center entrance."

"Roger that, sir," Agent Love affirmed. "A-one, center entrance, river."

"Apple Force Squad Two: West corner entrance."

"A-two, west corner entrance, river," Agent Jack confirmed.

"Apple Force Squad Three: South corner entrance."

"A-three confirms south corner entrance, river," Golf responded.

"Apple Force Squad Four, you will be held in reserve. I want you practically on the riverbank, but near the center entrance. Close enough to observe and respond, far enough away to stay out of any secondary splatter."

"A-four is in reserve, near center entrance, on the river," Agent Vessel of Alpha Thirty-Eight replied.

"Good copy. Be prepared for anything, guys," Echo said, somber. "And remember Fox's order: if any of you is grabbed by the wraith, eat your gun, or have one of the others shoot you. DO NOT get 'eaten' by this damned thing. You will not survive, and you don't want the repercussions. Either here, or hereafter."

There was silence; somber Apple Force members all

293

nodded.

"Good. Go load up on your airskimmers, cloak, and await my signal to take off," Echo said.

Apple Force moved away silently.

"Baker Force."

"Yes, sir!" Yankee said, snapping to attention. The rest of his force came to ready position.

"There are no usable entrances on most of the north side, and all of the east side, because of the power lines," Echo pointed out, "so you'll be wrapping around the west. Squad One, you have the northwest corner entrance on the secondary building, which most likely houses the control rooms."

"Copy that, sir; northwest corner, secondary building," Monkey answered.

"Baker Squad Two: river-side entrance of the secondary building."

"B-2, river-side entrance, secondary," Agent Jockey of Alpha Forty-Nine replied.

"Baker Squad Three: you are also on-site reserve. I want you on the greensward between buildings, on the northwest corner of the secondary building."

"B-3 confirms: greensward, northwest of secondary." Lugger, of Alpha Fifty, nodded.

"Baker Squad Four: You are aerial reserve support. Remember, once we manage to dislodge this thing from the plant, we want to herd it — without looking like we're herding it. So you'll become very important once the other squads have run it out. I want you in the general vicinity of the big antenna, or tower, or whatever the thing is — I can't tell in the dark. The big tall thing down by the river, behind the secondary building, at least relative to where we're standing."

"Copy that," Agent Windage of Alpha Forty-five noted. "Aerial reserve, stay mobile and orbit that big antenna-thing."

"What about Charlie Force, sir?" Tau asked.

"Stay put, keep an eye out, be ready to follow orders," Echo said. "I can't say what's going to happen when we tackle this wraith-thing. We may need you for reinforcements; we may need you to expand the perimeter. Or we may need you to help herd."

"Copy that, sir," Tau averred. "Charlie Force, stay put, be ready for anything."

"I won't repeat the warning I gave the Apple Force," Echo said, stifling a sigh; he had a very bad feeling that some of these friends and colleagues would not be going home from this fight. They were good, or they wouldn't be here, but the warpwraith was a complete unknown to them. "Just stay aware, watch each other's sixes, and let's get this over and done with. I want this damned thing gone from our universe."

They all nodded affirmation and agreement.

"Baker Force: Load up, cloak, and get ready to take off, on my signal," Echo ordered.

They headed for the airskimmers.

* * *

Echo waited until all the skimmers were loaded, then gave them an extra five minutes for everyone crammed inside to don gear and position themselves. He'd donned a subvocal comm neckband before departing the *Eagle*, and now he keyed it.

"GO," he ordered. "Report in once you're in position."

Almost as one, the ten airskimmers cloaked and vanished. Only the slightest humming whir denoted the quiet magnetic propulsion systems revving as they lifted off.

"Godspeed," he added softly, as the whirring faded into the distance.

* * *

One by one, the cloaked skimmers landed.

"*Crash Cart*, on the ground," India reported.

"*Break Five*, landed," Uniform noted.

"*Wind Chimes* on the ground," Nuts said.

"*High Flight*, landed and ready," Golf said.

"*Tow Truck* in position," Winch called.

"*Plain Sight* in position," Tare said.

"*Counting Trees* has landed," Kako reported in.

"*Ticket to Ride* is on the ground," Neptune said.

"*The Grunt* is where she's s'posed to be," Halliard called.

"The *Auger In* has augered into position," Fisher said.

"All skimmers report in position, Echo, sir," Romeo said then.

"Good. Debark squads and move to the entrances," Echo ordered.

"Debarking now," Romeo responded. "Should be in position in five."

"Copy that," Echo replied, glancing at his wrist chronometer.

* * *

Easy and Golf looked at each other and drew a deep breath.

"Here we go," Easy said.

"Yup. Keep your ass in gear and we should be okay," Golf replied. He glanced at the team, crammed into the available space in the crew cabin. "All right, guys, don goggle-glasses, initiate stealth mode; personal cloaking and sensor scrambler units on."

One by one, the squad faded from view.

A button depressed itself on the flight console, and Easy's disembodied voice said, "Hatch open. Begin debarkation."

* * *

Damn, this is eerie, Easy thought, as he moved, silent and invisible, toward the southeast corner of the building. The heads-up display on his goggle-glasses depicted his squad as codenames in brackets, superposed over the view before him. *Nobody in sight, dead dark, and dead quiet. I just hope this… thing…isn't the boojum Alpha One seems to think. If they're right, this is gonna be BAD. Maybe the worst thing we've ever faced, any of us.*

Within a few moments, the squad was in position to enter the building. Easy toggled his subvocal comm.

"Apple Squad Three in position," he subvocalized. The comm picked it up, transmitting it to Echo.

* * *

Echo listened intently to the largely-silent comm. Briefly he spared a thought for his wife and partner, and hoped Omega, as well as Myclestra and Surlianth, would be in position and ready…assuming his command could oust the warpwraith from the nuclear plant. Which thing, he realized, was not necessarily a given.

Abruptly the comm became active.

"Apple Force CO in position to command the fight," Romeo said softly.

"Alpha One medic in place, and prepped to handle any casualties," India's voice murmured.

"Apple Squad One at center door, ready for entry," Love said, sotto voce.

"Apple Squad Two at west door, ready for entry," Jack whispered.

"Apple Squad Three in position," Easy breathed.

"Apple Squad Four in backup position," Vessel muttered.

"Baker Force CO and XO in position to command," Yankee noted. "We're going in with Squad One."

"Baker Sqvad Vun in position for entry, northvest corner," Kako murmured.

"Baker Squad Two at secondary building rear entry, ready to proceed," Jockey whispered.

"Baker Squad Three standing by on greensward," Lugger breathed.

"Baker Squad Four standing by at the base of the tower," Windage said quietly.

Echo looked up from the comm, and glanced at Tau, who was listening to his own earpiece. He looked at Echo and nodded.

"Your people ready?" Echo verified.

"Affirm," Tau responded. "We're using a blockade model, with directional force wall projectors active."

"All right. All entry units, Condition Alpha Red One. Prepare for battle. Enter on my mark. And…GO."

And come back safe, buddies mine, Echo thought, biting

his lip in concern.

* * *

The entire plant was dark; only dim red emergency lights, powered by batteries, cast any illumination down the silent hallways and generator rooms. Wruthas would have smirked if he truly had a face. None of the plant's various video surveillance systems were operational, but Wruthas had extended himself to set a delicately layered series of magical warning spells. The arrival of the responding humans in their odd flying vehicles had been quicker than he expected. Those flyers concerned him. It was extremely difficult, nearly impossible, to actually see them, but their engines had a peculiar resonance to them that was irritating, nearly painful; they interacted with the local ley lines in a most unpleasant fashion. But his ability to peer into the strange world of the spirit and the soul enabled him to see the souls of the humans as they arrived, in despite of whatever it was hiding them, as they prepared to enter this place that had held such tremendous power. Power that was now his to wield.

Foolish humans, he nearly laughed aloud as the miniscule tendrils of magick near the entrances of this 'power-plant' slowly and carefully infiltrated into the thoughts and worries of the humans as they readied themselves to attack the building. *They do not realize my magics can detect their surface thoughts, and those thoughts are ones of fearful anxiety and even disbelief. They think there will be only ONE entity here, only ONE opponent. They could not be more wrong. My creations roam these passages, and they will feast and bring me man-flesh and souls. I shall feed well this night.* He pushed his will outward, awakening and alerting the…things…he had made. Things of which the merest glimpse would create terror and fear in these weakling mortals.

"Awaken, foul minions. Flesh and blood and souls come to be harvested. Go, slay those who would destroy your creator." His voice, dry and broken, a pitch and timbre of nails and glass being dragged through the screaming agonies of souls tortured in Hell, filled the Control Room.

According to their individual natures, his grotesque creatures began to move. Some gibbered and wailed, a discordant symphony of doomed spirits suffering the torments of the damned echoing throughout the silent halls. Others slid silently along floors or walls, and yet others scuttled behind piping and ceiling tiles. And some spread against walls and ceilings, blending into the red-tinged gloom, waiting for their prey to come to them.

* * *

Squad One of Apple Force was assigned the main entry control point of the reactor building. Led by Alpha Agents Love and Uniform, they hit the doors a few seconds ahead of the other four squads entering the complex. Fire Team One consisted of a pair of Delta teams, Diver and Ocean of Delta 128 and Delta 4's Gimel and Iota. They popped open the electrically locked doors and rushed inside, Gimel and Iota going left as Diver and Ocean went right. The flamethrower team, Beta Agents Ice and Jake were next, rapidly moving ten meters down the red lit hallway. The second Fire Team, Beta Agents Queen, Como, Reefer and Yacht, leapfrogged ahead of the flamethrower team, going into crouches at a crossing hallway.

"Apple Force Lead, this is Squad One Leader; we are in at Entry Point One. All clear. We have limited emergency type lighting in halls, no sign of opposition. Secure at this time. Over," Agent Love subvocalized.

"Apple Lead copies. Proceed as you see fit. Over," Agent Romeo responded.

"Squad One copies. Out." Love glanced at her invisible squad, their positions shown by her goggle-glasses. "Okay, let's move out. Slow and easy. Team One, left, Team Two, right. Flame team center. Go." Cautiously, the Agents moved down the main hallway, leading to the generator spaces.

Agent Yacht was the point, armed with a tachyon-splitter rifle. He heard something down the corridor and threw up a clenched fist; the signal had been programmed into the goggle-glasses display, and the squad's movement stopped. He pointed down the hall and they took what cover they could in the bare hall, the flame team centered and adjacent to Yacht.

"We got noise and movement, Apple Lead. Headed towards us pretty quick. Holding position. Over," Love barely breathed as she reported.

* * *

"Copy. Stay frosty. Over," Romeo replied, glancing at India. *It can't be this easy, can it?* he signaled her in their nonverbal code.

Maybe? I sure hope so, she answered. Stationed behind Squad One, just outside the building, the veteran Alpha Agents hoped and prayed it would BE that simple.

Their prayers would be in vain.

* * *

Hey, baby, where are you? Echo's mental voice came to Omega through the nd't'lq.

En route, fast as I can go, Ace, she told him, as the D1 *Prydwen* topped the peak of the parabolic arc and started down. *ETA, umm, about five minutes.*

Good. Because we're ready here, and about to enter the nuke plant, he replied. *After which, I kind of expect all hell to break loose.*

Yeah. We'll set up as fast as we can and start putting out an energy signature like nobody ever saw. Maybe that'll help, Omega said.

Good, because — OH SHIT!

What?! WHAT?? Ace? Are you there? Echo, what's happened?

But although she could pick up flickers of thought — enough to know he was still alive — he was apparently too busy to respond.

Grim-faced, Omega turned her own attention to the flight controls, boosting the speed of the *Prydwen* to its maximum safe atmospheric entry velocity, and maxxing out the shielding.

* * *

Agent Ice, carrying the German Flammenwerfer, saw it first, a roughly humanoid shape, big enough to brush the ten-foot-high ceiling. Other than the shape, it was featureless, a disturbing, glossy black mass gliding down the hall at little more than walking pace. Agent Ice triggered the hydrogen torch igniter for the flamethrower, preparing to cover the thing in burning napalm once it was within the weapon's thirty-meter range.

"Tachyon rifles, hit it!" Love commanded. Four tachyon-splitter rifle shots hit the thing dead center simultaneously, only to be absorbed with no effect whatsoever, when it should have blown off chunks of the creature. "Damn it! I was afraid of that! Plasma rifles, hit it!" Love and her partner, Uniform, added their plasma rifles to the fusillade. The plasma bolts splattered black goo all over the hallway. The monster shuddered and twitched, raising an arm-like pseudopod in a defensive reaction. Then, with a hissing shriek, it rushed forward, reaching toward the Agents.

"It SEES us!" Love exclaimed. "The cloaking and sensor scramblers don't work against it!"

"Didn't like that at all, didja?" Uniform shouted. "Roast it, Ice!"

The creature was easily within the flamethrower's thirty-meter range. Agent Ice filled the hallway with burning napalm, completely engulfing the thing. It screamed in apparent agony, flailing helplessly in the growing pond of flaming napalm. A horrendous stench assaulted the Agents, and Agent Como began to vomit continuously after getting a lungful of the noxious smoke. Uniform reached out and grabbed his collar, yanking him backward and sending him sliding away on the tile flooring.

The monster stopped thrashing as its body burned away. Ice poured fire onto it until the flamethrower's fuel tank ran dry. Ice dropped his cloak, and at Ice's signal, Jake swapped out fuel tanks, dropping the empty one behind him. By the time Ice was ready to fire again, only oily smoke and crusty, burned fragments of the monster remained. As they all relaxed, Queen voiced what they all thought.

"Man, THAT was what this Myclestra chick had all of us sweating bullets over? Whoo-boy, was she full of crap!" He wiped sweat off his forehead and chuckled. "Stinks to high heaven and the tachyon rifles didn't seem to hurt it at all, but c'mon, man! I'm thinking she's fulla crap and just playing us to get what she wants. They must make them dumb wherever she comes from!"

It was the last thing he ever said.

The real threat simply materialized out of the smoke-filled air. Huge and quadrupedal, an obscene neck lunged out of an armored torso, the horrific, circular, sucker-like mouth at the end of that neck engulfing Agent Queen down to mid-chest. There was a gruesome crunch as the thing crushed him into gory paste, the remainder of his body bouncing off the opposite wall, blood and organs coating the floor in a repulsive mix.

A foreleg, eight feet long, lashed out as the thing spun into the middle of the squad. The jagged, eight-inch-long claws tore Agent Ice open from throat to crotch, grabbing his pelvis and savagely shaking his body until it came apart. A kick from the horse-like hind leg punched cleanly through Agent Jake's body armor and then through his chest, leaving a hole a foot across in his body, destroying heart, lungs and spine in a single blow. His body skidded away.

The beast had a set of mid-chest arms, slightly larger and longer than a man's arms. The claw-like fingernails were redundant as those hands caught Agent Diver by a leg and opposite shoulder and simply tore him in half. It had no head at all, no face, just that hideous, worm-like sucker mouth full of rotating teeth at the end of that muscular, tentacle-like neck.

Love and Uniform hit it with plasma bolts to its center of mass, burning away huge masses of black skin, flesh and bone. It screeched, a hell-borne steam engine, before spitting an immense wad of poisonous mucus, mixed with gory bits of Agent Queen, at the Alpha Line Agents.

Their goggle-glasses saved their eyes, and their Suits and armor slowed down the acid, but any unprotected flesh quickly developed deep and serious chemical burns, exposing muscle and bone. Uniform went down as the acid burned into his neck. Love hit it again with her plasma rifle, burning away the worm mouth.

That injury sent it into a frenzy. It lunged madly about, knocking Yacht and Gimel down, the stomping, clawed feet smashing both of them into unrecognizable bloody smears on the floor. Screaming in rage at her partner's death, Agent Reefer shoved her plasma rifle into one of the gaping wounds in the monster's side and fired. The rifle exploded, the backblast killing Reefer and tearing the thing's armored torso open.

Ocean and Iota dropped their ineffective tachyon rifles and scrabbled in the bloody muck on the floor for a dropped plasma rifle or the flamethrower, still entangled in what was left of Agent Ice. Ocean recovered a plasma rifle and shot it, simultaneous with a hind leg kick from the creature that cleanly decapitated him. But the plasma bolt burned deeper into the guts of the thing. It leapt madly away from the blast. Iota got his hands on the flamethrower's wand, reigniting the hydrogen torch and firing at the leaping monstrosity. Coated with burning napalm, it shrieked a final time and landed on Iota with all four feet, rupturing the Flammenwerfer's nearly full fuel tank. The resulting explosion killed Iota, burning him beyond recognition, and shredded the monster into burning pieces scattered up and down the hall.

Agent Como sat up from where Uniform had thrown him, staring in horror at the burning wreckage of his squad. As they died, so did their cloaking systems, and the resulting carnage was clearly visible.

"Agen— oh God, Agents…Agents down! Oh my God, help us, they're all dead!" The smoke of the initial burning monster had poisoned him and left him with a damaged throat he could barely speak through. "Medic, oh dear God, medic!"

* * *

Outside the building, India threw Romeo a stunned look and bolted for the door, her partner and husband hot on her heels.

Chapter Nine — Hell in a Handbasket

Echo, along with the Alpha Forty-Two team from the Atlanta Office, listened in silence to the broadcast of the various squads as they slowly entered the nuclear plant.

"So far, so good," he murmured. "Still, I don't think they'll encounter the Big Bad until they get closer to the cor—"

He broke off, and all three men leaned over the speaker as Love shouted, "Tachyon rifles, hit it!"

"That's what I like to hear," Upsilon said…

…Then the comm turned into screaming.

"Oh, dear God," Echo breathed in horror, careful not to key the subvocal mic.

"It's a slaughter, sounds like," an equally shocked Tau whispered. "Maybe we found out what happened to the people who worked the plant? They all got ripped up?"

"No," Echo said, realizing the truth, based on what Omega had shown him of Myclestra's memories during their healing. "No, I think these monsters ARE the plant staff. Or whatever's left of 'em. Probably blended with shit from the wraith's original world, or plane of existence, or…whatever." He keyed his mic. "HEADS UP, ALL SQUADS! This warpwraith has monster sentinels positioned around the plant! They just took out most of Apple Squad One, by the sound! But they ARE killable. Tachyon-splitter rifles are useless; don't bother with 'em. And evidently the personal cloaking and sensor scramblers don't affect 'em, so don't bother with those, either. Plasma rifles and flamethrowers are the way to go. Repeat, use plasma rifles and flamethrowers. Be alert, be aware, don't get cocky, don't get overconfident. Just burn through anything you see, even if it LOOKS kinda like one of the plant staff."

There was a long silence, followed by India's, "All right,

I'm on scene, I — oh, dear Lord!"

"India, how many down?" Echo queried.

"Echo, I, I have three injured — Love, Uniform, and Como. Of those three, only Como is currently conscious, and all three are in bad shape. The rest..." India's voice choked, and broke off.

"Romeo to Echo," her partner's voice interjected, very quiet. "The rest are, um, well, they're sorta, uh, decorating the hallway, I guess you could say, along with what's left of at least one...thing, maybe two things."

Tau shoved a folding camp chair behind Echo, who sat down hard in it and put his face in his hands.

* * *

Three minutes later, the D1 *Prydwen* was on the ground in a very remote, mountainous, and surprisingly uninhabited parcel of land somewhere along the Tennessee/Alabama state line, northwest of the nuclear plant. Omega had zeroed in on a small valley that she, Echo, Fox, and Crutch had located, and decided that, given the nearest house was several tens of miles away, it would make a good site for their trap.

"All right," Omega said, unstrapping and rising. "Surl, have you been pumping some energy into the 'capacitor'?"

<I most certainly have,> he responded. <I feel a certain... strain...in the device now, so I believe it is as full as it should be, and needs to be discharged soon. I stopped when I sensed that a few moments ago.>

"Very good. Lemme see here." Omega pulled open a small door in the base of the pedestal and extracted a heavy-duty cable. She plugged one end into a special port that Madrid had installed once they'd reached the ship, then she plugged the other end into a socket in the base of the pedestal. "Okay, stand back, Myc," she told the Alontoran, who had come to watch over her shoulder. "Oh, and go ahead and withdraw Surl from the thing."

Myclestra did as Omega asked, then sheathed Surlianthet. "Done," she said.

"Annnnd…bam!" Omega said, as she flipped a toggle switch on the pedestal, taking a big step back.

There was a loud hum, as of high-voltage lines overhead, and the illumination on the flight deck brightened. An alert on the pilot's console began to beep, increasing in volume and frequency until it became a rather loud constant drone. The associated light went from red through yellow to green, then both light and alert switched off. Omega walked over to check the power gauge.

"Woo," she said then, with a grin. "Nice, Surl. I got power and to spare, to play with! You can't imagine what the ship's systems can do with THAT."

<Good,> Surlianth replied. <Now let us get me into position with that thing, recharge it for the beacon effect, and be ready.>

"Aaaaall over it," Omega said. "Myc, let me get this unplugged and the antigrav unlocked, then we'll trundle it out into the open and scout for a good place to put it…and the *Prydwen*."

"That seems like a very good plan," Myclestra agreed.

* * *

India had blood to her armpits and covering the front of her body armor as she struggled to save Agent Uniform's life. The creature's acid had burned through his jugular vein and she knew she only had moments to stop the bleeding and get at least some blood plasma into him. Love's burns were possibly worse, but none of them were immediately life-threatening.

Romeo was working on getting a strong dose of the galactic painkiller glatordanyl into Agent Love. Her burns were bad, but he knew the regen pods could fix it. As long as she survived to reach the medlab at Headquarters, at least. And the glatordanyl would help keep her from going shocky with the pain.

Como was sitting against the wall, an oxygen-enriched respirator over his nose and mouth, trying desperately not to hyperventilate from shock and horror.

It was Love who kept the next threat from killing them all.

She opened her eyes in relief as the pain meds took effect.

The homunculus was made of the same black, gelatinous stuff as the first two monsters had been. But it was just barely four feet tall, a tailed humanoid with spindly arms and legs. Its four-fingered hands were equipped with razor sharp claws, but physically it was no threat. Its head and face were the stuff of nightmares. Bony, corroded shoulders held a neck of wobbly, flapping flesh. There were no lips, only a horrible, insane rictus grin of an ape-like face and milky white eyes. Love described the thing later as a "deformed chimpanzee with no skin."

But Wruthas had put powerful magic into this creation, and a cunning intelligence. It was sly and malicious and wanted to hurt and maim and torture before killing. It hissed a spell and an immobilizing lassitude settled over India and Romeo. They lost focus on what they were doing, and neither of them comprehended that the sudden, draining weariness was not natural. Held in the grip of the spell, Alpha Two never realized what was happening. It chose India as its initial target, hating her for her beauty and healing talents.

Nearly microscopic black tentacles sprayed from its clawed fingers as another spell was released. India never noticed them twining around and around her body, slowing her movements even more. Romeo knelt next to Agent Love as he fell deeper into the grip of the first magic. Love raised her head as Romeo stopped talking, then slowed and finally stopped moving.

"Hey, Romeo, man, what the hell?" Love watched the alert wariness fade from his eyes. She didn't know what was wrong, but something was seriously amiss. Agent Romeo never shut up and rarely stopped moving. She sat up and braced against the wall, looking about in a panic. Love had paid attention when Myclestra had talked about magic and what could be done with it, and this sure looked like what she'd been talking about.

India had stopped her frantic attempts to stop Uniform's bleeding, and Uniform's gushing blood splashed onto her face. Love saw the thickening black limbs wrapping around her and then realized a third monster, much smaller than the first two, held the other ends of those black tentacles. Moving hurt like the torments of Hell in spite of the painkiller, but she got her plasma rifle pointed across her lap at the thing and yanked the trigger.

The plasma bolt blew the homunculus into very small, burning pieces scattered across the corridor and onto the walls, but not before the creature triggered the first stage of its cantrip. The magic erupted, tearing off India's left arm at the elbow and searing her left leg down to the bone in spots. Wherever the tentacles were on her face or body, they burned into her, leaving smoldering wounds wrapped around her like dreadful ribbons of charred and agonized flesh. Two of the 'ribbons' crossed her face, burning the left side of her face down to the bone, destroying her left eye in the process. The other set her hair ablaze and burned out her right eye. She collapsed across Uniform's body without a sound. Fortunately for Agent Uniform, one of the tentacles had crossed his neck and when it ignited, it cauterized the wound in his neck, preventing him from bleeding to death. That would certainly present problems down the road, but for now, it kept him alive.

"INDIA!" Romeo screamed, waking from the spell. He scrambled to her, his hands hovering above her body, afraid to touch any of the terrible wounds. "BABY, TALK TO ME! NOOOOOO!"

India remained silent, unconscious.

"OH SHIT!" It hurt to do anything, much less yell into her comm unit, but Agent Love realized that Alpha Two was combat-ineffective. "Apple Squad Four, GET IN HERE NOW! AGENT INDIA IS DOWN!"

* * *

Ten minutes later, the pedestal was settled in the center of the valley as nearly as Omega and Myclestra could determine it. Omega detonated the anchor bolt that would hold it in place until it was time to extract it, and then she turned to Myclestra and Surlianth.

"Okay, I'm gonna go get the *Prydwen* outta sight, probably

over there," she pointed to a nearby mountain. "Like, behind the flank of the mountain, there. Complete with cloaking, sensor scrambler, and solid hologram to make anything that wraith thing picks up look like part of the mountainside. Once I'm in position, go ahead and put Surl into the stand," Omega waved at the pedestal, "and Surl, you start rebuilding the charge in that thing. It's gonna take a while to get enough energy output to get its attention, I expect."

<Yes, it will, at least without melting down your device,> Surlianth agreed. <But only…mmm, perhaps fifteen of your minutes? It will not take long at all, now I have a feel for the device. And I know what the Warpwraith is looking for; I will ensure he cannot miss it.>

"Good. So once Surl says it's good, Myc, you need to hit the first switch that Madrid showed you on the way over to the ship," Omega instructed.

"Ah. Yes, I see," Myclestra said. "Then, when Surlianth says that it is properly charged, I hit the second switch, so that it begins showing up as a raw energy source, which the wraith will be able to sense…"

"Yup. And once you hit that second switch, you need to HIDE. Close, of course, because you need to be able to grab Surl and wield him, but you don't want the warpwraith thing to spot you."

"Of course," Myclestra agreed, nodding. "Which is why I think that rock outcrop over there," she waved her hand, and Omega glanced where she indicated, "will make an excellent hiding place. There is a gap there, and I should be able to fit into it."

"Ooo, there's a cave opening?" Omega wondered. "Yeah, that makes me think — let me double-check something real quick…"

She whipped out a small tablet-like device, and scanned the area.

"No, that's good," she decided. "Yeah, there's caves, because the rock is limestone, but they're down deep, here.

Nothing is gonna collapse under us. That's just a hollow, but you're right, it'll be a great place to hide." She looked up. "Are you two good with this?"

<Yes,> Surlianth averred.

"We are ready," Myclestra said.

"Then let me go jump in the *Prydwen* and hide," Omega determined. "You two be careful."

<And you,> Surlianth responded. <And I will do my best to aid your 'disappearing act,' as we discussed.>

* * *

"The ship has disappeared to my senses," Myclestra noted. "Can you spot it, Old Snake?"

<Mmm,> came the slow response. <It is…difficult. Yes, I think I can detect it, but the devices our Silver Hair has initiated make it very hard. I suspect I detect it only because I know where to focus my search. I think, if I have this much trouble and I am concentrating, our prey, being much more distracted, is unlikely to notice it.>

"That is good, then. Are you ready to begin building energies to draw it in?"

<I am. Place me in the capacitor and then hide, just in case. I will call you when it is time to flip the second switch.>

Myclestra drew the great sword from the sheath on her back and eased the blade into the slot in the pedestal. She flipped the switch on the device as she had been shown, then hastened for the hollow in the rock outcrop.

The dark night grew quiet, save for the sounds of crickets, cicadas, and tree frogs.

* * *

Alpha Seven — comprised of Agents Yankee and Tare — was the command team for Baker Force. The pair of veteran Agents decided from the beginning that they would go in with their lead team. Squad Two's entry point was a loading dock on the northwest side of the main reactor building. It offered the most open exterior, and the skimmers *Plain Sight* and *Counting Trees* grounded only a few meters away from fabric roll-up doors of truck docks. On the 'Go' command, Agent Butter used the door-mounted tachyon-splitter cannon to blow two adjacent loading doors into the warehouse area behind them. Squad Two, led by Monkey and Kako of Alpha Eight, charged through the cloud of dust obscuring the shattered doors. Fire Team One, Praetorians Topsail and Oyster and Beta Eighty-Four's Freddie and Dixie, followed immediately behind them, covering the right side of the entrance. Team Two, Beta Team Thirty-Nine, Agents Vast and Net and Beta Forty-Four, Agents Option and Unit took the left side. Tare, Yankee and the two flamethrower teams, Beta Ninety-Six, Agents Tide and Use carrying the British Lifebuoy flamethrower and Beta Forty-One, Agents Hotel and Mike, with one of the copied XM43s, took the center.

"Vell, zhat opened zhe door fast enough," Kako quipped. "You zhink zhey heard us?"

"Quiet, and look against the back wall, Kako." Agent Yankee pointed. "I think THAT was waiting for us!" Against the back wall of the loading dock, something huge twitched and clawed, trying to free itself from the crushed storage racks on which the blast had impaled it. The monster, dripping glutinous black slime on the floor, made no sound as it flailed, trying futilely to get loose. It was fifteen or twenty feet tall, a long, spindly creation of spider-like limbs attached to a twisted trunk that resembled a giant gorilla's mutated ribcage. An enormous human spine, vertebrae exposed, led to a giant-sized human skull that appeared to have been partly melted. It seemed to be only bone or perhaps fossilized wood. Nothing resembling soft tissue was visible anywhere on the creature.

"Oh, Boze moi," a wide-eyed Kako muttered to himself. "Shuttink up now."

"Tide, Hotel, incinerate that damn thing. I want nothing but ash." Yankee swallowed hard and turned to his long-time partner, Agent Tare. "We lucked out, buddy."

"I'll say we did. Brrr!" Tare shivered as the thing went up in flame and burned like gasoline-soaked dry wood. Within moments, it was only ash.

"Hey!" A voice shouted from the side of the dock leading into the main reactor building. There was an office there, probably used by the dock foreman. A human hand waved a white rag through a broken window. "Hey! Don't shoot! For Chrissake, don't shoot! I'm part of the staff here! I'm not one of these things!"

"Team One, watch our six," Monkey snapped. "Team Two, watch that entry doorway into the main building! Okay, whoever you are, come outta there, REAL slow like."

The man slowly stood up, revealing his blue TVA-logo shirt. He had darker brown hair, with a receding hair line and a neatly trimmed mustache and goatee. A TVA ID badge hung on a lanyard around his neck. He kept his hands in the air, pushing the office door open with his foot. He kept looking nervously into the corners and at the ceiling. Yankee thought he was maybe one step away from a heart attack, judging by the terrified look on his tanned face.

"Did you get them all?" His voice quivered. "The damn monsters can just pop outta the wall or the floor. They've killed all my team members. I don't know how I got out of the Control Room alive, but I got here and couldn't get past that thing. I jus—"

"Yeah, got it," Tare growled. "Now stop babbling and tell me your name! Monkey, Kako, keep him covered." Tare pulled his phone out of his pocket and opened the list of employees that had been downloaded into all of the strike teams' phones.

"Buckley, Joe Buckley, I'm the night-time Control Room supervisor. Just get me outta here before one of those monster things finds us!"

"He checks out, Yankee, he's on the list. Photo ID an' all."

There was a rending crash in the corridor behind the office. Buckley took one look over his shoulder, shrieked in terror and bolted toward the Agents. Somehow, they didn't shoot him in reflex action. Then their attention was riveted by what followed him into the loading dock area.

The first creature had a humanoid torso, and humanoid thighs descended from a sexless crotch to huge, goat-like cloven hooves. The torso's shoulders supported long arms that hung to mid-thigh, ending in three-fingered hands. Fingers that were mostly foot-long claws. Two shorter arms pushed out of the ribcage, with only a single, wickedly curved hook at the end of the wrist. A third pair of arms grew out of the thing's back, just below its shoulder blades. These arms equaled the monster's eighteen-foot height and it was using them to swing quickly into the dock, hanging from exposed beams and pipes like some horrific gorilla. The worst was its head, not even remotely human, simply an eyeless shark's head atop the shoulders. The mouth seemed to split the head completely in half, with jagged teeth fully six inches long grinding against each other as it snapped at the empty air. Without a second's hesitation, it charged straight at the Agents, close behind a panicked, screaming Joe Buckley.

Behind it, an obscenely huge blob squelched into the dock. The front half was armored, with sword-like blades sticking out in several places at the edge of the armor. The head that peered out from under that armor had a dozen yellow eyes, each one glowing eerily in the dim light. A gaping, tri-partite maw, large enough to simply swallow a man, revealed scores of razor-sharp teeth, flexing outward, then inward. Under those terrible jaws, half a dozen insectoid legs or perhaps arms moved nearly at random, sampling everything they touched, bringing anything small enough to be grabbed by their claws up to be stuffed into those serrated teeth. It squirmed along on dozens of tentacles, long, thick tentacles supporting a worm-like body the size of an African hippopotamus. There was a cunning, evil intelligence in the multitude of gleaming eyes. It stopped at the doorway, shaking and shuddering, as it released a deafening ululation that rattled the walls and was heard as far away as Echo's command post.

"Kill it, KILL THEM, FOR GOD'S SAKE, SHOOT!" Buckley squealed as he bolted into the protective circle of

Agents.

"Hit 'em!" Monkey suited order to action, his plasma rifle blasting chunks off the shark-headed thing charging them. Both flamethrowers gushed burning napalm over it, but not enough. Neither flame team had changed fuel cylinders after incinerating the spider-stick thing a few moments ago and the partly expended weapons couldn't put enough fire on it to stop it.

But the plasma rifles carried by Agents Yankee and Tare blew both of the swinging arms cleanly off its back. It crashed to the concrete floor, momentarily stunned. Five more plasma rifles blasted it across the polished floor and into the back wall, storage racks collapsing onto it. But as the squad concentrated fire on the sharkhead, the tentacled worm was free to act. And what it did next proved that it, like the homunculus slain by Agent Love, had magic in its black heart.

The forward half of the monster reared up until the head was twelve feet above the floor. The insect legs wove a fast, complicated pattern and with a hiss, a wall of black flame raced toward the Agents. The flamethrowers carried by Agents Hotel and Tide exploded, as the flame wall burned the two Beta Team agents into blackened skeletons almost instantly. Agent Mike, carrying the extra cylinders for the Lifebuoy, ignited, and his right side burned nearly to the bone. He collapsed, unconscious but still alive. Weakening as it traveled, the wall of eldritch flame was still powerful enough to cremate Agent Freddie and send Agent Yankee staggering away, right arm burned to bare bone, and blinded in his right eye. Agents Dixie, Option and Unit were all burned, but none badly enough to stop fighting. Monkey and Kako poured plasma bolts into the thing, but it was Option who flipped her plasma rifle to full auto and dumped the entire magazine into the worm monster, something Agent Madrid had STRONGLY advised against doing. She was lucky; the rifle didn't explode. The massive plasma bolt DID blow the worm thing completely in half.

Screaming in agony, it cast another spell, a bright blue

beam of pure energy shooting from its intact insectoid leg-hands. The beam left nothing of Agent Vast above mid-thigh and burned the left side of Agent Oyster's body away before punching a hole through the wall behind them. Tare, Topsail and Agent Net, who had dropped her ineffective tachyon rifle and picked up Yankee's discarded plasma rifle, all concentrated their fire on the spellcaster and burned its multi-eyed head away.

The three Agents stepped back and relaxed. But they relaxed too soon, and the sharkhead grabbed Topsail by an arm and a leg and ripped them off his body. He never had a chance to scream, as the shark mouth lunged down and cleanly bit off his head. Tare spun and fired into the wounded monster, as Net frantically changed magazines in her weapon. Tare's plasma bolts knocked it off its feet and it crashed into the tangle of crushed and fallen storage racks. Rifle recharged, Net leapt onto the pile and blasted the shark head's upper body into ash.

Agent Hotel looked up from where he was desperately trying to keep Agent Mike breathing.

"Is that the last of them?" he asked. "Please God, let that be the last! Someone get over here and help me keep Mike alive."

Those functional members left of Baker Squad Two immediately clustered around the wounded, trying hard to keep them alive. But they forgot one thing.

And it WAS a thing.

* * *

Behind them, Buckley grinned.

The grin morphed first.

Even as the hair disappeared from the head and face, the mouth opened wider and wider, until it seemed almost as if the top part of Buckley's head might fall off. Then the lips split in the middle and a second fissure opened up vertically; the bone of upper and lower jaws also split, and as the flesh opened up and the nose disappeared, it revealed the bone receding, leaving razor-sharp, dagger-like teeth. This new aspect of the mouth only stopped when it was between 'Buckley's' eyes on top, and nearly to his Adam's apple on the bottom. The resulting maw was fully capable of taking in an entire human head with no difficulty. At each 'mouth' corner, flexible insectoid mandibles extended, capable of helping direct that human head straight into the hideous maw. The throat opened up into a monstrous gullet as the neck expanded to the size of the creature's head.

Seconds later all semblance of humanity left the horrible face, as ears shrank into the sides of the head, most of the clothing seemed to dissolve away from the body, tanned skin paled into a leprous gray, arms and legs lengthened, and fingers extended into impossibly long, sharp spider legs.

The creature reached out.

* * *

Tare bent over his gravely-wounded partner Yankee, as that agent looked up at him and gave him a wobbly grin.

"Hey, p-pal," he breathed, shocky from the intense pain. "Damn, what a m-mission, huh?"

"Shush, Yank," Tare murmured, kneeling beside Yankee. "It's all right. I got this. We'll get you back to Headquarters and dunk you in a regen bath; you'll be good as new 'fore you know it. Remember what the medlab did for Echo. And he's out there, right now, directing this whole operation."

"Yeah, I know, I — TARE! LOOK OUT!" Yankee shouted.

Before Tare could react, daggerlike fingers dug deep into his shoulders, drawing blood as he cried out in pain. That cry was abruptly cut off, however, as a hideous, inhuman, doubly-split mouth engulfed his head and bit hard, then swallowed.

Tare's headless body, spurting blood from the severed neck arteries, toppled across his semi-prone partner, who was yelling.

"DAMN SONOVABITCH! SOMEBODY HIT IT! GRAB A PLASMA RIFLE AND TORCH THIS THING! IT JUST KILLED TARE!"

The creature grabbed Yankee's side, digging those sharp fingertips — there were no nails or claws, just what seemed sharpened bone — into flesh. Yankee screamed in pain and raw fury…

…Just as Net spun and unloaded her plasma rifle in full auto, as she'd seen Option do.

The remains of whatever had been Buckley — if it ever really had been Buckley — fairly exploded, as it came apart in the fusillade of plasma bolts. As the torso ripped open, something round tumbled out and rolled across the floor.

It was Tare's head, a look of shock and horror rictused on the face.

Yankee groaned, turned aside, and wept.

* * *

Outside the plant, at the command post, Echo, Tau, Upsilon, and the others listened in dismayed consternation and horror at the screams and shouting.

"Damn," Echo breathed. "Damn, damn, damn. Round Two, same as Round One. And the Alpha Line medic is down."

"It's cool, Boss," Tau murmured, laying a hand on the Alpha Line chief's shoulder. "We brought three extra medics from the Atlanta Office, just in case. They're in the craft patrolling the river; get the wounded out to the riverbank, outta further harm's way, and I'll call 'em in."

Echo nodded, then keyed his subvocal mic.

"This is Operation Takedown command to all units. Bring out the wounded to the riverbank as soon as you can evacuate 'em. Watch your six as you do. We have medics from the Atlanta Office on scene, and they're coming in to assist."

"Thank God," Romeo muttered on the comm, voice cracking badly. "Um, Echo, sir, gimme a chance t' get India outta here to th' other medics, an' I'll get, get back inna saddle, man."

"Understood, Romeo," Echo replied, keeping his voice low and steady. "Do what you need to do. Yankee, can you command from the riverbank, in absentia?"

"Uh…oh, damn, everything hurts. Damn, Tare, buddy, no no no…" Yankee breathed, unaware that the subvocal mic caught the comment. "Um, yeah, I mean yes, sir, Echo, sir. I think so. I'll do my damnedest, anyway. I…uh…"

There was silence.

"Echo to Yankee. Do you copy? Echo to Yankee."

"Um, sir, he's passed out," another voice responded. "He's pretty bad hurt. One eye gone, one arm, most of the shoulder, bad burns on one side, puncture wounds on the other…"

"Who am I talking to, and from what department?"

"This is Agent Net, sir. Field agent."

"Are there any Alpha Line agents left in your squad who are unwounded?"

"Uh," came a grunt from a vaguely familiar voice. "Sorry for the delay responding, Boss; we were torching some monster guts. Monkey here, Echo. Yankee's bad off, like Net said, and Tare is, is dead. But Kako and I are unhurt so far. Us two and Net are about the ONLY ones unhurt in this squad, though."

"All right. Pull back. Evacuate the wounded to the riverbank and medical help, then wait for my word about regrouping with the reserve units."

"Copy that, Echo. Pulling back and evacuating wounded."

"Shit hellfire damnation," Echo murmured without keying the mic. "For as vicious as that training room scenario was, Myclestra and Surlianth still didn't half prepare us for this thing."

"I'm not arguing that," Upsilon decided.

* * *

<Little One, I sense no one else in the area but the three of us. And it is time to flip the second switch.> Surlianth was positive on both counts. <I have the capacitor fully charged, or very nearly so.>

All right, Old Snake. Have you notified Silver Hair?

<Yes, I included her in this conversation, young one.>

Yup. I'm in the loop, Myc, Omega replied. *I'm ready here, and I'll notify Echo through our bond.*

<Very good, Silver Hair,> Surlianth replied.

Myclestra slipped out from her hiding place, headed to the

pedestal.

* * *

Echo, Omega here, and standing by.

Go, Omega, came the response.

We're in position. The Surlianthet Capacitor is charged. The beacon is ready, but the cloaking fields are still up. We're about to go live with the trap.

Good. I just hope it's enough. We're getting slaughtered over here. Literally.

Oh, no.

Oh, yes. We've lost some of the department, baby. I mean, I...well, it's bad. The deep, unsettled breath Echo drew was detectable through the nd't'lq, and told Omega a great deal. *There's even more to this thing than we realized.*

What do you mean?

It's generating monsters, and laying them in wait for our squads, Echo explained. *I think the monsters are probably remnants of the plant staff, modified by this wraith thing, but I'm not sure. Two squads are down; one has a hundred percent casualties, dead or wounded, mostly dead; the other has maybe three unwounded. And that second one was kinda luck of the draw, 'cause they didn't go in stealth, but blew the loading dock.*

Any get eaten by the Big Bad?

Honey, none of 'em have even REACHED the Big Bad yet. Given where I'd be if I were the thing, I don't think they're anywhere close.

Damn, damn, damn.

Exactly. The only good news is that the reactors appear completely cold, and I'm sure this thing has to be burnin' energy to create an' power all these creatures, so hopefully it's gonna notice a nice new energy source.

So go for it?

GO for it. ASAP. Or we're all dog chow over here.

Consider it done, Ace.

Good, baby.

* * *

<Perhaps wait for Omega to come back from her conversation with her mate, Little One,> Surlianth suggested as Myclestra reached the pedestal.

I had thought to do so, Myclestra replied, calm, as she paused beside the pedestal. *This is a joint military operation, after all, dual-pronged, and Echo is the commander. We need to know that we are doing this at an opportune time for the events at that nuclear plant, or it could be all for naught.*

<Exactly.>

Just then, Omega's voice came back into the telepathic conversation.

I think we need to do this thing, she told them, *before we lose anyone else.*

<Oh, that does not sound good.>

It isn't, Omega told the star drake. *Evidently this wraith thing is using what's left of the plant staff...* And she told them what Echo had told her.

<Yes, it is capable of doing such things, but it takes a great deal of energy...which it now has, I suppose, if it has 'killed' the reactors. And yes, those most likely are whatever yet remains of the personnel who staffed the plant. Forgive us; it had not occurred to either of us, given its attempt at the weapons depot, that it might do this here. That it COULD do this here.>

Good point, 'cause it only slaughtered the guys it encountered at the weapons depot.

<Exactly. At that time, it did not have the energy to do otherwise. But I should have inquired further regarding this power plant, else I might have realized the additional danger. Forgive me.>

It is what it is, Surl. I'm not sure it would have made a difference; from what Echo told me, the second squad went in knowing about the secondaries and still went down. We need to lure this thing over here and kill it. As soon as possible. Or ain't nobody over there gonna survive, I think.

And that includes your mate. Turn on the beacon, then? Myclestra confirmed.

YES. Do it, now, Omega answered.

Myclestra flipped the second switch.

Then she sprinted for cover.

* * *

In what could be thought of as the aether, a series of carefully-formed cloaking and force fields dropped around the core of the pedestal.

A kind of energy beacon ignited and grew in intensity, its brightness powered by the living soul of a Star Drake.

In the distance…something noticed.

* * *

The agents of both Apple and Baker Forces were learning quickly now, as they engaged the warpwraith's minions and guardians. The other squads had taken a bit more time entering the buildings than had the first two squads, and had the advantage of learning from their disastrous encounters. The fact that Echo activated some of the reserve units with specific instructions also helped; the reserves had listened closely to the comm and understood what was happening, and grasped how to counter it.

Squad One of Baker Force still lost Beta Twenty-Three, Agents Berta and Carmen, to a magical attack that sent lightning bolts jumping from agent to agent. Berta and Carmen were hit first and horribly burned. The rest of the squad survived with minor injuries and blasted the creature responsible into a black smear on the walls.

Thus warned of the rather simple tactics the monsters used, the plasma-rifle-armed fire teams and flamethrower teams took the lead and killed them before more than minor injuries could be inflicted, for the most part. Before it was over, however, most of the agents did have at least minor injuries, mostly limited-area burns and some broken bones.

But they were making progress.

* * *

Outside the plant, Agent Zulu waited in ambush. Echo and Omega had plotted the warpwraith's most likely course to the trap, and Zulu's Beast sat with a clear line of fire to that course, revved and waiting quietly. Zulu had demurred at rearming his vehicle with only a pair of untested plasma cannons. The Beast's main weapons were Agent Zulu's pride and joy. A turret-mounted GAU-12 Equalizer, a 25mm five-barreled rotary cannon, was flanked by a pair of M2A1 fifty-caliber heavy machine guns. Currently loaded with HEIAP — High Explosive Incendiary Armor Piercing — rounds in the M2s, and HEI, or High Explosive Incendiary, rounds in the GAU-12, Zulu hoped the mix of high explosive and incendiary ammunition would make short work of the monster.

While Zulu covered the low altitude track, Agent Dog in his personal airskimmer, the *Aces High*, waited to pounce from high altitude. Dog armed his skimmer with a pair of the new plasma cannons under the nose, and his door gunner, Agent Green, manned another plas-cannon on a flexible mount. Agent Hypo, his co-pilot for this mission — Quebec, the other half of Alpha Sixteen, had been away on personal business — handled the energy management to keep *Aces High* flying and those guns fed.

* * *

These humans in the black suits are becoming a problem. They are smarter than I expected; they are quickly learning to easily defeat my guardians. Guardians in which I may have unwisely placed too much faith, and more importantly, too much power. Wruthas sat at the center of all his spells, seeing through his creations' eyes as they fought and died. Each death drained a little more of his power and he noticed the loss, even with the immense amount he had drained from this 'power plant.' *There is nothing further to be gained here, other than perhaps being able to absorb the mind and soul of one of my attackers; it is a pity I cannot consume their spirits as well, and have done. But they are clever and careful and ridiculously well-armed with powerful fire weapons, so that is unlikely. I shall bide a bit longer, hoping to gain access to one of the leaders of these black suited humans. If I can do tha — What is THAT!?*

The Warpwraith's attention was suddenly riveted by the flare of an unbelievable fountain of incredible power to the north and west. Not close, but not overly distant either. And at least a majority of, if not all, that power was borne from the ethers of the arcane. In an instant of lust, gluttony, and greed, he decided he MUST have this new power.

He released all his spells, his creations instantly crumbling to dust, confusing the agents currently engaged in destroying them. He drew all his remaining new-found power into himself, changing form even as he erupted through the roof of the Control Room as a gigantic raptorial bird; the few local residents who saw it wondered if it was the legendary thunderbird, or if a California condor had somehow found its way east. His laughter shattered windows as he beat his wings, building speed to rush northwest and claim this power.

But in his haste, he never looked for any obstacles in his path.

* * *

Bullets won't hurt this monster, huh? It's what that woman said, and Alpha One backed her up. Okay, maybe normal, ordinary ball ammo won't leave an impression, but I beg to differ. I bet fifty cal explosive incendiaries at twenty-nine-hundred feet per second and sixteen hundred rounds a minute will knock this thing's ass sideways. And if that doesn't do the trick, the GAU-12U WILL! Twenty-five mike-mike at four thousand rounds per minute, High Explosive Incendiary rounds delivering thirty-five TONS of energy on target, per round, oh yeah, THAT'S GONNA LEAVE A MARK! Agent Zulu was practically dancing at the thought.

Zulu settled down into the gunner's seat of the turret mounted on the Beast and picked up the thing as it burst through the roof and started north. He slewed the turret onto the target, motors whining softly, almost silently, as the gunsight tracked the target. *Human weapons won't hurt it, she said. It might not even notice it was shot, she said. Okay, Miss Alien Universe*

Know-It-All, let's find out. Challenge accepted!

The monster was centered in his gunsight as it cleared the last building. Zulu squeezed the trigger, and his massively over-armored and over-armed M1114 shook with the recoil forces as all three guns fired simultaneously, and the Beast started to skid slightly to one side. But Zulu had planned for that and had already firmly set the anchor feet he'd installed in the Beast, and she stayed put.

The rounds from the turret guns all had tracer elements at the base of the actual bullets and it looked like a real science-fiction laser-death-ray battle as they, in fact, literally blasted the Warpwraith sideways in the sky. He kept the sight on the creature and pounded it with continuous fire. Wruthas screamed, a shriek like Hell's own steam whistle.

Zulu's only limitation was ammunition. Those monstrous guns ate ammo like a politician at a free steak-and-lobster buffet. He had two thousand rounds of fifty caliber, a thousand per gun, and another forty-five hundred rounds for the GAU-12, and roughly a minute after he started firing, he ran out of ammo. He flipped a switch and brought a pair of plasma cannons online; he'd decided they might make a decent backup, after all, but they weren't installed in the Beast as such, merely adjunct weapons he'd set up next to it. He also activated the M10-8 flame gun he'd gotten off a Viet Nam era M132 flame tank; its downside was a short range of less than two hundred meters. Fortunately, the wraith had just cleared the buildings and hadn't ascended much in altitude.

* * *

Wruthas shuddered in agony. Whatever those Hell weapons had been, they had HURT! Worse, they had managed to destroy part of his essence, and he had to use massive amounts of the energies he had taken from the nuclear reactors to heal himself.

That would never do.

He found the massive vehicle that had hurt him. Another one of the vehicles used by those men in the suits. Enough of this. A lance of energy speared from his talon-hand and

325

hit the vehicle. It rocked from the impact…but to Wruthas' amazement, its armor held. What was that armor MADE of?!

Howling in frustration, hand-like tentacles flung up and out. The spell did not target the apparently-impenetrable vehicle. Instead, thirty meters of concrete and soil vanished beneath it, and the Beast plunged into the resulting hole, turning turtle as it fell and landing nose-down on its roof.

* * *

Zulu, rattled but unhurt, shook his head as he climbed out of the instant cavern and watched the Warpwraith fly away.

"Well, shit," he grumbled. "Okay, I guess my guns couldn't kill it after all. I stand corrected."

* * *

"WOO-HOOOooo!" Dog shouted jubilantly, as he watched Zulu punch a hole all the way through the gigantic black, birdlike creature — though it sealed itself up again, once the incendiary rounds ceased. "Way to go, Zulu, man! Did you hear it scream in pain?! All right, guys, it's our turn!"

"Have at 'em!" Hypo cried from the co-pilot's seat. "You fly this bird! Me an' Green got the weapons!"

"All over that!" Dog exclaimed, setting up a strafing dive run. "Here we go, guys!"

The *Aces High* darted down from high above the warpwraith, and as it reached the range, Hypo opened up the onboard plasma cannons. They fired in an alternating ack-ack burst pattern, and another shriek from Hell rent the air. As Dog pulled up and they passed the wraith, Green opened up his plasma cannon door gun, fairly raining destruction on the black creature, which screamed again. Bits of black seemed to blast off the wraith with every plasma bolt strike, burning into nothingness as they fell away.

Dog maxxed out the magnetic 'throttle,' and the *Aces High* shot away, banking around hard for another strafing run.

* * *

NO! It will not DO! a furious Wruthas thought. *These pathetic little creatures barely provide me sustenance; they will not do me harm!*

He shot another energy lance from his talon-hand at the flying craft.

But Dog was an experienced dogfighter; it was part of where he had gotten his codename. As soon as the weapons aboard the *Aces High* had ceased firing, he brought up the force field, keeping it tight against the airskimmer's skin to provide for increased aerodynamics and smooth maneuvering. The energy lance glanced off and dissipated.

The craft swooped in again, blazing fiery death at the wraith, and he screamed in pain as he lost a wing and was forced to reform it. He watched in stunned amazement as the flaming remains of his wing fell, eventually burning out before it could hit the ground.

NO! I must reach that delicious energy! Then I will show them!

Another strafing run by the *Aces High* did woeful damage to Wruthas, who struggled to get away, darting and dodging this way and that, yet ever pressing to the northwest.

But this time, the wraith noticed something.

He saw the faint yellow halo around the aircraft, and he saw it flicker and die just before the shooting commenced... and he saw it pop back on when the craft had passed.

Ahhh, Wruthas thought, understanding. *A vulnerability at last.*

He waited until the *Aces High* was beginning its next strafing run...

...And fired an energy lance directly into the plasma cannons.

* * *

A tense Echo stood and watched the aerial dogfight from the command center, putting on his goggle-glasses and toggling them to night mode, telescopic vision, so he could see detail. He hoped against hope that his forces here, at the reactor plant, could take down the creature before he had to put his wife and their new allies at risk.

So he saw the energy lance strike one of the plasma cannons — and enter the device. Echo gasped, then held his breath.

Moments later, the *Aces High* blew up, as the fuel tank of the first cannon ignited and exploded, triggering the adjacent tank for the second cannon to explode, as well. A tertiary explosion occurred moments later as the door gun's tank blew.

Echo groaned softly. His goggle-glasses depicted flaming wreckage — and body parts — falling from the dark sky, as the giant black bird reformed its missing pieces and continued northwest, disappearing into the night.

* * *

"Agent Echo, sir!" came an urgent call on the comm just then. "This is Agent Fisher, Alpha Forty-Five in the *Auger In*!"

"GO, Fisher!" Echo, who had collapsed back into his camp chair, straightened up.

"Sir! Sorry for being late to the fight; we didn't realize what the *Aces High* was doing until they'd already started, and it took us a few seconds too long to join the dogfight. There's not a lot to do, but we wanted you to know that we managed to catch Dog in a tractor beam. He's not in the greatest shape, but he's alive…"

"How bad?"

"Missing both legs an' an arm, looks like, from here," Fisher responded. "Burned pretty bad."

"What about the others? Hypo and Green?"

"Um, no sir," Fisher replied, subdued. "Near as we can tell from what we saw, there…well, there wasn't really anything left to catch."

"Shit," Echo cursed.

He grabbed his tablet, which displayed the layout of the plant, and flung it across the road.

* * *

<He is coming!> Surlianth cried to his two companions, even as the sounds of the night silenced in an eerie sense of waiting. <Little One, to me! I will ensure you are hidden from

the Warpwraith. Silver Hair, be ready!>

On it, Omega replied. *And Echo confirms, it's on the way.*

"Old Snake, are you sure about this?" Myclestra sprinted from her cover.

<Positive, child.>

"And this…beacon…will still continue once I withdraw you?"

<If it was built as intended, it will. And I see no variation from our original plan, so unless it breaks down — there are great powers coursing through it now, after all — it should continue drawing in the Wraith.> Surlianth broke off. <Hurry now, both of you. He is coming swiftly. It is only minutes before he arrives.>

Myclestra reached for Surlianthet's hilt.

* * *

Behind the mountain's flank, Omega, sitting in the *Prydwen*'s pilot seat, activated the ship's inter-atmospheric drive — a minimized form of the saucer's interplanetary drive, intended to reduce friction and bow shock. Maintaining the full cloaking, sensor scrambler, and solid hologram, she also threw up the hardest telepathic block she knew how to produce, enhanced by a few basic techniques Surlianth had taught her earlier. *Hopefully,* she thought, *this'll keep the damn creature from detecting ME, inside the ship. Especially if it's hungry and concentrating on the beacon. Surl said he'd help as much as he could. Time for the magic word: OhmigoshIhopeitworks.*

She already had the sequence of commands she would need programmed into the console before her; she had done that while waiting for Surlianth to fully charge the beacon. All she needed to do was hit one button. *And here's hoping I get that chance, if it detects me,* she thought.

Then she pulled back on the stick, and the *Prydwen* gently lifted a few meters into the air, even as the solid hologram around the saucer adjusted itself, 'stretching' to compensate for the increased height of the 'rock outcrop.'

Omega tightened her straps and waited.

* * *

Wruthas headed up and slightly west of due north, aiming for the bright beacon of energy that had brightened into his conscious senses. Below him, the local populations faded away as he moved into an area of low, forested mountains, crossing — unbeknownst to him, not that he cared — into the adjacent state. The area was, from what he could adjudge, some sort of reserve or sanctuary, and there was no sign of intelligent life there.

But oh, there was some delicious energy.

At last he came to the site; a bright flare of light came from the broad, green valley below him. He paused, hovering above it, just long enough to do a cursory survey of the valley, but detected nothing…except that wonderful energy.

Perhaps something to protect this…sanctuary? he wondered. *If so, it is evidently malfunctioning. Maybe that is why it is radiating its energy so powerfully and invitingly. I think I shall partake.*

Wruthas dove down, landing beside the beacon and changing from a birdlike form to a loosely humanoid form, though without detail, and still with that deep, flat blackness, that absence of light.

He reached out to take the beacon in several pseudopods.

<*NOW!*> came the shout.

And suddenly all Wruthas' plans were set aside.

* * *

At Surlianth's mental call, Omega hit the switch on the flight panel of the *Prydwen*, and several things happened at once:

The *Prydwen* lifted off the mountainside, adjusting its solid hologram to reflect the night sky above it, and shot into position, directly over the beacon.

The *Prydwen*'s force fields activated, projecting out and down, then reinforcing itself…twice.

A secondary force field formed directly around the *Prydwen*, in addition to the tabernacle force field that had just closed around the warpwraith.

330

The beacon pedestal extruded one huge plasma cannon from an internal space warp, powered by the Surlianthet Capacitor. It took aim at the wraith, and fired in a continuous burst.

* * *

Simultaneously, in the scant seconds it took the *Prydwen* to move overhead and encase the Warpwraith in a tabernacle force field, Surlianth dropped the shielding he had been using to hide himself, Myclestra, and Omega.

Myclestra activated every cantrip she possessed, whipping Surlianthet around and pointing it at the Warpwraith, just as the plasma cannon opened up. She let out a roar, and unleashed a blast from Surlianthet.

* * *

Wruthas suddenly found himself facing down an old enemy, as well as a very large and incredibly powerful version of the weapons the little humans in black suits had been wielding to such good effect.

Literally swifter than lightning, he turned to flee, and abruptly found himself imprisoned beneath an oddly-yellow-glowing dome...a dome that would not let him jump along the ley lines, nor yet teleport outright.

Angry, he spun, preparing to unleash black fire on the plasma cannon, Myclestra, and her damnable sword.

But his instinct to flee had taken too long.

Both the plasma bolt and the energy release from Surlianthet caught Wruthas squarely in the center of what would have been a chest, and Wruthas felt pain so dreadful that he could not control his response to it. His whole being spasmed, what passed for a body instinctively pulling tight into a sphere.

But that only ensured that the discharges from cannon and Sword enveloped his entire form...which began to burn.

* * *

Using the tiny drones she'd set loose in the valley before the wraith's arrival, Omega watched overhead from the safety of the *Prydwen* and its holographic display, as the cannon fired, and Surlianth unleashed his raw fury at the abomination that was the warpwraith. She watched as the wraith pulled into a sphere, attempting to concentrate its energies…

…And then…SOMEthing…happened.

A blue-white light, seeming brighter than the Sun in the nighttime darkness of the deep forest, flared, filling the inside of the force dome until nothing within was visible.

Just then, an unearthly roar, audible through almost all sonic frequencies, fairly rattled the vessel in which she sat. There was a loud *CRACK!* as of a lightning bolt striking nearby, and then…

Nothing.

But the holographic display had been overloaded by the brightness of…whatever had happened…and she couldn't see anything, either.

Surl? she queried. *Myc? Myclestra! Battle-sister! Surlianth! Answer me! Are y'all okay? Is the warpwraith dead? Did you two make it?*

Nothing.

No no no no no, Omega thought, pained. *Myc? Surl? Don't tell me y'all bit it, too…*

Meg, baby? Echo's mental voice came in then, hesitant. *You're upset. But still alive. Did…did it work?*

I dunno yet, Ace, Omega replied, worried. *I'm fine, but my holographic display seems to be fried, and nobody's answering back when I call. I don't even know if the warpwraith is dead or not, and I'm not about to drop the tabernacle field until I KNOW. There was one helluva buncha energy flaring down there, I know that.*

I know. We could see it from here. I swear, it looked like a sunrise in the northwest, or maybe a nuke, or a rocket launch, or…something.

'Something' about covers it. But, Ace, Myc and Surl…they aren't answering.

Damn. Two more sacrifices, lives lost, to rid our universe of that monster?

<No,> came the answer. <Not…not yet. For-forgive me, Silver Hair, Agent Echo; my Little One is not herself telepathic, and I fear I was a bit…well, let us call it, 'out of breath.' We are here, we are intact, and the Warpwraith is no more. Though I expect the soil where it stood might want a bit of sterilization. Or at least a good, heavy rainfall.>

Not after the way you burned it to nothingness, Old Snake, came Myclestra's voice. *That was fascinating, and very interesting to watch…in a most satisfying way. But yes, I'm certain you're very tired, my old friend. And Omega, the giant plasma cannon was an excellent idea, else I am afraid my old snake might have had to sacrifice himself, of a certainty.*

<Indeed. The thing still had a great deal of energy left from sucking dry your 'power plant,'> Surlianth agreed. <Without the plasma cannon, it would have been…very difficult. Especially with screening Myclestra from the energies involved.>

And you're all sure the thing is dead? Echo pressed.

<As sure as I am of my own being,> Surlianth avowed. <I cannot sense the least bit of it anymore.>

Good, Echo said. *Meg, can you gather everything and everybody up and get over here? We've already sent off the wounded in our spacecraft — we started loading 'em as soon as the warpwraith vacated the vicinity, with help from the Atlanta Office and the Huntsville Station, but we need a little help with the cleanup and body recovery, not to mention getting everybody home.*

Wait. All the spacecraft? They're all gone over there?

Yup.

That many wounded?

Yup. And about as many dead.

Shit. Will do, Ace, Omega told him, dropping the force fields and moving to one side, so she could land and take on Myclestra and Surlianth, and fetch the miraculously still-intact Surlianthet Capacitor, never mind the battleship-sized plasma cannon.

Chapter Ten — Appointments

Four hours later, the surviving, uninjured forces had evacuated the area, and the Et Cetera teams were on site and hard at work.

It took a good bit to erase the blood and signs of battle from the Browns Ferry TVA plant, and a good bit more to explain to the world 'what had happened.'

In the end, Fox had his favorite offworld quick-manufacture firm gin up fresh fuel rods, and a team from Facilities, used to handling fissile material, install them, collecting what was left of the old fuel — which was bizarrely stone-cold — for disposal into a nearby uninhabited-system's flare star.

Then he put out a report that there had been a terrorist attempt on the reactor plant; the terrorists had killed all the staff, shut down the reactors, and attempted to make away with the fuel. After the recent events at Kirtland Air Force Base, which were likewise 'terrorist-caused,' it made a certain amount of sense. But in the wake of the Kirtland incident, the NSA had been proactive, and gotten a significant force on-site in a timely fashion; the end result had been some damage to the buildings, and the terrorists died rather than surrender, but the reactors remained unharmed, and there had never been any danger of meltdown, since all three reactors had been SCRAMed by the staff before they were killed.

* * *

Fox met with Myclestra, carrying Surlianthet, in his office with the bay windows opaqued.

"What is the problem, Director?" Myclestra wondered, concerned. "Is there something that did not get done in the aftermath of battling the wraith?"

"Well, yes and no, tekhter," Fox said with a smile. "It isn't quite what you seem to think, though, so no worries. I wanted to present you both with your bounty fees. Or at least, the first payment; there's considerably more on the way from higher-ups."

<Ah. For this we thank you, Fox,> Surlianth replied. <It may seem mercenary to you, but it is how we live, day to day.>

"No, I understand that," Fox said. "It's your pay. I get paid for my job; my agents get paid for their jobs. Now it's time to pay the two of you. I only hope it's suitable. Our budget is limited for such things. I do know that Pul is working out how to assist in that, however." He reached into a desk drawer and produced two cubical boxes, several inches on a side. Opening one, he produced a fist-sized pouch, a smaller, thicker, padded pouch, and a velvet-covered jewelry box. "Myclestra, I suspected you'd simply prefer coin or bullion. And silver is the easiest to get, at least in this country on Earth. So here's a goodly amount of bullion coins; the silver ones are called Silver Eagles, the gold, Gold Eagles, and they're worth a lot more each than the dollar amount inscribed on them, so don't let anybody fool you about their value." He handed her the smaller pouch. "This is a collection of gemstones in cases, mostly high-quality diamonds, but also some rubies, emeralds, and sapphires. By going offworld to source these, I could get 'em in quantity; there's somewhere between a quarter and a half a million dollars' worth of gemstones here." He handed her the larger pouch. "There's three hundred and fifty Silver Eagles and forty-five Gold Eagles in there. Based on current gold and silver prices, that's about a hundred thousand dollars in American money." He hefted the pouch. "That's about twenty-five pounds in Imperial weight units, and a goodly volume; I took the liberty of outfitting the pouch with a space warp and antigrav compensator to make it easier to carry, and less likely to burst the bag."

Then he addressed Surlianth.

"And here," he opened the other box and fished out two more, identical pouches, "is the same amount for you, Surlianth, in the same denominations and materials. And like I said, more is coming from higher up. This was as much as I could do, and I stretched the budget nigh to breaking, even so." He handed those to Myclestra, as well. "And then there's these."

Fox extracted another velvet jewelry case and set it beside the first. Then he picked up the first one. "Myclestra, this is yours. It's…well, I took my wife Zebra with me on the acquisition jaunt; we both stay very busy as you've no doubt noticed, and an opportunity to get away from Headquarters and go shopping and have a nice meal together in a fancy restaurant? We tend to jump at those. Anyway, she saw these in the same store where we got the bullion — the shop owner waited on us personally, and he's not from around here, if you understand me…"

<We do, Fox,> Surlianth noted with some humor. <He is not from Earth.>

"Exactly. Which is good, because I can be more specific about what I need, that way. Anyway, while I was transacting for the bullion, Zee spotted some jewelry that she thought was absolutely lovely, and insisted that you both have some — she liked it so much that I arranged for a set of necklace and earrings to be delivered to my office later today, to surprise her with it. It's made in an alloy called rose gold; this particular version of the alloy is a mixture of gold, silver, and a bit of copper, which latter is what gives it the reddish color alluded to. Myclestra, I know you won't know what that means, but I expect you'll be able to sense the difference. It results in a different look to the item from regular gold OR silver, and it's considered quite elegant on Earth." He opened the first box and produced a lovely but simple pendant of rose gold on a fine chain, with a fairly large star ruby setting in the center.

"Oh," Myclestra said. "Yes, I can detect it; that is, indeed, lovely, and the combination of metals produces a scent that I find intriguing. Is this a star corundum?"

"Yes, it's a ruby." Fox shrugged. "At least, that's what we call it. Rubies and sapphires are all corundum; we differentiate them by colors, which is meaningless to you. Ruby is the red corundum, which goes nicely with the reddish tint of the rose gold."

"Ah. I understand. It is very pretty. Thank you."

"You like it, then?" Fox wondered.

"Yes, I do, very much; please tell Zebra she has excellent taste. If you will let me hold the clasp so I can feel it and determine how it works, we can put it on."

Fox extracted the necklace from the box, and placed it Myclestra's open hand. She ran her fingers over it, then fiddled with the clasp for a moment, opening it and slipping the ring out of the lobster-claw clasp.

"Yes, I understand now," she murmured. "Director Fox, would you do me the honor of placing it about my neck?"

"Certainly, Myclestra," Fox said, accepting the pendant and moving behind the Alontoran to place it carefully around her throat, ensuring the clasp was firmly closed. "How does it feel?"

"Very good," she decided. "Not too heavy, not too light. And it rests in a comfortable place."

"Excellent. Now, Surlianth, it's your turn. Yours is similar, in that it's also rose gold and the pendant of a similar shape and variety, but I had the jeweler do a kind of heavy braided chain for you. It'll loop over the pommel of the hilt and attach to the cross-hilts, hanging just below that dragon-face sculpted in. I don't know that you can fight with it on, but if you have any need to, um, dress up, it would look nice."

<Never fear,> Surlianth replied, <I know how to attach it to my Sword so that I cannot lose it. I am quite eager to see it.>

"Can you see it from inside the Sword?"

<Not as such, but I use the senses of those around me. And since I once had eyes, I know what I am seeing.>

Fox produced the 'sword pendant,' as he thought of it, and held it up. "Is this okay? If you don't like the fact that it has copper in it, I can replace it with more bullion."

<No, I think it is quite lovely, and I rather agree with your

wife on that. I have not seen a precious alloy like this; they did not make it in the universe in which I originated, nor in my Little One's universe, either.>

"But…wait. You aren't from her universe?"

<No. But let that be all that is said of the matter, Fox, please. I trust you; I do not trust the Masters. Were they to find our whereabouts, the less known, the better, for all of us.>

"Understood, and I know when to shut up," Fox said with a grim smile. "Shall I put this on you, or give it to Myclestra to hold, for now?"

<Oh please, put it on me. I am eager to wear it.>

With Myclestra's assistance and Surlianth's permission to touch the Sword, Fox slipped the pendant on the large Sword, so that the ruby hung suspended against the hilt, under the chin of the dragon face that, Fox presumed, represented Surlianth himself.

<Oh yessss,> the ancient being practically purred. <That is very nice, Fox. Thank you very much.>

"You like it, too?"

<I do, yes. And just wait until you see what I do with it.>

"I…don't understand."

<You will, by tomorrow.>

* * *

The next morning, Myclestra brought Surlianthet by the Alpha Line Room. It was disturbingly empty; entirely too many Alpha Line Agents were in the medlab, recovering. But Alpha One was there, and at Myclestra's request, Echo called Fox and requested him to pop by for a few minutes.

Moments later, Fox had arrived, and Myclestra unslung the scabbard from her back, laying it on a nearby desk and withdrawing the Sword.

Surlianthet now had a rose gold filigree inlay worked through the hilt, especially along the cross-hilts around the dragon face, and around the base of the blade. The star ruby shone where it was now embedded in the pommel of the hilt.

<Do you approve, Director Fox?> Surlianth asked, as Fox,

Omega, and Echo gaped at the new designs.

"I…most certainly do, Surlianth," an impressed Fox noted. "This is beautiful. Now I understand about 'seeing what you do with it'! If you and Myclestra would come by my office right after second lunch today, I'd love to show Zebra, and she's joining me for lunch…"

Myclestra nodded, and Surlianth answered, <We would be delighted, Fox.>

"That's just plain gorgeous," Omega declared, and Echo nodded.

"No shit," he agreed. "Did you do that, Surl?"

<I did, young one, yes, from the tribute payment Fox gave me yesterday. You will see the mate around Myclestra's throat.>

"Ooo," Omega murmured, spotting the star ruby on Myc's neck. "Fox, you got good taste, hon!"

"Blame Zebra," Fox chuckled. "I was gonna just give 'em bullion, but she saw those and pitched fits, as Echo puts it."

"She done good," Echo averred.

<Many thanks, then,> Surlianth offered. <I will be happy to tell her so, when I see her this afternoon.>

"As will I," Myclestra agreed.

* * *

A couple of days later, when everyone left alive was either as patched up as they were going to get, or in the medlab for an extended stay — mostly the latter, unfortunately — a summons came from the Ennead…for Myclestra and Surlianth.

"You are respectfully requested to present yourself before the Ennead, that they may act on behalf of the Pan-Galactic Coalition," Fox read the summons to the two extra-universal beings, in the presence of Alpha One and Romeo of Alpha Two; India was still in the medlab with severe burns, being treated in a regen pod, though she had come to a few times before being 'dunked,' and passed on pertinent information to Zebra on other patients. "Division One Director Fox and Alpha One are respectfully required to attend, along with any others they deem needful, in order to debrief the recent events on Earth." He looked up from the transmission on his workstation.

<Mm,> Surlianth decided, <I suppose it is time to find out what they intend to do with us, Little One.>

"It sounds that way, Old Snake." Myclestra sighed; her sculpted face depicted unhappiness.

"Pulgey has had my full report on the whole sequence of events," Fox noted, "augmented by the reports from the Alpha Line and Field departments, not to mention the Atlanta Office and the Huntsville Station personnel. And he's a fair and just being. I think it will go all right."

"It will, if Alpha One has anything to say about it," Echo declared. "Fox, I think Meg and I can handle the debrief to the Ennead, especially if we can get a telepath to help out."

"Zz'r'p has already offered to assist," Fox informed them.

"Okay, then Romeo, you're in charge while we're gone," Echo said. "If you need to, though, I can pass that on to Golf, so you can spend more time in the medlab with India…"

"Um," Romeo tried. "Thanks, man. If, um, maybe you could give Golf a heads-up to jus', I dunno, help me with it? I can do it, I just…" He broke off and sighed.

"Sure thing, buddy," Echo said with a sympathetic nod. "Been there, done that a few times now, and I understand all too well."

"Then him an' me'll make it work. An' thanks."

"Good, and you're welcome, pal. If y'all get stuck, just ping Crutch; I'm sure she'll help out. Meg, you game for a jaunt offworld?"

"Sure am, Ace."

"Hold up, you two," Fox said, holding up a staying hand. "Surlianth and Myclestra haven't said they'd go, yet."

"Do we have a choice?" Myclestra wondered, surprise mingled with resignation in her tone.

<We have a choice, dear one,> Surlianth said, <if for no other reason than I will make one, if need be. But for the time, perhaps it would be best if we went and heard them out. We

have several friends in Fox's office, here, and they are the ones providing this Ennead its information about us.>

"I suppose. Very well; in this, I will follow your lead, Surlianth."

<Very good. Then yes, Director Fox, we shall attend, with you and Alpha One, and any others you wish, accompanying.>

"I'll call up the *Genesis* and have her ready to go in five hours," Fox said. "And I think Zz'r'p, Alpha One, and myself will do. Zebra might come along, but mostly to be with me, I think. And even then, I'm betting she stays here in the medlab, to work on the injured." He waved at the others. "Romeo, as Echo says, you're in charge. You, Golf, and Crutch can handle things between you; I'll let her know to consult with you two, and you can call me or Echo if something serious comes in that warrants Director approval. Alpha One, go do what you need to do to head to Aleancë, while I get our transportation ready."

* * *

The small group of six beings — Zebra did stay home; there were still too many agents in critical condition in the medlab for her to feel comfortable going offworld — was officially met by a full guard contingent at the docking gate for the *D1 Genesis* tender, the *Exodus*.

This doesn't look good, Ace, Omega told her mate through the nd't'lq.

I noticed. Armored and armed for full-up Cortian attack. Echo pursed his lips, considering.

<I have noticed also, young ones,> Surlianth told them in private. <Forgive me; I was not eavesdropping, but preparing to contact you both, to obtain your opinion on…this.>

It might be just a kind of honor guard, Surl, Echo noted. *Meg and I aren't used to showing up with what amount to celebrities, kinda — I guess Fox is a celebrity of sorts; they call him Lord Levy, after all, but he's also PGLEIA and we don't get that kinda treatment.*

What he's saying is, we're not sure, Omega said.

<I will not submit to being confined,> Surlianth warned.

Understood. But that isn't the way Pul works, Echo pointed out.

<You call him 'Pul,' not Lord Entiyti. You are friends with the galactic president?>

Of many years, yes, and we know each other really well, Echo confirmed. *If someone else were President currently, I'd be a lot more concerned. But Pul's a good guy, and very reasonable. Let's go on and see what happens. And what formation the guards take will tell me a lot.*

<Meaning?>

If they go before us, it's an honor guard. If they flank us, we got trouble.

<Aha. Then yes, let us see.>

When the guard fully encircled the contingent, however, it stymied even Echo.

Damn, Omega thought, watching. *Mostly in front, but some all around. Ace?*

I dunno, Meg.

Fox says to calm down, everyone, Zz'r'p said then. *This IS an honor guard, but a few of the more anxious sorts in the General Assembly requested handling matters so.*

Echo rolled his eyes.

I'd be willing to bet I know which ones, he grumbled.

I am certain you do, as do I, Zz'r'p said, his own mental tone sardonic in the extreme. *The usual suspects, as the Earth saying goes. But it is what it is. I expect, Surlianth, they are trying to bait you and Myclestra into reacting; do not give them what they want.*

It angers me, Myclestra declared, annoyed. *They disrespect us, after we risked ourselves.*

<And I agree. As do our friends, here. But that is what they want, Little One. As the good Ambassador here says, do not give it to them.>

Exactly what I would have advised, Fox commented in the telepathic conversation. *I know for a fact that Pul considers their worries rather decidedly overblown, given how the two of you have proven yourselves. There's some political gamesmanship occurring here, and we need to be careful not to walk into the wrong side's trap.*

Aha. I see now, Myclestra realized. *Very well. I am not as well-versed in politics as the Old Snake, here, nor yet Director Fox. But I will try to abide by the advice of both of you, throughout this visit. It will be…difficult. But I will do my best. However, I have my limits and I will NOT be pushed beyond them without response!*

Attagirl, Fox said, encouraging. *I understand how you feel, all too well. But there's a time to fight, and a time to grit your teeth and at least pretend to go along.*

And this is that last? Myclestra queried.

<It is, Little One,> Surlianth agreed. <Listen to me, and to Fox. With the help of Fox, Alpha One and the Ambassador, we will keep matters under control as much as is possible.>

Finally they arrived at the Office of the President of the Pan-Galactic Coalition. The guard in the lead opened the door, then stood aside, gesturing them all within the room.

But the resulting conversation went in a direction that neither Alpha One, Director Fox, nor President Entiyti, expected.

* * *

"Welcome, welcome," Pulgey Entiyti declared, rising from his desk and coming around to greet them. "Franz! Omega, Echo! It is good to see my family once more! Ah, Zz'r'p, it is also good seeing you, a fellow 'uncle' to Franz's family!"

"Indeed," Zz'r'p said with a smile and a slight bow to the galactic president. "It is always good to see you, Pulgey."

"Likewise, Pul," Fox said with a smile. "We have some special people we'd like you to meet. This is Myclestra of Alontora, and she carries Surlianth, the ancient being who was once a Star Drake in his universe. This is Pan-Galactic President Pulgey Entiyti, lady and gentlebeing."

"Yes, I have heard many good things about the newcomers," Entiyti said with a broad smile. "I am very pleased to meet you both. I want to thank you for what you have done to save one of the key worlds of our Coalition, as well as preventing the…let us call it a kind of infection…from spreading to other worlds in our galaxy."

Myclestra was silent for a moment, evidently discussing with Surlianth in private as to who should respond first, and how. Finally, and rather reluctantly, she bowed deeply to the Galactic President before rising and looking directly into his eyes, enigmatic behind her mirrorshades.

"It was ever our honor, milord," she said. "And I could not let my battle-sister come to harm, nor her world, let alone her family group."

"Ah, battle-sister; yes, I heard about that," Entiyti said, casting a glance at Omega, before looking back at Myclestra's inscrutable visage. "So effectively we have an addition to the family?"

"Of sorts, I think," Fox agreed, as Omega and Echo smiled, and Myclestra finally reacted, her face flushing a delicate rose hue. "I know I've found I tend to refer to Myclestra as 'tekhter' now and then."

"That clinches it, then," Echo said with a grin. "Myc, welcome to the family."

"I…I…am honored," Myclestra said then, in a soft, stunned voice, almost a whisper. "Milord President, may I present to you Surlianthet, the Sword of Surlianth, who is my Bonded." She drew the Sword slowly and carefully, and presented it to Entiyti.

"I am pleased to meet you…is it Surlianth, or Surlianthet?" Entiyti wondered, somewhat puzzled. "I have been a bit confused over that…"

<The Blade in which I am contained is Surlianthet, Lord Entiyti. I myself am Surlianth,> the mental voice of the star drake declared.

"Then I am pleased to meet you, Surlianth. I would shake hands, but obviously, I cannot."

<And I, you, Lord President. And the handshake is of

no matter. You know, you rather remind me of some of the few children of my fellow Star Drakes, though you are not nearly big enough for that. You make a very handsome dragon, however, if rather…I believe the term is, 'house-sized'… compared to what I am used to. But then, Star Drakes are in no wise able to fit into a house, to begin with.> Entiyti's silver-white face scales flushed, and there was a sense of gentle, even affectionate, amusement coming from the Sword. Then Surlianth added, <I gather that not all of the planets in your Coalition are entirely comfortable with me.>

"There is some difficulty, yes," Entiyti admitted, his horns crossing in his annoyance at those systems, "but we are working it out."

<Would it help if I could provide further assurance that I am here to help, not to harm?>

Entiyti, Fox, Alpha One, and Ambassador Zz'r'p exchanged startled, puzzled glances.

"It would," Entiyti averred. "But how do you propose to do so? More so than you have already done, I mean?"

<I have it to understand that you are waging asymmetric warfare with these…'Cortians.' These are the beings who tortured Agent Echo, are they not?>

"Yes, Surlianth, they are," Fox confirmed.

<You understand that they will never surrender?>

"How do you know that?" Fox wondered.

"Aha," Zz'r'p said then, ear-fins waggling. "That is what you were doing, when we were first detecting your telepathic probes. You were scouting the galaxy."

<No, say rather, I was exploring it. It was not a scouting expedition, at least in a military sense; by now you know from talking to Omega how I came to be in this sword, my blue friend. I was simply curious. I had what young Echo here calls 'down time,' so I took advantage of it to…look around.> Everyone in the room had the sense of a mental shrug. <And, quite frankly, I had been separated from my Bonded, who was in dire straits, given her wounds, and I was looking to find

someone to contact, to request I be returned to her, that I might heal her, while she could still be healed.>

"And Omega responded," Zz'r'p said.

<Yes. I had previously spoken to her, in the forest clearing when her friend and colleague was triaging the wounded, and knew she could hear me and would likely recognize me, if be a bit perturbed and confused. She did not yet know that I was anything but an ordinary sword, you see, so it was a quandary. But she was close by.>

"I wanna hear where he was going with the Cortian thing," Echo said, getting the conversation back on track. His face was grim.

<Ah, quite. So…do you, or do you not, realize that the marauding vessels have no intention of surrender, President Entiyti?>

"Yes, we do; we figured that out some time back," Entiyti noted. "Most notably, when the captains of the two ships involved in kidnapping Echo were interrogated. And every crew member of both ships said much the same. They somehow feel that they are in the right, that they are more… mm, righteous, perhaps…than anyone else, at least in the eyes of their personal deities, and that this means they are destined to prevail against us, no matter the odds. And they cannot be convinced otherwise. Every Cortian taken into custody since has given us that same response. It is frustrating, and a great waste, but it seems we will have to wipe out the ones already marauding in our galaxy. The homeworld, however, is slowly showing promise. We have it under a kind of benign blockade, mostly to prevent resupply or reinforcement of the marauders, and that lot are asking for more and more information about other, more benevolent, systems of government. And there is every indication that the various…I suppose we may call them polities, though it is more like regional warlords than nation-states, or at least, it was before we arrived…" He broke off, then resumed. "In any event, there is indication that at least some of the groups on the surface are attempting to put that governmental information into practice, trying out various forms of government in an effort to find what best suits them. So we have hopes for the Cortian homeworld. More and more, as time goes on, at that."

<Ah. That is good to know. So perhaps the Cortians will eventually become properly civilized members of the galactic community, after all,> Surlianth concluded. <In the meanwhile, would you like me to take care of the matter of the Cortian marauders for you? There are not that many left, perhaps a few dozen ships, no more; their inability to find supplies is slowly doing them in — several ships' crews have already starved to death, in the vastness along the galactic rim, and are apparently drifting in intergalactic space — but I can make it swift and more merciful.>

"What? How could you do that?" Entiyti wondered.

<I simply detonate their warp drives…>

"Wait, WHAT?" a startled Entiyti exclaimed.

"YOU CAN DO THAT?" Omega cried, shocked. Echo simply gaped.

<I can, little Silver Hair. All at once. From here. Right now. This is by way of a token of assurance that I am supportive of you. Assuming, of course, you offer me suitable…ornamentation.>

"Ohmigosh! It would be SO nice not to have to worry about one of us being kidnapped and tortured by those bastards, ever again!" Omega exclaimed.

"Alla that, baby," Echo agreed. "But…is that legal?"

"It would be, Echo, yes," Entiyti explained, "as essentially official executions, with only a minimum of formal paperwork to enable Surlianth, here, to be the official executioner. You and Omega were…occupied with your healing…in the aftermath of that hiigiissht gineest urr giisshttt…"

"Do wha?" Omega murmured.

"Damned pile of shit," Fox translated.

"Oh."

"Yes, and it was," Entiyti decreed. "A big one. But when the tribunals, all the way up to the Ennead, began to realize that the Cortian crews believed they could still win somehow, and that none of them intended to give up, give in, or relent, the Ennead knew that we must do something. They were causing far too much trouble, whenever they managed to actually attack, and they were embedding themselves in our cultures, which was how they came to capture Echo — and others — to begin with. We could not let it go on as it stood." He sighed. "And so we did two things. One: we officially declared another war on the Cortian marauders. Not on the homeworld, just the pirate ships. Two: we conducted a detailed investigation on each instance of their marauding we could find. Then we conducted a tribunal in absentia, and found them all guilty of war crimes. For there was not one instance that we could find of an interaction that was either well-intentioned, or without cruelty…of particularly egregious sorts."

"Damn," Echo murmured. "Why am I NOT surprised?"

"Lotta that," Omega agreed with her spouse. "So they already have convictions and death sentences hanging over 'em?"

"They do," Entiyti confirmed. "It is simply a matter of finding them and executing sentence…pun intended, if bleak. Which is why the instructions passed down from Chief Wux to the various PGLEIA Divisions has basically been, 'no quarter.' We have been attempting to ensure that there are no prisoners aboard, first…"

<Of course,> Surlianth responded, <as would I. Should I find prisoners aboard, I can always hold off and first draw to them one or more spacecraft under your control, to enable the rescue.>

"…But then, yes, provided there are no prisoners, the firing sequence that Alpha One developed in their encounters is being used quite successfully, with no attempt at calling for surrender."

"Aha! Now some shit I've seen in the division directorial feeds are making more sense to me," Echo said then. "So Surl, here, really could do that and it would not only be okay, but good?"

"It sure sounds like it, zun," Fox decided.

"Interesting," Zz'r'p said then. "It seems that the larger being has a proportionally large range and scale on his mental communication."

<I do, Zz'r'p,> Surlianth confirmed. <I had to, when I was a Star Drake, as that was typically how we communicated over the great intergalactic distances which separated us. It was how we were made by the Maker of All.>

"I see, and am beginning to understand a great deal more," Zz'r'p decided.

<Yes, I expect so, my friend. I hope so, at least. For of everyone I met on Earth, you and Fox were the beings with whom I felt the closest akin.>

"Fascinating," Entiyti murmured.

"Yeah," Omega breathed, eyes wide.

"Okay," Echo continued. "A few more questions, please, Surl — you said something about being provided ornamentation in exchange. What counts as suitable ornamentation? Ornamentation of what?"

<My housing. The Sword,> Surlianth answered.

"I…do not understand," Entiyti murmured.

"Us too neither," Fox agreed, after a glance at Alpha One. "I mean, I know you incorporated the necklace, but…"

<Ah. Of course; I never explained. It is relatively simple, really,> Surlianth explained. <I am confined to a sword, but I still expend considerable energies when I fight as I did against the Warpwraith. Were I left to my own devices, yet still used in this fashion, I should eventually exhaust my energies and die. It would take some time, though fighting a few more Warpwraiths would likely serve to do so! The Sword would dissolve away as this was happening…you could, I suppose, compare it to an organic being slowly starving to death, and this would reflect in ever-increasing corrosion and damage to the Sword. But by ornamenting the Sword — which I always prefer to do for myself — usually what happens is that a great

deal of gold, silver, and other precious metals are heaped about me, along with a few gemstones. I am then left overnight, and by the next day — possibly a day or two more, depending on the amounts provided — observers would see that the majority of these items have disappeared, and new decorations have appeared on the hilts and blade, as I choose. What has actually happened is that I have absorbed the materials as what amounts to 'food' to support my activity — effectively a more sophisticated form of mass to energy, which is largely how we Star Drakes consume, in any event — and used the little that remains to decorate my housing, typically including the gemstones in the decorating, as they are less dense than the metals. Were you to throw Surlianthet into the heart of a neutron star, I could eventually consume it all, though it would take a long while, many months, close to a human year, I expect. But I am already running a bit low on energies after the transition between universes, and multiple fights with the Warpwraith, for the Little One and I encountered it several times before Alpha One became involved, never mind our transition between universes — which was assisted by some in the other universe, else I might not have survived. And, while the bounty provided by Division One already did help ease my hunger after the Wraith's demise, the destruction of the Cortian ships' drives over so large a volume of space — most are currently at, or beyond, the galactic rim, skulking about — will be an even bigger expenditure...>

"Aha," Fox said in understanding. "You're hungry. You need to eat, to have the energy to do that."

<Exactly, Fox. I do truly like the way you think. You would have made a fine Star Drake, I suspect.>

Fox flushed, then grinned.

"Pul, we have a guest who's done a lot for us, is offering to do a damn lot more, and he's hungry," the Division One Director said then. "I think maybe we need to offer him a bit of sustenance."

"That...sounds like a plan, Franz," Entiyti decided. "Shall

we all sit down in my conversation pit in the corner, the better to be comfortable? Milord Surlianth, let us discuss precisely what you need for sustenance — specific materials, alloy types, even chemical elements, if need be, and also quantity required — then I will see what I can easily acquire for you. We should be able to obtain somewhat relatively quickly to ease your hunger pains — though it may not be what you consider gourmet, at least initially — with an eye toward providing you a proper meal soon. With an entire galaxy to 'grocery shop,' surely we can find what you need to abate your hunger. It may take a few days to gather a full meal, but we will ensure you do not go hungry."

<Excellent. My thanks, Milord President.>

* * *

The discussion regarding what could be safely used to fuel Surlianthet went for some hours, and everyone in Entiyti's office participated. This included Myclestra, who was pleased at how well she and Surlianth were being accepted by the galactic leader, and could offer her experience on the matter.

Omega, too, was fascinated, and brought her scientific knowledge to bear on the subject, discovering that Surlianth was capable of absorbing almost anything, but that the denser elements and materials provided the best fuel, which made sense to her.

<All metals are better than non-metals, because of the mass density,> Surlianth explained to her, <but the elements heavier than lead, most of which are metals anyway, are the best, though the silver and gold and such is very…I suppose you might understand it as 'tasty.' But the heavier elements are… more filling. It is almost entirely a mass-density consideration, you see.>

"No, I get that," Omega determined. "And the radiation of those heavier element isotopes doesn't harm you?"

<Not particularly. Were I not who and what I am, I suppose the metallurgy of the Sword might become degraded over time, but it is easy enough to take care of that at the same time as I

351

ornament it.>

"This is fascinating," Echo declared, and the others agreed.

"And I am learning so much," Myclestra said, in something very akin to delight. "My battle-sister is so knowledgeable, and so willing to share that knowledge! I never knew such things in my own universe!"

Omega smiled.

"I've heard it said," she noted, "that knowledge is power. You're strong, Myclestra, and you have a good brain. We need to teach you how to use it even better, I think."

"Which seems like a plan to me," Fox agreed. "I'll see about getting her some audio textbooks from the University of Aleancë. Lyddhu can probably help."

"Good idea, Franz," Entiyti said.

<She is very intelligent, my Little One. Now that her curiosity has been piqued at last, I think I can do a fair bit in that regard, also,> Surlianth averred. <If the august beings assembled here can provide assistance in that as they have said, my Little One will be impressively learnéd in no time.>

Myclestra fairly beamed, her smile was so wide.

Finally Entiyti called his assistant and had him order a significant quantity of silver, rhodium, and tin, all of which could be had relatively easily and inexpensively in quantity on Aleancë, to be delivered to the room provided for Myclestra and Surlianth, for the duration of their stay.

"And we will obtain more and better, once we have the opportunity," Entiyti promised. "But for now, you have 'food' in your rooms that should tide you over, be 'filling,' and relatively 'tasty,' into the bargain."

<For that, I thank you, sir,> a grateful Surlianth said, and they all had the mental impression of a bow.

"And now we all need to go to those rooms," Fox determined. "It's getting late, and tomorrow is going to be busy."

* * *

There were comfortable, even elegant, suites of rooms

waiting for Fox, Zz'r'p, Alpha One, and Myclestra and Surlianth.

Each suite had a sitting room with wet bar, entertainment area and conversational nook, a small kitchen with dining nook, already fully stocked with the appropriate foods — at least for the humanoids; Myc's kitchen was stocked with Earth foods, since they were similar to what she was used to eating. There was a bedroom with *en suite* bath in each, as well; both bedroom and bathroom were large and luxurious. Outside the bedroom in the suite assigned to the Alontoran, there was even a small nook in which Surlianthet could be placed to rest, and another room — normally a study — where his tribute could be placed and he could consume it in peace.

"Oh, great Mother Alontora," Myclestra whispered, as she surveyed the suite. "This is a small palace."

"You are appreciated, my dear, both of you," Entiyti noted. "Relax and rest well. I will have someone sent to fetch you mid-morning, before the Council convenes."

* * *

When Fox, Alpha One, Myclestra, and Surlianthet arrived in the huge Council Room the next morning, the Council was already in session; Zz'r'p sat on the dais with Entiyti, at the latter's request. The newcomers, likewise, were led to the dais by their liaisons.

"Good, good," Entiyti said, waving them to seats already provided in the rear of the dais. "Perfect timing. I have just finished detailing the help offered by Myclestra and Surlianth with regard to the Cortian problem, as well as the alliance that has developed between them and Division One. I have also explained the nigh-familial nature of parts of that alliance. This has all gone a great way toward easing the fears of many in this august assembly as regards the potential dangers inherent in the power of these two who have come from without." He paused, then added, "To that end, we have agreed via vote that we should proceed in an allied fashion."

He gestured, and Myclestra, wearing the Sword on her

back as usual, stood and moved forward. Then, at another gesture, she slowly withdrew the Sword from its scabbard. Behind them, the others rose and stepped forward to show support.

"Let us begin with a sincere and deep thanks to Myclestra and her bond mate, Surlianth," President Pulgey Entiyti formally decreed in the full Galactic Council, as Myclestra stood beside him, holding Surlianthet, the Sword of Surlianth. Flanking them were Fox, Omega, Echo, and Ambassador Zz'r'p ob Tii'rkin. "They brought us word of a danger we had no idea existed, chasing it from their own universe into ours despite the dangers. And when they encountered the local PGLEIA, they assisted them in destroying the menace, setting aside initial misunderstandings to do so."

Entiyti paused, and the huge room full of representatives enthusiastically applauded in various ways.

"Had they not done so," he continued, "the Warpwraith — heretofore unknown to our very universe — might have wreaked great devastation in our galaxy, beginning with Earth and moving rapidly outward. More, they helped train our Division One PGLEIA personnel in how to destroy such a creature, should one ever find its way into our universe again from without."

Another raucous round of applause went up.

"Even so, it was not easy," Entiyti cautioned. "Many good agents were lost in that endeavor, and even more gravely wounded. Let us have a moment of silence *in memoriam* for the dead, and a moment of petition for the wounded."

The huge room grew so quiet, each being could hear its own heart beat. The Agents upon the podium felt chills of awe.

* * *

"Now, it is my great honor to do a thing which has never been done before in this assembly," Entiyti declared, after a suitable time. "Myclestra, please step forward."

Startled, Myclestra sheathed Surlianthet and obeyed, as Entiyti produced a box from behind the podium.

354

"Myclestra, you have been of inestimable help to this galaxy," Entiyti pontificated. "As our ally, it is my deepest privilege to present to you the Cross in Platinum of the Grand Galactic Alliance. This is our greatest award and honor for valor in combat with enemy forces. With this medal comes a substantial monetary award, as well. And it shall be enhanced by an additional reward for services above and beyond that expected of a sentient." He opened the box, producing a silvery platinum chain with a large, deep-blue sapphire set in an equal-armed cross-shaped platinum medallion, then placed it over her head. "Henceforth you will be known in the Coalition as the Lady Myclestra of Alontora."

Myclestra stifled a gasp, but was otherwise speechless. She dropped a deep curtsy, bowing her head, and Entiyti smiled. The room applauded enthusiastically.

"Lady Myclestra, please present Surlianthet, hilts upward."

Myclestra drew and held out the Sword, blade down. Entiyti produced another box, extracting a second chain with an identical medal; however, this chain was much shorter, and just fit over the grip, sliding over the pommel and held up by the crosshilts.

"Likewise, do you, Surlianth, former Star Drake of another universe whose essence and power are contained within this Sword, Bonded to the Lady Myclestra, deserve the honor of the Cross in Platinum of the Grand Galactic Alliance. I hereby decree that you are the Lord Surlianth Surlianthet."

<I am duly honored, Milord President,> came the deep mental reply, 'audible' to all in the great hall. A soft gasp of surprise from multiple voices echoed in the Chamber. Then respectful applause once again filled the great room.

"Alpha One," Entiyti said, and the pair snapped to full attention; they had been busy applauding their comrades in arms.

"Yes, sir?" Echo replied.

"Step forward, please; it is your turn," Entiyti said with a grin. "And about damn time, too. The Assembly finally got the details of this award all worked out."

Omega and Echo glanced at each other in surprise. Fox, wily as ever, grinned from ear to ear.

"Gotcha," he murmured.

* * *

In short order, Alpha One had been given the Cross in Platinum, as well. They bowed, deeply honored, as a kvelling Fox threatened to pop shirt buttons in the background, and beat his hands numb applauding. After that, a few speeches were made, then someone called for a recess, another seconded it, Entiyti held a vote, and placed the coalition representatives in an extended lunch break.

"And now," Entiyti said, as the great assembly of representatives broke up, "I must ask you all to appear in the Ennead's council chambers, once we have all had the midday meal together."

Myclestra's jaw dropped in surprised dismay, and Echo and Omega glanced at each other, worried.

* * *

"Please stand in the center of the room, Lady Myclestra, and present Lord Surlianth, so that the being contained within may be considered as standing with you, as well," Entiyti said, once the Ennead ruling body had convened after lunch.

Myclestra turned to Alpha One. "Is..." she breathed.

"It's okay, Myc," Omega murmured. "It's not bad. Fox filled me in a little bit on the behind-the-scenes discussion, via Ambassador Zz'r'p, just now. I think the two of you are going to like it. And I've had an idea myself, though I dunno if either of you will be interested."

<Very well, my little Silver Hair,> a tolerant Surlianth told her, allowing only Omega, Echo, and Myclestra to 'hear.' <Let us see what they have to say, Little One. Do as Lord Entiyti says, please.>

At that urging, a reluctant Myclestra rose to her feet and moved to the center of the triangle, Omega and Echo flanking her in support. Once there, she drew the Sword from its sheath and held it flat-bladed, across both palms; the sapphire medal — whose chain was already 'welded' to the side of the hilt such that the medal rested below the dragon-head, as Surlianth began to make it part of his 'house' — dangled just below. Briefly offering the Sword to the high seat of the President, she turned it blade-down and bowed slightly.

"We await your word, sir," she said then.

"Very well," Entiyti said. "Please rise, Lady Myclestra. The Ennead has been deep in discussion on this matter, and we have had feedback from all the Coalition representatives; not all of them were in agreement as to what should be done. But then, you know that already. We understand that the situation is…difficult. Some fear for the consequences of Surlianth's existence in our reality, a reality in which he was not birthed, and with which he may not be able to harmonize, at least in the form he once possessed. Our initial response was to send him back from whence he came, assuming we could, or assuming he could…"

<I think,> Surlianth began.

"Hold a moment, please, Lord Surlianth," Entiyti said, raising a staying hand. "Let me finish, if you will. I do not think you will regret doing so."

<Very well. Forgive me; I am somewhat concerned.>

"And we understand that concern," Entiyti reassured the ancient one. "You are Bonded to Myclestra. Where one goes, the other must go."

<Precisely. And I would not have her go back to a place where the inhabitants would kill her as soon as they perceive her. But that is, unfortunately, true of all the places I have yet been before this.>

"Nor would we wish such a thing. The life she lived where she was created — I hesitate to say 'birthed,' given what Alpha One has told me of her life, and Omega understands that quite well, especially given her own life history — that life was not life, but existence, waiting for inevitable death. A horrible death, a painful death, a wasted death. That is NOT the way of the Pan-Galactic Coalition," Entiyti declaimed. "So we fully realize we must somehow help the two of you construct a life together, somewhere OTHER than that place. Those places. Somewhere that is likely to be within our own universe. This, we now hope we may be able to offer you."

<Interesting,> Surlianth murmured.

"Say on, please, milord," Myclestra said, feeling a light, reassuring touch from Omega's hand on her arm.

"We are willing to install you, Surlianth, as the controlling intelligence of a large starship," Entiyti continued, as the rest of the Ennead looked on in approval. "Omega tells me you are curious and wanted to explore; then we will help you do so. Given what Omega and Madrid were able to do with the Sword, for and during the battle with the Warpwraith, we now believe this will be possible, especially if you are willing to help them, and us. This starship — which we have already selected for you, and for which you will be the official, formal…'owner,' is already being upgraded to the highest power Alcubierre warp we can currently manage, enhancing the Alcubierre warp system to propel the wave function at speeds suited to traveling even intergalactic distances in mortal lifetimes. It will then be outfitted for such intergalactic exploration, complete with offensive and defensive armament, shielding against micrometeoroids, scientific instrumentation, astronavigation, and more. Your Bond Bearer, Myclestra, would, of course, go with you, hence the need for increased speed, to accommodate HER lifetime — which, the Division One physicians tell us, should be comparable to an Earth human lifetime, provided she is no longer risking herself in doing battle every other day. If you so wish, we can also send along a small crew of volunteers — we have already had some — for engineering, science and astrogation, and diplomatic outreach, as well as general exploration, and the logistical crew to care for them — food, medical, clothing, equipment, and so on. They would be there to assist, and to provide their own experience and expertise on what you may find. A scientific exploration team, if you will. We would like periodic communiqués regarding what is found, for our own scientists and engineers; we want to learn, also. Placing you — via the Sword — in the spacecraft, as an integrated part of it, should also give you an audible voice, as well as the telepathic voice, if you wish it. As the ship would belong to you, if you should wish to reconfigure it into something that you find more appealing, we would ask only that you consider the welfare of the other inhabitants as you are doing so — which, having now met and talked to you, I am certain you would do anyway." Entiyti paused.

<This sounds…intriguing,> Surlianth decided. <Please, Milord President, say on.>

"In addition to exploring our Great Spiral, I can say of a certainty that you have already had an invitation from the Persis Federation of the Andromeda Galaxy to visit…though Premier Hsrs Syrsh respectfully requests you do NOT appropriate his home galaxy as a hoard! He is a good being, a cheerful being, with an excellent sense of humor, but he leads his people as I do, compassionately but with great feeling and a desire to defend them, so it would not be a wise thing to do, in any event, I think. Far better to make a friend."

<Agreed. And the Persans were interesting, what I perceived of them; I think that might make a nice visit.>

"Should you find a galaxy suitable for using as a hoard, and decide to settle down and make use of it," Entiyti continued, "we would also request that you do not destroy any sentient life to do so, especially in the reconstituting of your drake body, and ensure that any sentients in that galaxy are willing to be part of your hoard. We would also like to request that you remain allied with the Pan-Galactic Coalition, regardless of your corporeal form." Entiyti paused again, patently awaiting a response.

<This all sounds quite reasonable,> Surlianth decided after only a moment to consider. <You are correct in that I chose to take this form in order to better explore All That Is. If I am actively doing so, and I have my Little One at my side, I am

unlikely to want to 'settle down,' as you put it, Lord Entiyti; I have always had a decided wanderlust, much more so than my fellow Drakes. Nevertheless, I understand your caution, and share it. Only *in extremis* would I commit such destruction to maintain my own existence, in any event, and that, purely instinctive…which is difficult to control. Yes, I would surely attempt — if need permitted — to choose an uninhabited system, for it were far better to survive without the taking of other life to do so. I suspect it would do me no favors, mentally or emotionally, to accidentally destroy an inhabited system for such purpose. And if you are willing to do this for me and my Little One, and given how well we worked with your Division One people, I see no reason why we should not continue our alliance with you. Little One? Do you agree?>

"Yes. I think it sounds very interesting, Surlianth," Myclestra admitted. "I find I am in no hurry to go back ho…" Abruptly she broke off and turned to Omega. "Battle-sister, must 'home' always be the place where one was created, do you think?"

"No, Myclestra," Omega said with a soft smile. "One of the things I've found is that 'home' is often not a place, but a person. Echo is that person, for me. Wherever he is, is home, as far as I'm concerned. We do a lot of traveling in the course of our jobs, so that's a really good thing; it means I'm comfortable wherever, as long as he's there. But the place that holds the beings who corrupted your species? That was merely a place of birthing, of creation. I don't think it was ever your home."

Echo moved over and took Omega's hand in his own.

"I'd have to agree with every word of that," he said. "Meg is home to me, too. And no, the place where you were created… isn't your home."

<Little One,> Surlianth said, <these two are wise far beyond their years. For they are correct. And so I have a request to make of you.>

"What, Surlianth?"

<Might I be your 'home' person? For what person I am,

at least?>

Myclestra's sightless eyes opened wide; her eyebrows shot up, and her mouth dropped open.

"Mother Alontora," she murmured. "You already are, Surlianth. You are the being upon whom I lean, as I have seen these two do."

<Good. For Silver Hair is right, and I am home with you, as well.>

Omega pressed her lips together, blue eyes sparkling, then held up a finger to Entiyti in a *hold one* gesture; he had cocked his head in an inquiry as to whether or not he should proceed. He nodded in response, and settled back in his chair to see what Omega was about to do. Likewise watching the interaction, the rest of the Ennead looked on in engrossed silence.

"Surlianth, Myclestra, like I told you earlier, I have an idea," she said. "I don't know if either of you will agree with it, and I'm not sure how we're ever gonna manage to do it, but after that exchange, I'm more inclined to think it…might work. At least mentally and emotionally."

<What did you have in mind, Silver Hair?>

"I know you both know what love is, though I have no idea if either of you have personally experienced it," Omega said, cheeks flushing slightly pink. "Not, um, intercourse, but actual, heart love."

"I…have," Myclestra admitted. "At least, what I think you mean. Romantic love, as between you and Echo?"

"Exactly."

"Yes. But as I told you, she was…killed…by the Masters, in a horrible fashion. I am…frequently lonely," the alien woman confessed. "Lovers, yes, from time to time. A mate? No. For I have had no opportunity, nor any time, to even try to find a mate. Let alone someone of my own species, most of whom are not free to take a mate, in any case. And Surlianth has been there for these many years, to alleviate some of that loneliness. He cannot hold me, but at least I have someone to talk to," she said with a wry smile. "We banter, we discuss, we ponder, we joke. He is a good companion, wise and understanding."

<The Star-Drakes of old,> Surlianth noted, <were made male and female, and there were matings from time to time. But it was rare, and there were never many of us to begin with, and only twice or thrice were there any young ones produced; though the little ones were very cute, creatures so large and so long-lived as we simply cannot have large populations, lest they decimate their environs. I, personally, never found a mate, though at one time I looked for one most diligently. And yes, I do enjoy communing with my Little One. When she listens,> he teased, and she flushed, then grinned.

"Okay, this might sound a little weird, then, and I hope I can get the concept across," Omega said. "But Surlianth, you already told us you could recreate your Star Drake body, but it would take a lot of material to do that. What if, after we installed the Sword into the starship so you could 'drive' it, you also tried creating a humanoid body, in addition to being in the starship? Maybe flesh, maybe android, maybe some synthesis of both? Then you and Myclestra could really be together," Omega added. "It wouldn't take nearly so much material to do THAT. And you could walk beside her and set foot on the planets you encounter, and personally explore them…"

<Ha! And come back and tell you all about them,> Surlianth chuckled.

"Well, I would hope you might visit your friends once in a while," Omega noted with a grin. "And I'm sure you'd have stories to tell! The plan is to make the ship fast enough to travel between galaxies in reasonable times, for those of us who don't live as long as Star Drakes," she ribbed.

There was another deep chuckle from the drake, then a long silence. Omega noticed that Myclestra was holding her breath.

<…I think I might like to try that,> Surlianth said then. <I can likely do both, run the starship AND walk beside my Little One, for the mind is as big as the body once was, if you understand me…>

"I think we do," Omega said, as Myclestra let out her breath. "And I think you might have made somebody pretty happy, here."

<Good. That…pleases me,> Surlianth said, mental voice quiet. <All of it. Yes, Lord Entiyti, you have my full agreement and cooperation. My word is my honor, and I give you my word, it will be as you have recommended to us. Myclestra, my Little One? What say you?>

"I am in agreement with my Bonded," Myclestra averred. "I give you my word, we will do as you say, and remain staunch allies of the Pan-Galactic Coalition, its Division One, and most of all, its Director and its Alpha One team."

"And no Alontoran ever went back on her word," Omega said with another grin.

"No, never," Myclestra agreed, matching her grin. "And this Alontoran never shall."

<And the ship, and the material for forming the body — perhaps with a bit extra to offset the remaining energy expended on the Warpwraith, which admittedly has tired me considerably, as well as whatever you decide to have me do about the Cortian pirate ships — shall be considered my full 'tribute,' my pay,> Surlianth decided. <The rewards already granted my Little One are her bounty.>

"They are," agreed Myclestra. "As well as the granting of titles to Surlianth and myself, and the realization that I finally have a true home…and trusted friends."

"As for the Cortian pirates and slavers," Lady Teela Krimnet, Vice-President of the Coalition and Entiyti's second, pronounced, as she rose to her feet, "let it be known that we, the Ennead, in joint council, have declared an allied Lord Surlianth Surlianthet our designated executioner. Provided there are no prisoners aboard the Cortian vessels, he is at liberty to execute judgement at his best convenience, preferably within the next few days but NOT today, so that we may have watchers looking for the ships as they detonate, the better to legally account for the executions. The Lord Surlianth may also contact myself,

Lord Entiyti, Lord Levy the Director of Division One, or either member of Alpha One, should he find Cortian vessels with non-Cortian prisoners, and we will ensure rescue is effected. After which rescue, Lord Surlianth shall perform the executions upon those last remaining vessels." She paused, then queried, "Do you accept this duty, Lord Surlianth?"

<I do so accept the duty, Madame Vice-President,> came the reply. <I have had some in-depth discussions with friends Echo and Omega about their experiences, so let me assure you that it will be my honor to ensure your spaceways are no longer plagued by their ravages.>

"Very good," Krimnet noted. "We, the Ennead of the Pan-Galactic Coalition, have a covenant with the Lord Surlianth Surlianthet."

"Then let the thing be done," Entiyti decreed. "We will write up an alliance and agreement, which will be ready by the time BOTH members of the bond are ready to sign it."

"It will be done as you say, Milord Entiyti," Lady Teela Krimnet declared.

"Then this session of the Ennead is concluded," Entiyti said.

* * *

That night, aided by Ambassador Zz'r'p in determining if there were other species aboard the Cortian vessels — which vessels Surlianth had no problems finding — the drake compiled a kind of telepathic list of the enemy vessels. This list was subdivided into two categories: those that only contained Cortian crew, and those that contained prisoners. This latter sub-list, complete with coordinates, was promptly provided to Fox, who — given that worthy was already in Fox's stateroom, reminiscing with him — passed it on to Entiyti, and the order given to PGLEIA Chief Gwag Wuxullian, who immediately sent out flights of spacecraft to intercept the Cortian vessels. Fortunately, there were only a handful.

Then the complete list was given to Lady Teela Krimnet, to ensure that there were observers capable of seeing the explosions, to verify the executions.

Surlianth? Zz'r'p queried then. *I have just thought of something.*

<Tell me, my blue friend. Let me add, consequent to nothing in particular, that your especial shade of dermis is a favored color of mine. My face scales were once that color.>

Oh! Thank you. I rather like it myself, yes. And I am certain your scales were most attractive, if they were shiny and iridescent like the Draconans'.

<Yes, they were. But I have diverted your inquiry; forgive me.>

Ah. You see, I know that, when Echo was captured by the Cortians, they had an embedded, disguised Cortian on the planet...which is how they came to capture him...

<Aha. I see your concern. We need to do a sweep to see if they are all in their ships, or not.>

Exactly.

<It will take a few hours, but I can do this.>

Good. What can I do to help...?

* * *

The next morning, Wuxullian reported to Entiyti's office, summoning Krimnet, Myclestra, Surlianth, Zz'r'p, Fox, and Alpha One.

"It took a bit of doing, and not a little assistance from Surlianth, Zz'r'p, and several other Deltiri in the Council staff," Wux noted. "Basically, we had to play some more of Omega's mind games with them in order to free the prisoners. Not all of the freed prisoners are in good shape, but they are getting medical treatment and counseling for their ordeals. We have them all, sir."

"Good," Omega said, seeing Echo's jaw set hard. "Nobody else needs to go through that shit. Ever again."

<Nor shall they, by the time I am through,> Surlianth said. The deep voice was cold, and hard as adamant. <Echo, my apologies; when we were discussing the matter the other night, your memories came to the fore on your capture, and I...

365

saw. Everything, I think. For a being whose communication is entirely telepathic now, it was hard NOT to see. It was not my intention, but it has made me very determined on this. You are friend, and family of a sort, after all.>

"No prob, Surl," Echo murmured then. "I…understand. I'm surprised Meg hasn't seen."

"I keep a block around that part of your memory, hon," Omega responded, soft. "Mm'l'n showed me how. Surl, here, didn't know, so it hit him unexpectedly; you asked me not to look before we ever rescued you, so I made a point of figuring out how to maintain your privacy on it. When you're ready to share it with me, you will…just like I did, with what Slug did to me."

"Oh. Thanks, then."

<I assure you, my wrath was great, Echo. I know that the specific ones who did this to you are already executed, but there was a battle to find you and Silver Hair a couple of annums ago, was there not? An entire fleet against an entire fleet? Friend Zz'r'p told me something of this…>

"There was," Fox confirmed. "It ended up taking two of our fleets against one of theirs; they're fierce fighters, and neither ask for nor give mercy, and as you've noted, they flatly refuse surrender. And if they'd found Alpha One, probably much the same thing as did happen to Echo would have happened to BOTH of 'em. Including rape, which they would have done to Echo when they had him, but couldn't figure out how to do with their limited resources, fortunately."

<Then I intend to ensure that my new friends are never endangered by them, ever again.>

"What about any embedded Cortians on-planet somewhere?" Entiyti wondered. "Zz'r'p contacted me last night to tell me the two of you were looking…"

<We found only three, disguised as a different kind of avian species, on two different planets,> Surlianth noted then. <Apparently your sweeps have been most effective, Chief Wuxullian. My compliments.>

"Thank you," Wux said. "What happened to those three?"

"We contacted the local gendarmerie," Zz'r'p explained, "told them what we had verified telepathically — I dropped my own name, here, as I am somewhat better known than Surlianth as yet, though not by much; I suspect it was the title more than my name that provided the influence — and we ensured the creatures were taken into custody and their Cortian natures exposed. Then, once witnesses were present, they were formally executed...mm, let us say, mentally."

"Ah," Wux said, comprehending. "Sudden brain death can be a very swift, effective, and relatively gentle method of execution."

"And it was," Zz'r'p confirmed. "We both ensured it was so."

<Lady Teela, Chief Wuxullian,> Surlianth said, <are your observers in position?>

"They are, Lord Surlianth," Krimnet averred.

<President Entiyti, is the 'tribute' ready? I will be very depleted once this is done...>

"It is, Surlianth. Some three large crates of material suitable to restoring you should be in the quarters provided for you and Myclestra by now, placed in the study. She need only take you back there, open a crate, and lay you on the contents. When that crate's contents are exhausted, she merely moves you to the next, and the next. If that is insufficient to refuel you, I have more already in waiting, and you need but ask." He paused to think, started, then added, "Oh! And I was told to tell you that none of it is radioactive, so Lady Myclestra will not be harmed."

<Very good then. We are ready?>

Entiyti glanced at Wuxullian; he nodded. Then he looked at Krimnet, who also nodded.

"We are ready," Entiyti declared.

<Good. If you have the special glasses provided for use around the memory re-encoder, you would do well to don them; this will be...bright.>

Myclestra positioned Surlianthet on a special pedestal placed in the office for this express purpose, then stepped back, as the others extracted goggle-glasses and donned them.

There was silence in the room for a matter of only seconds, but it seemed much longer. Then a brilliant flare of light emanated from Surlianthet; to the onlookers, it was as if a silent lightning bolt had struck, and nothing was visible for long moments.

<It is done,> Surlianth decreed. <You may now remove the shaded eyeglasses.>

Within seconds, bleats came from communications devices carried by both Krimnet and Wuxullian. They extracted them from pockets and checked the messages thereon, then glanced at each other. Krimnet nodded.

"It is indeed done, and very thoroughly and efficiently," Wux confirmed. "So complete was the destruction that there is hardly even any debris left, according to reports from the observers. Thank you, Lord Surlianth."

"Yes," Entiyti agreed. "Many thanks to you both. Lady Teela, would you and Chief Wuxullian be so kind as to escort Lady Myclestra and Lord Surlianth back to their quarters? I am certain Lord Surlianth is more than ready for a meal, at this point."

<I am, at that,> Surlianth agreed, sounding distinctly tired, as Myclestra hefted the Sword and slid it carefully into its scabbard.

"We should be happy to do so, Pulgey," Krimnet said with a smile. "Gwag? Shall we?"

"We shall," Wuxullian said, offering the much taller woman his arm. Teela laid her hand on his arm, and they escorted the Alontoran and the Sword from the President's office suite.

"And now we start adapting the starship to Surl," Omega noted, rubbing her hands together eagerly.

* * *

That night, after lovemaking, a contented Echo fell soundly asleep. Omega looked into his face and smiled, snuggled into his warm side, sighed, and slowly drifted into slumber herself.

As she began to lucid-dream, Omega became aware of two gigantic eyes, familiar, watching her with a warm, friendly, affectionate gaze.

<Mmm. Little Silver Hair,> Surlianth murmured. <You are a stalwart, fierce one. Intellect, great heart, determination, strong will. All for the good of those for whom you care. All for the cause of Right.>

"I try, Surlianth," she replied to those huge eyes. "I try. I'm not always right, and I'm not always successful. But I give it the best I can."

<You do, child, indeed. And you have done your best to do right by Myclestra and me.>

"Well, sure. You're trying to do right, too."

<We are, yes. Though sometimes I think our ideas may be a bit different from yours. Our experiences have been very different, after all.>

"True. But when you boil it all down, it comes out the same, I think."

<It does seem to, does it not?>

"Yup."

<But while I suspect that, in another reality, my Little One might have become what, on your world, some term a 'paladin,' I...am not so noble of nature.>

"What do you mean?"

<I am truly massive — or I once was — and used to looking out for myself. I am a Star Drake, and that means certain things, Silver Hair. Among those things are ego, a certain self-centeredness amounting almost to selfishness, and a bit of greed. 'Hoard,' you know. And I know these things about myself. I do not always like them — I see a certain dislike in Myclestra when they come up — but I cannot always restrain those aspects of myself.>

"Oh. Well, but to be honest, Surl, while I can see what you mean, personally I think you must have grown a lot over the years, where all that's concerned. You put Earth first. You put

Myc first. You made a point of taking out the wraith because it was the RIGHT thing to do. You could have demanded all kinds of stuff of us...but you haven't. And you explained that you actually physically NEED 'tribute' to survive, too. Which sorta puts a different spin on things for most of us."

<I suppose.>

"I think Myc has sorta rubbed off on you," Omega said with a grin. "She's good for you. And you're good for her."

<Now that, I must agree with. After the conversation in the Ennead chambers, I find myself seeing her in a different light, as well.>

"You love her, don't you?"

<I rather think I do. And I hope, based on her reactions, perhaps she loves me, as well.>

"I sure think so."

<It will be interesting to see how we react to each other, once I take humanoid form.>

"Personally, I think you'll just get that much closer. It wouldn't surprise me if you end up mates, of a sort, at least."

<Nor would I. And we would never have thought of it, were it not for you and Echo, child.>

"Aw. Hey, I got my happy ending with him; I just like to see it for others, too."

<Happy ending, eh? Tell me, child, what is it you wish for most in your life, that you do not have now?>

"Oh! I dunno," Omega said, caught off-guard by the question, and pondering it for long moments before replying. "I guess...Echo and I both want children, but right now we just don't dare..."

<Because of what this Slug did to you? How you were modified?>

"Yeah. See," Omega explained, surprised at how easy it was to tell this gigantic being these things that were so painful, "those modifications extended right down to my eggs, because if I failed to kill Echo for him, Slug had a plan to have the next generation of assassins kill him...and those would have been

my children..."

<Mm. Yes, I see it in your mind, where you show me. Poor child. And you WERE just a child when he abducted you.>

"*Yeah.*" Omega sighed. "*I mean, I've sorta come to a, a sense of, of peace, about what it all did to me, personally. And that's good, in a bass-ackwards kinda way. I don't like that it was done, or that I'm stuck with it, but I've been able to do good things because of what I can do, that most normal humans... can't. But I really wish Echo and I could look at having kids one of these days — probably not until a couple years from now, once he's Director and I'm the Alpha Line chief, and we're not out in the field, risking our necks — without the risk of his own kids killing him or something horrid like that.*"

<Can your physicians not correct the matter?>

"*Not so far, no,*" Omega admitted. "*They're having a hard time sorting out everything that got done to the eggs, see. And I'm, well...*" She blushed. "*I'm considered in the top percentile of human abilities and intellect. And apparently would have been, even without Slug mucking around with things. Echo is too, but I mean, they have to sort out what's my original genetics and what's tweaked, before they can do anything else. They want to take the eggs back to what they should have been, before...Slug. They just don't know how yet. And may never know, to be honest. I mean, I have faith in 'em, it's just...hard. Our genetic studies, even as a galactic culture, just aren't THAT advanced.*"

<I see. I have a question for you, Silver Hair.>

"*Whassat?*" She gave him a cheerful smile; the dream state kept her mood from deteriorating despite the previous discussion, somehow.

<Did you know that one of the abilities of a Star Drake is to manipulate time? It is limited in scope, but some of us have gotten quite good at what we CAN do...>

"*No, I didn't. That sounds...fascinating,*" Omega said then, perking up. "*I'd love to know how, and what you can do, and what the limits are, and oh, just ALL that! Hell, you and*

I flat need to sit down and talk for a bit, before you and Myc head off into the wild black yonder."

<I think I would like that, and I know you would. But I suspect you would like this more…>

The giant eyes suddenly glowed with a light that shifted through the spectrum, from a deep violet all the way to a dark red, and Omega felt something in her belly stir.

"Wha? What just happened?" she wondered, surprised.

"What would you think, how would you react, if I told you I reversed time on your ovaries, child, such that they now exist as they were before the rogue gastropoid manipulated their genetic structures?>

"I…I…WHAT?" Omega exclaimed. "Are you saying…?"

<Yes. What if I manipulate time in such a fashion that the changes to your eggs — JUST your eggs, so that your own 'enhancements' are unaffected — but the changes to your eggs never happened? That would make it safe for you and your mate to produce offspring, would it not?>

"OH! It sure would!" Omega cried. "Surl! That would be so wonderful! Oh, I'm so happy!"

<Indeed? Well, then. We shall have to see what happens.>

* * *

Omega woke up suddenly, completely alert and aware… and in full remembrance of the dream.

He didn't, she thought, stunned. *Surely not. That was just a dream…but it was awfully damn lucid! Maybe he DID.*

She sat in bed next to a zonked-out Echo for nearly half an hour, pondering what had just happened…or not.

Well, she decided. *Only one way to find out. I'll ask for a quick scan tomorrow. I wish India or Zebra were here. Hell, I just hope India's gonna be okay! Huh. It'll take some time to send back the scan to Earth for comparison, but if I can get scanned in the morning, I should know something by tomorrow night, provided the medlab's not too slammed. And I bet I know who I can ask for help.*

* * *

The next morning, while Echo was tagging up with Fox, Omega went directly to Lady Teela, and Krimnet promptly took her to her personal physician to perform the scan. It was sent straight back to Zebra on Earth, and by the time Omega and Echo had finished their all-day consulting session with the starship engineers about the means of integrating Surlianthet into the bridge controls, there was a message from Zebra waiting on her cell phone.

Meg,
Sorry, honey, no change. What made you think there would be?
Love,
Zee

Omega replied via text, explaining about the dream, then sighed.

She and Echo headed for their suite of rooms, provided by the Ennead for their comfort during their stay on Aleancë.

* * *

"What's wrong, baby?" Echo wondered later that evening, as they prepared for bed. Both had already stripped down, washed faces, brushed teeth, and they were turning down the bedclothes together. "You've been antsy all day today, and now you just look…blue."

"Um," Omega said, flushing. "It's…it's kinda stupid."

"I doubt it, but when you flush all over like that, it's really pretty cute."

Omega only flushed deeper, and gave Echo a wry grin.

"That's better," he said with a smile. "I got a grin outta you. Now tell me what's buggin' you. You know I'll never think it's stupid."

So she told him about the dream.

"…And I figured, if he can do what-all he did when he took out the wraith, maybe…" She sighed again.

"Aw," Echo said, understanding. "But the results came

back, same as always?"

"Yeah. So it was just a dream."

"Well, be patient, sweetheart. We got a great team back home, working the problem. They'll figure it out."

"I know…probably."

"Hey," Echo murmured, nudging her head up with his fingers, until he could look into despondent blue eyes. "They put Humpty Dumpty Echo back together again. They're puttin' together all the survivors of the nuke plant fight. They can fix this, too. They're GOOD, baby."

"I know. I'm just…"

"We've had a hard few weeks of it, and you're tired," Echo said, taking her in his arms. "I am, too. We've been beat to hell and back, dunked in the regen pod, beat up some more, forced to deal with concepts we never thought were real, had to stand by while friends died…it's been…rough. I mentioned it to Fox today, while you were in the middle of outlining the interface for the Sword, and suggested that maybe Madrid might come from Earth to fill in for you, while you and I take some well-earned time off for a mental break. And he said it was a good idea."

"Oh. Did, um…did he think I was antsy, too?"

"He did. And by now, he'll prob'ly know about the request to Zebra, and he'll understand."

"Yeah. It's kinda nice when your bosses are also family, sorta, I guess."

"Yup. Trustworthy sorts, all." He grinned.

"Ooo, don't get TOO full of yourself, now," she warned, and he grinned wider.

"What are you gonna do about it?" he demanded to know.

Then Agent Echo, Assistant Director of Division One, Alpha Line chief, the youngest and baddest of the Originals, let out a high-pitched, falsetto squeal, as Omega thoroughly goosed him in the ribs. He quickly clapped a hand over his mouth, stifling the sound, as he turned beet-red in the face in embarrassment. Omega bit her lip to stifle laughter, but it was useless; she broke into a giggling fit and doubled over. Echo, pleased to see his wife in a better humor, grinned ruefully, and plotted revenge.

He scooped her up, still giggling, and tossed her into the turned-down bed, then dove on top of her.

"Retaliation is in order, ya know," he told her.

"I was kinda hopin' so," she told him.

* * *

The next morning, Madrid arrived, having been notified by Fox as soon as Zebra told him about Omega's dream the previous night. Zz'r'p, as their counselor, had strongly recommended some time off for Alpha One after recent events, as well.

"And I have no problems with it," Madrid averred. "After all, I'm a designer, not a field agent. Per orders, I was at Headquarters through the battle; I didn't see what they saw, didn't lose close friends and colleagues in the battle. They did."

So Alpha One took a short vacation on Aleancë, and Madrid worked on the Sword interface with the starship engineers.

* * *

"But if we're gonna hit up some of the touristy places, I think we oughta invite Myc, if you don't mind, Ace," Omega told her husband as they planned in their suite. "I mean, she doesn't have to come along on ALL our jaunts, because privacy, but I sorta doubt she'd go out on her own. And you know, Pul said he was gonna put out that notice to everybody that the Sword was a person, so she can even maybe bring Surl, assuming he's not still feeding his face…uh, blade, I guess. He doesn't have a face, not yet, at least. Unless you count the sculpture on the hilt."

"I get it, and yeah, I think I'm fine with that," Echo agreed. "I mean, she's earned it in spades, from the sound. As long as you an' me get some private time together, I'm cool with it."

"Did you get that dinner reservation made for this evening?"

"The fancy restaurant? Sure did, baby."

"Okay, there's our first private time."

They grinned.

"Let's go see Myc and see if she and Surl want to go to a botanical garden with us," Echo decreed.

* * *

"Oh!" Myclestra exclaimed. "That sounds…very pretty. Yes, I think I should like to do that. Old Snake, are you still eating?"

The Sword rested, not unlike Excalibur, with its blade buried in a crate of metal ingots of assorted materials, in the study of their suite — which was being used as a kind of special dining room for the former Star Drake. The crate was no longer full; it was only about half-full. An empty crate sat nearby.

<I am, Little One, but I am nearly finished for the moment. I think I should like to pause my consumption and attend with you, yes. I also need to ask Omega's permission for something.>

"What's that, Surl?" Omega wondered, as she and Echo exchanged puzzled glances.

<You will recall that I had a small sample of your blood, in order to heal you after Myclestra's little demonstration in your simulation room…>

"Oh. Right; I'd almost forgotten. Yeah, I figured that was so you had my genetic structure to know HOW to heal me."

<More or less, yes. But now, I was wondering if you would give me permission to use it for myself.>

"Huh? For what?"

<I am not the Maker; I cannot create life where there was none before. I have been pondering how to best build my new, humanoid body. Were I to construct a new drake body, it would be no matter, for I made sure to have my own genetics encoded in the sword. I could use whatever biota was at hand, convert it to stem cells, and reconstruct it to match…>

"Oh, I know," Echo said then. "You don't have HUMANOID templates to use."

<Exactly, Echo. I was hoping my Silver Hair, here, would let me use hers as a guide and a basis for the construction. I

would study her genetics, then create a modified version of my own that reflects the humanoid development, replace her genes with my modified ones in the cells, convert the cells to stem cells, and begin to grow a humanoid form. Likely with a cybernetic skeleton, to speed up the process — I can construct that VERY quickly, from the raw materials I am eating. I have already developed a design for that, based on what I know of Myclestra's skeletal structure…which is very similar to your own…>

"You sound like you have a full-up genetics lab in there," Omega noted with a teasing grin.

<I understand there is a media series that is broadcast on Earth,> Surlianth said with amusement. <The time-traveling vessel is known for being bigger on the inside, much as is your Headquarters building. Surlianthet, for me, is rather the same.>

They all laughed.

* * *

"And you're sure you'll delete my genetic material and replace it with yours?" Omega verified.

<I will, yes,> Surlianth promised. <Be aware, however, that the modifications I make to my own code will be based to some degree on your humanoid form, and therefore similar. Are you accepting of that?>

"I don't see that that would be any harm, baby," Echo said then. "I mean, he has to get that info from SOMEWHERE. And it won't be YOU, it'll just be sorta-kinda LIKE you, because human."

<Exactly, Echo.>

"Yeah, I think that'd be fine," Omega decided then. "And glad to help, when you get down to it. Just realize that not everything that's there is necessarily actually human. Splice, remember."

<I know, and I should be able to identify the patterns in the coding that do not conform to the rest. I have a memory and knowledge that stretches back farther than your very galaxy, so the scientific knowledge is…well, let us say I have been

around the multiverse a time or twelve.>

"Oh, that's interesting," Omega murmured, thoughtful. "I might ask you to confer with my personal physicians in the medlab, one of these days."

<Ah. Yes, I see. And yes, I would be happy to do so, if you think it will help.>

"It just might."

"Okay, if that's settled, shall we go?" Echo wondered. "We have a pretty big garden to explore, and Meg and I have dinner reservations tonight." He cocked his head. "Myc, Meg and I plan to have a nice romantic dinner, just the two of us, but if you'd like for us to make reservations for you and Surl someplace, I'd be happy to. I mean, probably Surl would just have to be propped on a separate chair and sorta watch you eat, but…"

<I would not mind,> Surlianth said, <provided it will not cause trouble, 'Myclestra walking around with a big-ass sword,' as Silver Hair put it on Earth.>

"Not here, and not after the whole Assembly announcement," Omega pointed out. "I verified that Uncle Pul did put out that public announcement, so we're good. After that, everybody knows about y'all. You'll be celebrities, and welcome wherever you go."

<Then yes, please, Echo, I should like to take my 'home person' to dinner tonight. A reservation…perhaps at an all-she-can-eat buffet, for I do know my Little One's appetites…would be much appreciated.>

"I'll take care of it, then," Echo said with a smile. "And my Meg isn't really that far behind, where those appetites are concerned." Omega stuck out her tongue, and they all laughed.

"This sounds very enjoyable!" Myclestra enthused.

Chapter Eleven — Aftermaths

In the end, it was several months before the starship was outfitted. During that time, more 'tribute' material was provided to Surlianth, largely so he could produce the humanoid body that would enable him to walk with Myclestra and the rest of the crew, as they explored the Local Group of galaxies and beyond.

"And no one minds," Entiyti noted to Fox with a toothy grin, "because most of us think they have earned it several times over, and those few that are still afraid think, 'The sooner he is finished, the sooner they are gone!' and so no one complains!"

Fox's response was to snort in amusement.

"Playing both ends against the middle, eh?"

"Absolutely! It is galactic politics, my old friend!"

Shortly after they realized how long it would take, and once Alpha One had had their little holiday, Director Fox, Ambassador Zz'r'p, and Alpha One went home. Weapons Development chief Madrid commuted back and forth as needed.

Myclestra stayed on Aleancë, where she and Surlianth were frequently entertained by Entiyti, Krimnet, and other members of the Ennead. It was a considered thing, Entiyti had told Fox, to avoid Myclestra growing lonely without the rest of her new 'family,' and to keep both her and Surlianth mentally occupied, healthy and happy.

And, he added, the pair made for fascinating conversations, regardless.

* * *

Back on Earth, Headquarters and the Atlanta Office were both in a state of mourning; many good agents had been lost, including several in Alpha Line, and in addition to the fatalities, there were still quite a few casualties, most of whom were still in regeneration pods in the medlab. Alpha One had lost Agent

Tare, part of the Firewall Team; his partner, Yankee, was still in the medlab — unconscious in a regen pod — recovering from severe burns, a lost eye, and lost limbs incurred in the same attack.

"…And no, I don't know if he consciously knows Tare is gone," a tired, slightly blue Echo told Omega one night over drinks on their sofa. "I haven't had a chance to talk to him, or to any of the others, really. Not about…that."

"Counting Tare, we lost six Praetorians," Omega added, wincing.

"Yeah, an' one of those was my old buddy Queen," Echo sighed. "AND his significant other."

"Yup." A subdued Omega counted fingers as she listed the deceased. "Tare, Queen, Berta, Carmen, Topsail, and Oyster. Six good Praetorians, gone."

"Uh-huh. Plus eleven more dead, an' I lost track of how many wounded, outta Apple, Baker, and Dolphin Forces. I got no idea how many Charlie Force, outta Atlanta, lost…"

"Hey! I thought they were supposed to provide perimeter guard. First, last, and only!"

"Yeah, but when people started dyin', they brought in their medics, and people to evacuate the wounded, as fast as they could carry 'em out…" Echo broke off, then sighed. "And a bunch of those got taken out by the secondary monsters an' shit."

"Oh damn. And those reports don't come up our chain of command, so…"

"Right. You and I haven't seen 'em yet. But I DO know that, other than Yankee, we have four more Alpha Line Agents in the medlab — including India."

"Which means Romeo is down there pretty much constantly," Omega noted. "Our 'brother' and 'sister.'"

"Exactly. And that's just the people directly under you an' me. The Field agents took a damn beating. I've never seen Crutch almost in tears before, like that."

"Well, the joint memorial service was…" Omega broke

off and took a deep breath, but did not continue.

"Yup. Alla that," Echo agreed. "The funerals will come later, I guess, once all the partners can attend. Now we gotta rebuild, somehow." He shrugged. "It wasn't as bad as the Klydonian invasion, but it seems to hit closer to home, somehow."

"Yeah. But I shudder to think what would have happened if we hadn't had Myc and Surl on our side." She shook her head. "I dunno if anybody woulda walked away. And we'd probably have lost the whole planet to the damned thing. And THEN it woulda spawned, and started spreading out through the galaxy from here."

"No shit." Echo paused, then said, "There's more of those, out there someplace in the multiverse, aren't there?"

"Uh-huh. Not here, in our universe. But somewhere, out there."

"Can we kill 'em without Surlianth to zap 'em? I mean, you used his power, even for the plasma cannon…"

"Yeah, we can now," Omega averred. "He showed us how to gin that up, we just didn't have time to build it, Madrid an' me."

"Oh. That's good, then."

"No joke." She paused, then added, "But I don't know if that's the only consideration."

"Oh? What else?"

"Well, there's an ancient legend that's of some concern to me…"

"Spill."

"In the various indigenous nations of Central America — what anthropologists sometimes call Mesoamerica — there was a member of multiple pantheons, going way the hell back to at least the Olmecs," Omega explained. "And common to ALL the pantheons, even between unrelated nations, extending into North America. Even the Cherokee had a feathered serpent, called Uktena. Never mind the European and Oriental versions of dragons…"

"Ooh. Keep going," Echo said, attention riveted.

"The Maya called him Kukulkan and the Aztec, or more properly the Nahuatl, who came later, called him Quetzalcoatl."

"The feathered serpent god. Right."

"Yeah, but he may be older than even the Olmecs," Omega pointed out. "And he was a sky god. Some researchers think he may have been a personification of the Milky Way. Our galaxy. And he was, in effect, a dragon. A drake."

Echo stared at her in shock.

"Oh shit," he murmured. "You think Surl may not have been the first Star Drake to cross over to our galaxy? It would sure explain some of the oldest legends among the galactic races…"

"Maybe," Omega pointed out. "Which means Surl also might not be the last. But Echo?"

"Yeah?"

"If Kukulkan was a Star Drake…where is he now?"

Echo smeared a hand over his face.

"Damnation. Have you talked to Surl about this? I mean, if Kukulkan is still out there someplace…"

"Yeah, I have," Omega admitted. "When it first hit me, I told him. He said he'd keep an eye out; if anybody knows what signs to look for, he does."

"Well, that's something, then."

"Yeah. Meanwhile, we still have a mess here to clean up."

"We do, that."

They were silent for a moment, pondering, and remembering the dead. Finally Omega ventured to break the quiet.

"I, uh, I'mma go down to the medlab tomorrow and, and visit folks," Omega noted. "We shoulda done this a lot sooner, really. I mean, most of 'em are in regen pods, so they prob'ly won't know we're there, but…"

"Uh-huh, and yeah, we should've. Damn, but we've been busy," Echo said with a nod. "Um, mind if I come with?"

"Please do. It's…it's gonna be rough."

"Ain't that the truth." They both sighed.

Omega leaned into him and took a swallow of her whisky.

Echo wrapped an arm around her and knocked back his own whisky.

They were quiet after that.

* * *

When it was time to install Surlianthet into the newly-named SS *Surlianthet Antesh* — which simply meant 'Starcraft of Surlianth's Sword' in Alontoran, and it was registered in Division One of the Pan-Galactic Coalition, specifically registered on Earth — Fox, Zz'r'p, and Alpha One headed back for Aleancë. India, along with most of the rest of the injured, was finally out of the medlab, though most, including her, were on very limited duty, if at all; she and the others were in a recovery protocol with which Echo was extremely familiar. However, this meant that Romeo, with the aid of Alpha Four and his mate, could much more easily run Alpha Line during the short absence of the usual leads. This time, Zebra came along for the ride.

At the prearranged time, they all met with Pulgey Entiyti and Teela Krimnet on the bridge of the *Antesh*. Myclestra arrived moments later, with Surlianthet in his scabbard. Madrid, who was already there helping to finalize the receptacle for the Sword — which was heavily based on the Surlianthet Capacitor — made the last adjustments, then stepped back.

"All right there," he said, "I think this ruddy thing is finally ready to go. It's basically the same as what you used to draw in the warpwraith, except this time, we've tied it in with a right bloody lot of ship's systems. I hope Surlianth already knows how to fly one of these things, or we may need someone teaching him."

<That has already been accounted for, Agent Madrid,> Surlianth told him. <I have had a Deltiri pilot teaching me this entire time, as well as taking me for rides in her own spacecraft. I must confess, my first reaction, upon seeing your warp drives, was, 'Oh, how quaint!' — where I originated, and

by the time I left, the drive systems were considerably more advanced, but then, that universe was much, much older than yours, with corresponding time to develop — but that proved useful to learning to pilot and navigate. I even 'solo'ed' in her craft, and she said I did excellently well. I expect matters will go just fine.>

"Capital! Good on ya, mate! I'm happy to hear it," Madrid said with a grin; the others flushed in response to the 'quaint' remark, especially the pilots in the group. "Then this ought to be bonkers fun for you."

<I am looking forward to it, yes.>

"All right, Myc," Omega coached, "draw the Sword from its sheath, and put it into the slot, there, just like you did back on Earth, when we wanted to attract the wraith's attention."

"Very well."

Myclestra drew forth Surlianthet; it was so bright and shiny it looked new, and it was adorned with quite a few new bits of scrollwork inlay, much of it in the same silver-gold alloy of which Alpha One's wedding rings were made — chrysargyron, it was called, and it was intertwined with rose gold scrollwork in a beautifully contrasting design. In addition, the sapphire-and-platinum medal was now embedded face-out in the hilt, just below the dragon head where the crosshilts met. Above it, in the pommel, glowed a star ruby.

Then, holding it by the crosshilts so that the blade tip pointed to the deck, Myclestra carefully eased the blade into the silicone-padded slot in the interface housing; it was designed to allow the blade to rest comfortably, without damage to itself or the interface.

There was a pause, as nothing happened; abruptly, several lights on the interface flashed green, and a soft glow appeared around the visible part of the blade, then faded.

"Ah, that is quite nice," Surlianth's voice abruptly came from the intercom speakers. "Very well done, all of you. I see exactly what to do. Thank you. As Madrid says, this will, indeed, be fun."

"Would you care to take the *Antesh* out for a quick loop of the Aleancë system, Lord Surlianth?" Entiyti wondered. "If so, you will need to contact…"

"The drydocks control, yes," Surlianth noted. "Fox, I understand that you, Echo, and Omega are excellent pilots yourselves…"

"They sure are," Zebra confirmed. "All three."

"Perhaps you would like to station yourselves around the bridge, in case I find myself in difficulties with the new interface, or in handling the ship? It is not quite the same as J'd'th's…"

"We'd be happy to help, Surlianth," Fox said immediately, as Omega and Echo nodded.

The three took up positions at the helm and navigation consoles, as the Star Drake prepared to take to space once more — this time, in the 'body' of a starship.

* * *

"Aleancë Drydocks Control, this is Captain Surlianth aboard the SS *Surlianthet Antesh*, requesting permission to undock."

"*Surlianthet Antesh*, this is Aleancë Drydocks Control. Permission granted; we are releasing docking clamps…now." A soft thudding clang reverberated through the ship; the watching Coalition representatives thought they heard a slight giggle.

"He's tied into the ship now, including the sensors. I wonder if it tickled," Omega breathed.

<Yes,> came Surlianth's mental reply. <Considerably.>

Echo snorted.

Hey, you should know, Omega told him with a grin, and Echo promptly silenced.

Then the superstructure of the drydock began to slide across the viewscreen on the forward bulkhead, very slowly at first, almost tentative, then increasing speed slightly until the starship was free of the structure. The *Antesh* continued to move outward for a bit, then it stopped, rotated on its vertical axis until it was facing away from the drydocks, and moved away from Aleancë.

Once it was well past Armik, Aleancë's moon, the *Antesh* picked up considerable speed.

"HA-HA!" Surlianth's jubilant voice rang over the intercom system, and everyone grinned.

* * *

Some two hours or so later, and having traversed the small stellar system, then dropped briefly into warp to go to the nearest star system and back, the *Antesh* was properly docked at the orbital transfer station over Aleancë, as a live spacecraft.

"Come along, or stay?" Omega asked Surlianth.

"Ah, stay, I think," Surlianth decided. "I want to explore the systems routing a bit, at least for now." Myclestra's face fell slightly.

"Dinner tonight, my friends?" Entiyti wondered.

"I think we'd love that, Pul," Zebra said, after glancing at the others.

"Oh, I can't," Madrid said, regretful. "I have to be back at Headquarters by the morning, or my assistant chief will kill me! He wants to test the prototype plas-pistol we based on the Lady Myclestra's weapon, and it's a potentially dangerous test…"

"Just make sure you shunt any goof-ups through the blast tunnel," Fox noted.

"As always, Fox. But I do need to return in order to ride herd, as Echo says."

"Aw," Entiyti murmured, disappointed. "Well, I do understand; there is work to be done, after all."

"There is," Madrid said with a smile. "Perhaps next time. I enjoyed your hospitality very much while I have been here, sir."

"Good, good, and make sure there IS a next time!" Entiyti blustered, in good humor.

"I shall!"

And he was off, out of the ship and to another concourse,

to catch a flight to Earth.

"The rest of us will be there, for sure," Omega determined.

"Very good. Speaking of work, Teela, shall we go see what the Ennead has gotten into in the meantime?" the Draconan asked.

"I think that is a wise move, Pul," the Korian said, and arm in arm, the two good friends departed.

"Good," Surlianth said, once they had left the bridge. "I was wondering if…the rest of you…might come back to our quarters with Myclestra. I have a little something I should like to show you all."

"Sure thing, Surl," Echo determined. "Let's go, guys."

* * *

"I feel half-naked without the weight of Surlianthet on my back," Myclestra complained as they entered the suite of rooms assigned to the Alontoran and closed the outer door. "I suppose I shall have to get used to that, however."

"I believe so," Surlianth's voice noted before anyone else could answer. "I seem to be doing reasonably well on my own, today."

And the door leading into the study, which had been closed, suddenly opened to reveal a very humanoid form standing in it.

The being was slightly taller than Myclestra, fully formed, with long, platinum-blonde hair caught up in a clasp at the nape of its neck, and bright blue eyes set in a pale-skinned face, the features delicate, pink lips full, almost pouting; the body was well-muscled and strong, legs long and shapely, with the essentials hidden under a lightweight, pale-blue tunic. The hue of hair and eye were very similar to those of Omega, and the group standing there in shock fully understood that it was intended to be so.

For the humanoid body that Surlianth had formed was not a male body, but a female one. And a very beautiful, statuesque one, at that.

Um, Omega thought, surprised. *Girl?*

<Well, in appearance, at least,> came the private mental

387

reply. <It is what Myclestra is most used to. There are no male Alontorans, remember; the Masters eliminated them millennia ago. But as a roguish Fox told me when I consulted with him about, ah, anatomical details which you do not have, 'It's what's in the pants that counts.' And that, my dear Silver Hair, is very much…me. And I…am a 'he' in every way that counts.>

"Oh," Omega said aloud.

"Wow," Echo muttered; Fox just let out a low, impressed whistle.

"It's…it's kinda Meg," Zebra murmured, considering. "But…not."

"Correct, Dr. Zebra," Surlianth said softly. "I had Omega's genetic material to hand, and her permission to use it as a template. And I also had the knowledge that my Little One, here, has a…I think you humans of Earth call it, 'a type.' Alontoran males no longer exist, so if they have a relationship with a fellow Alontoran, it is of necessity female to female. And, though she only detects the subtleties with her…'other sense,' and has no eyes to see the exact shades, she prefers the pale skin and hair, and the blue eyes, such as our Silver Hair, there, has. So…I sought to please." He turned to Myclestra, and for the first time, they saw the Star Drake show uncertainty. "Was I successful, my Bonded?"

Myclestra stood there for long moments, completely speechless.

Abruptly, with a wordless cry she galvanized, running the few steps across the room to Surlianth and flinging her arms around him/her. In fractions of a second, they were kissing hungrily.

"Aaand I think we should slip out and leave these two alone now," Fox breathed.

The four tiptoed out, closing the suite door quietly behind them.

They made excuses for Myclestra to Entiyti at dinner that night.

* * *

A few days later, it was time for the SS *Surlianthet Antesh* to depart for regions unknown. The exploratory crew had already loaded their personal items and equipment, and eagerly awaited their departure. Pulgey Entiyti, Teela Krimnet, Ambassador Zz'r'p, Fox, Zebra, Echo, and Omega — along with family members of the crew — stood at the gate to say their goodbyes; no one knew when, or even if, they would see them again.

Myclestra and Surlianth — in his humanoid form — came up to each one and hugged or shook hands as was deemed appropriate. Echo and Omega both received hugs from each.

"Thank you, so much, for everything, battle-sister," Myclestra murmured. "I am currently happier than I thought it possible to be. The only disappointment is that you and Echo cannot come with us."

"For now," Echo noted, as Myclestra moved on to hug him, and Surlianth gingerly took Omega in his arms. "One of these days, when we both retire from doing the PGLEIA police work, if you swing back by here from time to time, you just might find two more crew members volunteering to come along."

"ALL of that," Omega decreed. "So don't forget to come back and visit once in a while."

"We shall not," Surlianth promised, moving on to hug Echo as gingerly as he had hugged Omega. Then, as they had already said goodbye to the others, Surlianth turned back to Omega, and laid a hand on her shoulder. "Oh, by the way, a little parting gift. Enjoy."

And Omega startled as she felt something stir in her belly.

"Wha? What just happened?" she wondered…

…As a powerful sense of *déjà vu* struck.

By this time, Surlianth and Myclestra were already passing through the hatch to the space bridge. He glanced back over his shoulder and grinned, just before he disappeared into his spacecraft.

"What is it, baby?" Echo wondered.

"You didn't," Omega yelled at the closing hatch. "You scamp, you DIDN'T!"

"Didn't what, Meg?" Zebra queried, as the others turned to look at the Alpha Line Agent.

"Move to the portals and wave goodbye, my friends," Entiyti decreed, interrupting before Omega could answer. "We are sending off two new family members into the vast unknown."

They did so, standing with the rest of the crew families to wave to the many faces visible in portals on the SS *Surlianthet Antesh,* a bright red head beside a pale blond head prominent in one portal. The big ship eased away from its docking port, headed outward, seeming to shrink as it grew farther and farther away. They watched until the tiny dot finally disappeared in the void. A collective sigh went up, and everyone turned away. The families began departing by small handfuls.

"Well, my dear, dear friends," Entiyti said, "we have work to do, Teela and I. I hope to see you for dinner tonight, one more time, but if you must return to Earth, I will certainly understand."

"We'd love to, Pul, but we need to be getting back, too," Fox said, clapping an arm around the big Draconan in a male hug of affection; Entiyti responded in kind. "I'll give you a call next week to set up that trade negotiation we discussed."

"Right, right," Entiyti agreed. "Come hug me, my family; it is likely to be some months before we see each other again, at least in person."

Hugs went all around, then Entiyti and Krimnet departed, and Fox, Zebra, Zz'r'p, Echo, and Omega turned and headed for the gate where the D1 *Revelation* was docked.

* * *

"So what was all that bit when Surlianth said he gave you something, Meg?" Zebra continued the earlier query.

"Yes, I heard that. Omega seemed rather startled," Fox agreed.

"Um, guys, remember the, uh, the dream I had, right

before everybody decided Alpha One needed a few days off on Aleancë?" Omega tried.

"Yeah, I — oh shit," Echo said, dumbfounded. "You don't mean…?"

"Your eggs?" Zebra hissed, and Fox and Zz'r'p stopped dead, staring, just as they arrived at their gate. "You think he really did, this time?"

"I dunno," Omega admitted. "There's only one way to find out."

"Get on board the *Revelation*," Fox shooed them into the sky bridge and away from prying eyes. "THEN Zebra can scan things!"

Moments later, in a quiet corridor aboard Echo's Assistant Director flagship, Zebra pulled her medscanner from a warp pocket and adjusted it for a very specialized scan, then aimed it at Omega's lower abdomen, while the three males clustered around in protective fashion. Only a minute or so later, Zebra gaped at the readouts.

"Oh. Dear. God," she deadpanned in astonishment.

"It's different? They're different? My eggs changed?" Omega pressed.

"Not only did they change, they…Meg, Zarnix and I have been busting our asses to determine what your nominal genome should be," Zebra explained. "And if this isn't bang-on the direction we were headed with it, it's even better."

"You mean…her ovaries are back to human norms?" Echo wondered.

"Well, Meg was never 'normal,' to begin with," Zebra said. "She was always gonna have eggs that carried her exceptional genetics. But yes, they're back to strictly human. I see no signs of what Myclestra called 'splicing' in those eggs' DNA. At. All." She shrugged. "I'll be able to verify that if you'll come by the medlab when we get home, honey. But right now, I'd say that was a helluva parting gift Surlianth left you two."

With a whoop of joy, Echo grabbed Omega and spun her around, as she laughed happily.

"HALLELUJAH!" Fox shouted, as gleeful as Alpha One, even as Zz'r'p beamed . "Ladies and gentlebeings, let's head for the bridge, so Echo can order us home, and then I propose we all retire to Zebra's and my stateroom for a small celebration."

"THAT…is a DAMN fine plan," Echo agreed.

The happy group headed down the corridor.

* * *

Many millions of miles away by now, and contained within a swiftly-speeding warp bubble, a statuesque blond humanoid, possessed of shapely feminine curves, sat on the bridge of the SS *Surlianthet Antesh*, another statuesque female, this one with bright red hair, sitting at his side.

In the mind's eye of the being that once was a Star Drake, the events that had just taken place in the corridor of the D1 *Revelation* played out. He watched as they jubilantly moved toward the bridge of that ship.

Smiling, Surlianth took the hand of his Bonded, and turned his attention to the future.

Epilogue — Loose Ends?

Ranger Roseanne Ramos took a deep breath as she carefully arranged the collection of evidence in the sturdy cardboard box on her desk. An old single action revolver in .45 LC, six rounds fired through it. Labeled and bagged samples of a very odd burn scar. Bagged samples of ground that had been liberally soaked with blood. Fur, bones and claws of some wolf-like creature. A thumb drive containing an audio recording of her talking to a young woman named Kim Hollowell about what had happened to her and her boyfriend. A recording VERY different from every other recording anyone else had of that conversation. Solid evidence, as good as she'd ever seen win a conviction in court.

But this evidence would probably never be used in any court. There were victims, Kim and her boyfriend, the latter killed by wolves as far as anyone else knew. No perpetrators, other than the supposed wolf pack. A wolf pack that had never been located. Wolves didn't get their day in court. Wolves who had killed humans just got shot.

Problem was, the US Forest Rangers responsible for the Gunnison National Forest, among a dozen other National Forests in Colorado, had not been able to find hide nor hair of a wolf, any wolf, within ninety miles of where Kim Hollowell had been found, naked and unconscious in an old fire watch tower.

But there was more to this conundrum, Roseanne knew. Whatever those men in the identical black suits had done to her fellow Rangers and the pair of Department of the Interior Special Agents, that had changed everything they thought they knew about what happened in the forest that day. At least, for everyone except her. She took a deep breath.

"Roseanne, chica, I hope you know what the hell you're doing. No one else remembers what you do. And maybe there's a REAL good reason for that, but I gotta talk to someone. Special Agent Holland will listen to me. I hope. I hope he doesn't laugh himself sick when I tell him we were all visited by the mythical men in black. And I remember, because I was in my truck, securing this evidence…and they never saw me, and those flashing, swirling light show things didn't affect me, because, because, because I hid in my truck." She sighed. "Oh boy, I sound like a nut even to myself." She picked up the box. "Well, here goes nothing."

She elbowed her office door open, walked down the hall to the elevator and took the old, cantankerous thing to the third floor. She turned left, went past the breakroom and around the corner to the door with the frosted glass pane window marked: US Department of the Interior, Special Agent Jon Holland. She knocked on the door and opened it at the muffled, "C'mon in," command from the occupant.

"Well, howdy, Roseanne." Jon Holland popped from behind his desk and gave her a hand with the box. "What's all this?"

"Sir, what this stuff is, well, what it is, that's gonna sound like some tinfoil hat-wearing loon who's had one Red Bull too many and been on the internet too long. But I swear it's every word true."

"Really?"

"Yes, sir. We really need to talk about what this represents."

Please leave a review.

Authors Notes

This one's a bit different. For the first time in the Division One series, I have a coauthor!

Tony has been a friend and fan for some time, and wanted to write. In fact, I've been paying it forward (Travis Taylor helped me get published) by trying to help him get published. One evening Tony and I were discussing an idea he'd had for a fanfic in the D1 universe, and wanted my permission to write it. "Tell me more," I said.

So he told me the story idea. The more I listened, the more I realized, "Whoa, whoa, whoa, no no no. This needs to be canon. This needs to be IN the D1 universe! But it's your idea. Wanna coauthor it with me?"

He agreed, and the result is the tome in your hands. So my deepest thanks, Tony, for a truly excellent story. I think this is GREAT!

But the idea he had was a bit different, and he wondered if there was anything providing precedent in the D1 universe. Which is when I told him about the short story I'd written for an anthology in Kate Paulk's VampireCon series. In the end the anthology didn't happen, but Kate kindly gave me permission to use the story in my universe. Thank you for letting me nudge my sandbox against yours, Kate! I'd planned, at some point, to issue a collection of my own short fiction, and still plan to do so, but Tony and I decided *Complications* might make an apropos prologue to this novel. Yes, it's canon.

Also my usual thanks to my beta readers, Evelyn Zinn, Dr. James K. Woosley, Randy Jones, and Kae Thompson. You guys catch things I don't, and you tell me if I'm off in the weeds on something or not. It's a good thing to have good beta readers in your life.

My hubby, Darrell Osborn, as usual, does the most bangin' covers. Love you, honey, and many many thanks!

And as always, thanks to my parents, Steve and Colene Gannaway, for bringing me up to believe I could actually do all this stuff I've done in my life. I don't know where I'd be without you.

~Stephanie Osborn
July 2021
Huntsville, Alabama

* * *

Wow. Me, a published co-author. I've been writing scenarios and home-brewed worlds for various RPGs for a long time. I read voraciously, since I was a kid. I've always scribbled world histories and character backgrounds. In high school, a friend of mine and I used to swap our stories back and forth, critiquing each others' stuff. She went on to be a very successful author and I joined the Air Force.

I met Stephanie Osborn at Imaginarium in Louisville, KY and after chatting with her most of the weekend I bought the first *Division One* book, *Alpha and Omega*, as an ebook. By the end of the month, I'd bought all of them. I really enjoyed her take on the old "men in black" urban legends. And after hanging out with her at a few more cons, I got this crazy idea. She'd said something about fan-fic and this idea just popped into my head. So, I suggested it to Stephanie and ZOOM, off she went, dragging me along in her wake, willy-nilly. And now, you have this book.

Lots of folks have helped me, encouraged me and booted me in the hind-end when I needed it. My 'Brother-from-Another-Mother' Troy Logsdon, who puts up with me on a regular basis. Lydia Sherrer, who has been a constant cheerleader for me and an author of no little skill herself. Lieutenant Colonel (ret.) Jon Holland, USA, and his lovely wife Veena Copeland, an Army Warrant Officer 4 herself, have provided tons of encouragement. Stephanie Osborn herself has put up with me quite a bit in the process of writing this book. And first and foremost, my lovely wife of 27 years, Kae Thompson, who has gone above and beyond the call of duty in keeping me on task and on time with this project. I love you, baby.

~A. G. Thompson
July 2021
Louisville, Kentucky

About the Authors

Stephanie Osborn is a former payload flight controller, a veteran of over twenty years of working in the civilian space program, as well as various military space defense programs. She has worked on numerous Space Shuttle flights and the International Space Station, and counts the training of astronauts on her resumé. Of those astronauts she trained, one was Kalpana Chawla, a member of the crew lost in the *Columbia* disaster.

She holds graduate and undergraduate degrees in four sciences: Astronomy, Physics, Chemistry, and Mathematics, and she is "fluent" in several more, including Geology and Anatomy. She obtained her various degrees from Austin Peay State University in Clarksville, TN and Vanderbilt University in Nashville, TN.

Stephanie is currently retired from space work. She now happily "passes it forward," teaching math and science via numerous media including radio, podcasting, and public speaking, as well as working with SIGMA, the science fiction think tank, while writing science fiction mysteries based on her knowledge, experience, and travels.

For more, or to subscribe to Stephanie's newsletter, go to her website, http://www.stephanie-osborn.com/.

* * *

Reared on a West Texas ranch, A.G. Thompson is a veteran of the US Air Force, having served during the Cold War and earned the rank of Staff Sergeant. He has Bachelor of Arts degrees in both English Literature and History from the University of Louisville.

Tony has been a competition shooter for around a decade, is an avid reader (as most authors are), and is extremely knowledgeable in military history, especially as regards World War II action; he has been known to use this knowledge in game-mastering exciting tabletop wargames.

He is currently a 24-year employee of UPS, a devoted cat-person with several fourfoots in his household, and has been married for the last 27 years to his wonderful wife, Kae Thompson.